Fatal Image

An Avery Sloane Mystery

Rhonda Lane

McNeely Solomon Media LLC

One

May 2010 – Bowmansville, Kentucky

Still unable to sleep after midnight, I picked up chatter on the "Blanchard County Fat Chewing" social media site. A man had been found dead after the horse show at the fairgrounds.

Wide awake now, I got in my car and headed out on winding country roads still gleaming wet from the sudden thunderstorm.

At the fairground's main gate, Georgia Fortner, the sole female deputy in the sheriff's department shoved out her palm for *halt.*

I snapped to alert. My first checkpoint since leaving Iraq. My first without a local driver or a translator. My first guard post not manned by a soldier armed to the teeth.

The deputy's badge glinted in my car's headlights.

I exhaled and lowered my shoulders from my ears.

She strode toward the driver's side window with a tight mouth and an all-business swagger.

My left hand jittered on the window control. The window whirred open and humid mid-spring Kentucky air rushed inside the car. So did the seesawing song of cicadas.

A departmental ball cap covered most of her hair except for the strawberry blonde military bun at the nape of her neck. I greeted her first. "Avery Sloane. *Blanchard County Tribune.* But you know that. Were you out in the storm?"

She swept her flashlight beam across my face before swinging it along the length of the dashboard. She said, in her official license-and-registration voice, "Press pass, ma'am."

She often worked the desk at the sheriff's department, so she knew full well where I'd been working for the past two months.

I put the car in Park. I imagined one of my brashest colleagues, in whatever hellhole she was covering, wishing me good luck with a hoisted drink and a jaunty smirk. Rumor had it she could forget her credentials and still get access.

"You'd think I'd have media credentials by now, right? But no," I said. "My bosses gave me the police beat, and then told me that," I used my fingers for air quotes, "everyone in town knows everyone else anyway." I raised my hands as if to say, *What can I do?*

The deputy shook her head. "No press pass. No entry."

Maybe I should've played the prosecutor's-daughter card even if my father had been no one the local talent knew. Even my memories of him before he died were hazy, except for stories from my mother and old family friends.

Law enforcement always struck me as all for one and one for all—except some lawmen and locals might insist that, as a journalist, I'd gone over to the dark side.

Time to double down. "Leave it to the brass," I added with a shrug and a shake of my head in hopes of sealing the deal. "Right?"

Fortner's stern mouth twitched in a momentary smile before morphing back to her poker face. "Put your car back in gear, Miss Sloane. Turn around."

I shifted into Drive so I could pull forward to turn around, just as she'd asked. With my foot on the brake, I said, "I'm sorry. Like my boss keeps reminding me, everyone here knows everyone else. Or is related to them.

So, that said, considering you probably know the person who died, I'm sorry for your loss."

That last bit had been sincere. Losing people in a close community broke open an aching wound. Been there, done that. Sometimes saw it happen.

She shook her head with a slight almost wistful smile and said, "I appreciate your situation, ma'am, but Sheriff wants everything done by the book. So, no creds, no go."

Ahead on the fairground's driveway, stood the century-old, covered wood grandstand. The arena silhouetted against the night sky stood tall enough to block out the stars.

At close to 1 a.m. on a Sunday, Lexington media hadn't had a chance to arrive. The *Lexington Journal's* reporter assigned to Blanchard County lived about an hour away.

Except for the occasional citizen journalist on social media and gossip over the phone, the *Tribune* was it. Maybe. With my foot still on the brake, I said, "Am I the only reporter here?"

"No press pass. No entry." She extended her arm and pointed toward the street I'd just left. "Now turn around or move aside. No blocking the road."

She didn't say, "Get out of here."

I moved the car off the road onto the grass shoulder, hoping that the ground wasn't boggy enough after the storm to suck in the tires.

I pulled out my phone from my jacket pocket and called the chief deputy's official departmental number for media relations. I didn't expect a return, but I had put an effort into channels.

Next, I called Gordon Hulett, my current editor and old Columbia School of Journalism pal. He answered the phone with a slurry groan.

The urge to rant about how unprofessional it was for me not to have a media credential, let alone how lame the *Tribune* looked when I worked without one, was strong. Let alone my itch to sing our "Told Ya So" song, but time was wasting.

"I'm sorry to wake you," I said, "but I need access to the fairgrounds to cover a potential homicide."

Silence from him, but a grumble in the background from his wife Shannon. The two high school sweethearts had been part of our college journalism group, so she understood the demands of the job, which, along with her more recent leanings toward domestication, led her to leave reporting long before I had hung up my Nikons.

He said, "We're a weekly, Avery. You don't have to work this hard."

I opened the car door. "I'm handing my phone to Deputy Fortner, so you can tell her I'm cleared to—"

"Go home." My old friend sounded like a boss. "Get some sleep."

My stomach shrank into a hard knot. I stood outside the open car door with the warning bell dinging like an auditory sledgehammer synced with my pulse. I didn't feel like telling him, again, I don't—can't—sleep.

Instead, I said, "I'm here now. Why waste the opportunity?"

He sniffed and coughed. "The state police there yet?"

A college memory surfaced—a story Gordon and Shannon had laughed about over pizzas and at least one pitcher of beer at John's on Bleecker St. All those stories of country kid shenanigans. So very Tom Sawyer when compared to my childhood in the Connecticut suburbs.

"Didn't you once tell me about how you and your brother used to sneak into the fairgrounds when you were kids?"

A hint of a warning entered his voice. "Don't make me regret this."

"Please." I flicked away his concerns like gnats. "I've done covert border crossings in the dead of night."

Two

After letting Fortner know I was just turning around the car, not backing up to storm the fairgrounds gate, I soon eased the car onto Fairview Lane which was lined with slumbering homes built in close formation for new families in the post-WWII boom.

Each house was a single-story ranch with a one-car garage or a carport. Narrow side yards offered neighbors enough room to block off their turf with a fence. Beyond the backyard, huddles of trees loomed in front of the darkened grandstand.

Four houses down, on the fairgrounds side of the street, a front-porch light glowed. Gordon had mentioned the specific detail of a blue house with a wagon wheel propped against a bird bath out front.

Parked in the short driveway was an older pickup truck with a cap, a newer minivan, and a tarp-covered street bike.

Among the vehicles stood a chubbier, tanner, and more heavily bearded version of Gordon. His older brother Buddy was bundled in a terrycloth robe with a saggy tee over what I hoped were baggy board shorts, not just boxers. He extended his arm at shoulder height to wave at me.

I parked in front of the house, leaving the driveway clear, and shut off my car. I didn't want to wake dogs who'd bark until all the houses nearby lit like falling dominoes.

Instead of using the chirpy key fob, I locked the car doors from the inside. Even then, when I eased the door shut, each click and latch sounded as loud as a shotgun blast.

To Buddy, I said, "Thank you for letting me cut through your yard."

"Let's make this quick," he whispered. He pointed with a tilt of his head toward the dark house about a bathtub's length away from his driveway. "Neighbors have big ears."

I didn't reply. No one needed to sell me on the tactical advantage of stealth.

He set off to lead the way. Every time his plastic flip flops smacked the soles of his feet, I cringed. A *thunk* to my right made me gasp. A mechanical hum followed—an air conditioner kicking on.

His sandals were muffled once he stepped off the paved driveway and into his yard. Behind him, next to a chain-link fence with privacy slats, oak branches still tipped with fresh green leaves, lay in a tangle—evidence of damage from the earlier storm.

"Follow me so you don't conk into the swing set," he said.

In his backyard to my left, under the dull, yellow porch light, a charcoal grill waited near a warped-wood picnic table. A faded plastic tricycle lay on its side, as if abandoned in a hurry.

The yard stretched farther past the house than the shallow front yards suggested. We headed away from the house toward an uneven wall taking shape out of the darkness. Bushes. Occasional tiny bright spots indicated light beyond the thicket of branches.

I clicked on my flashlight and scanned the beam across the row of vegetation ahead. A ragged gap showed where the shrub met the fence.

"The limbs ought to be weaker at the ends," I said, thinking aloud. "Right?"

"More give, sure, but stabbier. You sure you want to do this?"

Good question. I could go home, return to bed, and visit the sheriff's department at a civilized hour. Or I could crash through a hedge to gather first-person accounts from the remaining horse-show exhibitors and before the cops caught me.

I'd wanted a slower pace. No bombs. No snipers. No blood.

Peace and quiet both healed and suffocated.

I clicked off the flashlight and slipped it into my jacket pocket.

"Thanks for your help, Buddy." I unzipped my coat. "Your little brother owes you now. Make it good when you collect."

I shrugged my open jacket loose enough to tug over my head. By gripping the ends of the sleeves, I could shelter my face when I ducked.

I pulled my jacket up to cover my face like a wise guy on a perp walk. I gritted my teeth and closed my eyes before pushing myself into the branches.

From the other side of the hedge, a semitruck engine fired, then idled; air brakes released with a gasp.

Diesel fumes snaked into my nose, spun my stomach, and sent my heart juddering inside my chest.

The trucks were starting, and a convoy was leaving. Where the hell was my camera?

"Avery? Are you all right?"

A concerned Southern male. Had to be some country boy Marine. They don't trust me. Always looking for ways to give me crap. They'd leave me if they could, whether or not I'd been officially embedded by the military to cover their unit's activities.

Leaves tickled the back of my hand.

Leaves.

I wasn't on assignment overseas. I was in Kentucky. In a family home's backyard. Gordon's big brother's backyard.

My hand clenching the jacket over my head relaxed. My wrist rested on my head. I sucked in deep breaths.

His voice coming from behind me returned me to the present. "I'll get the chain saw."

"No." Too sharp. Too panicky. I heaved a deep breath and said, enunciating the words with care, "No chain saw. I'm fine."

I added through the bushes, "Thanks. You can go back to bed now."

With some twisting and pulling, I shook past the limbs to step free of the hedge.

I wriggled my shoulders and enjoyed lungs full of air without vegetation in my face. The night air cooled my exposed skin.

I almost stepped out into the path of a boxy white RV barreling along a narrow road running parallel to the hedge line.

I flattened myself against the branches poking my spine. My heart pounded hard enough it could have leapt out and smashed into the side window now passing inches from my nose.

The breeze in the motor home's wake ruffled my loose tendrils of hair. The square white block on wheels rocked away along the uneven road.

My knees quivered enough to almost spaghetti me into the damp grass. A road behind the hedge? Neither of the Hulett boys bothered to tell me. What else was coming my way?

Three

While my eyes adjusted, I heard a man's voice. "Dios mio!"

Still close enough to the hedge if I needed thrash my way back into Buddy's yard, I squinted toward where the voice came. I spotted a middle-aged Latino with a wide face standing next to a chestnut horse tethered to the outside of a parked horse trailer. A work light allowed him—and me—to see in the dark.

He wore what looked like a three-piece suit missing the jacket—with a short-sleeved business shirt and a loose tie—part of a show suit for riders who exhibit their horses in saddle seat classes. A towel lay draped over one shoulder.

He gaped at me from beneath the bill of his baseball cap. "Lady," he'd switched from Spanish to country southern English, "you like to scared me half to death." He glanced from side to side, as if he expected someone else to come out of nowhere.

I caught my breath and gulped before speaking. "Sorry for the scare. I'm Avery Sloane from the *Blanchard County Tribune*. I'm here to . . ." Gordon had asked me yesterday to dial back the brusqueness. "To find out more about the guy who died."

Next to him, the horse nosed a mesh bag of hay hanging from the trailer's side. By the man's rolled jodhpur legs, stood a plastic organizer tote bristling with brushes and combs.

"Pardon me," he said, "but I need to keep on working. I sent my family home as soon as I could." He walked toward the hind end of the horse where the long flaxen tail almost brushed the grass. "You're Mrs. Ward's tenant, right? I rent stalls in the big barn. Herb Olmos."

He pulled a wide-toothed comb from the collection of grooming tools. With his free hand, he scooped the tail toward him and carefully combed the bottom of the long strands.

"I thought you looked familiar. I'm glad we didn't scare your horse. Would you mind if I asked you—"

He swung toward me while gesturing with the comb. "I don't want my name in the paper. Not for this." He returned to dividing the long pale gold strands into thirds.

Okay. I'd find other sources sooner or later.

"No problem. Just background so I can get my bearings," I said. "Where did they find him?"

He finished braiding the tail, fast and tight, and then seemed to blow out resigned air from his pursed lips. Who did all that work in show clothes? A one-man-band horse trainer doing the best he can in unexpected circumstances, that's who.

He said, "The exhibitor's parking lot."

I glanced past him at trucks and low barns, and toward the grandstand in the distance on a property about the size of a community college campus. "And that would be where?"

His hand dipped into another pocket in the apron and pulled out a tube sock with a split top. "Keep going past the barns. You can't miss the grandstand. There's a parking lot off to the left. Just be careful poking around in the dark."

"You're doing your job. I have to do mine." I stepped away from the truck. "Nice to meet you."

Herb lowered the braid into the sock and tied the tabs that had been the elastic top together. "If you like horses, maybe come down to the big barn at the farm. Meet my wife and boys. Just be careful tonight. No telling who's out there and what kind of meanness might be about."

With a wave and a grin, I set off with my boots squishing in the wet grass.

Ahead lay a scattering of low barns with floodlights hanging above the open doors and nearby parked trucks. The faint strains of country music wafted from a radio punctuated by an occasional whinny or banging kick against a wall.

My eyes adjusted to the darkness. I passed several groups of people going back and forth between the barns and trucks. Along with seeing the occasional glow of lit cigarettes, I overheard phrases of conversation in voices dripping with scorn. *Brought trouble here. That element.*

Torn between wanting to ask questions and needing to get to the crime scene, I kept moving. A tall wiry man led a spirited black horse out of the barn and under the floodlight. The lamp over the open barn door misted light down onto the two.

Too bad I didn't have a real camera anymore. That I'd not even taken the shot with my phone confirmed photojournalism had left my soul.

The horse, wrapped for travel in a scarlet blanket with matching padded leg bandages, pranced and swung out before charging into the trailer with horseshoes clattering along the ramp and disappearing beyond the walls. The handler kept pace, entering the trailer as well.

As I approached the trailer door, I heard thumps and stomps, along with a firm but nasal male voice saying, "Quit," dragging the word into two syllables.

Interrupting this guy with an excited horse inside a tin box seemed reckless. Not safe for anyone involved. *Pass.*

A muffled sob to my right startled me. I peered into the deep shadows by the trailer. A woman stood with her head bowed low and her arms folded tight, as if to hug herself.

A tinge of sadness immobilized me against intruding on her private moment.

She murmured, and I heard, "Please protect and comfort his family. Amen."

While on assignment overseas, I carried tissues to offer, along with words of comfort, before introducing myself. How I had tactically ingratiated myself for stories made me a little ill.

But my brand-new personal ethics hampered my job performance.

The woman crying moments ago emerged from the shadows and stalked toward the open door of the trailer.

Her energetic change attracted my attention and interest. Slender and blonde with an ivory complexion and a sleek low bun over her shirt collar, she also wore horse show clothes, except her long white sleeves ended in French cuffs.

She stomped onto the trailer ramp and stood outside the open door. "No wonder we didn't place," she said into the horse trailer. "Sitting as deep as he was. Looking a lot like a bad-image horse. I'm surprised you weren't shown the gate."

The man who'd led the black horse swaggered out of the trailer. "The old man likes 'em that way. He's the one signing my checks, punkin."

For that last sentence, his voice turned playful with an edge of condescension. His body shifted as if he'd popped an exaggerated teasing wink at her.

Her shoulders stiffened as if she recognized his patronizing tone. She stepped forward. "Not if we don't win. You know bad-image horses do us no good. And if you've been helping them?" Her voice rose into a threatening question, but he interrupted her.

"Stop crying. I know why he won. You know why he won. Those people stick together. We should've never . . ." Something in his gaze stopped him. He squinted at me, as if he'd just seen me listening among the shadows.

"Can I help you?" he said, his voice bristling with confrontation. A deep scowl creased his face when he peered at me through small hard eyes.

Whether out of training or habit, the old electrons sparked to life inside my brain and activated my mouth. "Avery Sloane from the *Tribune*. Terrible night."

"Indeed, it is, lady." His jaw set under the ball cap brim. "I got horses to get home." With a dismissive huff, he swerved wide to walk past me toward the barn.

The woman gaped at me as if her boots froze to the ground. Then, her initial open-mouthed stare of surprise morphed into a southern hospitality smile.

"Yes. Such a tragedy." She switched gears and sounded very Dolly Parton-Goes-to-Harvard. "Are you Daddy's new hire? I'm Josie Kinsale. Clark Kinsale is my father." She stuck out her hand.

Next to her on the trailer wall, glittery reflective letters spelled out "Kinsale Farms." Below the farm's name, smaller letters sparkled "Reg. Bluegrass Ambling Horses" followed by a local phone number.

Kinsale. My newspaper's owner/publisher's daughter. His farm. And even Gordon's uncle. The big boss.

No way could I use them for quotes. Too self-serving, even if Kinsale did own half the county.

Way to go, Avery. Salvage this. I completed the handshake. I'd expected a charmed-I'm-sure handshake from Kinsale's daughter, but she pumped out a firm business handshake.

I said, "What do I need to know before going further?"

"Oh no." Josie tugged a tissue from inside her French cuffs. Her slender fingers fluttered it to her face. Her fingertips pressed the tissue beneath her nose. "I can't do this." She backed away. "I'm sorry." She ran past me into the barn.

More people led horses to load into trailers. Stern faces with narrowed eyes and tight mouths tracked my progress with cold forbidding stares. I had sent their princess packing.

The grouchy man strode past me again. "Somebody up and killed the horse show judge. Happy now?"

If he expected me to wilt, he faced the wrong woman. "So I hear. How do you know? Do you know who it was?" Not an official confirmation but leverage or a diversion if the cops confronted me later.

He headed toward me. "You reporters always talk a good game then do a tree-hugging hatchet job on us and our horses." He stepped into my personal space, close enough for scattered saliva specks to land on my cheek. "Is that your plan, too?"

I studied the deep crow's feet etched around his eyes and tan, leathery skin—a farmer's face. Lines around his mouth suggested a long-time smoker. The silence around me, even from the horses, told me everyone waited for my reply.

"All I care about tonight is the murder. I think the *Trib* ran an announcement about some guy from Nashville judging the show. Is that who's dead?"

Josie emerged from a stall and said, "Oh, mercy, Uncle Dwayne," to the grouchy man half threatening me.

She brushed past him. A fresh tissue fluttered from the fingers of her right hand. "Please accept my apologies, Avery, is it? Daddy told me he'd hired a go-getter from New York. Y'all get to the point in a straight line."

The man who'd loaded the horse into the trailer, who Josie had called "Uncle Dwayne," huffed and slouched into another stall, leaving me with his niece.

"The judge we'd hired couldn't come up," she said. "He's in the ER with a kidney stone. No one on the grounds wanted to step aside and judge instead of showing their horses tonight. After all, this horse show is the main fundraiser for the VFW to donate to our local military families. We called an old family friend."

From inside the barn, as if he'd been close enough to eavesdrop, Uncle Dwayne chimed in again, "Which is why we get so upset when you liberal media types go off and write stuff when you don't know what you're talking about. These horse shows raise money for charity. Now, I have to stop jawing and get back to work."

Josie sighed and studied her tissue. Even in the dim barn light, tears glistened on her cheeks. "Cyrus filled in as judge. How unfortunate. He was nice enough to come down here to help us, but that's our Ambling Horse family. Always willing to help. I can't imagine what those poor schoolchildren in Lexington will do without him. For too many of them, he was their only hope. Let alone his poor momma."

My stomach fluttered a warning. Someone named Cyrus with schoolchildren. Let alone one who'd offered guidance away from the lure of the street. Way too familiar. "Cyrus who?"

"Cyrus McCoy. Wait—was it you, or Wilbur, who wrote the article in our paper a few weeks ago about Cy winning Teacher of the Year?"

I shuddered but couldn't place the source of my unease. Too much, too much. Emotions clogged the words in my throat. I stepped into the shadows so my face couldn't be seen or read. My voice returned, but only for a brief exhaled sentence. "I wrote the story."

Josie filled the dead air by huffing a socially appropriate response about the tragic loss, but my brain couldn't grab traction with her words. Inside my head, too much blood pulsed and swirled with memories.

Towering bookshelves, soft carpet, and light jazz on the sound system. Sunlight streaming through an arcing wall of windows tall enough to draw me to the view of the landscaping outside but also put me on edge. A lotta glass. The aromas of coffee brewing with hints of warm cinnamon and vanilla. The moderated hum of conversation with the clatter of cutlery.

Through the maelstrom of images swirling in my mind, Cy's voice surfaced. "Check out the wall of books by Kentucky authors," he'd said with excitement and pride. "It'll blow your mind."

Now, a different male voice chimed in. A honeyed, bourbon baritone saying, "Avery. Sloane." as if it were single-word sentences, pronounced in a way that said, "bus-ted."

Four

I turned to face Blanchard County Chief Deputy Marvin Taylor. Much younger and fitter than the elected county sheriff, the chief deputy dealt with press and didn't have to worry about re-election.

He stood with his feet planted shoulder-width apart and his pale hands resting on his utility belt. He projected the image of The Immovable Object personified.

"Hi, Chief. Has the family of the deceased been notified yet?"

"That's an ongoing investigation." He changed tone from official to teasing with an alarming edge. "Look at you, all when-in-Rome, hanging out at an ambling hoss show."

So, this was what a mouse cornered by a cat felt like when the cat was more in the mood for fun.

"What about the coroner?" I stood tall to disguise needing to lean against the doorframe for support. "Is she here yet?"

In the dim glow of the stable lighting, my fingers slipped into the pocket for my notebook and pen. In a now-instinctive move, I slid them out and held them in a clear silent announcement of "we are on the record now."

He unclipped his mic from an epaulet and raised an index finger to suggest I wait a moment. Then he raised the mic to his mouth. "Send a deputy in a car to Barn Five." He'd dropped the exaggerated accent for his usual speech, more midwestern than southern.

A scratchy "Roger that" came through the tiny speaker.

He responded, "She's here. Been here. She showed a horse." Before I could ask my next question, he folded his arms and looked down his nose at me. "I didn't pass your car when we came in through the gate. Where did you park?"

That he knew my car was no surprise. I seemed to drive the only Mini Cooper in Blanchard County.

But no way would I give up Gordon's brother. Always, *always* protect a source. "I was in the mood for a walk."

"After that thunderstorm?" He said, "Show me your press credential."

That again? A sheriff's department vehicle was on its way. I'd be leaving soon, right after I'd arrived.

I kept my tone even—as well as I could through thin breath. "Nothing personal, if the *Tribune* didn't pay me to see you every day, I wouldn't make the effort."

Marvin tilted his head to study me, maybe deploying x-ray vision to determine my intentions. He also played my old trick, let them fill the silence.

He said, "That's a long-winded *no.*"

I took the bait and added a twist. "My chain of command left me hanging."

"I see. That's unfortunate. Does Gordon know you're here? Or Mr. Kinsale?"

"Josie may tell her dad," I said with a *so what?* smirk.

"Let me count the possible charges you might face. You came through an enclosure."

As he listed my potential legal issues, I steadied my breathing. I had no police record. I could be given a warning or a stack of them.

He ended his litany of possible criminal charges with a possible criminal mischief charge for damage to the Hulett house's shrubbery.

I kept my mouth shut about permission. Snitches get stitches. Or end up in ditches. And I doubted he'd seen the Hulett house shrubbery, but I didn't want to call him on that bluff. Yet.

Finally, Chief Taylor started wrapping up. "And folks in these parts aren't fond of media people. Gordon, Wilbur, and the others? People've known them all their lives. But you? From New York City?" He paused, then added in a confidential tone, "You might as well be a minion of Satan himself."

Remembering all the tracking stares I'd received moments earlier, including grilling by Dwayne Kinsale, I said, with the expected amount of resignation, "They're all gathering pitchforks and torches." Then, I switched gears, leaned toward him, and said, "To defend themselves from the *murderer* you guys have yet to catch." A step away, and I said, "Some perspective is in order here. I'm not the bad guy."

A golf cart with a Kinsale Farms decal on the front rolled up. The new deputy, all long legs and pale arms, scrunched behind the wheel.

The butterflies in my stomach spun into another gear—chaos mode. A golf cart, owned by my paper's publisher, not a patrol car. Deputized.

The chief deputy ordered the young deputy driving to get out and man the perimeter. The new deputy nodded before shooting a wary glance my way. He unfolded his long legs, arose from the cart, and stepped aside.

Marvin pointed toward the direction from which I'd come. "And go down there to keep an eye on that perimeter, adjacent to the Fairview Lane backyards."

The deputy nodded and headed off toward the Olmos trailer and the Hulett hedge.

Marvin swept his arm to direct me toward the golf cart. "You'll be happier if you just get in the front seat."

I'd be riding in an open golf cart, feeling the breeze pass over my face instead of sitting in the rear seat of a police car behind the cage. An odd nagging quirk poked at me. "Don't you have better things to do than drive me out yourself?"

"This is both quicker than walking you out and a job I need to stay done."

"I see." I perched on the gray vinyl slab that didn't quite pass as a cushion. The cold plastic sent a damp wakeup chill through my jeans. "Thanks for the lift," I said, meaning *thank you for not arresting me.*

He walked around to the driver's side, all the while eyeing me like a German Shepherd gazing at steaks on the grill. The chief deputy slid in behind the wheel. The cart beeped in reverse until we moved forward with the weak excuse for headlights swatting at the dark.

"I'll take you as far as the fairgrounds gate," he said. "You'll stay outside the gate. You won't come back in. If you do return, you will go to jail."

I tucked my notebook and pen into my pocket before regaining my seat on the golf cart. At least I wouldn't be shot on sight. But I wouldn't have been able to gather much news from a jail cell, either.

We took off with a lurch. I grabbed the shallow handle that ran alongside what passed for a passenger seat. We bumped along on an old asphalt driveway toward the grandstand on the way to the gate.

I asked a question, and I knew I wouldn't need my notebook to record his answer. "Can you confirm or deny that the deceased is Cyrus McCoy of Lexington?"

The chief deputy kept his eyes front and his poker face steady. "The case is still under investigation."

"Of course." I had to ask, and he had to lob the expected reply in the game of Cop Keep-away, a game with its own rules and gambits to elicit subtext, which couldn't be printed as news but could serve as leads to something else. Especially for high-stakes pro-level action like this, a murder case, or in a war zone.

We bounced and jostled through a village of gloomy empty horse stables with open stall doors reminding me, as we drove by, of a smile with missing teeth. In more populated areas, I spotted truck-and-trailer rigs and RVs. Closer to the grandstand, men and women in tees and jeans were packing unsold merchandise and collapsing folding tables and tent canopies, adjacent to trucks and vans, in what appeared to have been a makeshift flea market.

I asked, "How many people were here tonight?"

"You'd have to ask the sponsoring organization. The VFW."

Also, not an unexpected answer. High stakes.

The driveway took us closer to the largest truck, emblazoned with the name of a Lexington tack shop. Two men, with their ball cap brims pulled low, smoked in the dark. Each drag of their cigarettes sparked the glowing tip and illuminated their strong chins and grim mouths. One glanced up as we passed with his stare tracking our progress.

I said in more of a conversational tone, "A lot of money changes hands at these events, I guess."

"I wouldn't know about that." His terse reply hummed with resignation.

Time to change the rhythm, to interrupt the Q&A. "Horse show Murphy's Law," I mused. "When you're in a hurry, the equipment you need most will break. Or you'll realize you forgot to pack it. Been there. Seen that. My little sister showed hunt seat."

The glow from a streetlight revealed a smile on his mouth with a nod of familiarity. "Show specials aren't usually on stuff you need, if you get my drift. Typically, impulse purchases. So, you borrow from who's next to you. So, you didn't ride? Your sister did?"

"I can ride. I didn't show." A lot of fuss over ribbons and points. For what? I loved the horses, but I knew I had to move on.

The underpowered golf cart chugged up a hill, a rise on which the massive grandstand loomed to our right, but we veered to the left, away from the main gate.

Alarm spiked along my spine. Long after midnight at what I used to know as *zero-dark-thirty,* I was riding into the night in a golf cart driven by a man I barely knew, a local authority, who now held additional power over me.

I jabbed my thumb as if I were hitchhiking. "I may be new around here," the words scratched out of my throat, "but isn't the gate over there?"

Five

Shadows hid the chief deputy's face as he drove the rickety golf cart toward what I'd presumed—even hoped—was the fairgrounds gate.

By noticing the front grill of the vehicles headed our way, I grounded myself. I reminded myself I was stateside where a veneer of civilization remained, not like in a war zone. Here, I couldn't bribe local officials, nor could they trade access in exchange for special private privileges.

The new deputy had seen me get into the cart with his boss. If it came to the chief's word against mine, I knew where the rookie deputy's loyalty would lie.

Whether the wall was olive or khaki or desert camo, it was still a wall and it took care of its own.

But I wouldn't go down without a fight. The Master Sergeant had taught defensive tactics to us journos headed for the desert, let alone a combat zone. If I could only remember his lessons better than his snark.

"Are we headed for a gate I don't know about?" I managed to say. I turned to make sure he was watching the road and not me when I pulled my phone out of my jacket pocket to hold by my side.

Stables lay ahead. To our right was a parking lot.

"One rule. Don't get out of the cart or you'll be a guest of the county at taxpayer expense. Worse, you'll explain your choice yourself to Mr. Kinsale."

"All right," I said. My voice sounded cold. Hard. Tough. "What do you really want?"

I'd been in this position before. I'd seen how war set loose human darkness, as if we could fight darkness with darkness.

Ahead, over a rise, glowed some light.

The chief deputy gripped the top of the steering wheel with both hands "What I want," he said a bit louder than necessary, "is to get you off the property so I can get back to work."

"That's it?" *No handcuffs? No trading sex for access?*

No longer in a war zone, either.

He gunned the cart engine, causing it to grind its way up the small hill. Then he slammed on the brakes, jerking us forward. "I'm throwing you a bone, Scoop."

Yellow police tape marked off the crime scene's perimeter. The glow I'd seen earlier came from powerful work lights for the crime scene.

He said, "You've got sixty seconds. Tops. Stay in the cart."

Under the lights, near a flatbed wrecker, a group of workers in protective suits—cops or evidence techs—worked around a late-model two-door sporty red coupe I recognized.

Not an official confirmation, but the same make and model of Cy's car.

A small criminalist in a white hazmat suit squatted by the rear passenger door and faced what might have been the driver wearing a dark business suit and sprawled face down in the grass.

My focus zoomed in on white cuffs between the suit jacket and the man's hand. The arm stretched out and led to the back of a man's white dress shirt collar, almost glowing against his dark walnut brown neck under his short and crispy black hair. An eighty percent confirmation of I.D.

An inky brown pool, like thick sludgy stew, peeked out in the grass surrounding his head.

Old compartmentalization skills kicked in. The phone camera was on and up to my face.

Fast, fast, fast. Get the shot, Avery, before anyone realizes you're here. And framed so the work light wouldn't futz with the meter.

The golf cart took off with a whir and a lurch. I rocked backward with arms up and elbows out. I grabbed the rail with one hand while the other pinched the phone with sweaty fingers.

The chief deputy said, "You had to take advantage, didn't you? I should've known you'd pull out a camera phone. Delete that photo now."

I yelled over the clatter of the golf cart on the driveway, "You told me to stay in the cart. You said nothing about photos."

I twisted as best I could to look back as we drove away, but the crime scene receded from view and the ride got bumpy. I couldn't be certain that if I fell out, I wouldn't be arrested anyway.

"Do you ever wonder why people don't like reporters?"

"Not sure if you pay much attention to national news, but cops aren't so popular either." I made sure to add, "Especially when we're both doing our respective jobs."

We zoomed past the grandstand and headed toward the other side of the checkpoint at the main gate, all the while shouting at each other over each *thunk* and rattle.

He said, "Is that why the messenger always gets killed?"

"Not always. Sometimes, we recover." *Voice of experience, pal.*

We rode through the gate past a scowling Deputy Fortner. About twenty feet past her, the golf cart clunked and jerked to a halt.

"This is your stop," the chief deputy said. "Head on over to the old Hulett house for your car." He leaned across the wheel and tilted his head. "They say it's a nice night for a walk."

I tottered, stiff and achy, from the cart. "Yes, the famous 'they.' They say a lot of things. Thanks for the lift."

He pointed at me. "Don't sneak back in." Then he called out, sounding more official, "Deputy Fortner, see to it that this reporter stays out of there." Then to me, he said, "See you tomorrow."

With my feet on the asphalt, I said, "It is tomorrow."

He shifted the golf cart into Reverse and swung it around in a clunky J-turn. He returned to the fairgrounds, toward the grandstand and back toward the crime scene.

I watched the cart recede into the dark, like my story access. From behind the grandstand where the golf cart had disappeared, came headlights and orange reflectors outlining an approaching semitruck.

I turned to Fortner who stood her post.

I held my phone so she could see. "Is it too late to order pizza?"

She countered. "Stay on this side of the fence."

On the outside looking in. Except I watched the long truck headed our way.

The big rig came closer to the fairgrounds gate. The paint job suggested it wasn't Kinsale's mostly white truck. Blurry-at-a-distance markings on the side might be information advertising the farm.

I pulled out my phone with its lit screen and opened the voice recorder app. The phone camera couldn't take useful photos in the dark even with the flash, which could obliterate the writing on the vehicle walls under a splash of glare. Definitely not enough light for writing in the old-style paper notebook, either.

When the truck passed, I read the farm name and town off each vehicle that passed in front of me. The drivers ignored me or gave me the stink eye from under the bill of a ball cap.

Fortner called out, "Aren't you leaving?"

"I'll stay out of your way."

"Stay out of *their* way. Don't block traffic."

Vehicles passing me included a minivan, a motorhome with the old boxy living quarters, a couple of family sedans, and more pickup trucks pulling horse trailers. Some rigs, even the small farm horse-haulers, gleamed new under the lights. Others looked faded and old enough to have hauled Secretariat.

On almost all, whether on a door panel or a front license plate, was a silhouetted logo of a high-stepping horse. The horse's head looked as if it were pushing into a strong headwind with its tail flagging out in its wake.

The region's ubiquitous symbol of the Bluegrass Ambling Horse was everywhere. On license plates. Mailboxes. Over wide barn doors. On T-shirts. Ball caps.

A white heavy-duty pickup truck pulling a horse trailer passed me and then pulled off to the side of the road. Printed on the truck door was "Olmos Stables" with the ambling horse emblem. A browner than tan male arm with a wristwatch and curly arm hairs ended in a short-sleeved dress shirt and rested on the bottom of the open window.

"Where's your car?" Herb called out to me. "Are you stranded?"

A glow from the dash on the older truck attracted my attention. A small screen, not a nav system unit, but a video monitor showing shadowy horses tugging hay from net bags hanging in the trailer.

"Oh. Thanks. I'm good." I offered a brisk wave with a smile. "No problem."

We exchanged more nods and smiles, and he was off again, and not a moment too soon. I didn't want to miss any other trucks exiting, except a white Cadillac sedan slowed down and eased onto the shoulder near where I stood and stopped.

Now what? Music, a male baritone crooning country rock, had to be loud to be heard outside a hermetically sealed luxury car. The music faded. The window hummed open. A feminine arm in long sleeves ending in French cuffs seemed to float out and beckon me over.

The night kept getting weirder.

I headed over, my boots crunching on the pea gravel along the shoulder of the road. In the movies, killers favored black SUVs. In real life in Iraq, I'd seen them in crappy cheap pickups loaded with gaggles of men waving AK-47s and itching for action.

Josie Kinsale rested her arm along the base of the open window. "Once I regained my composure, I realized you're new to our Bluegrass Ambling Horses."

The "our Bluegrass Ambling Horses" grabbed my attention. Why that phrasing? "I'm new here. Period."

Her nervous laugh tinkled like a wind chime made of spoons. "We owners and ambling horse fanciers are a community. A family. We're often misunderstood by outsiders looking in."

I'd done a little online research. Misunderstood was an understatement, but I needed to cover a murder. "Most families are misunderstood." *And dysfunctional*, but I left that silent.

Another truck rumbled my way. I didn't want to miss its information.

"This is both an industry and a way of life," she said.

"Okay." I nodded like a woodpecker on meth. "Like boating," I offered way too cheerily.

A squeaky whimper came from inside the passenger compartment. A pile of fabric on the passenger seat shifted and revealed gleaming black eyes peering at me. A tiny mouth yipped, then growled, showing pointy white teeth.

"It's alright," Josie cooed at the raggedy . . . terrier? Or was it a shih tzu with a short haircut? "Go back to sleep, baby."

Then she handed me a business card. "Call me if you have questions," she said, no longer talking to her scruffy little friend. "Or need anything else."

The window raised its glass boundary between her leather upholstered luxury and the country road. She put the car in gear and waved with fluttering fingers before easing back onto the road.

I slid the business card into my hip pocket. "Princess," I said to the SUV rolling away from me. Her mascara, after all that crying, remained flawless. I should've asked her what brand she wore.

Another white vehicle drove by; a windowless van, but with the round blue, gold, and white Blanchard County seal. Below it, black letters said, "County Coroner."

My dictation hung in the air with my fingers clutching the phone. My chest tightened around my lungs. I tracked the blocky van like a panning TV camera.

That's why I was there. That's why I was anywhere. Even when it wasn't a conflict zone. Loss. Violent loss. Grief. Consequences.

The coroner's van drove away from me. I blinked tears welling to spill. The red taillights blurred in my tears.

Compartmentalization?

That was a work in progress.

Six

I hung tough while watching a few more vehicles exiting the fairgrounds until close to dawn. A deputy I didn't know arrived to relieve Fortner. The relief deputy nodded with raised brows shooting a question my way, but Fortner shook her head and waved her hand as if to dismiss me as a problem.

Just great. Of course, I belonged there, but to outright dismiss me? Insulting. *Geez.*

After I'd almost fallen asleep waiting for the last rig to leave, I checked my phone for messages. None. Big surprise.

I walked the way I'd driven earlier, around the corner and past the still-slumbering houses of Fairview Drive to get my car; I was half-surprised the Blanchard County Sheriff's Department hadn't towed it for sport.

I headed out along the country roads into Bowmansville, the county seat of Blanchard County. My dry eyes took in the pink and gray streaks of the sun rising over trees and hills. Mist lingered in the hollows as if laid by hand.

Outside my car's windows, lay lush horse or cow pastures with old trees—maybe even like what passersby saw a hundred years or so ago.

The sunrise cast a pink glow on the county courthouse's sandstone Greek revival columns, suggesting a temple of supposedly benevolent power and authority.

My approach to the town's sprawling cemetery on the left side of the street indicated my proximity to home. Or home for here. Good thing. My aching eyes threatened to swoon back inside my head. Maybe I was tired enough to sleep without nightmares. Today, I'd skip my morning run through the graveyard, which I found to be safer than running alongside the busy state road with no sidewalks.

I drove past a mailbox with "Ward Farm" painted on its side. Close to the road, the white barn with its tall sliding doors already open, showed silhouetted people puttering around inside. Outside near the entrance was the Olmos Stables pickup truck and Herb's rig, disconnected and off to the side.

Across the lawn, past a riding ring, my landlady's white-frame two-story house stood tucked in a grove of maple trees. A shady porch held a swing and some white rockers, as well as hanging baskets of pink petunias above bushes with white peonies.

Past the other side of the house, I nosed my car up a short gravel driveway. I parked next to a white mobile home with cornflower blue shutters.

I shut off the engine in time to hear the screen door to the house smack shut. Had she been awake and watching for me?

Sure enough, my landlady Hazel Ward bustled outside in powder blue capri pants and a Nashville Music City tee. She gathered sticks from the lawn, strewn by the previous night's storm.

She stood with one freckled hand clutching the bundle of twigs and the other shading her eyes, as if she were scouting a better trail for a wagon train. Or instead, looking for news to share on the phone or Facebook.

"Mornin'," she called out. "Are you just getting in?"

My face buzzed from lack of sleep. A shower would clear my head and then a couple of hours of sleep would re-build my game face. *Just smile, wave, and keep moving.*

"Hi," came out of my mouth. "Late night at the office. Gotta grab some shut-eye."

"Come in for some breakfast before you hit the hay." Hazel looked way too perky for the hour. "You'll sleep better."

A light breeze sent me a whiff of coffee brewing. The aroma wafted into my lungs, floated toward my stomach, and dragged me by my belt.

A cup of coffee and maybe some eggs wouldn't kill me. Let alone a little time outside my head, even if I had to pay for it with a little RUMINT, what the troops called "rumored intelligence."

I followed Hazel and the trail of coffee aroma up the two crooked concrete steps to her screened-in porch. The screen door squeaked when she pulled it wide for me.

"What a terrible, terrible thing. A murder at a horse show. With families there." She stopped at the threshold to change her shoes from sneaker loafers to scruffy blue slippers. She pointed at my feet. "Don't worry about your shoes."

I was already unlacing my boots in the speedy way I'd learned in Iraq. Removing shoes at a home's threshold appeared appropriate in Kentucky farm country, too.

"The cops are still there," I said before padding into the house in my socks.

Inside Hazel's kitchen, white lacquer cabinets and new appliances sparkled, even though Hazel was in the middle of breakfast preps that would have left any kitchen of mine littered in dust, grease, and rubble. A table and chairs stood in the middle between the sink and the stove. A hanging shelf, covered in a lineup of ceramic frog knickknacks, seemed to monitor our activity.

She scuffed over to the stove topped with two cast-iron skillets. "I heard the state troopers came in and took over everything." Her voice bristled with indignation.

She spooned white flour into a skillet already shiny with a glaze of grease and studded with chunks of meat.

My stomach quivered and so did my arteries. *Just coffee and eggs for me.*

"Blanchard County doesn't have a crime lab," I said. "The state police does, thanks to you taxpayers."

"I bet your daddy still won cases back in the day without all that CSI stuff." She stirred the gravy in the skillet with a whisk. Her cheeks pinked from the stovetop's steaming and sizzling pans.

A shiver of tension hit me. The chitchat when I'd rented the place had included a short family bio, which I'd kept to my mother, stepfather, and late father. Little did I suspect the precision of my landlady's retention of details.

"I don't remember much about him. Mom told me he was pretty aggressive in court. I think he would've traded *me* for a shot at DNA evidence back in the day."

Hazel hissed a *pshaw*.

I peeked into a basket lined with a napkin to see about a dozen biscuits tucked inside. A buttery aroma wafted my way. I patted the cover closed.

The screen door creaked open and banged shut.

"Oh, good." She grabbed the dishtowel from the drawer handle and blotted her hands. "Norwood can join us after all."

I heard the one-two plops of big boots hitting the floor by the row of shoes. When Hazel's son stepped over the threshold between the screened-in porch and kitchen, he spotted me. "Oh." Energy fell from his voice. "Hi, Avery."

Whoa. *Good morning to you, too.*

Norwood lowered his lanky frame, clad in jeans and an indigo polo shirt, into the end chair of the dinette set. He slouched, shielding most of his face under the bill of his hunter green cap with the logo of a Lexington racetrack, where his mother had once said he'd been one of the veterinarians.

His mouth twitched among what had to have been yesterday's five o'clock shadow.

Hazel pulled coffee mugs from another upper cabinet. "Did you see each other at the fairgrounds last night?"

"Was he there last night?" I asked.

His fair skin made his bleary eyes look even more red and tired. "What? He who?" Clean hands or not, his dark hair and fair skin made him look sooty.

Still wearing the cap, too. Wasn't keeping a man's hat on in the house a social gaffe especially in the ultra-polite South?

Hazel bustled over with a mug and placed it in front of him. "Did you see Avery last night? She was out at the fairgrounds, too."

He shook his head. "No." He glanced at me with eyes so droopy he looked stoned.

My stomach growled in hunger or protest. I looked over the selections on the table. My mind ran the nutrition math. A platter of scrambled eggs cooked in an unidentified grease. A basket of biscuits. A bowl of cream gravy. Plates of bacon and sausage links. The only edible plant matter untouched by animal fats? Orange juice and white sugar.

While pouring Norwood's coffee, Hazel prattled about "the tragedy."

The screen door banged again. "Hello?" called out a woman's cheery nasal voice I heard five days a week.

Hazel called out, "Come on in, Laverne. We're just sitting down."

Her friend Laverne, the office manager at the paper and one of Kinsale's sisters-in-law, launched into talking before she left the screened-in porch.

"Was down at the Quik Stop. They fired up their coconut doughnuts for the season."

She bustled in bright-eyed as if it were almost noon instead of shortly after dawn. Her fuchsia lipstick matched her nails and her track suit. Around her neck, she wore a nest of gold chains which included a cross and a high-stepping Miniature Pinscher, a charm that looked at first glance like the emblem of the Bluegrass Ambling Horse.

Her puffy ash-blonde helmet of hair always suggested she visited a hairdresser often. She greeted her friend's son with a hug around his shoulders. "Hi, Norwood. How you doin,' shugah?"

In silence, he patted her hand.

She turned to me, "Well, hello, Avery." The cheer had left her voice. "I didn't expect to see you here this morning."

Likewise. I said, "Good morning, Laverne."

Laverne bustled over to the coffee pot and the cabinet with the coffee mugs.

Hazel pulled another place mat from the drawer. "We were talking about what happened last night," she said with the excited breathlessness of someone from a sheltered life working to avoid mentioning a particular unseemly event like a murder. "Were you there?"

Laverne shook her head while helping herself to a mug of coffee. "Just to say, 'hello' and then watch Josie show in the early classes. We can't stay up for those late classes and make it to church anymore."

"This is terrible of me," Hazel said, "but I just can't place who Cyrus McCoy was."

A chill hit me. Was Hazel having memory problems? I said, with a slight smile, "A couple of weeks ago, I wrote a story about Cy McCoy for the paper after he'd been named state Teacher of the Year."

Laverne blew past me with her steaming mug and chimed in. "You remember Louise? One of the household help for Clark and Polly?"

Drawing a blank, Hazel scrunched her face and shook her head.

Laverne continued with some mock patience, "Louise was the housekeeper and Mavis the cook. Cyrus helped in the barn and on the grounds. Even showed some of Clark's older horses in the juvenile classes."

Hazel tapped her index finger on her chin while deep in thought, "Louise's boy. Now I thought he married one of Mavis's girls?"

"No, Mom." Norwood sounded exhausted. "They broke up. And she wasn't Mavis's daughter. You know . . ."

They launched into an extended session of "Country Connect-the-Dots." I struggled to follow along in case some useful information came out, but the convoluted provenance gave my tired mind mental whiplash. In horse country, even human pedigree mattered.

But I sensed no sadness, no feeling of loss from the death, let alone the shock I'd seen erupt when violent death dropped like a boulder into a quiet pond.

My stomach quivered. Maybe I should've grabbed some scrambled eggs to go with that coffee. Something I couldn't place was off. Out there somewhere. Almost like Hazel's tip of the tongue memory, just out of reach.

Fatigue catches up sooner now than it did when I was younger.

I said, sounding as tired as I felt, "The recent Teacher of the Year?"

"Yes." Hazel's eyes brightened as she connected all the stories. "I remember him now. He did real good for himself. A shame he had to die so young." As if someone had tripped a switch, she said, "Mavis did real good, too. Even got her family going on educations."

Laverne turned up her nose and flipped a wave of dismissal. "She had to hit the lotto to do it."

Hazel said, "Cyrus was such a nice boy. I just hate to hear he got mixed up in one of those gangs."

What?

I jumped into the conversation. "But he worked to help kids avoid the streets. Hello? Teacher of the Year?" I managed to resist adding how *Louise's boy* was an adult.

Laverne dumped two sugars into her milky coffee, tilted her head and shot me a grin that chilled like vodka from the freezer. She then said, "I hear tell it was one of those drive-by shootings," in a patronizing you're-cute-but-clueless tone.

Gunfire? No one mentioned anything about hearing gunfire. Not even on social media.

Eager to hear what she'd say—would she be sincere or patronizing—I leaned toward Laverne and then said, "Who told you it was a shooting?"

"That's what I heard." Laverne rapped her spoon on the edge of the mug like a judge's gavel. No more questions.

I'd have to ask the sheriff's department later. "Had any of those *theys* worn a badge?"

Their silence let my mind consider what I'd considered unthinkable. Had a crew taken issue with Cy's work with their potential recruits? Or had he been collateral damage in a hit gone wrong. Had there been another target?

But why drive all the way out here to do it?

I broke my own rule and filled the silence with my own observations. "No one I talked to at the fairgrounds said anything about hearing gunfire. I didn't see it on social media, either."

But how many people had I talked to before the chief deputy drove me to the gate? I had to consider any new lead, no matter how whack. I hated chasing leads rooted in gossip—or worse—stereotypes. My job demanded I extract rocks from the dirt to see what lurked underneath.

I swiveled to the other potential on-the-scene witness, who'd been eating and drinking but not talking. "Norwood."

He startled when I addressed him. "You were there. Did you hear any gunfire? And you knew him, too. Do you think he was killed in a drive-by shooting?"

Norwood wouldn't look at me or respond. He studied his eggs as if they offered the secrets of the universe, like how to get me to shut up. "I need to go."

Wuss. "You're going along with them believing rumors, maybe even outright lies?"

Norwood shoved his chair from the kitchen table, causing the screech of wood on vinyl flooring. Hazel and Laverne gasped.

Hazel said, "Norwood, honey, you stay put," offering the plate of bacon to him. "Are you ready for some more?"

He waved her off with a tight-lipped downcast shake of his head. "I have to get back to work." He stood.

Laverne laid her palm over my forearm as if she were about to lay some truth on me. "Those street gangs have used those MAC-10s and AK-47s and who knows what else now *for years*. Cy worked with that element every single day. Going in and out of those neighborhoods. Those gangs were bound to get even with him for interfering with their recruitment practices."

My blood pressure hammered like a troupe of Japanese *kodo* drummers. I locked my gaze on her cold blue eyes and then dragged mine to stare at her fuchsia gel nails on my arm.

I lowered my arm to dislodge her firm but steady grip. I raised my gaze back up to look into her eyes. "Maybe I should look up what constitutes a hate crime in Kentucky?"

Hazel rested her open palm on her throat and said, "Lord, have mercy. No one here *hates*."

Laverne cooed at me as if I were five. "Won't you be glad when Crystal has her baby and comes back to work so you can go back home?"

I wadded the paper napkin and dropped it into my plate.

I am here for a short time. I may be among them, but I am not one of them.

My mantra on being an embedded photographer with the military, as well as for checking on civilians in the Sandbox. Did it have to apply in the States, too?

I stood, grabbed my plate, and then toted it to the sink. "I should go back home where I belong?" I added a sneer before saying, "With live theater and chai lattes?"

Laverne tapped her nails on the table. "And muggings. And garbage in the streets." She smirked.

Behind me, Hazel said, in an attempt at spin control with niceness that made me itch, "Avery was up all night working. I'd be cranky, too."

"I don't think so." Laverne wagged a scolding finger at me. "She's just stirring up stuff for attention." She added, "And in a private home. Shame on you. That's no way to treat your hostess."

I leaned against the edge of the counter, holding the sink. I should've been out the door by now, but no way would I give Laverne the last word. From talking about a man who'd been murdered to maybe perpetuating racial stereotypes—or was I misreading—and then making it all about my lack of manners.

"You and I? We both work for a *newspaper*." I uttered the last word as if it was holy. To journalists, it is. But maybe not to the office staff. "We're supposed to be objective. Show respect for everyone. Except not so much for those pulling the societal strings at-large. Have you heard the saying about journalists comforting the afflicted and afflicting the comfortable?"

Laverne swiped the air in front of her face and scowled with distaste. "Aw, honey. No one here wants to read that crap. And you think your behavior," she gestured to encompass my space in the kitchen, "is objective? Let alone respectful of the dead? You're just after a *story*. Talk to Clark like you've talked to me. See what happens."

Fatigue sagged my body. I thought about Iraqi women scarved and silent. *Way to impose your values on the community, Avery.*

I braced my hand on the countertop behind me as if I were leaning in a casual and cocky stance.

To Hazel, I said, "Thank you for breakfast. It's just not sitting well."

I couldn't resist shooting Laverne a hard glare I hoped would make her flinch.

Instead, she leaned away from the table, folded her arms, and returned my gaze down her nose with entitled defiance.

On my way out I snatched my boots from the collection of shoes. Pulling them on would take too long. I just wanted out before I lost my temper. I carried my boots while padding along in my socks on the cool painted concrete flooring through the screened-in porch.

Once I touched the screen door, I realized I didn't want to trek home through the damp grass in my socks. I plunked my butt on the threshold, still out of their sight. I fumbled with the laces on my boots.

Behind me, from the kitchen I heard Hazel say, as if spitting out the words, "Well, thank you very much. Now she thinks we're awful."

"So what?" Laverne said, "It's a free country. We can talk about whatever the blue blazes we want. Little Miss Prissy News wants us to respect other people and free speech? Well, she needs to respect ours. She has no idea how we live our lives here. She's a little too mouthy for my taste."

Hazel said, "Maybe so, but you don't have to be so snippety about it. And I always did like Louise, Mavis, and Cyrus. Mavis and I exchange Christmas cards every year."

Laverne's voice veered into loud and teasing. "Forget her. You'll never guess whose car I spotted last night parked at the First and Last. She'll be hungover at church today, if she makes it at all."

With that, they flipped the conversation to gossip.

I turned around, pulled the screen door open and slammed it shut. Petty, but satisfying.

Seven

With the screen door still quaking, I jumped from the top step and over the two crooked steps to the grass.

In the trees above me, birds tweeted with saccharine merriment. Somewhere it was five o'clock.

I trudged through the grass and mulled over the previous night. Er, morning. And I called a halt to mentally kicking myself for losing my cool.

Had shots rung out at the fairgrounds by the time I'd arrived at Gordon's brother's house, every home within earshot would have been lit with people hovering in their backyards to compare notes. In that family neighborhood with houses close together, a fired gun would wake up everyone. Let alone all those horse people; I would've seen outbursts about gunfire on social media.

In the side yard toward the riding ring was an older teenage boy wearing a tank shirt and baggy khaki shorts. He sported the kind of muscles you get from weightlifting. He gathered post-storm lawn litter into a pile. His muscled legs, sticking out of baggy khaki shorts, looked paler and way hairier than his arms. He spotted me and gave me a double take with a lingering gaze at my chest.

Great. Walking hormones in a pair of Timberland boots and baggy long shorts. Just what I needed after all the prejudice with a coat of good manners. Now, sexism too.

Full all the way to my throat with what lurked in the shadows of southern hospitality, in confrontational mode, I stomped over. “Hey. You. What are you looking at?”

His mouth compressed to whiten the olive skin around his lips. His face flushed red. He heaved the armload of branches to the ground and off to his side. What had been a tidy bundle landed so hard some bounced away from the grouping.

Then, he blinked hard. A mix of confusion and panic fluttered over his face. Could’ve been rage or could’ve been embarrassment.

“Lady,” he said in clipped tones in an accent I recognized but hadn’t heard since I’d moved south. ”*You’re* the one with the problem.”

A New York accent in a rural Kentucky backyard? Curiosity and a spark of connection shifted my attitude more.

“Yeah,” I said. “I have problems. Who doesn’t?” I offered a crooked grin with enough of a twinkle to smooth the vibe and lower the threat level more.

He pointed to a spot near where my feet had been headed. “You almost stepped in a big gopher hole dug by some freaky country rat. Alright? I was gonna wave you off, but you went off, so I didn’t get the chance. So go ahead. Step in it. Fall down. You’re welcome.”

I slid my gaze across my previous path. No shadow, but a raised area with coarse grass. “Oh,” I said in what amounted to an apology. I hadn’t ruled out the possibility of him viewing life through a filter of testosterone. “I feel the need to mention your eyes weren’t looking there.”

“Geez, lady. Your team T-shirt logo. You bleed Yankees blue, too. There aren’t many of us here. The whole freakin’ joint here is drowned in Wildcat blue.”

My gaze dipped toward the Yankees logo on my T-shirt. After a murder, my thwarted job performance, and the Polite Ladies wing of the John

Birch Society, two homesick souls of different generations connected over sports.

The kid sagged at the shoulders, looking as exhausted as I felt. It was too early in the morning for a teenager. And too early, or too late, for me after pulling an all-nighter on the job. He'd been a good target for my frustration, and I'd made him drop all those sticks he'd gathered. By hand.

I said, "Sorry about my outburst. I was up all night. The next time I see you, we'll talk pinstripes and dirty water dogs."

He popped a resigned shrug with his broad-pumped shoulders like a kid who's heard a lot of benign white lies from adults. He doubled over to gather the scattered tree litter and said, "I miss going to the beach. A real one. With the ocean."

He sounded so forlorn. No wonder—hundreds of miles from the ocean, let alone the Yankees.

I hopped forward to help collect the twigs. "Let me help you. This is on me." I added, "I hear there's a lake with some beachfront in town."

He scrunched his nose, shook his head, and cringed. "It's not a beach. It's a patch of sand. You need ocean for a real beach."

"You got a point." I bundled my sticks into one hand and offered the broken branches.

He mumbled words of gratitude, and I pivoted toward home but paused to call out over my shoulder, "You're doing a great job. Keep it up."

Sunlight hitting the white siding on my mobile home hurt my eyes. I climbed the few steps to the deck at the rear door of my trailer. Before I unlocked my door, movement off to the side attracted my attention.

In the pasture behind the barn, mares with round bellies grazed while foals bounced as if their spindly legs hid springs. My blood pressure receded, cooling my fevered brain.

A man in a ball cap and jeans I suspected was Herb, led a black horse past a spreading oak toward a pond ringed with clusters of yellow wild irises. Following them was a young teen boy. He carried a long white pole pointed like a shepherd's staff.

Herb switched out the lead line clipped to the horse's halter for one end of the pole. Then he walked away and stepped onto the dock jutting out toward the middle of the pond while sliding his hand along the pole attached to the horse.

As tired as I was, with my hand on the door, I couldn't help but watch. The black mare sniffed the water near a cluster of the yellow blossoms and took a dainty sip before walking in. She sank to her chest, then to her head out toward the center where I could only see nostrils, eyes, ears, and a wake trailing behind her.

The boy joined Herb on the dock as the men tracked the horse swimming in an arc around the end of the dock. She emerged on the other side and shook like a sopping wet Labrador retriever with water flying and arcing with the blur of hummingbird wings.

The men stepped backward away from the shower. Their shoulders rose and fell in laughter I couldn't hear. The boy tilted his head to dry his face with the sleeve of his T-shirt. Herb patted the mare on her glistening shoulder and stepped in closer. She lowered her head and arced her neck around him.

I left them to their lovely scene and went on inside. I logged onto the *Lexington Journal* site to see a front-page story, a single column below the fold, about the suspicious death of the recently named state Teacher of the Year. No photo, thank goodness. Not sure I could've handled that yet.

Judging by the dateline on our website, Gordon had posted a basic story about an untimely death at the fairgrounds with identification of the deceased pending notification of family.

As if it weren't already on social media. Or sizzling over phones.

My head tried to swoon around, in a spiral of fatigue. Forget the shower. I'd collapse under the water. Straight to bed.

The book on my nightstand caught my eye only to punt me deep into the land of memory— a trip to the bookstore where I'd found a familiar face.

Cy had led me from the bookstore's periodical section to a wall of shelves, from ceiling to floor, filled with books by Kentucky authors. "Try this one," he'd said while pulling a book from the shelf. "A period piece set around the Civil War that'll move you with its beauty one minute and then enrage you the next. Written by a former war correspondent, like you, but a dude in the Spanish-American War."

I'd said, *no matter what else changes, war stays the same.*

So, no reading my new book in case it set off my hair trigger. I burrowed deeper into my pillow and threw a T-shirt over my eyes to black out the insistent morning light.

Under the cool darkness, my mind raced faster than my fading body. As soon as I'd get vertical, I'd make some calls. The sheriff's department, the coroner . . .

The relentless sun blazed and braised me into a stew of my own sweat. Through the *niqab's* peephole slit for my eyes, I scanned the market.

A fruit seller. A basket maker. T-shirts hanging over a table covered in brass pots and pitchers. Hagglers gesticulating their dismay at the quality of goods, then the seller's version, with timing like a call-and-response. Glaring sunlight, endless shadows.

Panic zinged. How was I alone in the market? Where was my translator?

A whip-slender youth in front of me turned and shot me a smile cultivated by the best orthodontists in Detroit. Hassan—except all of us in the bureau called him Sandy—flashed his eyebrows high.

My nerves spiked.

Too public. Too casual. Our American-forged mannerisms too ingrained.

My sister is mute, is how he'd explain my silence to curious locals. I knew a little Arabic and Pashto. Some would remark upon his good fortune in having a sister who'd never mouth off.

I slumped, lowered my head, and shortened my steps to keep my American stride from giving me away despite the veils and the long skirt. A handbag as big as a sink carried my Nikon and weighed down my forearm.

Then, Sandy spun, held out his hands, shook his head. *No, no, no.*

A whistle leading a mechanized scream flew over our heads only to end in an earth-shaking boom. I dropped and curled.

Fruit and brass flew. People with mouths open wide scrambled. Dirt, rocks, and moist clumps rained on my head. Smoke burned my eyes and clawed into my nose.

I couldn't just stay hidden. I had to get up. Grab my camera. Pictures. I had to get pictures. *Get your ass up, Avery.* Except I lay paralyzed on my side.

I curled tighter into a ball. A howling siren cut through the muddle between my ears, also allowing screams of panic and moans of pain access in its wake inside my head.

If I burrowed deeper under the veil tenting my body, its quilted softness wadded by clutching fingers, maybe I'd just disappear?

Wait. *What?*

A quilted *niqab*? Too heavy. Who'd walk around under a duvet?

The yowl of the siren faded. The noon whistle from the Blanchard County Fire Department located about two miles away in downtown Bowmansville faded.

A remnant, Gordon had told me, of the days when Blanchard County was covered in tobacco farms. Convenient, too, for tornado warnings. But a siren at noon meant, well, noon, and tradition in a place that revered tradition.

Oh, hell.

I blinked awake in a film of sweat and tears. I flipped up the duvet.

No smoke. No fire. No carnage.

Just a white ceramic toilet beneath a window decorated with frilly gingham curtains I wouldn't have picked on a prank.

The siren's wail dissipated. Only the hum of an air conditioner remained.

A hot shimmer of *not again* coursed through my chest and spread through my veins. I sagged against the tub's shower wall in my trailer's second bathroom.

The one more likely to remain standing if the rest of the trailer collapsed after a mortar attack.

Which wouldn't happen in Kentucky. Nor would I be in a mobile home in Iraq.

Again, I'd gathered up bedding and while I'd slept.

The Master Sergeant's training on how to survive a hazardous assignment hadn't covered what to do when the work followed us home like a ravenous ghost.

Eight

My blurry vision picked out spotted, dark-flower outlines floating like chunky motes of dust.

Blinking through the hangover provided by the nightmare, I'd stared through the ruffled gingham curtains at the horizon. The afternoon sun had backlit the embroidered daisies.

Over the coffee pot, a ceramic clock made in the shape of the sun complete with yellow sawtooth rays, smiled at me like the demented product of a child's cartoon.

The country *sweet* was enough to make you puke, even though I should've been glad I no longer lived in a hotel room with bullet holes or suspicious brown stains.

With my breakfast eggs long gone, I munched a sliced apple with almond butter. I washed it down with some coffee made from my freezer stash of good beans ordered from a shop in Greenwich Village.

I sat to check for updates on the murder at the Blanchard County Fairgrounds in the *Lexington Journal*. Nothing new yet. Then, I played my voice mails.

"Hey, Avery." Gordon sounded more awake than he had earlier. Still, he drawled his words, sometimes dragging them into three syllables. "Come over for supper. You can get me up to speed on the murder before we eat."

I couldn't help but smile. Only journos and cops have such odd dinner convos.

The next number caused me to brace myself for the message.

"This is Doris Caldwell. I wanted to know what you thought of the horse show." She sounded breathless, manic, and gossipy enough to have fit in at Hazel's breakfast table. "Disgusting, wasn't it?"

For a moment, I thought she meant the murder. "They act like they've changed their evil ways, but they haven't," she said. "And they know I know they haven't." Which made me wince at her smug paranoia. "That's why I'm not welcome there anymore."

Nope. Not talking about the murder. Maybe she hadn't heard.

She continued, "And then they murdered the horse show judge. Probably for tying the wrong horse." She rushed to add, "That means, picking the horse that wasn't slated to win."

Her condescension irked me. "I know what it means," I said as if she could hear me.

Taking competition too far was a new theory. I welcomed anything other than a repeat of the local gossip about the murder having been drive-by shooting.

When everything sounded outrageous, maybe others accepted it as the norm.

"Anyway," she took a deep breath, "You never know with that horse show bunch. Call me back when you can."

I cleared all the messages. I called the county coroner. Her brisk greeting of "Cathy Epperson" sounded as if she knew she had to answer the phone but had other things to do.

I identified myself and then said, "Any news yet? A cause of death for Cyrus McCoy?"

"Too early to tell." Cathy sounded more midwestern than southern, and today, more harried than usual. "The state pathologist just finished conducting the autopsy."

My mind flashed to rooms I wish I'd never seen. The coffee and apple chunks in my stomach gurgled in warning. "He's in one piece? Right?"

She sounded startled. "Yes." A moment, as she remembered she was talking to press. "Officially, I'm in no position to make a statement." Her voice shifted to the solicitousness of her other job, managing other peoples' emotions in legal matters. "Are you alright?"

Relief sagged my shoulders. "Yeah. I'm fine. When can we talk?"

"Come by the house tonight. About eight. Our usual contact mode."

A procedure we'd established early in my short tenure at the *Tribune.* I'd covered a couple of traffic fatalities as well as an untimely death the autopsy revealed as having been the result of undiagnosed heart disease.

"Got it." She ended the call.

I needed some fresh air. Perfect time to head for the fairgrounds.

No more sheriff's department radio car and no more Deputy Fortner standing post at the main gate. Hanging on the chain-link fence beside the fairgrounds sign was a banner fluttering in the slight breeze: "Race today! Free practice rounds for Cancer Society R.C. Car race at 2!"

I drove along the entry driveway I'd been blocked from earlier. A couple of rows of cars and trucks had parked nose-in toward the grandstand on the coarsely mowed grassy knoll rising from the chain-link fence. I parked at the end of the row next to a minivan.

When I left and locked my car, hard rock music blared over a loudspeaker from the grandstand. I bypassed the wooden arena and headed straight for the line of crime scene tape on the top of the hill above where Cy, his car, and all the evidence techs had been.

I stood at the top of the ridge with my toes under the yellow tape. Near a post supporting the tape sat grocery-store bouquets of flowers, pictures of medium-blond Euro Jesus, and even a teddy bear. Below, a white tent big enough to surround the car, obscured my view with its fabric walls.

A pale, pudgy boy in baggy shorts and a pro-wrestling tee scurried up beside me. He whipped out a cell phone and took a selfie, complete with duckface and his free hand throwing the double deuce, using the crime scene as backdrop.

He yelled to those behind us, "Ma! I got it."

"Show some respect," popped out of my mouth instead of his mother's. Which, considering my job and especially my old job, was rich, but I didn't stoop to selfies in the war zones, even if almost everyone else shot them. Even when one of the photo editors in New York requested I send them some to "put a face on the news."

Pudgy Selfie Taker turned so his mother couldn't see him flipping me the bird. He pivoted fast-break style to join his family walking toward the grandstand.

I turned my attention back toward the crime scene area. I'd check social media later. The kid couldn't have been the only one snapping pics or selfies.

"Everything's under the tent now." The male voice behind me snapped me into a startle—even a freeze.

Salaam aleikum almost popped out of my mouth.

Old habits.

Breathing into my jangled nerves, I faced the glasses, sandy hair, and sun-free ivory skin of Pete Livingston, the *Lexington Journal* reporter covering Blanchard and two neighboring counties. So nice of him to swagger up more than twelve hours into the story.

I made my voice sound bright and said, "What brings you here on a Sunday afternoon?"

"The same reason as you." With the first two fingers of his right hand, he shoved his glasses onto his nose. "Small town. Murder. How's it going?"

Not a polite conversational inquiry, but the first line tossed out in a fishing expedition.

"Isn't this your day off?"

"Your co-worker Wilbur is into that old-school scoop and competition mentality, too." He tilted his head as if he were sizing me up. "But I give you a lot of credit."

Healthy paranoia among competitors made me want to grant him nothing. "Why?"

"Everyone has to start somewhere, even you change-of-career reporters. Too bad this is a tough time to start paying your dues."

Paying my dues? Scars on my legs, hidden under my jeans, let alone the award my photos had received, said I'd paid in full. I folded my arms and hoped my poker face held. "I like a challenge."

"You've got one. Publications everywhere are falling like dominoes." His tone veered from snarky to smarmy. "Also, I swear you look familiar. Are you sure we've never met before?"

Him, too? Flirting? With the reporter from the lowly Podunk weekly?

If he kept up with industry awards, he'd probably seen my face with shorter hair.

"Nope. We never met. Look, neither one of us has time for this."

Livingston added, as if we were gossiping, "McCoy was an animal abuser, or he wouldn't have been at this horse show. Let alone judging. I wouldn't be surprised if one of those morons didn't kill him over a ribbon."

Anger snapped behind my eyes. A few weeks ago, Cy had saved cocktail shrimp for a take-home bag while telling me about his mother's Persian cat. He'd smiled like he did when talking about his students. "Even after I wash my hands, she knows I've had shrimp and didn't share with her?" His voice raised in the inflection of a question. "All kinds of hell to pay."

Animal abuser, my ass.

Instead, I said, "What happened to objectivity?"

Pete nodded a knowing smile. "I get it. I really do. You had to drink the Kool-Aid to placate the advertisers, let alone your boss. You'll have to get over that eagerness to please when you move on to The Bigs."

Adrenalin shot up my spine so hard my head hurt from the sparkles firing inside my skull.

"The Bigs? Like the *Journal*?" An urge rode over me and drove me to add, "Here's some advice. Cash out what savings you have. Get a good camera, a sat phone, a laptop, and a flak jacket. And then pick a hot zone."

He gaped, a classic open-mouthed, wide-eyed stare. But it wasn't enough. The whiff of psychic blood sent me in for the kill.

My rage swelled, and my mouth kept going. "Get used to seeing, not only bony cart horses beaten and bloody after they've fallen while pulling a heavy load, but children and old people starving and maimed. Or dead. And get this—they're the lucky ones. Or are the dead ones really the lucky ones? You're never quite sure."

He eased into a silent laugh, complete with a you-had-me-going finger-wag. With a you're-full-of-it-but-you're-entertaining smile, he shook his head.

He said, "Just be careful on the hillsides. Some spots are still damp and slick from that storm last night. High winds took down power lines in Harrodsburg, you know." He walked away.

I said to his back, "Thanks for the tip."

Nine

Later that afternoon, I soaped my hands in Gordon and Shannon's seashell-themed powder room. To avoid the ivory towels embroidered with gold seashells, I wiped my hands on my jeans.

I stepped out the door into a hallway on the main floor of their house, too big for two adults and one small child, as if Shannon and Gordon had intended to fill it someday, but time and their ages seemed to mock their dreams.

In the kitchen, filled with all stainless-steel appliances and curtains with ivy prints, Shannon sliced celery at the counter by the sink like a sous-chef, with the blade making machine gun whap-whaps on the cutting board.

Her oversized walkathon freebie tee draped over her denim shorts, which showed tracks of blue veins tracing sporadic branches on her pale legs—like a road map of time and pregnancy.

At school in New York, we'd all been classmates and friends sharing tips about professors and productivity tricks, as well as beer and pizza. Then we graduated, went our separate ways to greet Life head-on; except our respective dreams had their way with us.

She swept aside her bangs with the top of her wrist. "You and Gordon need to finish your talk about the murder before Teddi comes home."

"Sure." I put my hand on the screen door and stopped. "Is everything okay?"

She spoke, facing the upper white cabinet with her hands stilled but in position to slice more celery. With a *thwock*, her knife halted on the cutting board. "A man was murdered at our county fairgrounds. Isn't that enough?"

I rocked back on my heels, but not at her snappish tone. So far, Shannon was the first person showing an appropriate amount of shock and sadness for the tragedy in her town.

The wall phone hanging over the stainless-steel dog feeding station rang. Shannon pointed with the knife at a stack of paper plates with a pile of regular cutlery on top. "Be a dear and take these out to the picnic table," she said. She snatched the phone off the charging station and added a dash of cheer to her "Hello?"

Be a dear? Hazel, who had to have thirty years on Shannon, didn't even talk like that.

I cradled the tableware and nudged the screen door open with my elbow. The setting sun cast long shadows across the lawn from the sturdy wood swing set toward a vegetable garden with tidy rows of young green plants. With any luck, if I were still around in a month or so, some surplus veggies might make their way to me.

In his backyard, Gordon Hulett dropped creamy yellow chunks of breaded catfish into a deep fryer next to the end of a picnic table. At his end of the table, cookout tools, utensils and plates lay aligned like surgical instruments on a paper towel-lined tray.

Like Shannon, Gordon's frame had softened since graduation, but more gray showed in his short, wavy brown hair. He also seemed to look more like Shannon, or maybe it was the other way around.

Over the front of his Kentucky-blue golf shirt and khaki cargo shorts was an apron he'd once told me they'd inherited from Shannon's grandmother. Depicted over his chest was a Precious Moments-looking couple standing apart and bending at the waist to kiss on the lips above the slogan: "Kissin' don't last, cookin' do." He also wore shorts showing paler, yet-to-tan skin, and flip flops.

He grabbed his bottled beer from the table and stared into the vat of burbling oil as if he were about to tell my fortune. The family's red and white pit bull stared at the kettle as she lay sphinxed on the lawn. Gordon said, "When do you talk to the coroner?"

"Right after I leave here." I sipped on the iced tea I'd left at the table and eyed the hot oil. "How do you and Shannon stay thin?"

Shannon dropped off a plate of raw veggies—broccoli, cauliflower, carrots, and the guillotined celery she'd just chopped. "Fewer carbs." Her voice sounded lighter now, younger, as it had in New York. Not as it had sounded in the kitchen when we were alone.

"Are you sure I can't help with anything?"

She plucked a carrot stick from the plate she'd placed on the picnic table. "You guys are working." She rested her hand on Gordon's shoulder and let her arm slide along his bicep. Then, she scurried away toward the house.

I lowered my elbows to the tops of my legs unlike theirs, covered in jeans, and leaned in closer. "Is she pissed off at me because I called late last night?"

His mouth compressed into a flat line. He shook his head but concentrated on poking catfish lumps with a pair of metal grill tongs. "Having a child drops you into a whole other dimension of worry."

He glanced toward the house. "Did you see if she's making hush puppies? Little blobs of fried cornbread with onion? She makes 'em for company. Man, I miss hush puppies. All this low-carb stuff all the time sucks."

A little catch hit my throat. "I'm company now? After all these years?"

He waved the tongs as if to swat away a bug. "When it's not just us three."

I fidgeted with the carrot stick. We needed to stay on task. "Besides this drive-by talk, I've heard some speculation that the horse show judge might have been killed over a ribbon. Are horse shows that cutthroat?"

He capsized the sizzling balls of fish and cornmeal batter. "Competition, money, and ego. A triangulation of fire." He poked a lump. "Did I get that one right?"

I sang out, "Good boy." Then added in a more conversational tone, "But cool it with the military lingo. You don't want Teddi to pick it up. That'll spin up Shannon more."

"Keep in mind, I don't know much about horses," he said, gesturing with the tongs. "I'm not a horse Kentuckian. More like a basketball Kentuckian. What I see is the economic impact horses have on the area."

"Do go on," I said.

He set the tongs on a platter already lined with a paper towel. "Horse shows may look like a hobby, but families—generations—have built careers out of this. They don't call it the horse business for nothing. Sure, there are families with a couple of horses they show just for fun." He reached for a plate. "But, if you have a breeding or training program, horses out showing and winning is good marketing. Factor in travel expenses, multiple horses, gear, training, vet bills. It adds up fast. So does money from stud fees and colt prices."

"Is the money big enough to cheat, bribe, or threaten judges? And what about Doris Caldwell who hates the horse shows? And Pete Livingston from the *Journal*, who's not objective about your horse culture?"

"Oh, yeah. The antis are another business interest. Like Doris. Pete, too, huh? You don't say? He arrived on the scene a few weeks before you did. Good to know where he stands on the horse shows."

An odd observation for him to make. Why would Gordon need to know what Pete thought about the horse community? Before I could ask, the door to the kitchen smacked shut. The dog raised its head from its outstretched paws while staying down and gazing at the house. The tail lifted and wagged. A child's voice with a girlish lilt shifted his energy and attention. "Hi, Daddy!"

A small blend of Shannon's curly hair and Gordon's skin tone skipped over to us.

Gordon placed the tongs down and stepped away from the deep fryer. "Hi, sweetie. Don't get too close to the fryer. Did you have a good time with grandpa and grandma?"

She wrapped her arm around his waist for a half hug with him between her and the sizzling air from the fryer. "The *best*."

Then she said, "Avery!" She launched off him and dashed toward me. The blow of a soft fifty-pound tackle slammed into my lawn chair. She ducked her curls into the side of my face and breathed out bubble-gum breath, "I'm so glad you're here!" She dropped onto the grass beside my chair and folded her legs.

Gordon said, "It's not too soon for chiggers, hon. You might want to get a lawn chair."

"Daddy, you didn't tell me Avery would be here tonight," she said.

A memory of the morning's nightmare punched me from the past. My fixer Sandy's little sister finding a bloody, dusty handbag.

I blinked away tears and intoned, "My invitation to dinner tonight was a surprise."

"Nooo," Teddi tossed her curls as she shook her head with a gleeful face that said yes-yes-Yes. "This is *supper*. Not dinner. That's how city folk talk. You're country now."

My good friends had made this little human with the best of themselves.

Gordon cast us a sly smile. "Teddi, Mommy needs help carrying stuff outside."

Shannon appeared without the slam of the screen door to announce her arrival. "Yes, Mommy needs help with the ketchup and tartar sauce, too. Avery and Daddy have to finish their *boring* work talk as soon as possible."

Teddi ran toward the house. I leaned to mutter to her dad, "What were you going to tell me about the antis and business?"

Gordon ladled the catfish from the burbling oil with a flat mesh sieve. "Later." He placed the first glistening breaded piece on a paper towel-lined plate.

Turns out, I wasn't the only master of compartmentalization.

Ten

From my car in Gordon and Shannon' s driveway, I texted Cathy, the Blanchard County coroner, to let her know I was on my way. I eased my car out of the tidy new subdivision for a county road lined with wide pastures and long fences.

Except for the occasional pickup truck and beat-up sedan, the two-lane state road into Bowmansville, was empty on an early Sunday evening.

With each property line, the fencing changed, from wire and wood to black three-plank fencing to some low, drystone walls. On the edge of the downtown business district, offices and homes mixed in with large Colonials, Greek revivals, and Victorians left over from a more prosperous time.

Epperson's Funeral Home allowed customers to say farewell to their loved ones in a grand house. A modern addition with a picture window showcased a gleaming, black, horse-drawn hearse. Track lights aimed from the ceiling cast glints on the black lacquer and polished brass trim.

Cathy and her husband lived upstairs above the funeral home that her husband ran with his brothers.

Across the street, I pulled my car into the empty funeral home parking lot and checked my messages in case Cathy needed to wave me off. I preferred being considerate of my sources, not treating them like information vending machines. Working at a weekly granted me that freedom.

A golden porch bug light clicked on. Cathy Epperson, funeral director's wife and three-term elected coroner of Blanchard County pretty much 24/7, shut the back door of her home behind her. I flashed my car lights. She tightened a nubby blue knit shawl around her plump 50-something shoulders, then headed toward me in her A-line dress and sensible flats. The light glinted off her strawberry blonde hair.

I watched her wait for traffic that wasn't coming before she crossed the street. I rolled down my window and opened my mouth to speak, but she spoke first. "Can we go for a walk?"

"Are you okay with me recording our conversation?" I held up my phone. "It's too dark for me to take notes."

She twisted her mouth, as if she had to make up her mind. Then, she nodded.

Up whirred the window, while my mind did a quick calculation. I grabbed my phone and stepped was out of the car. I locked it with the remote.

She looked at my car and pulled the shawl even tighter. "I used to think it was funny, that you lock your car here. Now? Not so much."

"That bad?"

We left the parking lot by walking across the strip of grass toward the sidewalk. Cicadas filled her silence, until we neared a house with open windows and a loud TV turned to a cop show.

"People stay and move here because they want the safety and quiet." Glum, she continued warming up to talking to me. "They want their kids riding their bicycles on the streets or playing with dogs and ponies."

Despite my thirst to know, I let her work through her wistful mood. I'd rather she felt relaxed and generous, even though my deep breath hitched enough that my reined-in impatience almost slipped.

I bit my lip to let her fill the silence.

"I've been cooped up all day between the drive to and from Frankfort and the autopsy room," she said. "You know, I hate going there, because of what it means, but I owe it to them. I probably knew them unless they're from someplace else. Then, I feel like I owe it to them as guests of Blanchard County."

"The after-life edition of Southern hospitality," I observed as gently as my impatience allowed.

She cringed but smiled, as if she didn't dare laugh. "It's nice to have a grown-up doing your job. Clark's usual temp hires don't get it. Junior year interns, or fresh out of college. You understand dark humor doesn't mean we don't care. "

Been there, done that. "Otherwise, we'd care too much." Except I was already way past the point of enmeshment. I opted for a little clinical distance and chose my wording with care.

"I got to the point where I was glad when they didn't die in pieces. Sorry. TMI. What did you want to tell me?"

"Cyrus and his mother may have moved, but they still have lots of friends around here. Did you know that?"

"Did they? Really?"

Her shoulders stiffened. "He did die here. Unnatural causes."

Time to cut to the chase, a little stronger this time. My idea of prejudice looked different from the general local standard. "A rumor going around town is about a drive-by shooting. Loose talk?"

"He wasn't shot." Her firm answer came quick with a punch of disgust. "People around here need to mind their own business. They need to use their imaginative powers for good for a change. Or join a book club."

"Have you determined the manner of death?"

"We're still investigating."

A standard answer, not unexpected. "Are you leaning toward homicide?"

"I should go inside." Like a switch, she pivoted and turned around toward the house.

One step forward, two steps back. All faith and respect aside, I needed her for information as much as she needed me to cover her exploits to keep voters happy. Time to politely provoke her.

"I'm sorry, but you can help the public determine if people need to worry about someone coming along and killing them. If that's what happened, if it had been a random attack, we need to post it on the *Trib's* website. We can't wait for pub day."

She halted. "Avery, the man was beaten to a pulp. He's a big guy. He had minimal defensive wounds on his hands. Someone with a lot of strength and a lot of rage pulverized him, not with their fists, but a tool." She leaned in and swept her hand as if she were clearing a table. "And all that's off the record. I should've said that first. It'll come out later, but please hold that."

My breath shallowed, only filling my chest to a hair below my throat. "But he was a man in the prime of his life! How does that happen?"

"Ambush? Someone he trusted? Do you really want to go down the speculation road?"

"We're still off the record." Full-voiced, I added, "You know I don't burn bridges. Not to the ground, anyway. Some kind of tool, you say?"

No laugh, no smile. "Still, please keep this to yourself. Not a knife. Not a hammer. The M.E. and I were thinking maybe a chopping tool, like an axe or a hoe or even a shovel. A couple of blunt force traumas to knock him down, but chopping?" She shook a finger at me in warning as if I were a naughty child. "If you print any of this. I'll make sure my husband pulls all our ads."

Ah, leverage from advertisers—the Achilles' heel of the news business. With money yanked away for whatever the reason, news organizations took casualties every day. As a small town, family-owned rural weekly, the *Tribune* remained among the last of the dinosaurs.

I said, "His injuries suggest someone just plain went off in a rage on him." I played my wildcard. "Could his murder have been a hate crime?"

She halted again and drew the shawl more tightly around her shoulders. "No." Under the streetlight beam, I could see her tighten her mouth as if to consider telling me the rest. "Again. Deep background. In a hate crime, a killer or killers tends to do something degrading to the remains. I won't go into detail."

My gut told me secrets lurked. Ugly, centuries old, shoved out of sight, secrets. "Unless the attacker was interrupted."

She pivoted and confronted me. "Is it appropriate for us to brainstorm?"

"Sorry. Probably not. We've both seen too much we can't unsee."

Eleven

The next morning, the office manager, Laverne, blocked my path between the desks. She shoved out a closed shoebox painted white. Visible through the white paint on the cardboard was "Easy Spirit, Size 9."

"You said H-E-double hockey sticks." Laverne tapped the center of the lid, decorated with a gold painted cross. A cut-in coin-drop slot darkened the nexus. "Now pay up." She tapped the lid of the box near the glitter. "One quarter."

Really? Her taking me to plantation school in Hazel's kitchen remained fresh in my mind.

While staring at that sparkly cross with a money slot, I said, "A man got pulverized at the fairgrounds this weekend, but you're hellbent on penalizing me for swearing."

She shook the box, prompting clanking. Someone else had been caught earlier, too. "Tiny missteps pave the road away from salvation."

I almost blurted out, if she really wanted to police us, a dollar fine made more sense. Except I'd have to hit the bank every morning for singles like a dude planning lunch at a strip club. On second thought, demanding a quarter was part of the genius of her annoying plan. Nuisance factor, plus juvenilization.

With my lips clamped tight, I dug into my pockets. Then, I said, "You do love the sound of coins clinking. It's the sound of false moral victory."

She waved toward the long plate glass window, almost the entire front wall of the office. "Innocent children and good Christians walk in here off the street. I won't have them exposed to that New York City trash talk."

Sharp pain popped behind my eye, feeling like an MSG headache from too much bad Chinese takeout.

"You wouldn't know 'New York City trash talk' if it walked up and mugged you. Or spat on you. Or peed on you. The list could go on forever, just on body fluids alone."

Her face flushed red under her platinum blonde bouffant hair, but she stood her ground. The knuckles on both her hands whitened as she clutched the cuss box. "You just doubled it. Good job. Now pay up."

Our fearless leader, Gordon Hulett, wearing a blue blazer and gray slacks, walked through the glass entry doors.

At least he wasn't wearing a shirt and tie, but a polo shirt underneath.

"What's with the jacket?" is how I greeted him.

Carrying a travel mug in one hand and a folded *Lexington Journal* tucked under the other, he walked down the aisle between the desks. "Get it over with," he said to me. "Pay the fine." He headed for his cubicle, an alcove behind a partition in the far end of the office.

Seeing the *Journal* reminded me, even though Pete had been nosing around at the fairgrounds, he hadn't reported any more than I had. Odd for the murder of a man who'd recently received a state honor.

Laverne blocked me again and shook the box with insistence.

I slid a folded dollar into the coin slot and itched to make a wise crack about strippers. "Consider it an advance."

"Penalty for sass." Laverne flashed a smug smile.

I headed down the aisle toward Gordon's desk for the upcoming Monday staff meeting. I shot over my shoulder, "This isn't over."

Unlike the other desks jutting out from the wall at right angles, I'd managed to turn mine so I could see both exits. A side glance gave me a view of the massive surveyor's map of Blanchard County, occupying a chunk of the adjacent wall. Sometimes, I meditated on the map, tracing roads and musing on their names, often reflecting the area's history in hopes it would give me more insight into the lay of the land.

"Alright, folks." Gordon projected his voice from his desk. "Let's do this."

Along with my cell phone, I gathered my notes on the case. I headed through the center aisle of the open bullpen. One of the two other reporters on duty, Wilbur T. Abernathy, as his by-line always stated, rewrapped his half-eaten peanut butter and jelly sandwich—carbs and fat his body would never store—and shoved his black BCGs, what the troops had called Birth Control Glasses, higher on his big nose.

Across the aisle, our sportswriter, Justin, scrolled through the night's baseball matchups on his laptop. With his arm on the desk, his rounded bicep with its University of Kentucky logo tattoo in the correct shade of royal blue, flexed in full view.

Funny how you could live a thousand miles away from other sports fans who claimed to *bleed blue* except those fans bled a different shade.

On the other side of the only cubicle wall that gave Gordon and his staff an illusion of privacy, I claimed one of the mismatched chairs aligned so their occupants could face his desk. I liked the corner chair by the water cooler for its broad view of the rest of the office, even into the rear rooms with the long-abandoned darkroom equipment and the old-school file cabinets that comprised the *Tribune's* "dead tree" library, AKA, its morgue.

Gordon flipped through some paperwork. He spoke low enough so only I could hear. "She wants to raise the fine to a dollar," he said.

"Nah. She'll never do that. She likes the clink of the coins. The sound of victory."

He murmured, "She's got a point. This place is a fishbowl." He flipped through some new mail on his desk. "Lookie here." He ripped open an envelope and handed me two laminated cards. "Your state police press credential. And a parking pass." He presented them with a goofy exaggerated *ta-da* smile.

I accepted them with the hand I'd scratched while barging through his brother's backyard hedge. So intent on making the crossing, even through my panic attack, I'd ignored the injury until my shower the next morning. I couldn't even look at him. "Tell me again why they can't issue these online so we can just print them out," I said, more than asked.

He called out louder to the rest of the newsroom, "Come on, people. Let's do this."

Wilbur stretched out his long legs. Muscled, compact Justin seemed to overwhelm the chair he sat in. I often wondered how Crystal, who was on maternity leave, fit in with the boys' club.

At his desk, Gordon filled in the rounded letters on the *Lexington Journal's* masthead with blue ink. He began the meeting with, "What do we know about the murder?"

My cue. "As you see in the *Journal*, the cops released the victim's name. Cyrus McCoy. Yes, the state Teacher of the Year as we reported three weeks ago. The full coroner's report with the labs won't be done for a while. I left a message with show announcer Harlan Davenport who's working now at the Fairmont House."

My peripheral vision noticed extra movement in the front by the window. At her desk, Laverne turned to gaze at the door. She stood and smoothed her skirt, all the while watching the door.

A man's arm braced the glass door open to admit a fortyish woman in a sleek black dress, more Tribeca ladies-who-lunch than a local style. Her light brown highlighted hair swung as she walked. She dipped a brisk nod at Laverne and then peered beyond her into our bullpen. Her flinty gaze landed on me and locked on.

She said, "Never mind, Clark." Traces of Jersey, of all places, powered her voice. "I see her."

Kinsale—or, rather, *Clark*—our owner-publisher, followed. He was tall, with a full head of silver hair setting off his started-in-mid-winter-elsewhere tan and built upon through country-gentleman pursuits like golf, boating, or show horses. Clad in a lightweight charcoal gray suit impeccably cut to fit his military bearing, he breezed in and gave his sister-in-law Laverne a chaste hug.

With his nephew in charge, Kinsale had been a hands-off boss. I whispered to Gordon, "What's he doing here?"

Gordon raised his gaze to meet my own and held it. "Whatever he wants." His stillness chilled me in warning.

Wilbur said, "It's about that murder." He clicked his pen open and shut like castanets. "No good can come of this."

Kinsale's melodic southern baritone sang out, "Avery, can you come up front for a moment?"

I stood to face my boss's boss. The last time I'd seen a man that entitled, he wore gold stars and a chest full of fruit salad. Around me, Kinsale's staff gave him silence. I sensed heads swiveling between us, as if to say, "What did she do this time, and what's he going to do about it?"

The woman he'd escorted into our office spoke. "Oh, yeah. You're Clark's New Yorker." She stuck out a slender hand decorated with hand-crafted gold rings, as well as a wedding set glinting with diamonds. A distinctive sculpted gold collar glinted below her tanned throat. "I'm Sylvana Dobbs." Her calloused hand oddly suggested she did manual labor.

Who was this woman to have such pull with the big man? Her diamonds and gold placed her firmly among the country club set, except for her New York tristate accent and all that Manhattan black.

I returned the handshake. "Avery Sloane. No offense, but this is an awkward time. We all touch base before we go out on our rounds." I could do the polite rituals laced with time constraints along with the best of them.

"That's our Avery." Kinsale's booming voice made him sound merrier than Santa. "Always so hard at work. This will only take a moment, and Mrs. Dobbs can be on her way, too. Then you can join us at the meeting."

Our Avery. Eww. A nervous twist hit my stomach. *Everyone else's time is more valuable than ours, which we already knew from our pay.* Message received.

"Absolutely," I said with too much emphasis. "I'm sure Mrs. Dobbs also needs to get on with her day." I folded my arms and hoped he could read my mind. *This had better be important, Clark.*

Kinsale boomed a laugh. "Perfect. I'll let you two take care of business while I confer with my nephew." He excused himself from us womenfolk to go talk business with Gordon.

My fellow reporters, mostly fellows, turned to greet the big boss, and I felt cast out again from the boys' club tree house. The big man loomed over Gordon's desk. Gordon cricked his neck to hold the phone hands-free while he shuffled papers like a good assistant.

When I faced Sylvana, her smile tilted into a smirk and a roll of the eyes, as if to say, *what a tool.* "Mrs. Dobbs is my mother-in-law. Call me Sylvana. My new arts group for teens is about to break with the end of school. I wouldn't mind some coverage."

Hmm. *Thanks for setting me up for a puff piece, Clark.*

"Sounds interesting, but, as the new reporter on staff, and a temp, I don't usually land such plummy assignments. I'll have to run it past my editor. At the meeting. In progress. May I have a card so I can get back to you?"

On a slow news day, maybe I'd leave it for Crystal, a softball piece to ease her return to work in time for back-to-school.

Sylvana reached into the top of her chic, ginormous leather bag. She held out her business card, presented edge first between her index and middle fingers like a blade. "Ever so helpful, Clark gave me your contact info." I struggled to avoid returning her slight smirk. "I'll be in touch."

I glanced at the card that said, "Youth Arts Crew" and "Sylvana Dobbs, Director," along with her email and requisite social media contacts. Before heading out, she strode deeper into the newsroom to swing by our end of the bullpen. "Clark, sorry to interrupt."

Four male faces turned to her, but one spoke. "Yes, my dear?" No one could bring the southern smarmy charm like our Supreme Fearless Leader.

She lingered by the door. "I just wanted to thank you and let you know I'll be in touch." She waved at everyone else, then pivoted on her stilettos and strode out the way she came in.

I flipped the business card onto the top of my desk where it could wait. Then, I hurried to return to the meeting so distracted I'd just realized Kinsale had taken my chair.

Not gentlemanly, sir. But message received.

I leaned against the partition between the bullpen and Gordon's area. Our owner-publisher gestured a "come here" to me, with a sweeping gesture to me in my chair, a weird mix of southern chivalry and dominance.

With a shake of my head, I waved him off and mouthed, "I'm good."

The meeting was progressing beyond the murder investigation. "So, Justin," Gordon said, "What's going on with the discussion about the county fair's horse show?"

The sportswriter cleared his throat. "With all due respect, sir," he looked as if he was having a bad shrimp day. He cast a sidelong glance at Kinsale, "Sir, I'd think you'd be more wired into those developments than me."

"Don't worry, son." Kinsale patted the back of Justin's chair. "The fair program book comes out later this week. An early bird told me there are no changes from last year." Our very proper boss winked.

Why the hell did he hire us to collect news if he knew everything already?

I interrupted. "I haven't finished presenting my status report about the Cyrus McCoy murder."

Kinsale intoned, "Such a tragedy for Blanchard County."

I wouldn't defer like Justin. "Residents out there are buzzing with wacked out ideas about this murder, even before Lexington media picked up the story."

"Out of respect to the family," Kinsale said, "I don't think we should dwell on the unseemly details of this matter." He turned to Gordon and said, "Graduation is coming up—"

What the hell kind of newspaper owner punted away from murder coverage? Fuming, I said, "We'd never sensationalize or exploit this story. It's news. People are talking about it. We can squash the rumors."

Even though the police had been stingy with released details, I managed to keep a straight face.

Kinsale cast me a sly grin. "You would cover a murder investigation with not a smidge of New York's fine tradition of tabloid journalism? Is that feasible for you?"

The sting of insult pinched my mouth shut hard enough to tighten my chin. New York's biggest tabloids were still alive and kicking. At least one seemed to hold views echoing his own. Except his provincialism wouldn't allow him to pick up a New York tabloid to find out.

But I had to admit; part of my heart agreed. Another friend, even though I hadn't known him long, was dead. I, too, wanted reporting, not salivating—nor, holy crap, gossiping—over the juicy details.

"Yes, sir." He'd appreciate the good manners. Let alone confidence. "I can do it."

A warning creeping along my scalp made me wonder if truth might get trampled under competing agendas. I said, "The state's newly honored teacher of the year, who grew up here, was murdered here. The news angles make it news."

Kinsale turned to Gordon. "It's time to run the list of graduates of the town and county high schools. People expect to see the good news in their community."

If I had to type a list of high school seniors graduating, I'd grab two bottles—one of Percocet and another of Jack—then drive faster than a stealth bomber speeding to Baghdad to the closest stretch of railroad tracks.

Time to propose a mutually agreeable solution. I said, "Here's a way we can take the high road and still cover the story. I'm probably not the only person unaware of McCoy's involvement with horses. He didn't mention it in our interview. Remember? What if I wrote a sidebar about his history with local equestrian activities?"

Before Gordon could respond, our boss chimed in. "Cy McCoy grew up here. Many long-time residents are acquainted with his equestrian accomplishments." His smarm lilted with pride. "Many of them occurred under my employ."

Dude, you own most of the county. Then, the realization hit me. He hadn't said *no*. He'd be open to a pitch.

My newly minted conscience squirmed, but the predator sleeping inside my heart stretched and flexed with anticipation.

As if he were a general brimming with power and command, I played to his ego. "Lexington media won't have the easy angle we have of his life as an equestrian."

Gordon spoke first. "She's got a point. Lexington is all about thoroughbreds first, and then saddlebreds. They even gloss over the harness racing at The Red Mile. We hold this news peg."

Wilbur shoved his glasses up his nose with a finger pushing at the bridge and seemed to revive. "Lexington only covers the bad news with our breed of horse. They've been hard on the walking horse bunch, but they double down when it comes to us."

Pete's warning about "morons" killing each other for a ribbon surfaced inside my mind. That the local angle shaped up into horses kept me free to work, yet not reveal the biases I suspected.

Time to bring the discussion to a close.

I said, "This sidebar could be a nice tribute. We can do that for him. Here. His home. We are uniquely qualified to produce this tribute."

The funny part? I needed to do this for Cy. That he was murdered after judging a horse show at the fairgrounds made his life with horses a part of the story. Which also should've been part of my interview and profile of him. Why hadn't he mentioned horses during the interview? I'd asked, what are your hobbies? Maybe he loved the horses so much they were more than a hobby. Or maybe he'd been teased so much as a guy who loved horses that he'd learned to play it down.

But more than the horses, even larger than the horses, I suspected a deeper, more insidious issue, deeply ingrained in the culture and economy of the area. Maybe I was missing something, but I got the feeling the locals, without my prodding, would prefer to overlook the murder of a black man. Even a man they'd insisted they admired.

That I hoped I was wrong about that made me wonder about my own objectivity.

Wilbur's voice almost cracked. "Why should *you* write the story? What do you know about the horse business? McCoy's life as a horseman is a sports sidebar to a news story. That would be Justin's turf."

The sportswriter waved his hand as if he were pushing away second helpings at dinner. "Don't look at me. I know less than she does about this show horse stuff."

"Hello," I said. "I'm still here. I spent my teen years around riding lesson barns."

Wilbur continued, waving his hands more than I ever did. "Just because she lives on the Ward Farm doesn't mean she's got an *in*. You can't learn the horse business and our culture by osmosis, let alone in a span of two days. My gramma always said, if a cat has kittens in an oven, that don't make them biscuits."

No way would I lose this story to Wilbur.

I doubled down. "I was on the fairgrounds after the horse show ended early Sunday morning. I made contact with several horse show exhibitors, some of whom are willing to help."

Even if her father wasn't keen on us writing the story, Josie had volunteered with her business card. "I have a head start, plus I can make the story classy and tasteful and maybe even elegiac."

Note to self: look up "elegiac" so I wouldn't renege on a promise.

Our owner-publisher's chest rose and fell as if he were hiding a laugh. "It's only a sidebar, not an epic poem." Still, the room temp dropped a few more degrees. "Keep in mind that I will not allow my newspaper to cover this murder on the front page every week until a verdict comes down in the trial."

Even though everyone in the county would be talking and fretting about it until a murderer was locked up. Or, maybe not, considering the general disconnect with the crime.

I clamped my mouth shut to stop talking while I was ahead.

Gordon cleared his throat. "I won't let it monopolize our news hole. Avery's just saying readers might be interested in reading about McCoy's history with the horse business. It's a part of the story only we can do justice."

Kinsale looked at his wristwatch, a fancy gold number befitting his status as a pillar of the community. "I also don't want us to forget about the feature about our local boy who just came home from deployment. Miss Sloane, I think you could add an element our other staffers cannot. In time for Memorial Day."

Leave it to me to have to poke the bear while I was ahead.

"Memorial Day is about those who died in war," I said with a furrowed brow implying *pardon me* but not. "Veterans Day is about those who got to come home. The troops are aware of the difference." I think I even batted my eyelashes at my boss.

Gordon chimed in, "Didn't he just get home? Maybe he'd want a little time to re-bond with his family before we barge in?"

Kinsale tilted his head as if he were imparting wisdom to his younglings. "It's not 'barging in' when you've been invited. Our readers love to hear about the young men, and now women, who honor our county."

"I'm not trying to duck this one," I said, pushing my luck into a corner, "but troops are trained not to talk to media. Voice of experience, as you might say. He's still liable to turn me away whether his family members invited me or not."

But Kinsale returned to Wilbur to talk about coverage leading up to the fair in two months.

For a newspaper owner/publisher, he had poor news sense. Aside from revering the military yet being tone deaf about military-inspired national holidays, he was limiting our coverage of a murder case? Why the hell would he do that?

Twelve

Getting out of the office to go on my daily rounds to check in with Blanchard County's chief deputy should stop my ruminating about Kinsale's motives for blunting our story coverage. For once, Marvin and I had a big case to talk about. Or talk around.

Between us, his desk with a closed laptop and neat stacks of folders served as a net over which I'd serve up questions about the McCoy murder. Over his shoulder hung a display of diplomas as well as photos from his life, from local school sports to candids with army buddies.

After we covered autopsy questions, where the evidence was being examined, and when police would release the scene at the fairgrounds, I had a new question to serve. One that would wake him up. "When is the press conference?"

His left eyebrow lifted, a crack in his poker face. "Excuse me? The what?"

Mission accomplished. Interrupting the rhythm of Cop Keep-Away where I ask questions and he lobs replies, not necessarily answers, in return. Rinse, repeat.

I paraphrased the headline. "Lexington community activists have been calling for a swift investigation into the murder of Cyrus McCoy." I wanted to see how he'd respond, but my gut stirred with a not-great idea vibe.

"A press conference would be a way to gather us in one place," I said. "You wouldn't have to field separate calls."

On second thought, me calling for a press conference was a lousy gambit. For whatever reason, Marvin liked me enough to encourage a first-name basis and swing us by the crime scene when he'd been escorting me off the fairgrounds. A press conference would dilute my advantage.

Way to go, Avery. Whatever kind of cold Kinsale has that's stopping up his nose for news must be contagious.

"The case is still under investigation."

A different tactic. Low, but usually drew out more info. "Is there anything you or the sheriff would like the paper to say to reassure the public about its safety?"

His mouth quirked in a that's-a-new-one smirk. "I'd tell citizens to just go about their everyday business." He smoothed an already straight stack of paper files. "Speaking of everyday business." He rose in front of his wall of criminal justice and public safety administration diplomas—my cue I was about to be escorted out.

I gathered my gear but lobbed a fast shot. "Odd to have such a big case in town, but the big boss isn't re-assuring the public himself. Where is the sheriff anyway?"

Halfway around his desk, the chief deputy stopped. "Busy. That's why he has me deal with the media."

"A quick question, not directly about the case." A question I didn't want to ask. "At the fairgrounds the other night, why did you drive me the long way around and let me see the crime scene?"

With all my internal radars on high alert, I watched his face for a leer or a wink or any sign of a flirtation. Or something more subtle. No matter how square his jawline or broad his shoulders, I hoped that had been a favor I wouldn't be expected to pay back.

"Professional courtesy," he said with an impassive face. "You're not the usual wet-behind-the-ears-dying-to make-your-bones *Tribune* temp."

On the wall opposite his desk, what he could see as he worked, hung his personal gallery of the West. To the left of the door, a poster of the Crazy Horse Monument with the statue facing and pointing toward the exit.

The other side featured a cluster of framed photos of him, a woman, and a bunch of kids on ponies with western tack surrounded by greenery, more Kentucky than South Dakota.

"Before I forget, I'm working on a feature story about McCoy's life as a horseman. Would you like to add something? A quote? An anecdote?"

He leaned against the front of his desk. "You're writing a puff piece? And you want a quote from me?" His mouth quirked and his head tilted.

"Why not?" I parroted something Gordon once told me, "Feature stories are the lifeblood of community news." I swept my arm to encompass the photos. "Besides, you ride. You grew up around here. You had to know him."

"The horse business isn't a club with a secret handshake."

"What about the Blanchard County Saddle Club?"

He graced me with a you've-got-to-be-kidding shift of his eyes. "You didn't press this hard with your specific questions about the case. Are you playing detective?"

Not sure I liked where he was taking this, but I wouldn't cut and run. "You know the drill. I know the drill. Your answers, unless kept close to the vest, might compromise OPSEC; i.e., the investigation." I flipped an exaggerated shrug. "But I still have to ask."

The chief deputy opened the door. He did a lot of escorting me from premises. Even though I knew the way out, he couldn't let me free range through the sheriff's department. Plus, it had to be the southern hospitality thing to do.

While we walked, he said, "Don't get carried away asking questions out there. Stick to what you need for the story—your little feature about

McCoy as a horseman." A whiff of condescension wafted my way. "Don't stray onto our turf."

"Fine with me," I said and hoped I sounded tired and overworked. "You can hunt the murderers. I've got horse people to chat up." I left, half queasy and wondering if, on impulse, I'd shown him my hand.

In the lobby, Deputy Fortner, who'd been standing post at the fairgrounds gate the night of the murder, sat at the desk behind the glass. Her gaze flicked toward me. The left corner of her thin mouth crooked, either in smirk or dismay.

No point in burning bridges. I stepped closer to the glass and the speaker. "Hey, Fortner. Thanks. Have a good shift." I pulled my mouth into a jaunty smile. *Bygones, dude.*

Her mouth tilted into a full smirk. She flipped her wrist in a wave of dismissal.

I headed for the doors. If I hurried, I'd make it to the Fairmont House before lunch. Show announcer Harlan Davenport hadn't returned my calls. Rumor had it, he had political aspirations. Unlike the county sheriff, who seemed to believe he could ignore the media, for a new candidate for office, dodging calls from the media was bad business.

Unless he had something to hide.

Thirteen

When I drove to the Fairmont House, I expected a classic antebellum mansion with columns. I drove along the long driveway flanked by pristine white plank fences toward the red-brick Fairmont House.

No classic columns, but three levels of white woodwork trimmed porches and balconies.

Around town, I'd heard couples from moneyed families in the surrounding counties used its events calendar to set wedding dates; unromantic strategic planning for photos someone would torch in a fit of pique within ten years tops.

Harlan Davenport, horse show announcer and skilled phone-call ducker, ran the joint, which would be gearing up for the lunch hour. That meant he'd be on site and eager to get rid of the press. We'd have a quick chat, and I'd be out of there and parked somewhere with my fingers in my ears in time for the noon siren.

I climbed some wooden steps, then across the deep veranda with white wicker furniture between tall windows. I smelled roses when I'd passed the bushes heavily in bloom.

Just inside the entrance, a teenaged girl with sleek blonde hair and a toothpaste-commercial smile stiff-armed the door open. "Hi." Her chipper greeting stretched into three syllables. "Welcome to the Fairmont House. May I direct you to your party?"

I stepped inside. The parquet floor in the foyer welcomed me with an old-money creak. "Avery Sloane from the *Blanchard County Tribune* to see Harlan Davenport."

"Just a moment, ma'am." She touched an earpiece under her hairdo to announce my presence by name to someone unseen. I watched her so-far-unlined facial skin with its country club tan.

Her megawatt smile flickered, then she said, "Is he expecting you?"

He damn well better be, after ducking my calls all morning. "I need a quick quote from him for a feature story. A walk-and-talk would be great." I gave her my merriest social smile.

She held up her hand to listen to her earpiece. Her eyes sparkled. Apparently, she'd heard something she could say to be hospitable. "Please follow me."

We glided through ornate parlors with substantial cherry furniture with curving lines. No photography on the walls. Audubon-style prints showed birds larger than life. Tall portraits of southern gentlemen and their ladies peered down upon us. Some British-looking sporting art of horses, regarded us with a sliver of white around their wary eyes.

The hostess led me to a dining room with floor-to-ceiling windows overlooking the golf course, what used to be farmland.

Nervous energy crept along the hairs of my neck. I used to like bright rooms with big windows overlooking scenic views until I found out what explosives could do to plate glass. I had left places where that was all too possible, only to have their memories follow me home.

Servers in white shirts and khaki pants assembled place settings over white linens on the tables. A lone diner, a woman with burnished curls and a sleek black dress, scrolled through her phone at a table overlooking the golf course. No Harlan in sight.

My dry mouth made the sounds. "How long will he be?" Instead of, *how long before the siren?*

"Mr. Davenport is unexpectedly delayed. Please enjoy a beverage of your choice, our compliments, while you wait."

Each table had been draped in white tablecloths, perfect for hiding knobby knees, stashed weapons, and stowed IEDs. Cutlery arranged into precise place settings made great shrapnel, as did the glass itself, shattered and flying.

I searched for the restaurant's exit. Nope. Blocked by servers beating a path to and from the kitchen.

"How long did he say he'll be?" I managed to ask. Man, I had to get a grip.

"Yo. Avery." A woman's voice with a Jersey accent. "Avery Sloane."

I was startled with a shiver of nerves dancing down my spine.

The lone diner said, "Leave her with me and get her some iced tea."

The hostess said, "Sure thing, Mrs. Dobbs. Coming right up." Then she said to me, over her shoulder, "We're famous for our iced tea. Sweet with a wedge of lemon and a fresh sprig of mint. Like a julep but for teetotalers. Or before five," she added with a juicy secret twinkle. She hurried off as fast as her flats would allow.

Sylvana Dobbs, who I'd met at the news office, stood facing me with her hand on the back of a chair carved or molded to resemble bamboo. "Today's luncheon hell will be officers of the local women's club." Her curls bobbled with her shrug of resignation. "You'd be a lot more fun."

I sank into the chair, but perched on the edge away from the table. "I'm here to see Harlan. I'm not staying for lunch." Just cut to the chase and get it over with, as far as she was concerned, I said, "I'll come to your youth group before school's out. Okay?"

She leaned down as if to dig in her tote bag. "Whatevs."

Appearing at my elbow stood a tall glass of iced tea with a sprig of mint big enough to have roots. The server set a black coffee in front of Sylvana and then left.

She dug in her bag. I heard things bump together as she pawed inside without looking. "Don't you ever crave a decent pie?"

I knew she wasn't talking about apple or blueberry. "Lexington has brick oven pizza," I said. "You guys have the college kid hipsters to thank."

"But not coal-oven pizza. With all those coal mines an hour or three away?"

I winced. "I don't think Kentucky coal miners sell direct to consumer."

From the recesses of her bag, she pulled out a silver flask, opened it and poured clear liquid, probably vodka, into her coffee. Then, still open, she tilted the bottle my way. "Want some?"

I waved her off, even though she continued to wiggle the flask at me in case I changed my mind. I ignored her offer and said, "What made you move to Bowmansville?"

The flask disappeared into the depths of her tote. "My husband manages an anchor store in a mall in Lexington. We have two children. A boy sixteen and a thirteen-year-old horse crazy girl. She can show horses at a level in this circuit that would bankrupt us up north."

What a great lead-in to Cy. Maybe this delay wouldn't be such a waste after all. "Were you and your family at the horse show Saturday night? When the judge was murdered."

Her shoulders sagged and she shook her head like a disappointed mother. "Yes." Her brow twitched in grief or dismay. Then, she smiled with slyly amused pride. "God forbid my Lexi miss a championship stake class, even if it is the last class of the night and happening around midnight. That one was a doozie."

A man had been murdered, but she wanted to talk about the horse show. Just like everyone else.

If I stuck around, would I go native like that, too? Yet, I remembered Pete's and Doris's cracks about Cy's horse show judging choices being a possible motive for murder. "I heard there'd been an upset."

Sylvana dabbed her mouth with her napkin, managing not to leave lipstick on the linen. Her eyes lit up. "An upset? An upending, really. Get this. Kinsale's big black stake horse, his prize stallion? I forget his name, something to do with Tribbles, but I don't think it's a Trekkie thing. Anyway, his prize stallion lost to his former housekeeper's new horse."

I'd missed fast-talking people, let alone this touch of home so far away, but the tingle in my mind told me to pay attention. "The housekeeper has a show horse?" came out of my mouth.

Sylvana leaned in, "This is Kentucky. You'd be surprised at who owns horses. Anyway, Mavis, the Kinsale housekeeper, hit the lottery a couple of years ago. She left Kinsale's, bought houses," she ticked off her fingers, "educations for her family," another finger ticked, "and then she set them up in businesses."

Mavis, the lottery, and her practical generosity to her family—all echoed part of the chitchat in Hazel's kitchen.

Instinct reminded me this was good stuff and to lap it up as long as possible, but my nerves nagged at me to leave. If Harlan was delaying me, I could delay him, too. I could call him after the siren.

I couldn't resist the good stuff. Someone who wanted to talk to me. To keep her talking, I said, "Buying a show horse is kind of frivolous, isn't it? The whole eating while you sleep thing tends to be the very definition of a classic bad investment."

"But not just any show horse." Sylvana may have been sipping spiked coffee, but she was on a tea-spilling roll. "Mavis went to a big ambling horse farm outside Aiken and bought a horse capable of beating her old boss's champion. What I don't understand is why she sent him to Herb."

The mention of the family man horse trainer pinged my radar. "Why not Herb? Too brown?" Oops. Too blunt. Had that flask wafted out some intoxicating fumes?

But Sylvana, an artist and a New Yorker, had to notice the local miasma of prejudice under a veil of manners and dispensed through behavioral sleight of hand.

Behind me, a crash. Dishes. Glass. My pulse geysered into my spine. Sparklies flashed behind my eyes. Distant shouts faded behind the whipped tide of my panicking blood.

Somewhere under my ragged breathing, Sylvana's voice. "Whaddya know? Dinner and a show." Then, a shocked, "Avery? Where did you go?"

I slid my arms from my face. The tablecloth felt cool and dry on my wet cheeks.

Crap. I was squatting under the table.

I swiped my hands over my face and sniffed hard to blunt the tears before shouldering my way out past the fabric. "Dropped my napkin," I mumbled.

"Oh, *please* don't pick that napkin up off the floor, ma'am." The man's voice, said to be famous across three counties, drawled. Black leather Oxfords topped with sharp creased dress slacks stepped into my view. "We'll be happy to get you another one." A tan man's hand snatched up the white fabric puddle on the floor near where I knelt. "Oh." Surprise lilted his voice. "It's you."

Harlan's white hair looked stark against his deep tan. For a moment, his smile slipped from his eyes. I'd meant to ask Gordon or Hazel how old he was. He could've been fifty or thirty-five. My compliments to his cosmetic surgeon.

His office in the Fairmont House showed off the expected local sports collectibles from the Blanchard County Demons, a UK Wildcat, and an EKU Colonel, a wide swath of local sports showing he liked everyone who might grace his office. His hero wall also included more posed awards presentation photos from horse shows.

In one, a sweaty gleaming show horse stood facing the camera at the end of a line of presenters, mostly women of all ages, ranging in attire from evening gowns to frilly Easter dresses. Smiling teenage riders wearing three-piece suits and dapper hats raised the reins and smiled for the camera.

"Your children?" I said. More like grandchildren, but deal-with-the-brass mode called for generous guesstimates. Especially when he'd found me ducking and covering under one of his dining room tables.

"Our grandchildren. We try to keep them out of the shows where I announce—conflict of interest, you understand—but I'm at a show pert-near every weekend. But I still get to see our grandbabies ride."

He waved to offer me a chair in front of his spacious walnut desk, perhaps cleared of intriguing papers before bringing the reporter inside. He sat opposite me in the power position with his hands folded on top of the desk.

Ten minutes til noon. Had to get a move on to get out before the siren.

I pulled out my notebook and rested it on my lap. "I'm working on a story about Cyrus McCoy, about the equestrian part of his life. Because I saw your name listed as horse show announcer and your statement about announcing a lot of shows, I thought you might have something you'd like to add."

His face scrunched into polite sadness. "The death of Cyrus McCoy was a tragedy for our town, our state, and our Bluegrass Ambling Horse family," he said as if he recited from a prepared statement.

That phrase again—ambling horse family. I made a show of jotting down a version of his quote which I never intended to see print. A glib dude like Harlan could do better. "I was told he used to ride horses for the Kinsales?"

His shoulders clenched, as if an invisible arm squeezed. "Yes. You should ask Clark and Dwight about that. Or even Polly." That had to be Pauline Kinsale, Clark's wife.

I waved my hand as if to erase the question from the air. "I'm looking for a more personal memory you have of him with horses. I realize I've put you on the spot. Maybe a favorite comes to mind?"

He sat straight and gazed off to his right, toward the EKU Colonel bobblehead that looked like a young Mark Twain. "Let me see . . . he showed this big old blue roan mare, lit up with lots of chrome—I mean, a silvery gray female horse with a bluish cast set off with a black mane and tail and a big white blaze and long white socks. Pardon me. I don't know how much you know about horses. Do you ride?"

"Used to. When I was a kid." I waggled the pen between my fingers to suggest he continue. In case he hadn't noticed the body language, I said, "Please go on."

His shoulders eased away from his ears and his eyes brightened from a social smile to genuine amusement. "Well, that old mare had a thing for Sunnydale Bakery glazed doughnuts. She could tell the difference, too, so you couldn't pass off any old glazed doughnut." His eyes went soft as his mind focused on his memories.

He was winding up for a great story, but the clock was marching fast toward noon. Note to self: never see, call, or contact Harlan Davenport within half an hour of the noon siren. If for no other reason than he liked to linger over tales he told.

Harlan continued, "If you cheaped out, she'd drop that doughnut back into your hand and then flatten those ears before giving you that grouchy mare stare. I know you know the one. Cy was fall-through-a-soda-straw skinny then, probably about fifteen. He'd mow lawns to keep that horse in her special doughnuts."

He shook his head in a private joke. "Mares." His shoulders bobbed in a silent laugh. Then, his face straightened into a more business smile. "I shouldn't have said that. You'll take that the wrong way."

"I get it," I said. "Mares get a bad rap by people who don't want to put in the effort. You have to earn a mare's respect. Each one has different rules she expects you to figure out." Time to swerve back on topic. "So, what did you do right after the horse show Saturday night?"

That question wasn't part of the story. But it fit into the conversation. A good interview is a directed conversation. In my photog days, I'd paid attention to the reporters. The ones who got the best quotes were trusted.

And I kept the clock in my peripheral vision. Five til.

He replied, "I got my things wrapped up just before that storm hit but not soon enough to leave. The rain just hammered down and the wind blew the rain sideways, so I stayed under the gazebo until it cleared. I think I ruined my sport coat. That nubby silk you can't find anymore."

The clock ticked closer. I had to ask. "Was McCoy still in center ring with you?"

"Naw, he'd left by then. You know, I'd figured he would've been driving home to Lexington. But I reckon not. A shame he wasn't." He cocked his head and those shoulders of his hovered around his ears again. "What does where I was have to do with your story about Cy as a horseman?"

Bus-ted.

I put on my best innocent face. "That he was at the horse show. Judging." I could salvage this. "How long had he been doing that?"

"I don't rightly know. And why did you ask me what I did after the show?"

Aw, crap. "Look at the time. We're both very busy. Thank you." Another day, I'd tell him he'd better get used to odd questions if he planned to run for office.

"I don't see what my whereabouts has to do with anything. How will that fit into your story?"

"Don't worry about that. You're gonna love it. Fitting the story together is my job."

"Are you married?" he said more as a challenge than a question.

A sharp right turn into way too familiar territory. I'd learned not to counter with an *unimportant* or *none of your business*. "Not anymore."

"Do you have children?" The hint of a sneer in his voice suggested he already knew the answer.

Except I gave him a slightly different one. "It's best I didn't." Let his sense of family man superiority switch to pity or shock. I'd be happy with either or both, if it meant I'd be out the door sooner.

"Do you have any idea how difficult it is for families to have activities all ages can enjoy together? Well, these horse shows are family affairs. Horse lovers of all ages ride and show. Children just old enough to sit in the saddle. An 86-year-old man who comes up from Tennessee. They all ride in our horse shows." He raised his right arm and swept the air as if to include everyone everywhere. "Local charities benefit from the proceeds. Local businesses benefit from the influx of people. That a murder happened? A murder of our horse show judge? Just deepens the tragedy."

"Your point?" Tick tock went the clock. But Harlan was on a roll. Primo stuff. Unlike Kinsale, I wouldn't ignore it.

"Ms. Sloane, I don't want to see any more bad news attached to our horse, the Bluegrass Ambling Horse." We weren't talking any more about the murder at the fairgrounds.

Was he going to challenge me, like Dwayne the Kinsale trainer asked me at the fairgrounds, if I planned a "tree-hugging hatchet job?"

I also suspected he wasn't only protecting the reputation of his beloved breed of horse.

While easing toward the door, I said, "The murder happened. It's a matter of public record. If I don't pursue it," I added with the Pete Livingston's competitive smug face in my memory, "someone else will."

Harlan stood. "That's a job for the police."

"The cops are after the facts. I want the story behind the facts."

I ducked out so I could have the last word before the noon siren went off and sent me taking cover again: an encore performance of me "hunting for my napkin."

Fourteen

I rushed out of the Fairmont House and hurried down the steps. Once on the paved driveway, I broke into a run, yanked open my car door, and then sealed myself inside. My hands slapped over my ears just before the noon siren wailed. Covering my ears only blunted the yowl.

I latched my stare onto the rose bushes. I counted each scarlet head. One, two, three. *Stay. Here. Now.*

The siren faded. I lowered my hands from my ears to rest them on the steering wheel. Started my car. Cracked my neck from side to side. I slid the gear into reverse to head out for my next stop, Kinsale's farm, to meet with Josie about photos for the story. I wasn't all the way down the Fairmont House's long driveway before my phone rang.

Through my ear buds, Gordon said, "How did things go with Harlan?"

Extra meaning weighted his words, telling me Harlan hadn't wasted time calling Gordon about my extra line of questioning.

The soft clicking of his typing filled his pause to wait for my response.

"I didn't kiss up to him, but I wasn't rude." The fencing I passed went from black plank to wire with black cattle dozing under a tree near the road.

"He said he found you under a table. Hiding."

My eyelids squeezed toward shutting, like emotional blast shields. Except I popped one eye open to see the road ahead. *That rat bastard Harlan.*

"Avery?"

An overloaded truck teetering with bales of hay approached on the other side of the almost two-lane road. I edged my car closer to the right side while avoiding the steep incline to the adjacent drainage ditch.

"I dropped my pen." Oops. Wrong lie. "I mean, my napkin."

Damn multitasking. I should've told him I'd return his call.

Gordon said, "Ya know, I just heard the siren." His sentence trailed off as if he were waiting for my response.

"No worries." My voice sounded hoarse. "I was in my car."

A massive close call, but I didn't want to tell him about the dropped dishes setting me off considering he was fretting about me being out in public during the noon siren.

"Are you coming back to the office now?"

"I'm off to get photos. I'll come home after that, mom."

He lowered the volume of his voice and then said, "Harlan's an egotistical asshole." I imagined Laverne hovering nearby with her cuss box. "Be careful. Please try not to spin up anyone else."

I spotted a big sign proclaiming "Kinsale Farms," complete with the black silhouette logo of a high-stepping Bluegrass Ambling Horse. A smaller shingle hung from the bottom of the mailbox and said, "Visitors Welcome."

I eased the car down a driveway that looked more like another smaller country lane. To my right, mostly black or chestnut mares with round pregnant bellies grazed on one side. On the other side of the car, slimmer mares with spring foals lolled or romped across the grass.

I said, "I don't know what you're saying. Just spit it out. Stop being passive aggressive oblique."

"Word around town is, you can be a little brusque with folks."

This again?

Ahead, at the end of the drive, stood a white Greek Revival mansion complete with tall columns supporting a portico, very Tara Meets the White House.

I said, “When did you forget how to be direct?”

I could almost see the sigh on the other end of the line.

“I live here. My family lives here. Teddi is growing up here. But you get to move on. Know what I mean?”

I made a game show buzzer sound to make light of the unease squiggling through me. “Dude. Didn’t you mean to say, you get to live here? What happened to the hometown booster boy, selling us heathens in Gotham your version of paradise?” Before he could answer, or to save him from answering, I diverted us to a professional update. “Hey, I’m at Kinsale’s to pick up photos for our story from Josie.”

I drove past the big house, as Josie’s texted directions had instructed, and swung the car out toward the long barn off to the side. I pulled into the small parking lot with a pickup, a sedan or two, and three SUVs. Under the white rail fence, a line of purple irises bobbed in the breeze. Dogs barked in the distance.

“Pick up?” Gordon sounded grouchier than he had before. “She can’t send it email because ...?”

“I don’t think the image is digitized. A photo of McCoy riding. An old picture.”

A groan of impatience. “Can’t she just take a picture of the picture with her cell phone and send it to you?”

"This story needs art. Do you want to depend on someone with maybe iffy photo skills?”

"Just get back to town ASAP. This isn’t your only story. You don’t have the luxury of working on only one story at a time.”

“You realize not all the news happens in town.”

"Just get that picture." He ended the call.

I got out of the car and locked it with the key fob. He'd been a lot more fun when he wasn't saying what was on his mind.

I approached the barn to hear the rhythmic squeak of leather, the jingle of metal, and the thuds of hooves beating a four/four time. At the open barn door, I stood outside and peered in enough to allow my eyes to adjust to the natural light provided by the tall doors opened at each end and a beam shining from a cupola skylight.

I scanned the shadowy depths for more traffic before stepping inside yet stayed next to the wall to get my bearings. Old-school country music played on the radio. Away from me, a horse and rider headed down the extra-wide barn aisle. At the end, they pivoted and headed my way again. The hoofbeats, metal clinking, and leather shifting grew stronger over Loretta singing about life as a coal miner's daughter.

The aromas of horse and leather, not manure, surrounded me. A warm childhood memory of grooming ponies surfaced and embraced me as if to welcome me home.

Too bad I couldn't linger. Work to be done. Impatient, moody editor waiting.

"Loosen him up." The sharp nasal twang suggested Dwayne Kinsale was in the house. "You got him all froze up in the mouth." I'd arrived during a riding lesson, where I could get a glimpse of his training style. My eyes found him in the shadows by a hallway branching off from the barn aisle. "No, that's too much. You still gotta take hold of him."

Horse and rider, a plump mid-life woman with poufy red hair and jeans, pivoted again. "Oh. Lookie here. It's Lois Lane. You snuck up on me." He leaned down the hallway out of sight. "Josie," he called out, "that reporter's here." To me, he said, "She's in the crosstie room. Down that hall. But watch your step and stick to the walls. We don't want to run you over."

Then, he called out louder into the barn aisle, "Loosen up and slow him down."

I sidestepped my way along stalls and watched for an equine nose to emerge to take a chunk out of me. I ducked into the corridor surrounded by a variety of bits, like D-ring snaffles, and curbs with shanks of various lengths and some with Western ornamentation, all hanging like wall décor with hooks on pegboard.

Heading past me in the other direction was a lanky liver-colored hunting dog with a graying muzzle and eyebrows. His raised wagging tail thumped against the paneling as he passed.

The hallway opened into a bright, bustling grooming salon for horses. Floor-to-ceiling square columns of golden oak sectioned off the open frame booths with black rubber-mat flooring. Shelves of equine beauty supplies, including curry combs, brushes, cans, and bottles divided off each workstation.

A sleek black horse spotted me first. He angled his graceful ebony head with delicate perked ears with their tips curved inward. He stood at attention, both to greet his new visitor and assess my threat level.

A tall, thin man in a red ball cap and a khaki jumpsuit had been gazing along the shelf of equine beauty products until he noticed the horse paying attention. The man with splotchy freckles and a need for dental work turned to face me. "Can I help you?" No stranger danger stare, no "reporter scum" vibe, just a check in.

"I'm here to see Josie."

"Over here." She peeked around the horse's head. She must've grown about a foot. "Come on around." She reached her arm around the horse's neck and patted its side near me. The horse relaxed its ears.

I walked over. The man selected a spray can from the supply shelf. "Don't worry. He won't get you." He shook the can and the mixers rattled.

"Unless you have gingersnaps in your pockets, then I won't be able to save you." His grin showed some yellowed teeth missing. He added, "Just from a horse nose frisk. He won't hurt you."

"No worries. I'm clean." Despite the metallic clacking from the can, the horse returned its perked ear attention to me. Might have been the word "gingersnaps."

On the other side of the horse, Josie stood on a short step ladder with red and white ribbons streaming from her hands. "We're getting our stallion ready for his new conformation photo." She wore a sleeveless blue riding blouse and indigo jeans. Her long blonde hair trailed in a long French braid.

The riding student led her horse into the grooming room. Dwayne's voice followed. "A conformation photo is for his computer dating profile. He's a breeding stallion."

Josie tinkled a genteel laugh before saying, "Uncle Dwayne says the darnedest things."

I said, "He's Dorothy Parker in drag." Oops. Gordon would hear about that one. Change gears fast. "Thank you for the photos. I can take them and be on my way."

Josie's smile widened when she waved me over to the horse. "Come meet our champion stallion."

Oh, crap. Another delay. Yet, Gordon's disappointment that I'd been rude to another source prompted me to pull in my claws. I said, "I don't want to monopolize your time."

Josie climbed off the ladder. "Are you afraid of horses?" Was that amazement? Or maybe a passive-aggressive dare?

I breathed into my impatience. Pet the horsey. Get the pictures. Then, go back to town like an obedient reporter.

The horse stood tall with only a faint white star on his gleaming black brow. A red-and-white braid of ribbon ran down between his ears and swooped under the brow band of a fancy halter and draped along his face.

"This is Midnight Tribulation." His mistress's voice lilted with pride and affection. Despite the crossties, the horse lowered his head to his blonde beloved, who stroked his satiny neck with long smooth strokes. "But we call him Ol' Trib." Before I could add the pithy observation about how Daddy owned the *Trib*, she added, "Pun and in-joke intended."

My hand stretched, but hesitated. "I don't want to leave fingerprints on his coat."

"He won't bite," Josie said. "Not even for gingersnaps. Some people like to tease new people." She shot a pointed stare at the groom and tsked with sly sass.

My palm touched the satiny neck. Warmth and life spread down my arm like a current. I flashed into a world of ponies, then bigger horses, their memories flashing through my mind like a flipbook.

Tears teetered on my eyelashes. How long had it been since I'd touched a horse? Middle school or sometime in high school?

A distant voice, male and Southern said, "'Scuse me, Josie." One of the grooms rattled the can mixers again. "Time to pretty up those front hooves."

I yanked away my hand and my mind. What the hell, Avery? Are you fifteen and trying not to be horse crazy again? Time for business.

"I need to get that photo of Cy McCoy." I blinked away a tear and sniffled. "I'll let you guys get on with your day." Sniff.

She gave the horse a couple of graceful caresses along his mane before stepping aside. "Well, it's good timing before I start the second braid." She backed down the ladder. "The photos you want are over there." She turned to gesture toward a wall.

Whispery aerosol blasts suggested the stallion's pedicure was underway. A quick glance showed me hooves gleaming like patent leather. The sharp metallic tang of paint wafted my way. When the stallion shifted his feet, delicate black crescents of paint remained on the barn floor.

No wonder I hadn't set foot in the barn or on the pasture rail since I'd moved to Kentucky. I couldn't keep my mind in the present, let alone get anything done.

Still, of all the memories haunting me the most often, with so many sweet ones filed away, why did the ones that visited me the most have to be ugly images of war?

Fifteen

Josie led me, and her little dog following on her heels with a sassy trot, to a sunlight-bathed lounge attached to the barn. Where I grew up in the north, viewing windows showed the riders working horses in an indoor arena. The Kinsale barn used its wide aisles as an indoor arena and overlooked the grooming area.

Open windows between Glen Plaid curtains let me hear Dwayne drawling at the grooms and allowed me to appreciate the leathery musk of nearby horses. Another window opened out to an outdoor ring, complete with a center gazebo.

Josie pointed to a small round dog bed of matching Glen Plaid print and ordered the little dog to stay. He climbed aboard the upholstered cushion from where he watched her with his button eyes. I'd heard of "ugly-cute," and he was an example.

In the lounge with its upholstered chairs and wet bar, high on the walls, hung framed action photos of high-stepping show horses and trophy presentations. The changing fashions of the women's clothing and hair suggested almost five decades. So did the color fading from display in a sunny room.

Also, in the photos, every rider and presenter was white.

No Cy there.

In one photo, a young rider with long blonde hair made me think of a younger Josie with a rounder face. Over to the side, almost behind a cabinet, I also spotted a couple of faded rectangular gaps suggesting missing photos.

Josie sang out. "They're over here."

I followed her to a tack trunk by a cabinet. The framed photos had been facedown against the Kinsale Farms logo on the lid.

Josie said, as she lifted the frames to a standing position, "We've had them hanging in here for a good twenty years."

I studied them. A teenage Cy, the only black rider in the photos. He'd been all lanky like Harlan had described, riding a flashy show horse, gray with a black mane and tail, with tall white stockings on her legs. A blue roan, like a gray but with a bluish cast, lit up with lots of chrome, like Harlan had described no more than an hour ago.

The other photo, an award presentation with the same horse turning its face toward the camera, showed its wide expanse of blaze between its eyes.

With Harlan's story in mind, I said, "This morning, I heard a story about a mare that loved a particular brand of doughnuts. Is this her?"

Josie's gray-blue eyes went wide. She said, "Why, yes. She showed for Cyrus like she didn't show for anyone else." She stepped closer and said, in a half-smiling conspiratorial tone, "Are you telling me he gave her doughnuts? *Treats?*"

She cast a side-eye toward the open window leading to where her uncle was busy haranguing one of the grooms about one of the horses. "Mercy," her voice went breathy and conspiratorial, "Uncle Dwayne would have a cow if he knew that."

I couldn't help but grin. In the north, trainers scolded us kids when they caught us sneaking treats to lesson ponies, too. Uncle Dwayne seemed like a no-treats trainer, but Josie seemed more like a soft touch for big eyes, perked ears, and a lilting nicker.

While watching him to make sure the trainer didn't invade the conversation, I leaned and said, "Harlan told me at the Fairmont House this morning. It's an awesome anecdote for the story."

She tilted her head with a dreamy gaze. "We always knew he had a way with her. She was a mite particular about her riders."

"And particular about her doughnuts, too. Or so I heard."

With a wide grin and a shake of her head, she said, "It all makes so much sense now. Hindsight."

Dwayne broke off his convo with the stable hand. Maybe he could hear us as well as we could hear him.

I lifted the paper's classy point-and-shoot digital camera and said, "I'd like to make a still-life photo illustration, but glare from the glass frames could be a problem." I glanced around the room designed for less horsey parents or spouses of students or spouses wanting to keep an eye but not be immersed in the activity.

"No problem," Josie said with a breezy voice. Then, "Oh, dear."

She'd opened the frame on the action shot and destroyed the image. One hand held the 8x10 photograph, now with a long splotch of white where that section of the image had stuck to the glass.

"Oh, no. I should've warned you first." I picked up the still undamaged photo in its frame to protect it. "The photographic emulsion on those photos has been expanding and contracting with the weather for years. No wonder it stuck to the glass."

I wouldn't let this remaining picture get damaged.

A ringtone of Elvis fast-talking about less conversation interrupted us. "Oops," she said. "Pardon me." She dragged her phone out of her jeans pocket. "Hello, Momma." Josie excused herself with a raised index finger. She stepped away to open the exterior door, stepped outside, and then didn't quite close the door behind her. Her small dog whimpered as his eyes tracked her.

The photographer in me mourned for the damaged photo, an irreplaceable piece of personal history. The long, ripped splotch ran from the hoof of the horse's high-stepping front leg and slashed all the way across to the rider's face.

Out of the glass, yes, but now rendered useless.

Who didn't know you don't yank out a photo touching glass for years from old frame?

The action shot may have been beyond rescue, but the static award presentation photo remained safe behind glass.

Aboard the horse, in the irons, sat a serious-faced, thin, teenage Cy, all decked out in a three-piece suit with a snap brim hat covering much of his brow. His intense eyes surrounded by geeky wire-rimmed glasses peered from beneath the brim.

Distantly, Dwayne said something sharp, telling Josie to hurry, the photographer was almost ready. Josie opened the door wider, poked her head into the room, and sang out with the phone in one hand how she'd finish braiding in a minute.

"You're not Eye-talian." He teased her in response. "You don't need both hands to talk. Even an old fart like me knows Bluetooth don't bite."

She replied, "But multitasking does." Her voice returned to the murmur of her phone conversation. "Sorry, Momma."

After a few minutes, Josie returned to the crosstie room, but still on the phone. "I promise to reconsider." She ended the call, then changed her voice to speak to me. "So unfortunate about that photo. That old mare sure could break level and reach over the rail," she said in a voice lilting with admiration. "Maybe you know a specialist in photo repair."

A cordial but hollow ring in her voice made me feel she didn't sound as sorry as she should have. Had she not wanted me to take that action shot? It would've been the best picture. Or was the horse stepping too high for good press? I'd probably never know.

I couldn't resist offering free advice. "When you guys redecorate in here, don't take these old photos out of frames yourself. Take them to a pro framer. Extra points if that company also offers photo restoration." I waved to encompass the paneled lounge. "My Spideysense tells me you guys can afford it."

She flinched. "I am aware of your deadline. I took the risk. I'm sure you've taken risks counter to conventional wisdom."

Had she and her father talked about what happened in the *Trib* staff meeting? Or my old job overseas? Which on paper made me look great, but also taught me to lean into risk.

"Point taken." I'd have to be more mindful of Josie if she had a tendency to complain to Daddy. I added, "And thank you for providing these. I appreciate it." I really did. Otherwise, no photos would go with my sidebar. Or elegy, as I'd pitched it to her father.

"Well," her downcast gaze and slight smile suggested I'd soothed over my sharp east coast barb. "If you need anything, just holler."

I noticed the window overlooking the outdoor ring streamed a narrow beam of light with floating motes of dust. "I have an idea for a photo illustration using the framed win picture." I tilted my head to point with my chin toward the picturesque corner. "Do you have some spare tack? Things I can arrange for a still life around the picture?"

Her gaze riveted to the corner. Her eyes brightened with delight. An artist's eye lurked under all those manners and makeup. "Props? Unique to our horse?"

My turn to be delighted. “If it’s not too much trouble.” I pointed to a dusty wooden stool. “Can I use that for staging?”

“Sure,” she called my way. “I’ve got some great stuff in mind.” She returned with a tricolor rosette streaming ribbon and a tight braid of red and white ribbons attached to an alligator clip. “If you need more, I can find things. I didn’t want to make the image too busy.”

I accepted them with, “These are great.” And they were. I couldn’t help but grin at the alligator clip. “Thank you.”

Smiling and fidgety, as if she itched to help arrange and set up, she backed away. “I’ll leave you to make your magic,” she said.

I arranged the items on the stool in the light coming from the window. Maybe I’d prop up items, instead of shooting a flat lay. Or I could do both and determine later which worked better.

I could still hear men working and talking while horses pawed and stomped on the rubber stall mats with a radio soundtrack of a woman singing about being famous in a small town.

While I happily tweaked positions and determined the framing of the image, Dwayne’s voice called out to Josie, “What did Polly want?”

She called out, as if she were away from him, “Momma told me about Cy’s funeral arrangements.”

Just because my hands were busy didn’t mean my ears weren’t open. Cy’s funeral arrangements?

Of course, I should go, but not with Josie. Arriving with the privileged blonde at her family’s former employee’s funeral? Sketchy optics.

But, then again, she didn’t invite me.

Dwayne spoke again with a squint and a sneer. “He gonna be up at Epperson’s?”

“No. Lexington.”

I kept my mouth shut and took my photos. I slowed and tightened my movements to blend into the background. I could be seen through that window into the grooming room, which also allowed me to watch what proceeded.

He said, as if she were a kid, not a grown woman, "Did you forget how they shot up one of their funeral homes a few years ago?"

"Uncle Dwayne. Please," she said with a dismissive sniff. "That was Louisville. This is Lexington. And the service is at a church, not a funeral home."

But I kept my head down and my eyes busy arranging an image.

"Saturday's the Lawrenceburg show," he said while doubling down in intensity. "You can't be in Lexington all day Saturday."

Josie's voice took on a pleading tone, "He and Louise were like part of the family. I'll be done in time for the horse show."

"Wait. *I'll*? Isn't Polly going with you? She's letting you gallivant alone off to a dangerous part of town?"

I didn't know Josie's age, although I'd guess almost a decade past twenty-one.

"She's considering attending," Josie said, still finger-combing the horse's mane.

I didn't know Josie well, but I sensed she was telling a fib.

"I'm going." I could almost hear the necks swiveling, as I proved I'd been eavesdropping. "If it's not a private service. You could ride to Lexington with me."

As soon as the words left my mouth, I wished I could take them back. Not two minutes after I'd told myself I didn't want to go with her, my itch to stack the deck against Dwayne had overwhelmed me like an undertow.

Her southern hospitality smile and vocal cadence returned. "That's so sweet of you, Avery. I appreciate you asking. Even though I'd love the company, I'd probably need to leave sooner than you will." She paused a couple of beats and then said, "Horse show night."

I suppressed my sigh of relief and re-arranged my equestrian stuff, but Dwayne said, "And you, Miss Nosy Reporter." He spoke directly through the window. "You barely knew him, but you're going to the funeral. Did you know they have all-day funerals? The music'll be good, but that's a big chunk of time."

"She's working, Uncle Dwayne." Josie's voice held an edge.

I said, "Attending would be part of my job."

I tweaked the framed photo so the beam wouldn't glare off the glass. I took several shots, at different angles, both horizontal and vertical.

Realizing I'd felt a bit shaky among all the unsubtle power plays, I wished I'd had a tripod, but knew I could make do.

I parked my tush on the floor and braced my elbow against the adjacent wall. I ignored chitchat between the grooms, controlled my breath, and reshot the photos.

"I'm not saying he wasn't a good kid." Dwayne's voice sounded close. "It's a damn shame he got killed."

I turned, craning my neck to look up at him. "Are you talking to me?"

He nodded with a sniff. "I hear tell you can take care of yourself, but don't you go egging on our Josie. She don't know how to handle herself in extreme situations. Word is, you do."

I sensed he'd just worked in a veiled insult at me, let alone cloaking his prejudice toward Cy by calling him a kid instead of boy. A two-fer.

Good thing I was largely finished shooting.

"Right," I said. "My time overseas in conflict zones." I couldn't resist adding, "I'm sure you served and saw much of the same things."

With his elbows leaning on the windowsill, as if he'd been eager to savor my comeuppance, his face flushed and his expression froze.

So, he hadn't served in the military, despite his region's fondness for military service.

I'd hit a nerve. I'd pay for it. But worth it.

He said, as if he'd been speaking to children, "I meant when you lived in New York City." His shoulders bobbed as he laughed at his own joke. He turned away from the window as if he had delivered his parting shot.

Before I could trade more barbs, Josie chimed in. "Uncle Dwayne, you know full well that I've not only visited New York with Momma and gone to shows and even a gospel brunch in Harlem, but I've also gone by myself. Shopping and visiting and everything."

I suspected she meant for her voice to sound triumphant, but to me, the subtext played as *I'm a big girl now.*

But I'd also noticed Josie wasn't the only one treated with condescension from her elders. I'd seen Hazel waiting on Norwood as if he couldn't manage for himself.

Come to think of it, I knew a lot of northern families who saw their offspring as children, long after they'd left childhood behind.

I needed to get my images before getting kicked out. I scrolled through and expanded them to check for any blur from camera shake.

Sharp, even in the contrasty light.

Pleased with the images and itching to leave, I headed out to my car and checked my phone. A text from Gordon, directions to my next interview on the other side of the county.

The hometown hero story. The I'm-wasting-my-time-because-he-won't-talk-to-the-likes-of-me story.

I drove through what amounted to a tiny ghost town—vacant storefronts, a blink-and-you'll-miss-it place even in better days. More cattle than homes.

While I drove, I called Gordon. "I found out Cy McCoy's funeral arrangements." I told him the details, as Josie had reported them. "The online obit says public is invited, and I want to go to the services."

On the phone, the faint clicking of his typing. "Is he out at Epperson's?" AKA, in town.

"No. Lexington. Where he lives. I mean, lived. Saturday morning." My head felt foggy. I knew better than to skip lunch.

The background noise of the faint clicks of keys filled his silence. Then, he said, "On your time off?"

"What else am I gonna do? Play golf?" I made sure my sneer sounded playful.

"You could, I dunno, rest. It's not a short drive, and this will be a full-day trip."

I took the opening. "But Gordon, it's the funeral for a murder victim. On our turf. He was a respected man. A big church funeral. With multiple speakers. And music. I can video a song or two for our website."

My boss said, "Okay. Don't stay all day. Get what looks good, slip out, and take in some of Lexington. Get some quiet time. Maybe visit a horse farm. Have you done any of the tours yet? I bet you'd like that."

I didn't remind him I live on a horse farm. I let him believe what he wanted.

Saturday was my own time. He had no say in how I spent it.

One entity did. I called the funeral home, identified myself, and then asked about media coverage.

The woman who answered the phone said, "We welcome media attendance."

Sixteen

I walked from my car to the three painted wooden steps then up to a front porch punctuated with baskets of scarlet geraniums. A porch swing dangled from the ceiling at one end. Through the front screen door, I saw straight through to the back screen door.

Not being able to sit facing the door in his own home could put Terry Johnson, a US Marine home from deployment, on edge. I bet he sat where he could see the route through the house.

From inside the house came the sound of a sports announcer calling an afternoon baseball game, as well as the deep voice of a young black man. From his energy, I'd arrived mid-conversation. He said, "I know what to do. What to say. How to act. I'll be fine." His emphasis gave the words weight and punch.

I placed my hand on the thin, painted white wrought-iron banister and froze. Then, I returned to the ground, all the while looking into the house through the screen.

A midlife-woman's voice, brimming with faux optimism. The woman said, "You're a veteran. That ought to count for something."

Engrossed in their conversation and with the cover of an energetic sports announcer, let alone organ music playing a cavalry Charge, they hadn't heard me drive up. He may not like surprises any more than I did.

I froze with my hand on the banister with one foot on the step.

Inside the house, a little girl with skin the shade of an acorn spotted me. Her hair had been twisted into stubby knots, but her mouth was full of shiny wet fingers. In her matching shorts set with printed blue flowers, she stared with uncertainty.

Lousy at guessing a child's age, I decided she was a preschooler. I waggled my fingers at her and stayed at the base of the steps.

"Lord have mercy," said the woman's voice inside the house. "I didn't hear her pull up."

The ball game went mute. I heard a thumping shift, making me think of a recliner closing as its occupant stood. "Mom." He drew out the word into two syllables spoken in a *we've talked about this* edge. "I told you. I won't talk to her."

Too bad I didn't have my phone out to record him for Gordon.

Bright orange shifted into my field of vision. Terry Johnson's mom, Grace, wore an orange Blanchard County High School Demons sweatshirt. A spiral of black hair hung loose from her low ponytail and drifted along her high cheekbones. She swept it away from her face with a huff and shot a sidelong glance toward the right out of my field of vision.

Then, she straight-armed the door open and stood aside with a gracious smile topped by harried eyes. Closer, I could see some gray through her black curls and some darker acne scars dented her face. "Do come in and have some iced tea."

"Thank you. Call me Avery, please." I engaged my own ultra-polite mode, after you-ing like those cartoon chipmunks. "Perhaps this is an inconvenient time?"

"No, please. I work around men all day. I miss visiting with other women." She patted the little girl on her shoulder. "This is Terry's baby, Shanice."

No telling how much time I'd waste, for few or no results. Still, I thanked her again and stepped inside the farmhouse.

She gestured to a big sofa with doilies on the seat back. "Please. Have a seat." She deployed her Mom voice: "Terry. Sit down."

My interview subject, Marine PFC Terry Johnson almost overwhelmed the chair where he sat, but he wasn't fat. Yet. His shaved head gleamed above his gray Marine Corps T-shirt and black sweatpants.

The little girl climbed onto his lap. He cuddled her like a teddy bear. He watched the muted ball game. I also noted he had me, who I'm sure he saw as a potential threat, in his sightline.

Grace headed toward the kitchen. Even though I'd photographed firefights and recently had barged through a hedge to get a story, I couldn't get out of that living room fast enough.

On her heels, I said, "I'm more of a kitchen table gal." Just one more lie in service of the truth.

"Well, then, Avery, what's a parlor for without guests to entertain?" She gestured to the couch set off to the side and perpendicular to the TV. "How do you take your tea?"

"It won't work." Johnson's voice came out deep, rich, and edgy. He wouldn't look my way.

His mother shook her head as if to shake off the bad vibes. "Don't pay him no never mind. Your tea, Avery? How do you take it?"

"Straight up." Uh, oops. No. "Plain's fine. No sugar or lemon."

Johnson turned up the volume on the game. Otherwise, the silence would've been oppressive.

With bright, blinky eyes, the little girl raised her head to peek at me again.

Peek a boo? Really?

Instead, I made friendly eye contact, smiled, and said, "Hi. I'm Avery. Do you like baseball?"

She flashed me a brilliant but soggy smile before turning her gaze of adoration to her father. She ducked her head to snuggle into his neck and muttered something.

Little kid jabbering sounded the same in any language. My actions switched into routine, so I grinned to play along.

While staring at the TV, Johnson said, "She said you're pretty. You should say 'thank you'." His tone said reporter scum. He tucked his head to whisper to her.

Still, a connection. A switch inside me clicked as the previously impossible started feeling possible.

My turn to ignore him. "Thank you," I said to Shanice. "How many are you anyway? I'll show you how many I am." I flashed all my fingers of both hands, fluttered to inspire her to laugh and engage. If her father engaged, then fine, otherwise, we'd entertain each other.

She raised her hand and unfurled three fingers. She giggled and twisted to look up at him, as if for confirmation. He glanced down at her with an adoring smile then stilled his face and chilled his demeanor when he gazed at me for the first time. "Don't you have somewhere to go?"

"Your mom's making me iced tea. Bugging out would be rude."

"I got nothing to say to you. Let alone for the paper."

I leaned forward with my elbows on my knees. "Here's the sitch, Marine. Your boss," then I waved toward the kitchen where his mom was making tea, "called my boss. We're caught in the middle. Do you think either one of them is going to cut either of us any slack if we don't make this happen?"

With the arm that didn't encircle her, he stroked his daughter's braids. "You people just don't get it. You take things out of context. You get good people in trouble. You have your own agenda."

Good. That was finally out of his mouth. At least, he hadn't said, get the hell out of my house.

I pointed to the window overlooking the driveway and said in my best child-friendly voice, "Hey, Shanice. Would you please go to the window, look out at my car, and watch out for a giant butterfly? My car's so tiny a giant butterfly can steal it right off the parking space. Please go watch out for it, for me. Okay?"

"Really?" he said in a voice as dry as summer in Ramadi. "That's not gonna work, either."

But Shanice swung her legs over his lap to hop down. But first, she glanced at her dad and beamed an eager smile for permission.

He gave her a yeah-whatever nod and patted her on the shoulder. Her little sneakers padded toward the window.

To me, he said in a voice as cold as a high desert winter, "Don't you mess with her."

I said, "Not on my agenda."

When she leaned over the windowsill to brace herself for a closer look through the screen, I bent to roll up the hem of my jeans. My breathing went shallow, whether it was from the bending or nerves or even having become too accustomed to air-conditioning. No telling.

"Seriously?" He hissed softly enough not to distract his daughter from her sentry duty. "You're playing that card? For a minute there, I thought you might be smart."

Thanks to the line of my bootcut jeans, I rolled the denim past the tight laces of my hiking boots, over the top of my sock. I exposed the skin of my lower leg.

He wasn't watching TV anymore. He stared at my leg. But not in the way men used to stare at my legs.

Most women my age don't have unmarked legs anyway. Many have varicose veins from sitting with their legs crossed at work. Or carrying a baby, or multiple babies, to term.

More Marines than mommies have marks on their legs like mine. Shrapnel scars.

"Where'd you get those?" His voice and tune had changed.

Before I could reply, his mother gasped so hard glasses rattled on the tray. Another clunk.

I ducked my head to swing my gaze toward her. She'd set the tray of full iced tea glasses on the dining room table. She stood next to it with her body twisted away. She'd averted her gaze, but not enough for me to miss seeing her fingers pressed over her mouth and her eyes squeezed shut.

Heat flushed from under my tee to roil along my neck to my cheeks. I rolled down my pant leg.

He was right. Civilians didn't get it. Or maybe I was unfit for polite society after all.

I straightened and slapped the top of my thighs once. "Look at the time." My chest tightened so my voice came out thin and distant. "Thank you. I'm so sorry. I need to take a rain check on that iced tea."

Through the screen door, Terry Johnson called out, "Yo, Sloane. Where you going?"

Seventeen

By the time I returned to the office, the sun had sunk behind the buildings across the street. Gordon sat alone at the front workstation to edit copy and cover Laverne's desk. Everyone else had left for a dinner or what they called "supper" break before we put the paper to bed. An old newsroom term I never understood. If we're publishing the paper, we're distributing the news, and bringing it to another version of life, so to speak, and into public discourse.

Too bad for me Gordon hadn't left yet. I had a story to write under a tight deadline. But, first, I could tell by his grim face, I had some explaining to do.

I didn't need an audience, especially one fond of gossip. "Laverne's gone?" Let alone another civilian who didn't get it. The memory of Grace Johnson's revulsion sent my skin crawling.

"Left early to go to the dentist." His gaze stayed on the monitor. His fingers clicked at a steady pace on the keyboard. "Grace Johnson called. She says you didn't do the interview."

My stomach clenched. And here we go. Could anyone in this town resist grabbing a phone to gossip and tattle? Why did they need a newspaper?

I dropped my tote bag onto my desk. I dragged my rolling chair away from its nook under my desk. I raised my eyes to the county map and mentally traced one of the streets around the lake. "What else did she tell you?"

"You got through to him." Gordon continued to type. "Then you left."

I thirsted to hear more about what a crappy job I'd done—a validation of the mental tongue-lashing I was giving myself.

With all the swagger I could muster, I yanked open the top drawer of the desk and plucked out a small bottle of headache meds. "It's all part of my evil plan." I popped the lid and shook two tablets into my palm. "Now he can't wait to talk to me." I bluffed a wink.

As his habit, which he'd shared with us as good advice, Gordon clicked the Save button before he stood. "If you say so."

"But if you'll let me get to work, I'll blow your mind with this story. Wait until you see the photo illustration."

He logged off. "I'd been holding space for Johnson's story." He pushed his chair away from the desk.

Subtext being, you crappy failure, you. You let me down. From my friend. Who was now my boss.

My fingers clutched around the dry tablets still in my hand.

"Johnson took forever warming up to the idea to talk. By then, it was too late. He had to go to work. I'm not going to make a guy late for work."

With a wrinkled brow, he said, "Are you still insisting on going to the funeral?"

"News is news, and Saturday is mine to do what I please." I rubbed the back of my neck.

"I'm concerned about your health." He furrowed his brow. Then added, not like a boss, but like a friend, "Your nerves."

I couldn't help but smile at his use of the genteel blanket term for anxiety or any other emotional upheaval. For once, I appreciated Gordon's habitual indirect statements. I wasn't ready to talk about what was or wasn't happening with my health, physical or mental.

I countered with a redirection back to the point. "How often do you get a murder story in this county?" Okay, that sentence rushed out a little harsh. "Kinsale will probably give us this week—tops—to cover it until an arrest is made. Then, he'll just want news briefs for court updates. He'll comply with the old 'if it didn't happen here, it doesn't go in our paper' line. This is a slim window of opportunity."

He folded his arms and drilled through me with his gaze. "A two-hour drive each way— starting in the early morning—to a crowded, emotional, and long funeral."

I dared a dark-humored grin. "Because those are always the best and the newsiest." The words soured in my mouth. I'd admired Cy. He deserved better.

"Even though you couldn't get through a simple feature interview?" Gordon headed for the door.

I followed him through the newsroom and continued my pitch.

"Maybe I'm playing a long game. Johnson's still in play. He didn't say 'no way.' You're familiar with the dance between reporters and reluctant subjects. Hell, if you want this done fast, send Wilbur. They could've talked man-to-man."

I tried to imagine our wiry nerdy reporter connecting with Terry the muscly Marine.

With his hand on the door pull, Gordon stopped and turned to listen. With his renewed attention, I continued. "They both grew up here. Wilbur's probably known the Johnsons for years. Which makes me wonder, why did you and Kinsale insist on sending me, a stranger?"

I couldn't stop talking. I went for the maybe outrageous, maybe not. Go big or go home. "Or does Wilbur have a problem with black people? I've seen a lot of that around here. People work hard to hide it, especially around a stranger like me, spreading on a coat of good manners like paint, but whoops there it is."

Gordon dropped his hand from the door handle, turned to me with his facial muscles all agog.

I'd said too much. Too fast. Too soon.

He said, explaining as if I were Teddi, "I sent you because you'd been over there, too. I thought you'd make a connection. You're the only one in this office who's come even remotely to being in the military."

A laugh rose like a belch, but I suppressed it.

"Gordo, even if we'd crossed paths in the Sandbox, my experience was vastly different from his experience. Maybe not in your eyes, but unquestionably in his."

My editor halted and pivoted toward me. "You still insist on attending the McCoy funeral? And chatting up mourners at the funeral?"

"I don't plan to chat up anyone at the funeral. Just watch and listen and take notes. See who the speakers are. What they say. Maybe video a song or two. I'll blend in. I used to do it in Iraq. You know good photojournalists are ghosts, and I've got an award that says I'm good. You know I can do this."

He rubbed his right hand over his grayer-by-the-day stubble. "That's the problem. You're not a photographer anymore."

I blinked hard and flicked my gaze onto the county map hanging on the wall. Maps could ground me. They had logic.

My gaze zeroed in on Bowmansville Lake, a major feature and a man-made lake, like in that old George Clooney movie with the hillbillies re-enacting the Odyssey. Small towns, modest homes, trees, and farms, all submerged for a reservoir. A rural American Atlantis.

"You left the city because you can't stand crowds. This'll be a noisy, emotional crowd."

"I've been in protests and riots and gone to Fenway for away games." I added, going for the dark humor journos, nurses, cops, and troops appreciated. "In Yankees fan gear."

That had been before I'd gone to Iraq, but that also proved his point, which didn't help me.

"The thing is—" He rubbed under his shirt collar. "Mr. Kinsale won't want you to go. Let alone for us to cover it."

"Mister? You mean, your Uncle Clark? When did you get so cowed by The Man?"

"You heard him at the meeting. He doesn't want us sensationalizing this story." He focused on tidying a stack of papers. His message? Case closed.

Not on my watch. "First, he's got no say in how I spend my time off. Second, a murder in our area of a hometown guy is hard for us to ignore." Did I have to keep repeating that? Maybe it was time to get to the root of the problem.

"So," I said, "what is the big deal? That Cy wasn't a resident in our circulation area? Or that he's black and most of our readership isn't?"

I came close to mentioning the discussion I'd just overheard about "driving while black," but this conversation needed to pertain to the funeral.

My old friend's voice vibrated with tried patience. "Avery—" He paused as if he were about to say something else. "It's not a race thing. It's business." Gordon gave me a pointed look down his nose. "I need to be able to authorize your travel expenses. It's paperwork. Unc—He thinks like a businessman. But I'm thinking like your friend."

The words tumbled out of my mouth. "My own time, my own dime. Unless I find something newsworthy, Kinsale doesn't need to know. Tell me it's not sounding better all the time."

The concern emitting from his eyes and pulsing from his posture almost made me cry. "I know," he said, his voice sagging and his gaze down at the swinging door in front of him. “I hope you make a different choice. No one will think less of you.”

As he headed out the door, a sad smile tugged at the left corner of my mouth. “But I will.”

Eighteen

The *Blanchard County Tribune* hit the streets, store shelves, and email mailboxes on an overcast morning. On my way to work, I went around the corner to the Quik Stop, the local greasy spoon breakfast and lunch joint, for a cup of plain oatmeal and raisins.

From behind the cook's pass-through, the Quik Stop owner and cook called out, "Nice article," and gave me a thumbs up.

I couldn't help but smile. Funny to feel so proud of a feature sidebar to a news story, a fluffy cushion for hard news.

On the way out, I caught a glimpse of the courthouse. With its tall Greek columns at the top of the wide steps, the Blanchard County courthouse had been built in a time when only a temple was suitable for meting out justice. The trial of Cy's murderer would be held there—whenever that would be.

My phone rang. On another generous whim, I answered.

A male voice brimming with New York rushed out loud and brisk. "Mason Russo, editor *Outdoor Challenge* Magazine. I've seen your stuff. You're a natural for us, maybe even give us fresh eyes with a gritty spin. We've got a shoot scheduled for Baja. Motor sports. Video and still. Interested?"

How I'd missed the crackle of New York English, like a shot of sriracha in a steaming bowl of pho.

I shifted my gaze to watch red geranium blooms bob in the breeze. From Blanchard County to Baja? Outdoor adventure photography? After my years of spot news, let alone hard news?

"Sorry, pal. Wrong number."

"This is A. S. Wharton, right? Wait. Sorry. I heard you go by Sloane now. My bad. Divorce. It sucks."

"How did you know—"

"I get it. You've had enough desert for twenty lifetimes. No problem. It's a big world. What about recreating the Lewis & Clark expedition with a saddle horse and a pack mule? Or you could pitch something else." His rising voice suggested desperation. "We can make you staff. Give you bennies."

A magazine offering a staff position with benefits. It didn't make sense. Besides, Russo must have blown through his short list to get to me. "Why me? How did you get my number?" Which helpful friend had written my phone number, not on a men's room wall, but on internet help wanted sites?

On the call, the fast-talker from New York continued. "Listen, we're looking to expand to a female market. You'd make a helluva bridge. Whaddya say?"

A staff position with benefits. No more blood and guts, shrapnel and fire. No more small-town chit-chat. Back to New York. But a staff gig at a magazine based in New York? In this economy?

Maybe that's why I didn't jump at the offer.

Crystal, whose spot I filled, would return in a few months. Maybe.

Marvin and the sheriff's department would catch Cy's murderer. Maybe.

Maybe even by the time I left.

The editor on the other end of the call was silent for a moment. "Word has it you're cooling your heels in Pennsytucky." His words no longer reflected his own desperation but sympathy for me. "Leave the banjos and come home to decent pizza."

An elderly man wearing a red plaid western shirt with faded overalls shuffled by, made eye contact, and tipped the brim of his ball cap with an acknowledging courtly nod. His smile had been warm, not patronizing.

I thought of Gordon, Cathy the coroner, and Hazel, who had her moments of warmth. Okay. Hazel had plenty of moments of warmth.

The glimmers I'd see from people like them gave me hope their views hadn't contracted and hardened them against the rest of humanity, humans who weren't like them.

Into the phone, I said, "Dude, you're the photo editor of an adventure travel magazine. Learn some freakin' geography."

Had my pulse not been pounding in my ears, I might be more certain as to who ditched the call first.

Little did he know, he almost had me at "decent pizza."

So, it was true.

I was going to finish this job and see Cy's murderer come to justice. The first might be a matter of months. Let Crystal's baby come to term, give her a month or two maternity leave, but the cops bringing a murderer to justice could take two or three years, depending on whether I'd stay for the trial.

Did I really want to stay here?

When I shoved open the inside glass door, my gaze skimmed past Laverne on the phone and Wilbur speed-typing with two fingers. Gordon held a phone to his ear with one hand and flicked a wan wave toward me with the other.

I headed toward my desk. Laverne called out, "Doris Caldwell is calling off the hook, saying you're not answering your cell." Our office manager hit the mute button. "Good for you. Ducking her calls." She punctuated her sentence with a smug nod.

Her approval sent me to my phone to return Doris's call. If Laverne approved of a choice, I needed to reexamine.

There's no motivation as strong as spite.

After three rings, Doris's said. "Cyrus McCoy used to be a good man," Her voice quivered with outrage. "When he was a boy, he didn't know any better, but going back as an adult? When he knows what he knows? He could have excused a horse from the ring, made an example of that owner and trainer, but he caved and let them stay. Money talks. But you know that. It certainly spoke to you and overrode your New York values."

She hung up before I could respond.

What the hell? My New York values?

Laverne's voice boomed from the front. "Lord have mercy, Doris Caldwell's on the warpath again. We got a new letter-to-the-editor, too. Gordon's gonna have to do a lot of that 'editing for length' before Clark sees it." She even hooked her fingers for air quotes.

Someone was having a busy, manic morning.

Before speaking, I made sure only *Tribune* staff was around. "So," I said to Laverne, who could be counted upon for gossip, "what's the deal with Doris anyway?" That'd be enough to prime the pump.

I settled into my chair, settled my elbows into a relaxed position, and arranged my face into a "tell me more" smile.

Laverne came out from behind her desk with forward posture; ready to dish.

"When she and her husband showed horses that were winning, Doris couldn't get enough of them. Now she hates the horse shows. Oh, she's all lawyer slick about it. All but says Clark is a criminal just because his horses win. She's lawyer enough to know how to run up to the line and then scoot away."

I nodded more to get her to continue. Anyone suspicious of Clark Kinsale won points for superb intelligence in my private book. Yet, I'd seen the show horse Josie Kinsale affectionately called Ol' Trib earlier in the week. With his sleek coat and handsome muscles, let alone his doting attitude toward people, especially Josie, he didn't look or stand like an abused horse —especially to someone like me who'd seen skeletal cart horses laboring in the Middle East.

At my elbow, Gordon said, "I have a dentist appointment. Walk with me to the car."

We walked out the door in silence while I fretted. Just like me to push it when things were going well.

Out on the sidewalk, we passed a young mother with a baby on one hip and a toddler gripping her other hand heading toward the bank.

As soon as we got past the closed newsroom door and Laverne, I said, "Sorry, man. You know how much gossip bugs me, and here I go dishing it out."

"Has Doris been harassing you?"

I'd been ready to explain myself, but this was new. Doris? "Doris has an agenda, but who doesn't? Just about everyone who contacts us of their own free will has an agenda."

"You'd tell me if she went overboard?"

"Hello? You know where I'm from. I have no meter to measure. We're pushy for sport. She must drive you southerners batshit." As soon as the words left my lips, I almost rocked back on my heels. "Do *I* drive you batshit?"

"Present tense noted. You're a lot more impulsive than you were before . . ." Distress crowded his brow. He wouldn't say the words. Just two words, three little letters each. The. War. Instead, other words rushed out. "I see a lot of you in Teddi." He opened the door of his minivan.

"That's biologically impossible."

"Somehow you got in there. I reckon having you around now is good training for me and Shannon for our future with her."

What do you say to that? "Then, I'm going to warn you right now about when she turns seventeen."

"Hoo boy. Don't let Doris play you," he said over the hood of his van. "Laverne's not wrong. Doris once said the only way to clean up horse shows was a few good Baptist funerals. She's too blinded to see the line, and someday she's gonna cross it."

Nineteen

Late? How the hell could I be running late? On a Saturday morning. Even on Lexington's version of D.C.'s Beltway, New Circle Road. Worse? For an event I was determined to attend.

I hadn't needed my phone's GPS to tell me I had arrived at my destination. Parked in front of a massive brick church stood a Victorian horse-drawn hearse with a team of two black draft horses with smooth legs, probably Percherons. A long line of mourners streamed from the rear parking lot to the church door.

My instinct to dress up had been correct. Mourners arrived in their best or the best they could manage that day to send off Cy. He'd been a sharp-dressed man whether meeting a reporter by appointment, or at work, or running into said reporter during his down time. Women wore hats with their suits or dresses. Men wore suits or shirtsleeves with ties. Also, some teens wore black tees, the deep black of new shirts, with a picture over their chests—an image I couldn't identify from behind the wheel of a moving car.

I eased my way into the parking lot in a futile search for an open space, even a gap for my tiny car. No luck.

On my way out of the block, I glanced again at the line. Sunlight glinted off the edge of a tall black hat. While waiting to pull out onto the street, I got a better look at the woman with a black pillbox hat embellished with a dramatic black lily, its petals outlined in black sequins glinting in the sunlight.

I glimpsed high cheekbones reminding me of my mother's old smoky quartz ring. I noted the lady's position and decided her place through the line would work as a timer.

Finally, I exited the parking lot to circle the block. The voice on my GPS insisted I make a U-turn, so I punched it off. Last night, I'd done some internet recon for the trip, getting my bearings from an online map. The church's neighborhood was laid out in visitor-friendly grids, like New York City blocks, but not as long.

While cruising for a parking spot, I drove through a residential neighborhood with lush trees and a variety of architectural styles mixed together. Some of the buildings had seen better days, and I had to slow my driving speed to preserve my car's suspension on the street's uneven surface. On-street parking narrowed the roadway.

Every time I passed within sight of the church and the line, I checked on Lily Hat. She'd advanced about halfway toward the steps.

If the church filled to capacity, I might be shut out. If I had to, I'd wait on the street.

I almost drove past a spot in front of a duplex, a two-story wood house we northerners would call a two-family home or a double-decker. I eased the little car into the space, popped open my dash and pulled out my media parking credential. I set it on the dash in clear view of the window. Maybe useless, maybe worse if someone with issues with the media walked by.

I left the car, locked it, and then set off. I glanced back to set my memory of where I'd parked my car. In front of a sage-green sided double-decker across from a gray Craftsman bungalow.

At least I didn't have to worry about car bombs anymore. Or finding my car blown up as a precaution.

I had a bit of a schlep ahead. Good thing I'd worn dressy but low-wedge shoes, not heels.

But I'd also made enough of an effort to fit in with the crowd. I'd subbed my usual civilian life photographer's "uniform" of slacks, silky tee, and hikers or sneaks for a black sleeveless sheath dress, my last find at a Manhattan sample sale before I left for the frontier. Black lacy hose blended away the scars on my legs.

After what would count as my cardio for the day, I made it to the corner of the street and noticed Lily Hat was nowhere to be seen. She'd made it inside the church.

From the tote bag over my shoulder, I pulled out my laminated press credential and looped the lanyard around my neck. I tugged my hair out from under the chain. Might've been a good idea to have done that when I was in the car using the mirror.

Finally, I rounded a corner and approached the church. In case I got stuck outside, I glanced around for a place to wait, preferably a public place with an uphill grade so I could see over the hearse. If I couldn't get inside, I'd catch the recessional.

Down the street, I spotted a slight rise on the sidewalk with a view of the front of the church. I could photograph from there if necessary.

A group of teens lingered on the front steps. The girls in dresses teetered on their high heels and dabbed at flushed shiny faces. Their arms swept in graceful movements. The boys slouched in line with some laughing and talking, just representing, as if it didn't bother them—the tough guys. None of them wore the black T-shirts I'd been unable to read earlier.

Still on the sidewalk, I slowed to take a wide shot, with kids backlit in silhouette and framed by the porch's columns and ceiling. The frame even included the church's spaghetti board sign behind glass stating Cy's full name, time of services, and then, on the line below it, the quote: "I am the resurrection and the life." Plus, the ornate rear door of a tall Victorian hearse.

The kids and their body movement, their shoulders, their tilted heads, gave an energy to the static image. The silhouettes granted the teens privacy, which Old Me might not have fretted about. Besides, the obit had invited the public. And I'd confirmed with the funeral home.

If I got no other picture, this told the story. Mourners and kids.

I imagined Gordon's voice saying, *Okay. You've got what you need. Get out of there.*

The tallest boy wearing a black tracksuit crumpled into sobs. A girl with glossy hair and a short dress hurried to him as fast her chunky platform sandals would allow.

My heart sank with the weight of witnessing deaths and maimings years away and halfway around the world.

I hadn't anticipated crying kids, let alone teens near enlistment age. I'd been so determined to cover the event and expand the story, I hadn't thought about my own deep visceral reactions and how they might manifest while I was on the job.

Had Gordon been right all along? Was I up for this?

But, story or not, I was there for the farewell to a kind man who'd made a difference in many lives, including my own while I browsed a bookstore and wondered what the hell I'd been thinking when I'd moved to rural Kentucky.

I loved seeing the horses, but my days didn't involve horses. My days involved people cloaking their anger and frustration in social graces. The people around me relished talking about other people, and there came Cy who was happy to talk about books. My intellect starved for conversation lapped it up. But he also kept his love of and work with horses a secret.

Closer, through the open door came the strains of an organ playing gospel hymns. From time to time, over the music on a public address system, came an older woman's voice saying Bible verses pertaining to the afterlife, mostly from the gospels.

As I approached the still open door, I walked past the scrum of teens and glanced for the T-shirts I'd seen earlier. No tees. No luck.

I walked through the open doors of the crowded sanctuary and entered the end of the center aisle. The soft murmur of conversation also filled the high ceiling space, featuring stained glass windows soaring toward the ceilings of the long sides of the chapel.

Along the sides, at four strategic positions among the standing room attendees, stood the stiff legs of TV camera tripods staffed mostly by white dudes in baggy khaki pants and faded tees. I also spotted another white news photog with a pro digital camera with a long lens hanging around his neck. I tried to place him, figuring he was with a publication, and wondering where Pete Livingston of the *Lexington Journal* might be in all this.

A young man with a high fade topped with short curls offered me a program, a single sheet of paper folded in half. To keep my mind focused on where I was, I met his gaze when I thanked him and then murmured my condolences.

I couldn't hear him, but his tight smile loosened into words that looked like "thank you."

From the front, some mourners, with heads bowed, walked down the center aisle and then slipped into their standing places at their seats in pews. I couldn't spot Lily Hat.

Past the massive crowd, some seated and others standing and swaying to the music, I noticed some gaps in the seating toward the center of the pews. The seats weren't worth climbing over mourners to reach.

A quick survey, even with so many people in attendance and my obstructed view, told me fewer than a quarter of the crowd was white. If Josie was there, she was somewhere I couldn't see her.

With seating in the pews now out of the question I turned to see my closest exit options. Flanking the door leading to the center aisle, two single lines of men stood, leaving space in front of the door.

Glad I hadn't worn heels. I firmed my resolve to stand. I stepped into a space toward the end of the line. The men shuffled sideways to admit me.

The fine wool of a nice suit brushed the skin on my arm. "Ma'am?" A voice next to me. A tanned white dude maybe a little older than me stood at the end of this particular line.

On alert, I twisted to face him to speak, but we locked gazes.

Electricity shot through me, from the tingles on my scalp to my toes, already annoyed about standing in thin flats.

The sparks faded into creeps. Flirting at a funeral. A new low even for War Zone Avery, who, for a while, seized the day by the shirt front or even the belt.

His eyes were different. Heterochromia, having eyes of two different colors. One brown and one green with flecks of brown. A trace of a suppressed smile twinkled around his face and eyes with sun lines radiating from his eyes.

He spoke. "Can we trade spots? I may need to leave early." His voice sounded familiar, but I couldn't place him.

As he spoke, his sizzling grin cooled fast. His brow furrowed and a flush rose from his white collar.

The moment was over. Good. He must've been as embarrassed as I was.

My blood needed to circulate all the way to my brain. To think clearly. To be able to report. To behave in a manner befitting a funeral. Not like someone reminding herself that, in a world of war and death, life still sparked.

If he had to leave, I'd have the spot by the door again. Provided no one else arrived and packed me in.

"Yeah. Sure," I said.

We shuffled around each other. I didn't look at him, except for his feet in black shoes under the midnight navy suit trousers.

He said, "Thanks, Avery."

That's why his voice had sounded so familiar. The handsome white dude in a midnight navy suit and tie was my landlady's son. Norwood Ward.

Without his usual ballcap. Or his cloak of perpetual exhaustion. Or maybe he just looked better rested in that he'd appeared to have time to shave?

How had I not noticed him before? Did it take him wearing a suit? Was I that shallow? Worse, tacky? Feeling attraction at the funeral of a murdered man?

Before I could berate myself even more, the music faded out. Over the PA, a man's resonant voice intoned. "We have come together for a dual purpose today." Wearing vestments, he stood behind the pulpit to the right of the casket. "Both to mourn the loss of a life sent home too soon," he said before a pause holding space for weeping, "and to celebrate a remarkable God-given life."

Twenty

After the services, a woman's rich contralto sang a triumphant "Take Me to the King" as the minister preceded Cy's casket on a wheeled bier as it turned toward a ground-level side door. Most of the mourners followed, led by Cy's delicate and chic mother flanked by two sturdy women each with an arm on her shoulders. Just the speaker list for the funeral revealed his family had been much larger than his mother and Mavis.

The rest of the attendees filed out behind them, slow and steady, with the front rows going first. I gazed at the people—young, old, people of color, and some whites—passing me. The size of the crowd told me he'd touched many lives and been part of many communities. What I knew or thought I knew was just a corner or a tip of an iceberg peeking over the top of a murky sea.

To get more perspective, I needed to speak with people. Today, with emotions high, was not that day.

With empty pews and the end of the line in front of us, Norwood gestured me to leave in front of him, even though I had to step around him. As the last of us walked out, the woman singing transitioned to humming the tune and then fading with the piano.

"Amen," she said, the microphone sending her spoken voice across the chapel and out the doors. "And thank you."

Mourners hurried to their cars as best they could in slick-soled dress shoes or high heels. Digital chirps happened over conversation as phones switched on and car doors unlocked. Men exchanged elaborate ritual handshakes closed with teary hugs.

Norwood and I stood, him checking his phone and me feeling numb, except for the odd sensation of us being stationary stones in a flowing stream.

Watching TV reporters corner various family members for standup interviews made me grateful to work for a dinky weekly newspaper. Even if I felt guilty about avoiding the scrum of newshounds. Part of me thought, I should be among of them. Intruding. Delaying.

Pardon me. May I have a moment of your time?

Um, no.

I grabbed some more photos with my phone. A young man had lifted a boy toddler to pet the hitched Percheron on the street side of the hearse. The giant black draft horse with its gleaming harness lowered its head, bobbing the feathers on top of the bridle of its funerary harness.

To me, that said so much about what I'd observed in my short time in Kentucky, families gathered and found peace with horses. Basketball was for excitement and distraction. As Gordon insisted, Basketball Kentuckians outnumbered Horse Kentuckians. Yet, horses still called to them.

Next to me, Norwood scrolled on his phone.

I said, "Where's Hazel?" I made sure my sleeveless arm didn't make contact with his jacket.

"What?" He gave me the *did you say something* look. "Sorry," he said. "She's volunteering for a kids' thing in Harrodsburg."

His voice had sounded hoarse and itchy with tension. He cleared his throat and I gazed at him, not so much in a "wow, does he clean up well" way but as an interested listener encouraging him to elaborate.

He didn't disappoint

He shook his head and stared out in the distance. "She'd promised the kids at school a long time ago. Big class trip. She knew there'd be a lot of people here. His mom is at least vertical. Mom will contact Louise after the crowds and family—"

"Just stop." I'd raised my hand to stop him. Or, rather, put him out of his garbled misery.

He still looked like he had heartburn.

"So," I said, "here you are, while your mom is off with the local kids. Fine. Why did you let them go on so much Sunday morning at breakfast? Do you agree with them? As in, let's slap up a veneer of good manners over the ratty old particleboard of bigotry?"

A pink tint climbed his neck above his white collar and tie. He swiveled his head from side to side as if to see if anyone had heard me. "My mom's not like that," he said with a thousand-yard stare crossing the parking lot.

My gaze went out to where his appeared to be. A blonde, white woman dressed in a sleek black suit and a dainty pillbox hat opened the driver's door of a white SUV.

I couldn't leave well enough alone. Just like the other sharks here, I was drawn to blood in the water, especially emotional blood.

I swerved my gaze from her to him. "Looked like she's here alone, too." His gaze remained locked on her. "She may be out of your league," came out of my mouth, along with a "Too bad," said to the tune of womp, womp.

The pink tinge on his neck deepened to crimson. A jaw muscle in his cheek twitched. "I've known Cy since we were kids," in a voice implying *are you out of your mind?*

"So, I heard." If he stayed put, so would I. This time, it wasn't my lady hormones drawn to him but a vibe of secrets I could sense.

He turned to me and said, "I believe it's important to witness."

The air went thin and my breath hitched. My skin crackled with electricity. I managed to croak out, "That's why I've been," my turn to scramble sentences, "to all the places I've been." And, even, if I'm being honest, here.

"Really?" He stepped closer with his jacket open and both hands on his hips, but more of a confrontational vibe. "Or be the first with the news? The big heroine?"

"No." Now my turn to be taken aback. "I'm a true believer. People's lives—everyday people's lives—matter. I just report the story."

That electricity sparked again, deep inside. From all my travels, I'd racked up hundreds of thousands of loyalty points for several hotel chains. Some had hotels in Lexington. With blackout curtains and room service.

A woman sobbed loud, and then said, "No. Not her. Not here."

I heard an older man say, "No. No good can come of this. Get in the car and let it go."

Feeling guilty about looking but unable to look away, I glanced toward the voices.

From across the parking lot, a woman with long box braids hurried my way as fast as her pencil skirt and stiletto heels allowed. Her stare and her determined stride locked in on me like a missile.

Inside my mind, the Master Sergeant berated me for dropping my situational awareness.

Norwood stepped forward, as if to intervene in gentleman mode.

Without looking at him, I raised my hand to ward him off. "Who is she?"

He said, "Cy's ex."

She halted about six feet from me and then folded her arms across her chest. Her bloodshot eyes blazed at me over tear-glistened cheeks. "Why would you come here?" She sounded aghast. She shook her head while staring at me. "Is it New York *nerve*? Bald-faced shamelessness?" Her volume and anger rose with each sentence. "With a face you believe entitles you to go anywhere? I don't understand."

My pulse drummed behind my eyes, which dropped like a spotty diffuser filter over my view of the cars, the people dressed to the nines, and their murmured conversations with furtive glances at me.

From the parking lot, voices. "She's upset." Murmuring voices. "Can you blame her?"

Almost as a reflex, I stepped one foot backward for balance and flexed my knees. I've been where a crowd wanted to turn on me.

Of course, when I needed to think of tactics, the Master Sergeant's voice had gone silent.

I moved my hands out wide and open in a gesture of surrender. "I'm so sorry for your loss."

"Loss?" She shook hard enough from rage her braids trembled. "Too little, too late from you." Her rage roiled with a tinge of betrayal and humiliation beyond shame.

A gasp from someone in the crowd of mourners sent my attention wider. Some had slowed their progress to their cars, as if they didn't want to miss out. Some even had phones out with the cameras pointed our way.

They all were way ahead of me. I didn't know but held a strong suspicion.

Only one kind of betrayal caused that flavor of passion, one I knew from the inside.

I said with all the compassion I could muster and hoped she didn't take any of it as pity, "I think you've mistaken me for someone else." Which felt as lame to say as it sounded.

"No. I *know* it's you." She tapped the nexus of her clavicle as if her heart was sure.

I remembered being sure, when it happened to me, that everyone I met knew and, worse, pitied me in a world where the strong preyed on the weak. Even the so-called good guys. The whole situation made me feel crazy. Add grief on top of that?

Just loud enough for her to hear, and no one else. "Hey, it happened to me. Years ago. My husband cheated. Big time. I understand. But what happened to you wasn't me."

From under her braided bangs, she studied me with pursed lips. Then, she said, "You wouldn't be the first white lady to lie to my face."

I lifted my media credential, still hanging around my neck, for her to inspect like evidence, "A few weeks after I interviewed him, I ran into him at a bookstore. We grabbed a fast, casual lunch in the store. Broad daylight. Nothing physical. Not even sharing French fries."

Her steady gaze suggested she was listening. My words may have been sinking in.

I used her silence to continue. "He saved some shrimp for Salome. Then, we went our separate ways."

Her hard stare softened at my mention of her ex's mother's Persian cat.

An older woman's voice rich with command but warm with love said, "Celia."

The crowd of onlookers parted for a short and sturdy older woman in a sleek and short black wig, no hat, and a tailored ebony suit skimming her ample curves. A wide collar embellished with matching black fabric roses framed her face.

The older woman said, "That's not her, child." She took both of the younger woman's hands. The elder lady cocked her head toward me and said, "This is the woman reporter from that county paper. You're thinking of someone else. That one's not here."

Was this the Mavis Clement, lottery winner and angel investor to family members, let alone show horse owner?

Over Celia's shoulder, the woman who may be Mavis Clement, shot a pointed look at someone and gestured a "come here" flip with her chin. The older man who'd tried to discourage Celia from confronting me stepped forward and encircled her shoulders with his arm.

With Celia being tended, Mavis pivoted to shoot a hard stare at the line of upraised phones. "I better not catch how y'all posted live with any of that."

The phones lowered and those holding them turned as if they were scrolling.

She returned her attention, but it landed just past me. "Hello, Woody," she said in a melodic voice. "Thank you for coming. It's so nice to see you again, except for the circumstances."

Woody? People called him Woody?

"Likewise, ma'am." Norwood's dignified nod, more like a shallow bow, projected formality beyond his nickname. "I'm very sorry for your loss."

She glanced my way. "Ms. Sloane, I'd like a moment alone with Dr. Ward. Please."

The steel in her voice forged her words into an order, not a request.

"Of course," I said, "Ms. Clement?" As if there could be more than one Mavis.

She tilted her head at me as if she were waiting for me to move away.

"Yes. I'm Mavis Clement. My apologies, miss, but I'm talking to him, not you. If you would be so kind?" She tilted her head away from the upcoming conversation and toward where she suggested I go.

"Of course." I stepped aside, ostensibly to check my phone, near a strip of grass by the sidewalk but close enough to watch.

With her back straight and her head held high, the older woman locked her sight line onto Norwood's and advanced toward him. Her firm posture softened with a tilt of her head and a wistful smile. She raised her right hand, glinting with rings, and offered her palm to him.

Norwood accepted her hand. Silent, his attention riveted on her and her words, his broad shoulders slumped. Pain rippled through his face, radiating from his glistening eyes to his compressed lips. His grief made my own heart squeeze.

Who had he been to Cy? Was he part of the story behind the story? Considering how distraught Norwood—er, Woody—was, could he and Cy have been lovers?

Yet, I'd seen alpha males in full battle rattle sob at memorial services. Dudes who'd sought my attention until they found out I was media or worse, assigned to cover their units.

All the sparks I'd felt earlier must have short-circuited my gaydar.

And I could be as mistaken about that as Celia had been about me.

Mavis and Norwood broke up their private conversation. He'd turned away to check his phone while she headed toward me.

She extended her hand, not for a handshake but to encompass the length of my outfit. "Thank you for making an effort. Most members of the media did not."

Like the guys in faded tees and khaki pants for whatever a day on the job threw their way.

"Please let me know if there's anything I can do to help." Which sounded empty and hollow, and as an observer, I probably shouldn't have even said. Then I added, "I'll look you up in a few days."

She pivoted on her sensible pumps to express an afterthought.

"Too bad your boss won't let you run anything you submit today." She stepped forward. "Still, watch your back in Blanchard County," she said loud enough just for me to hear. "You're new here. Just because you're white doesn't mean you're safe."

A chill resonated through me.

She left and headed toward a sedan. The muffled chuff of late model car doors shutting *thwupped* over the uneasy silence in her wake.

To Norwood, who rubbed the back of his neck, with a "close call" grimace on his face, I said, "How did Cy and Celia break up? He cheated on her. Right?"

The teacher of the year. A man killed in his prime by unknown hands. A man whose life we'd just celebrated.

Norwood said to me, "Now who's being inappropriate and speaking disrespectfully of the dead?"

Ouch. Maybe I'd deserved him echoing my parting shot to his mom and aunt at breakfast.

But I'd also found out another motive for murder in the angst of Cy's ex. More likely than people killing each other over horse show blue ribbons and stud fees.

Twenty-One

Despite what Dwayne Kinsale had said about the funeral lasting all day, it did not. Just into the early afternoon. I took Gordon's advice by staying in Lexington. More or less.

For a late lunch, I headed to a busy coffee shop with Wi-Fi. I ordered a turkey sandwich on wheat and an unsweetened iced tea. I shifted the plate to my left hand, in hopes it'd catch the crumbs while I ate, set up my laptop, connected my phone, and got to work.

Driving and changing my location helped me process the day and the service enough to write about it with the detachment necessary for news writing. My old compartmentalization skills distilled the day into images and words.

Before hitting Send, I texted Gordon to let him know a story was coming for the website. I chowed down while my story, photos, and video uploaded. Not only did I feel the glow of a job well done, but I'd been out of Blanchard County for that damn siren.

My phone buzzed. A text from Gordon. *Call me ASAP. Sooner.*

As soon as he answered, assuming he'd seen the pictures, I said with my old bravado, "Does momma still bring the magic?"

A pang of guilt hit me and made me wish I could pull the words from the air. Boasting about my coverage of a funeral.

My new standards of compassion were getting in the way of my job, even though I liked to think they helped.

"Get back ASAP." His voice sounded tense. "I need you for a story."

My stomach twisted. What the hell had happened? Another murder? A big fire? Some political disaster?

After all his big talk about me taking it easy and relaxing in Lexington?

While powering down my laptop, I said, "What's wrong?"

His voice snapped. "Just get back here. You need to be at the library for a program." He hung up.

Shocked, I blurted out in astonishment, "The library!"

Blanchard County only had one library, no branches. I knew where to go, but what could be going down at the library that'd be so important I had to rush?

My foot pressed the accelerator harder. If I didn't hit traffic, I'd show up a few moments late. Maybe.

No time for road construction or accidents.

No time to go home to change out of my funeral clothes.

No time to speed so fast I'd get pulled over, especially with my attractive out-of-state plates.

I kept my eye out for state troopers with speed traps and sped to Bowmansville, all the while struggling to focus on the road rather than memories of fire, smoke, and blood.

To keep my mind busy, I tapped the phone mounted to the dash and called Gordon. I needed to know what I was getting into, considering it was a rush assignment.

The call went straight to his voice mail. I lost count on how many times I tried, but I added a few more just for spite.

Then, again, what kind of disaster would keep him from texting? A disaster at the library?

As I hit the Bowmansville town limits, I started scanning the horizon for rising smoke I wished not to see. Some wishes come true. I pulled down the street where the library sat, parked my car, and hurried up the walk.

The automatic glass doors whooshed open. I ran into the high-ceilinged library lobby, my shoes ticking on the tile.

Several young mothers with tots in tow walked as slowly as tiny legs would allow and headed for the elevator to the children's department.

No one rushed, except me.

Panting and bracing my hand holding the phone against the stitch in my side, I leaned against a tall bookshelf of New Releases.

A silver-haired lady with an ashen complexion gathered a stack of books and turned to head for the door. Her departure revealed the brunette librarian working the circulation desk. She squinted at me through her black plastic cat's eyeglasses.

"I almost didn't recognize you," she said. "You look different dressed up. Super nice. Wait. That didn't come out right." She furrowed her brow and then tilted her head. "Hey, are you alright?"

"What's happening?" I managed to wheeze out over my burning toes after rushing in my shoes. "Is everything okay here? Gordon sent me. He's too busy to tell my why. Do you know?"

"Let me check the schedule." She side-stepped over to a computer terminal. "The only thing going on now is story time," she leaned in to share, "and we love the coverage, but you really don't need to cover it again this soon." After which, she returned to her normal voice, "Oh. Wait. The Youth Arts Crew meeting is downstairs in basement community room B. It started at 3:30."

Rats. Sylvana Dobbs's youth arts group.

Gordon had scrambled me out of murder coverage for a feature story. A fluff story.

The librarian leaned in again, tucked brown hair behind her olive toned ear, and said, "Are you sure I can't get you a drink of water?"

Waiting inside the library's meeting room were three bored teenagers around one side of a rectangular table. A freckled boy with stubby brown hair and silver wire-rimmed glasses hunched over an open laptop.

A pudgy girl with light brown hair in an unfortunate perm and glasses scrolled on her pink phone. When she shifted, I spotted her Taylor Swift concert tee.

A goth brunette with purple highlights and smoky eye makeup smirked at something on the screen of her smartphone, its case embellished with a Templar cross.

But no fearless leader. No Sylvana Dobbs

I folded my arms, leaned against the wall adjacent to the only door, and joined the kids in silent surliness. She got what she wanted. Coverage for her group. Or, rather, me covering her group.

Time to take a closer look at the group itself, none of whom had noticed me. The goth brunette reported on the progress of growing out her hair for the county fair and what a *pain* it was to the other girl who kept pushing her glasses higher on her small nose. The boy, staring with dreamy eyes, never shifted them from the goth girl.

This was it? Sylvana Dobbs's "exciting" new Youth Arts Crew, the group I'd been scrambled out of Lexington for, from the time off Gordon liked to yammer at me about, to visit? Three teenagers?

They still hadn't noticed me. When I'd worked only as a photojournalist, disappearing into the background worked to my advantage. But I had a new job. Time to calm myself and get to work. From a funeral for a murdered man to a library kid program.

"Hey." Even after my attempt at deep breathing, my voice cracked sharp like a snapped whip. "When does this start?"

The three heads stirred and stared at me. The girl with glasses flushed pink and doubled down on her doodling. Fair enough. It was an arts group.

The boy said, "Mrs. Dobbs will be here soon." His gaze slid over to the brunette, as if to check her reaction or see if she had something to add.

The scratchy click of hard-soled shoes on tiles preceded the entrance of a tornado of gold ombre curls and a black summer jumpsuit with gilt accents.

Sylvana Dobbs exhaled more than spoke, "I got stuck behind a tractor." She dropped a tote a third the size of the folding table on the floor.

Louder and fast, before I could respond, she said, "Guys, we have the *Blanchard County Tribune* with us. I hope you made Ms. Sloane feel comfortable and welcome."

"As only teenagers can." I waved my phone camera. "Let's make this quick. I have other assignments."

Someone had better present me with a decent photo soon so I could leave.

Sylvana swept a bangle-braceleted forearm to encompass the windowless meeting room. "Where is everyone else? We have media here. Finally. On our last day before we break for the summer."

So that prompted the mad rush to get me here. But Gordon's misleading me? After he'd been so insistent on my relaxing? I'd deal with him later.

I circled the room in search of camera angles and lighting that didn't include the recessed ceiling lights. I'd also get some quotes from each kid. Our readers would love it.

The shy girl with glasses spoke in a soft voice I strained to hear, "A lot of us aren't allowed out of the house until the murderer is caught."

The boy said, “The killer’s not gonna bother us. Unless,” he crouched low, as if sharing a secret, “he’s a serial killer.” He glanced toward each of us, as if to check for our laughter, except even I didn’t laugh.

His gaze landed and lingered on his crush, the goth girl, but she twitched her nose in distaste.

She said, “To kill us all, he’d be a mass murderer. Besides,” she added, while contemplating her glossy black fingernails, “who says the killer has to be a man?”

Sylvana, with awkward scrunched brows, praised the goth girl for thinking out of the box. “That’s another purpose for art,” Sylvana said, “to open each other’s minds to unexpected possibilities.”

I took photos of everyone yakking with great animation. If nothing else, the photos showed the kids got along great and shared a connection with their group leader.

Sylvana called for order by asking how projects were going. The kids dug into tote bags and cardboard boxes beside them on the floor. I circled closer with the camera. Finally. Something visual.

The boy extracted a sculpture of a horse. The high stepper he’d shaped from clay looked like the logo of the Bluegrass Ambling Horse. The girl with glasses flipped through her sketch book.

The goth girl accessed an app on her smartphone. Then, she set her phone on the table and said, “That guy getting killed sucks.”

The boy said, “When we were little, he’d come home summers and help around Mr. Kinsale’s barn. He didn’t teach, because he wasn’t the trainer, but he taught me a lot. Little things to watch for with the horses, like horse psychology. Stuff my dad doesn’t notice.”

“Or doesn’t care about,” the goth girl added, “as long as they do what he wants and he wins.”

His face flushed pink again. He mumbled, "My dad loves the horses he trains like he loves our own horses."

The girl with the glasses chimed in. "One time, when I was little, Mr. Dwayne yelled at me for the entire lesson. 'Show him who's boss. Hit him like you mean it.' I started crying. He just yelled more. Louder. How horses don't respect us til we show 'em who's boss." Her voice thickened with emotion. "I loved Tater. I couldn't hit him."

Jerk. Dwayne Kinsale was a pre-natural horsemanship dinosaur.

But I kept my yap shut. I'm a reporter, an observer. And, when taking photos, I'm a ghost.

Sylvana said to the girl about to tear up again, "Please continue."

The girl said, "When I led Tater out of the ring after my lesson, I was bawling. Cyrus checked to see if Mr. Dwayne was around and then he explained how to show Tater who's boss without hitting him. 'It's all in your mind. Make up your mind where you want to go. Make sure you look at that point. Then, pretend your legs are squeezing the movement out of him, like toothpaste from a tube.'"

I heard a sniffle and realized it came from me.

The girl wearing glasses wiped her eyes with the back of her hand, sat taller, and said, "Cyrus was nice and should've taught riding. Mr. Dwayne is mean."

Somehow, her jittering gaze spotted me. Her voice changed gears to reedy and high-pitched. "Oh, no. I shouldn't have said that."

The girl's face flushed red and her eyes, behind her glasses, spilled tears. "I—I didn't mean to say that. Mr. Dwayne was strict. He was a good teacher." Tears streamed down her face. "Oh, Miss Sylvana," the girl sniffed hard and wet, "I didn't mean to say that. She won't put that in the paper, will she?" She shifted her attention to me and begged, "Please don't. Don't let Mr. Kinsale know I think his brother is mean."

Her eyes beseeched me. No longer was I a ghost at work.

After Dwayne Kinsale had confronted me at the fairgrounds on the night of the murder, I didn't doubt her assessment. I knew better than to make promises I couldn't keep. I wouldn't rat her out in print, but I'd keep an eye out for confirmation to get the info from an adult. Some day.

Sylvana dipped into her giant tote bag and pulled out a packet of tissues. "It's alright, honey." She passed the entire packet to the weeping girl. "Use as many as you need."

Sylvana glanced at me with a pointed shrug that could only be interpreted as "cut her some slack."

I had enough action photos, so I tucked the phone in my folded arms. "I won't write that, but here's a grown-up lesson. When a reporter is around, whatever you say or do could be like posting it online. It can be forever. Everyone you know – and people all around – could know what you said or did."

The girl with the permed brown hair wiped her face with tissues and stared up at me with begging puppy dog eyes.

I added, "Besides, Mean is Strict's evil twin."

Over to the side of the room, golden highlighted curls bobbed. Sylvana had tucked her head and stifled a laugh.

The goth girl chimed in, "Dwayne Kinsale is just plain mean. But Mr. Cyrus was alright." As if a lightbulb had clicked on, she added, "O.M.G." She popped up from her seat and held out her hands. "Let's think of a community project to honor him."

Sylvana leaned against the front table and said, "Go on, but remember the school year is almost done. Whatever we come up would need to be tabled for fall." She added, with a wistful brow ripple, "I don't have to tell you to not forget about your art over the summer. Okay?"

The goth girl said, "We could keep up with group texts. Send each other pictures. Updates on our work."

Sylvana paced as if her moving feet propelled her thoughts. "It'd have to be a group project. It might need funding. Outside funding."

The energy left the room and maybe took the air with it.

"Yeah. Funding." Sylvana's words dropped like a heavy wet blanket. "Or lack of funding. That remorseless killer of many a great idea." She folded her arms and jerked her head toward me. "We still have media here. The *Tribune* could spread the word."

Three stricken, glum teenage faces met mine. I liked these kids. They wanted to do the right thing, even though geography and culture tag-teamed their destinies.

"Okay," I said. "Off the record, it is. But there's an exchange. The *Trib* gets the exclusive for behind-the-scenes. You can promote the event to other media. But we get the skinny."

Considering the polite veiled and openly snarky racism I'd seen, I wasn't sure the parents wouldn't squash this project like a fly buzzing a pecan pie.

To manage the kids' expectations but not squash their generosity and optimism, I added "Keep in mind there's nothing to stop your parents from pulling the plug at any point along the way."

"She's right." Sylvana chimed in. "You're already getting lessons in how to conduct yourself with the press. This could involve a lot of work, but a group event would be great experience and look good on a college or scholarship application. Fundraising is a crucial aspect of public art and a valuable business skill."

While the kids mulled over the amount of work, their leader shifted her gaze up to her right while she tapped her chin. "Not insignificant money, either. You'll need to buy a lot of candles. You'll have to get permissions, too. Local ordinances might even shut you down. Candles and fire on county property, or what not. If you want to do large scale art, you have to get permits. Look up Christo," she spelled it out, "to get an idea. You're not wrapping an island in pink, just a fairgrounds in light."

I chimed in before I could stop myself, "You could try crowdfunding."

Twenty-Two

Toward the evening, I pulled out my phone, scrolled to a number, had second thoughts, and then cleared the app. Then, I reopened the app, re-clicked through the entire sequence twice more. My second thoughts looked more like waffling. Finally, I steeled my resolve and punched "call" on Doris's number. After three rings, she answered.

I squeezed my eyes shut before identifying myself, even though she had caller ID, too. "Got a minute?"

I braced myself to listen to what she'd say next.

"You were at the fairgrounds for the murder but not the horse show." Her statement landed flat, like a smack. "Why didn't you follow up on my tip?"

Inside my mind, potential lies lined up. I had other plans. I had cramps. I didn't feel like being in a crowd, which was the truest of all.

In that moment, though, I realized I didn't trust her. Had I let the opinions of others around me sway mine? Or had my time in the Middle East given me an aversion to zealots? Especially one-note wonders like Doris, talking hard and tough about matters that weren't life and death. Or were they? Had a man been killed over a horse show?

I said, "You told me you weren't going to the horse show, either," with a whine I didn't bother to control.

"That would be supporting the horse show." She hissed a noise of contempt, an added layer to her opinion of my cluelessness. "Then there's the matter of trolls online telling me I'd better not show up at a horse show. Threatening me. I wouldn't put it past these ambling horse trash to kill a man who got in their way. Hypothetically speaking," she added in a rush, "of course. Then again, maybe they did."

I'd remembered a streetwise detective on a TV cop show once saying there were three reasons to murder someone. Revenge, money, or sex. I'd glimpsed possible examples of two of those options.

As a dare, I said, "Loose talk for a lawyer." It was a bit past past five o'clock, so liquid courage may have been at play. "Maybe I called at a bad time."

"I am . . ." she paused as if searching for words, "dispirited." Her voice deepened gears. "You just don't understand." Her voice quivered with rage.

Frustration, I understood. Then, the curious reporter mentality shoved aside my better angel, let alone the fear. "Then tell me."

"Not over the phone."

Crap. Had to go out again. But what was I going to do? Sit in the trailer and surf the web?

"So, tell me over beer why you think some of the horse crowd is capable of murder." I spoke as fast I could before one of us freaked out and hit End Call. "Meet me in that bar over the county line, the First and Last."

Silence met my suggestion. Considering the local zest for gossip, I switched gears.

"If beer's not your style," I said, instead of *maybe you don't want to be spotted at a dive bar*, "there's a truck stop a couple of exits away. Tell me over coffee." I sweetened the deal. "And pie. Or fries." Sweet or salty, whatever bait it took.

I heaved a deep breath and offered out into the silence. "And if you've already enjoyed an evening cocktail, I can come meet you." I didn't want to tempt her onto the roads if she had no business driving.

I waited, my breathing shallow. Had she hung up while I was talking?

"The truck stop," she said. "Half an hour."

At the truck stop, my corner booth by the window gave me a great view of the parking lot and door. I'd see Doris coming in and flag her down from my table.

The scent of diesel fuel beckoned me into my past. I clutched my mug of black coffee to my face so I could inhale its aroma to anchor me here.

From my booth, I saw tanker trucks at the blazingly lit gas pumps. They and the pumps themselves could make humongous bombs. I tried not to imagine exploding fireballs and flying shattered plate glass.

Good thing I'd ordered decaf.

Headlights from trucks sweeping around the curve at the truck stop entrance lit me several times. Maybe I'd picked a bad table? We'd be super visible. Spot lit in the goldfish bowl.

The clientele at the tables and the counter turned over at least once. Several truckers I suspected were veterans sat as I did, facing the door with ready eyes and braced elbows. The country rock on the sound system and the garish lights in the night gave the truck stop a Southern Edward Hopper diner vibe.

I eavesdropped as best I could. None of the diners, some truckers and some families on the road, griped about traffic or any unexpected meteorological events. All of which would make for a great excuse for Doris's lateness now looking a lot like absence.

I checked my phone. Gordon had posted my funeral package on the *Trib's* website. To see what other Lexington media did, I clicked over to their websites.

Despite all those cameras on tripods in the sanctuary covering the funeral of the recently honored Teacher of the Year, the sites carried nothing except for standard funeral footage. They showed the coffin being loaded into the hearse and edited in a quote from Mavis Clement, identified in the font as family spokesperson:

"He has gone home to his ancestors. We will miss his courage and kind heart." She shifted her piercing gaze from the reporter to the lens of the camera. "And we demand justice."

Amen. "You tell 'em, Mavis," I muttered to the video on the phone.

I searched the other social media outlets while dreading finding video of Celia confronting me. I've been called names in various languages. She didn't need that. But the absence of anything that looked familiar suggested people had heeded Mavis's warning.

And still no Doris.

I clicked over to texts and voice mails in case I'd overlooked a notification.

Nothing.

That I wasn't worried about her gave me a little rumble of guilt. I'd suspected she'd blow me off. My invitation to come and spill all had been more of a dare. Put up or shut up.

Still, she'd been after me soon after I'd arrived in town to tell me all about the cruel and horrible people showing horses, but she never showed up to make good on her offer. Especially after someone had been cruel and horrible enough to murder a man.

Maybe she wasn't being wimpy but prudent.

When my red-haired server passed again, instead of asking for more coffee, I asked for scrambled egg whites and rye toast.

She nodded and then said, "I was afraid you'd be ordering Tums or Maalox next."

A beefy trucker paying his check waved at me and then tipped the bill of his Peterbilt cap with a wink and an unmistakable leer he probably thought was hot.

Great. Maybe I'd just leave cash on the table and then bug out.

Except Doris could arrive after I'd gone only to leave me a "Where were you?" message or text.

Time to get to the bottom of the Doris situation. I dialed her number.

After four rings, a man answered and gave me the southern, multisyllabic extended version of the phone greeting.

"Hel-lo." He sounded mellow, like a man unconcerned about a wife who was out late at night or even enduring a home invasion with armed criminals.

I said, "Is Doris home?"

"She is," he dragged the words out into four syllables each.

I took a deep breath to ward off anti-social swearing. "May I speak to her?"

"Well." There was that drawl again. "She went upstairs half an hour ago and went to bed."

The air left the room. Not that long ago, she'd been ready to dish the dirt. I managed to draw in enough oxygen to say, "Are you sure?"

"Yes, ma'am. It's late for her. She gets up early. I'll tell her you— "

It was either cut him off or swear. The waitress left my plate of eggs that looked like a white rubber toupee and wan brown toast.

I pulled out a twenty to leave on the table for my meal and an ample enough tip to qualify as "booth rental." I'd catch my server's eye before heading for the door. Better yet, I'd hand it to her.

A youngish trucker with good teeth and thick sandy hair ambled into the restaurant past the rack of maps and headed straight to the counter. He swung a denim-sheathed leg over the stool and rested his elbows on the counter. His red western-cut plaid shirt made a nice V into his faded jeans. He glanced at the reflective wall behind the counter and caught my eye, giving me a long slow nod with a wistful smile.

Yeah, I had to get out of here. For a lotta reasons.

Then, a woman wearing all black, from her ball cap to her sneakers to the humongous leather tote slung over her shoulder, hurried in. She looked familiar, but her Manhattan black made her conspicuous among all the camo overalls, khakis, and jeans.

Wait. What? Manhattan black?

The cap funneled Sylvana Dobbs's hair into a bushy ponytail poking out like a tail. Of course, she spotted me and did a double take. She gave me a wave like she'd spotted an old pal.

Crap.

I gave her a wan "I see you too" wave. She'd be over like a ninja to pump up the Youth Arts Crew. Stuff like, when would the story run? Or which photos might we use? Or even to see the article before it ran.

Man, I hated when subjects asked for pre-pub approval. Who did they think we were? Puff Piece Palooza?

But I was no longer involved with hard news. Except for the rare murder.

She pivoted my way. Sometimes, I hate being right. Where the hell was my server so I could pay my booth rent and get out?

Sylvana stood before my booth. She eyed each side of the table, obviously set for two but only used by one. "Don't tell me you're waiting for a date. Here."

Double crap. "Not that kind. I'm leaving." Where was my check?

"I've seen several possibilities who'd be happy to be your Plan B Date." She slid across the table into the empty half of the booth, without invitation—a nervy move I might have taken. "One over there might be fun for a little catch and release." She flashed a sly smile before tilting her cap and curls toward the handsome young trucker sitting at the counter with his back to us.

How long had she been standing at the register? "What are you doing here?"

"Jonesing for strawberry pie. It's a specialty here. I don't make it at home, otherwise I'd eat it all." She frowned at my plate. "Scrambled egg whites? Are you a health nut? Or anorexic?"

Lousy timing for my server to go on break. "Brave of you to venture out this late with a murderer at large."

"Please." She propped her right elbow on the table and flicked her wrist with a dismissive flourish. "Where we're from, that's any day that ends in y."

Annoyance slipped out as a resigned sigh. "All right." I flipped both hands in surrender. "I don't know when the story will run."

"Ah. Forget that." She waved her hand as if to erase the words from the air. "My husband's out of town, and my kids are away, so I've been working a lot and didn't plan well. Obviously. Or I wouldn't be here. What do you say to some *pinot grig*?"

She'd pronounced *pinot grigio* like a New York tri-state Italian, dropping the final two syllables. "Or *pinot noir*, if that's more your style. I picked up some good bread and olive oil in Lexington. Fresh bruschett," also with the dropped a like any New Yorker who knew the way to Arthur Avenue, "with nice tomatoes. You don't want to eat that egg frisbee! Whaddya say?"

My gaydar wasn't just off but broken. "Sorry. Not gay."

"Me, neither." She waggled her left hand with its sparkling gold band. "Look, I don't know about you, but I'm sick of gossip and conformity and trying to figure out who the hell someone is by who they're related to. You can't tell me you're not bored here, too."

I knew better, but I put the twenty on the table. "I like *pinot noir*."

Twenty-Three

I couldn't catch my breath. Tears spouted from my eyes. I clutched my chest and doubled over. "Oh, no, he didn't!" I wheezed through the laughter. Best of all, I didn't spill my wine.

Earlier, I'd followed the taillights of Sylvana's SUV away from the freeway and the glare of the truck stop lights out into a twisty labyrinth of secluded roads leading to her lake house. The way fencing didn't change along the road until I entered the neighborhood near the roads named for waterbirds made me think the Ward Farm ran almost to the lake, making the property appear as big as Kinsale's.

We sat out on the rear deck of Sylvana's home overlooking the lake. Moonlight shimmered through the trees onto the water. Bullfrogs and other night creatures boomed and skittered, filling the rare lapses in conversation, with their echoes bouncing off the water.

"Ohh, but, yes, he did," she said while suppressing her own laughter. "How could I not fall for such a sweet mope? Come on. So, what about you?"

I'd seen a picture of her "sweet mope" on the wall serving as family photo gallery. He didn't look like a man an Italian glamazon like Sylvana would fall for. Balding, pudgy, and glasses.

Maybe he'd been hot before the weight gain and hair loss because their older boy was kind of a heartbreaker. I'd recognized him as the kid who'd been mowing Hazel's lawn the morning after the murder and asked me about my Yankees shirt.

Sure enough, there'd also been a photo of the Dobbs family posed at Yankees spring training camp, all pinstripes and palm trees. The boy Sylvana called Rick, the kid who'd been working in Hazel's yard, posed with a bat, a confident grin, and sparkling eyes. A smaller girl who distinctly took after her father smiled for the camera, but I bet she was eager to get to Ocala horse country instead. To the Yankees camp, she'd worn a T-shirt emblazoned with the logo of the high-stepping Bluegrass Ambling Horse.

"Do you have enough bruschetta there? One thing this part of the country has in its favor is fresh garden tomatoes for weeks before we get them back home. Now, dish. I won't let you off the hook. What's a nice girl like you doing all the way out in the sticks eyeing truckers?"

I steered the conversation to her. "Does your husband travel a lot?"

"He manages Wharton's department store, the anchor in the big mall in Lexington. He keeps a dinky place there for easy commutes. We live out here where we can have a bigger house to pursue our interests and keep Lexi in a relatively economical horse world."

Rick's insistence he'd been staring at my Yankees tee, not my chest, while he'd been tending Hazel's lawn, reminded me. "What about Rick? A thousand miles from Yankee Stadium. Aside from you, what's here for him?"

Even through the dim light, I could see her sad grimace. "Thanks to his athletics and his looks, he's a big man on campus. Still, he dreadfully misses life in the north. I send him up to his grandparents for school vacations. Each time, he comes back with old school tri-state attitudes that doesn't serve him well here in the land of 'please and thank you.'"

I sensed more than saw her gloomy mood.

"After he graduates," I said, "maybe he can go to school there."

She'd shifted her face from regret to a social smile. "Nice try with the conversational diversion. I believe I asked about you."

The index finger of her hand cradling the bowl of her wineglass pointed across the patio table at me.

"Maybe I don't want to kill my buzz." I steered us into another topic. "What's up with you having an RV parked out by the boat shed? You strike me more as someone with a hip silver bullet for glamping."

"If you could see the restroom facilities at some of these horse shows, you'd bring your own, too."

Determined to keep the conversational table from returning to me, I said, "But a boxy Mom & Pop rig?"

"The boxy rigs are cheaper, especially secondhand. Leaving more resources to change décor on a whim."

"You must be paying that contractor double secret overtime so he'll work this late." When I'd pulled in behind her, I'd seen the big dark pickup parked in the shadows next to the RV with lights inside glowing.

She shrugged but kept her fingers on the wineglass. "He comes and goes when he can. I can give you his contact info, if you need work done."

"I rent. Not sure how much I can change. Let alone how long I'll stay." I tipped my glass again. "At least there aren't bloodstains on the wall."

Damn it. That slipped out. Back to me. Time to spill. I swigged another gulp of pinot noir, half for courage and half as a toast to who I used to be.

"After I was injured, my ex freaked out," I said. "Tubes, bandages, and beeping machines. Crashed his Hemingway dreams of 'War Correspondents in Love.'"

Good thing bullfrogs filled the silence. I knew better. Just because a weak moment let me feel like talking about it didn't mean listeners were ready to hear what I had to tell them.

Sylvana raised a napkin to press under her nose and sniffled.

Yeesh. The last thing I needed was pity. I added in a hurry, "I'll have you know," I waved my wineglass, "that story just kills in certain bars in Kuwait."

She didn't respond. Had I just cracked the most tasteless joke of the week? City people appreciated dark humor more than country people, even those who spent time in big cities like Gordon and Shannon. Besides, like I'd stayed in the Middle East long enough to party in Kuwait.

"Well, the past is past," she said. "When we're lucky and smart, it's not even prologue, just a teaching moment from which to move on. What about now? Anything interesting to you?"

I was taking another sip of wine when my brain noted "anything" not "anyone."

"All right." Surfing along on a wave of rich tangy liquid California sunshine from a glass, I said, "I covered Cyrus McCoy's funeral where I ran into Norwood Ward. You know, the veterinarian. My landlady's son. The dude lives in ball caps and perpetual fatigue. But in a suit and tie without the cap? Wow. Unrecognizable. My hormones wake up like the Fourth of July."

I shifted my gaze from the shimmering water to the woman sitting next to me at the patio table. "Is there a reason why people call him Woody? I mean, his name. Sure. But?" I let the question trail off.

"Beats me," she said. "Who the hell names their kid Norwood anyway? Must be a family name. Do go on."

Surfing the good vibes and the wine, I returned my gaze to the shimmering water past the deck.

"I felt a connection, too." Until he recognized me. My ego stung too much to share that tidbit. I gulped a little more *pinot noir*.

I added before she could jump in, "Back in the day, I racked up loyalty points to every business class hotel chain. I almost grabbed him by the belt and suggested we go somewhere quiet with room service. I came this close," I raised my thumb and index finger as if to pinch a cherry tomato.

Instead, I picked up my wineglass and mock-toasted her. "Good thing I didn't." I left out the part where he'd mocked me. I'd already blabbed too much. "Somehow, Gordon went into panic mode to summon me to your program at the library like the joint was on fire or something. I mean, really. I was pissed then, but thanks."

"Had you followed through, you might not've been eyeing young truckers. I arrived tonight in the nick of time."

Hypnotized by the ripples breaking the sheen of the lake and the moonlight I kept talking, and she let me.

"I may have been looking, but I wasn't feeling. That's what's weird. I haven't felt . . . anything. A crush. An itch in the night. Nothing. Not until that funeral. Until I saw, of all people, Norwood Ward in a suit. Without a ball cap. And he smiled at me. What a smile. But that was before he realized he recognized me, too. I think we both felt the connection but then thought, 'whoa.'"

I swung my gaze to her. "You know what? I had dinner a couple of weeks ago with Cyrus McCoy. But it wasn't a date. I ran into him in Lexington. One of those, 'it's time to eat, if you haven't eaten, let's eat together' things."

I couldn't see her well in the shadows, but she murmured an encouragement to continue.

"Ya know, when I saw his picture on the cover of the funeral program, he was a handsome dude. So, why didn't I get sparks from my time with him?"

She shifted her view toward the water, took a sip of wine, and then said, "Maybe he wasn't your type?"

I asked, while watching her face, this woman a little older than I was and who'd also been raised in the north, "What if it means I'm really a bigot?"

She gulped hard, almost like a spit take. Then, she heaved a deep breath, steadied, and said, "If you have to ask, you probably aren't." She clinked the side of her wineglass against mine. "But if you are a bigot, then you've come to the right place. Wait. That didn't come out right. Not here." She waved her index finger to encompass us and our surroundings, "but around here."

How much wine had I drunk? I tilted the glass. A deep inky pool of red wine remained in the bowl.

My mouth went dry before I spoke. I held the glass in front of me. "This looks remarkably like the same amount I started with," I opined to the glass as if it were Yorick's skull. "Someone has been pouring when I haven't been looking."

Don't knock it back, Avery. Put it down. Walk away.

"I've adopted that famous Southern hospitality thing," she said breezily. "Fun. Don'tcha think?"

I eyed the bottle of wine. Once we'd set up the wine and the bruschetta, she hadn't left the deck. Not even to pee. We were still on the first bottle?

That I had to ask told me I was done.

"Oh. Look at the time," I set the wineglass on the table. "Thank you. Unlike you, I don't work out of a home studio or welder's shop. I have to work in town."

To get to my car, I had to go through the house. I popped to my feet, took a steady step, and then walked toward the sliding glass door.

Behind me, the growl of a metal chair shoved across wood.

I pulled open the sliding glass door. Cool dry air soothed my *pinot noir* flushed cheeks.

From behind me, she grabbed the door and said, “Hang on. I’m right behind you.”

I stepped into the combo kitchen and family room—a utilitarian great room. Good thing she’d left all the lights on.

My shin clunked into a hard edge. I doubled over to see it was that heavy glass coffee tabletop on a stand she’d made of repurposed fireplace tools.

While I leaned over and rubbed my leg, a plate clunked onto the thick glass beside me. More slices of bread with garlicky, tomato-ey topping.

“Eat more bruschett,” she said, still dropping that last syllable on those Italian words. “You need more blotter in your stomach and more garlic on your breath if one of the Barney Fifes catches you. Thank God you’re still glib.”

She had a point. I’d compensate for the lack of protein elsewhere. I reached for more bread and tomato mixture.

“Good thing I keep a pot of coffee going. Let me get you a mug. Sit down over there.”

I eyed the plush leather sofa and assessed its soporific capabilities. “If I sit and get comfortable, it’s game over.”

“I can’t figure this out.” She slid a small stack of paper plates next to the snack platter. “You have no family here. You aren’t in a relationship here. You haven’t mentioned horses once. And you covered war in the Middle East. Why the hell are you working at the Mayberry Gazette?”

I grabbed another plank of the Italian bread, along with a tiny paper appetizer plate to hold under the snack in case it dripped in transit. I wasn’t so buzzed I didn’t care about someone else’s flooring or upholstery.

“That’s a story for another time.” I semi saluted her with the food. “Thank you for a lovely evening,” I repeated for good measure, “but time to hit the road.”

I headed for the front door. My shin still rang. I had to get out the door before I blabbed more, even if I had to pull over to the side of the road and tuck my tiny car among some trees.

Sylvana called out behind me. “This was fun. Don’t be a stranger.”

Twenty-Four

At work the next morning, ready to confront Gordon about scrambling me back to Bowmansville for a feature story, Laverne's glance of greeting was more side-eye than welcoming. At their desks, Justin and Wilbur stared at their computer monitors as if hypnotized.

Gordon sat behind his desk. Kinsale hovered beside him. The owner-publisher's height made him tower over Gordon and emphasized their lots in life. The Big Man who ordered around the Little Man. More proprietary than uncle and nephew.

The impulse to take the offense, to take control by taking the initiative, occurred to me.

Gordon spoke first.

"Avery." His gaze blinked a slight wince, a tell. "Join us."

This time, I would be the confronted, not the confronter. For what, I wasn't certain. Could've been half a dozen things I hadn't considered. No telling what I'd done this time.

Down the central aisle between the desks, past my colleagues so absorbed in their work, I breezed my way to Gordon's cubicle zone. "What's up?"

Kinsale answered for his editor. "Circulation, my dear. The Quik Stop ran out of copies by noon. So did the filling station." He gestured for me to sit in my spot by the water cooler. "Even the truck stop store."

That he'd directed me where to sit after speaking first, reminded us all who was in charge here.

For a hot second, I almost said, *Murder always sells papers.*

Instead, I decided to lob a prop for Gordon, while using formal BS-speak.

"As a veteran of many newsrooms and news bureaus, may I say that Gordon has steered us through a week of big news stories with quiet authority, dignity, and taste."

The subject of my compliment didn't raise his gaze, although one side of his mouth twitched. Good. He was in there somewhere. But hiding. Not so good.

Trying to let the silence ride, I glanced over to the corner of Gordon's desk where he kept his family photo. All I could see was the back of the frame, but I knew it was a selfie he'd taken while sledding with Shannon and Teddi after a blizzard. Unlike other businessmen with family photos on the desk, he kept his where he could see his family's faces, like a North Star he could consult.

The photo he loved enough to live with at work was a photo of them having fun together.

Gordon had everything, including everything to lose, in this one-horse—metaphorically-speaking—town. The hometown girl. The house with the backyard, the garden, and the gas grill and deep fryer. All his dreams.

For me, there was nothing in Blanchard County I couldn't find somewhere else.

How had I not seen that all along.

Bad idea, to let my mind wander when I'm supposed to let a conversational partner fill the silence.

Kinsale spoke. "Our Gordon is much too modest. He had the gumption—or should I say foolishness—to send a reporter on an out-of-town assignment for which he updated the website as if it were real time-sensitive news."

There it was. A pat on the back with a thin blade between the ribs. For both Gordon and me.

I gazed at the deep bags under the publisher's blue patrician eyes, suggesting possible health issues lurking beneath his outdoorsy tan.

Local businessmen like Gordon who worked with Kinsale probably feared him, but not me. Facing down that entitled feudal lord would be a piece of cake.

Appealing to his ego and business acumen was the way in.

"We sold a lot of papers with a story people all over town are talking about. I'd say that's a good day's—week's—work. We should be wondering what we can to build on that momentum."

I risked a glance at Gordon, who stared at his doodle on his desk. Inking in the round letters in the *Lexington Journal's* masthead.

His eyes and mouth drooped in sadness, like a fortune teller unable to control emotions after glimpsing a future of bad news. Maybe he was watching his cute little house with the gas grill and the yard full of kids' toys shrink into a tiny dot at the center of that metaphorical crystal ball before winking out.

Kinsale solidified those fears by saying, "I told you both to not waste resources on this unseemly story."

I sucked in a deep breath. Time for a sharp change of tactics. I had to draw Kinsale's fire away from Gordon, so he could keep his little house.

"Begging your pardon, sir, but I don't think resources were wasted. I went on my own time with no expense to the paper. You know as well as we do, we don't get to be picky about what's news and what's not, especially with breaking news. Let alone a murder story in our backyard."

My hands waved and I fast-talked in true big-city fashion. "What if it had been a hate crime? The funeral video suggests people in Lexington aren't convinced it wasn't. Don't we have a moral mandate to report, even show posted comments on that story? Ya know, I still managed to fit in a feature story about—" *Careful, Avery, don't say 'white people' or you'll lose him.* "Locals."

Kinsale's voice was as sharp as his glare. "Which also references the tragedy." As if I'd proved his point.

I countered. "Because people in town and within the county, heck even in Mercer County, are talking about it."

Come on. Leave Gordon alone. Fire me. You know you want to.

Kinsale straightened his spine before saying, "You and Gordon made unfortunate executive decisions above your pay grades. While my better half and I were in Hilton Head this weekend, irate subscribers texted and messaged me that a sudden story posted to the website over the weekend signaled serious timely news—except it was a video of children singing."

He shook his head in distaste.

Cy's high school students? Teenagers? Some old enough to enlist?

"So, what you're telling me is," I said while I gathered my composure, "readers objected to teenagers in an *a capella* group singing harmonies for a hit pop song by a boy band from ten years ago?"

Kinsale continued. "Many readers objected to the T-shirts."

"The T-shirts? What about them?"

He all but spat out, "What they said." He pursed his lips and shook his head.

"*Why?* and *Why there?* are valid questions. We should be asking them, too."

"I ordered Gordon to take the story down."

The words spilled out of me. "Every local news organization recorded the entire service. Everything. But all they ran on TV, even online, was footage of the casket going into the hearse. Ours was the only record of that tribute from his students. It's an exclusive."

My cell buzzed for a text. Buzzed again.

I grabbed the phone and glanced at it. Hazel texting me, in two separate texts. *Police here*, said the first one. Then, *Now*, almost as an afterthought. Or a shaky hand unaccustomed to texting hitting Send prematurely.

My spine shot cold chills.

Did she mean "here" as in her house or here as in my trailer? And why hadn't she called her son Norwood, instead of me? I'm just her tenant.

I waved the phone in my hand. "Something's going down. I need to check it out."

Gordon's head snapped to attention. "Seriously?"

"Terse message. Might be something. No details yet." I shook my head while texting, On my way. "I need to go."

I circled around the barrier between Gordon's alcove and the rest of the newsroom.

Kinsale's voice also stiffened. "Ignore it."

"The message involves cops. Did you hear anything on the scanner? I didn't. The silence tells me it's big. Otherwise, we would've heard the ten-codes. I need to check it out."

I didn't want to throw Hazel to the gossip wolves sooner than a police matter became public record. Laverne and the rest of the newsroom may have been faux focusing so they could eavesdrop.

Kinsale again. "Then the prudent thing to do is to contact the police department. We can return to our conversation. You realize, by running out that door, you're proving our point. That you are perhaps unstable."

The big man was a coward. A coward who'd played on Gordon's concerns about my state of mind.

I imagined Kinsale with a military uniform decorated with fruit salad and launched off into my response. "Sir," I said in a crisp, military voice while I gathered my tote bag and gear, "if the cops have an operation in progress and we call them, they won't tell us jack. That was a reader who called. A reader who trusts *me*. I'm going."

Hitching my bag over my shoulder and halfway to the door, I heard Kinsale said, "This isn't over Miss Sloane," as if he expected me to stop.

"I hope not. I have more to say."

I shot a glance toward Gordon whose mouth quirked into a slight smile and an almost imperceptible nod. In return, I maintained eye contact a moment longer. His approval would be our secret.

Gordon was one of the last people I thought I'd have to protect.

Twenty-Five

I headed for Hazel's screen door. Unlocked during daytime, even with a murderer at large. I all but tiptoed and whispered, "Hazel?"

Her voice sounded tense. "The living room window."

Still in her PJs and robe, Hazel hunched near the window where she could peek past the drape of the sheers toward the riding arena and the barn. Some of her shrubbery and trees next to the house obstructed the view.

Outside the open barn door sat a fleet of police vehicles. Blanchard County Sheriff's cruisers lined the outer perimeter whereas Kentucky state police cars and a couple of cube vans parked closer to the barn door. Had I driven in from the other direction, I would have seen them.

My fingers itched to pull out my phone, camera app open, but I could blow my insider status by going into reporter mode. Hazel would freak. I needed some background before I went down to the scene. Instead, I folded my arms to tuck them out of trouble and asked, "How long have they been here?"

"Georgia Fortner, the woman deputy, knocked on my door about sun-up and told me they'd be searching the barn. She gave me some paperwork, then went on to join them. I'm surprised they didn't come to your trailer."

Because they knew where I was.

While she spoke, a man wearing a bulky orange diving suit emerged from the clutch of cube trucks. He waddled in his so-called dry suit toward the barn with black flippers in his left hand and then disappeared down the wide aisle.

No way.

I needed a better view. Closer would get me punted too soon. I muttered, "I need to use your upstairs bathroom." I pivoted from the window to run up the stairs.

"Avery?" Hazel's voice called after me. "Are you sick?"

Upstairs, I powered down the hall and barged into the bathroom with a window overlooking the field behind the barn.

By the pond where Herb had been exercising a horse a few days ago, a second diver adjusted his mask while another guy in a navy polo and khakis had strung a line of yellow tape, its color echoing the lemony shade of the wild irises on shore.

What the hell could they be looking for in the Ward Farm's pond?

In a move practiced on a larger camera, I yanked the phone camera from my pocket and clicked the power switch while raising the viewfinder to my eye. Granted, the shots would be nothing special, high-angle wide documentary shots, but still exclusives. Even if I didn't get permission from Hazel to print them, I'd have them for reference. I snapped a couple through the window before barreling down the hall to an open bedroom with another window, another angle.

The stairs creaked with Hazel's careful and deliberate steps. No telling how long I'd be alone. I clicked photos panning the camera across the scene toward the parking lot of police trucks.

The higher angle revealed the identifier decal on the dive team's truck, Louisville Metro Underwater Search and Recovery, and spun up my thoughts. State troopers, I expected to see, but not Louisville police. What could they have been looking for in the pond? It had to be serious to require the extra manpower and resources imported from hours away.

Another body? Here?

To the left of my view, in the riding ring, Herb led a black mare, her coat gleaming with sweat. When they'd stop, she pawed the sand arena. She sagged as if she wanted to lie down, but her trainer encouraged her forward. A brown foal on springy gangly legs trailed her.

"Avery, what's wrong?" The timbre of Hazel's voice suggested she'd arrived at the top of the stairs. She'd be beside me soon.

The cops. The divers. The sick horse with a frisky baby. Outside the sand practice ring, stood a veterinary truck with the low built-in bays for equipment.

Norwood Ward, also wearing coveralls and a ball cap, bent his head while holding a stethoscope to the mare's barrel just behind her left front leg. She pawed with that foreleg in front of the stethoscope's round chest piece disc. Her doctor lowered the stethoscope and turned to consult with Herb, whose brow furrowed and mouth tightened. Norwood moved in again to check the mare's heart rate.

Despite the gravity of the situation, my heart gave an unwelcome squeeze. Biology cared not for an appropriate time and place. Let alone that he was probably gay.

I swung the phone around to see a lanky Blanchard County Sheriff's deputy standing outside the gate.

The mare raised a white-socked hind hoof and banged it on her belly, as if she were pounding on the ceiling to get the upstairs neighbors to turn down the loud music.

Technically, colic was just a stomachache, but it could kill a horse and, in this instance, orphan that foal, while police searched the barn and probably kept the farm help at bay.

In a world of no coincidences, this was a whopper.

I stowed the phone. I said loud enough for the words to leave the bathroom and travel down the hall to the stairs. "Were they working on the colicky mare when the cops showed up?"

Hazel's arm reached past me. I caught a whiff of roses when she brushed the sheer window covering aside. A swash of guilt sluiced over me and left sweaty trails on my palms.

"Oh, dear. Missy's not getting better. Norwood might have to operate. Herb doesn't have that kind of money." She'd come closer. "That's Wesley's filly. Herb's older boy. He's so proud. He used years of paper route money to pay for the stud fee to Ritz." With each sentence, she sounded more worried. "People will think those boys do something they don't do. They don't hurt those horses for a ribbon. We're all judged by the actions of the same bad apples."

"Are you talking about horse show controversy?" With each word, my voice had risen in sharp inflection. What about that fleet of police vehicles at the barn? I dragged in a deep breath and stabilized my voice. "Dive teams aren't called out to execute warrants on animal abuse charges." I made sure to watch her reaction, "But they do for murder."

She shivered with nerves or dismissal. "You just don't know what it's like to be lumped in with the worst people who do what you do."

Not the time or place to mention I'd heard curses shrieked at me in five languages and in as many dialects. Instead, I said, "Your lawyer's on the way, right?"

Which was worse? Sneaking photos or hopscotching around boundaries? From journalist to chitchat to suggesting legal representation.

Good thing I faced the window so she couldn't see my face.

"Of course." Something about her attitude sent my skin creeping. Was she really more worried about public perception about their show horses than a search warrant served on her farm?

Maybe I could drag her back to reality without a snap-out-of-it slap. "Didn't the cops give you a copy of the search warrant? It tells where they're looking and what they're looking for."

"It's downstairs. Come on. I'll show you." Our steps thudded down the staircase. "Oh, were you taking pictures?"

She asked so casually. *Oh, was it raining?*

A lump massed in my throat. I'd rather she'd called me 'dirt' in Kurdish before shrilly ululating her lamentation in my face.

"Yes." I said no more, as if I were testifying in court, just answering the specific question.

"Taking pictures and finding out what's happening is more than a job for you," she said to me, from over her shoulder. "Isn't it, hon?"

"God help me, yes."

"Norwood feels that way about his job, too. He can't not help."

Guilt wormed its way through my gut. "Maybe you'd better save showing that warrant to your lawyer? Not to me."

"I already took a peek. It's for the barn, the pond, and Herb's vehicles. They're looking for a shovel. Someone called in a tip."

A shovel. Reminded me of the coroner's description of the wounds.

The only crime scene tape I had seen was around the pond. Nowhere else.

So, I needed to get going. Commuters driving the road by the barn would see the fleet of police vehicles. Gossip would be wagging over fill-ups and fast food. "I have to get down there."

"You should stay here." Her gaze shifted, suggesting she didn't want to wait alone.

No time for handholding. I yanked my new press pass from my tote. "This says I can get closer." Time to test its clout. I hung it around my neck.

"Oh." Past her wire rims her brow wrinkled. Her fingers fiddled with the hem of the lace curtains. "This will be in the paper?"

My stomach slithered in guilt. Heat rose up my neck and cheeks. Déjà vu all over again. I was a reporter, only an observer, surrounded by participants, and not one of them, even when exposed to the same dangers.

"The warrant is a matter of public record," I said. "Other media outlets, like Lexington TV might cover it, too. Plus, you said it yourself. This is what I do."

My throat swelled, making the words come out thick. "Even if I weren't here, the chief deputy would tell me eventually." My throat felt parched, but the truth clawed out of my gut. "And if this is part of a high-profile case?" I let the question hang there.

Her brow shifted with uncertainty, and her lips moved to purse and unpurse.

Did I have to spell it out for her?

She had no idea how big and ugly this could get, far beyond town gossips, straight into statewide media and even national if a cable news crime show took an interest in the murder of a black Teacher of the Year murdered in a Kentucky town that was predominantly white.

"Hazel." I said her name with a snap. When she made eye contact, I felt her energy shift as if she mentally engaged.

I said, "Until your lawyer gets here, screen your calls. Let your attorney be your contact with the media." I gulped. "Once I walk out that door, everything will be different. I'll be a reporter. Full on. After that, please don't trust me."

"Avery," her voice sounded shaky, and her eyes went watery, "you're scaring me. No one here has done anything wrong."

"Call your lawyer." Before I headed outside to the police perimeter, I had to add, "The truth doesn't set you free. It sets you up. Even when you're innocent."

Twenty-Six

With the sun climbing higher in the sky, I made my way toward the makeshift veterinary hospital and cop convention by the barn.

But first, I stopped on the opposite side of one of the shingled outbuildings in Hazel's yard, the side opposite the barn, and then tapped my phone's earpiece to call Gordon. Talking to him would help me stay in the present and keep my loyalties clear.

The first words out his mouth: "What the hell?"

"Police are executing a search warrant at the Ward barn. I'm on the scene."

The squeak of his swivel chair. "Your place? Why?" Then, "What do you need?"

I spoke before I could wallow in relief. "Is Big Daddy still there?"

"He's gone." He added, "To you," his voice trailed with an audible sneer, "that would be Mr. Big Daddy."

A geyser of joy chased away any guilt I'd felt about Hazel. An important story breaking in my neighborhood. Even better, Gordon and I were a team again.

"Officially? I don't know yet. Sources tell me," I scanned the area to figure out how to approach the action behind the barn and overhear something, "the cops are looking for a murder weapon. They've got a dive team from Louisville. I think they're searching the pond. What do you hear on the scanner?"

"Not a peep. This must be big if they're doing this on the down low. Do you want me to make a call to confirm?"

"Hell no. That'll only show them our hand. They'll shut me out for sure. I have to go now."

To my right, vehicles rumbled down the road, including rickety tractors and trucks. Drivers slowed as they checked out the cop convention in front of the barn, as irresistible as a wreck along the road. Word was getting out. I had to be quick.

"Be careful," he said, and sounded as if he meant it. "Keep in touch. And stay out of jail."

I couldn't help but smile as I ended the call. I was back in familiar territory and part of a team with shared goals again.

Movement to my left in the sand ring attracted my attention. Herb no longer stood at the horse's head. The lead rope he'd held was draped around her withers.

Norwood stood at the horse's head with it raised high. He raised her lips to press her gums to check her hydration levels and for anemia.

Where was Herb?

With all that was happening, let alone all that kept a barn operational, come to think of it, I hadn't seen farm hands to help, especially with an active foal. Maybe the cops held them at bay to keep traffic in the barn to a minimal level.

Cold logic hardened inside my mind. My ticket in, if I could talk my way inside. Close to the action, maybe I'd see some of the comings and goings from the cop motor pool, instead of being cordoned out of sight. "Do you need a hand?" I called through the fence.

From my right, a young male voice, said, "Stop right there, Ms. Sloane." The young new deputy who'd brought the golf cart to Marvin at the fairgrounds, headed my way. He was so new he didn't have his authoritative swagger down yet, almost as if he needed to grow into it. No wonder he'd been assigned the perimeter.

Still, he hadn't said, "get out of here." Not my job to teach cops precise speech. I stopped and wrapped my fingers around the wire cross hatch on the fence.

With a face tight with suppressed jitters, he approached and said, "Ms. Sloane, you need to get out of here before—"

"Who's that woman? Where'd she come from?" A male voice ringing with military authority came from the direction of the barn. He wore a blue nylon raid jacket over a white shirt and black tie. His blond high-and-tight haircut also suggested he'd served.

Deputy Fortner and Marvin, the chief deputy, joined us in ready stances, hands open, eyes hard, mouths grim. It just got real. I was about to be punted, even arrested, if I didn't watch my step.

I raised my press pass, complete with its handy official Kentucky state police seal. "Avery Sloane, *Blanchard County Tribune.* But they also need another pair of hands with that mare and foal. I can do that. That'll keep me out of your way, too. Win, win."

The state police detective turned toward the medical team. "Where did Olmos go?"

"Right here." Herb walked around the veterinary truck. "What do y'all need?" he asked more like a host than a possible police suspect.

"We've got questions for you," the detective said.

Not a "come with us." Not a reading of the Miranda warning, advising him of his rights.

A conversation with them was about as casual as a conversation with me.

Herb, as innocent and cooperative as Hazel, nodded with acceptance and headed toward the gate.

Norwood followed Herb but swerved off to face the detective and chief deputy. "First, you run us out of the barn," he said to the cops across the fence, "and now you take my other pair of hands?"

Marvin stepped forward. "Back off, Woody. Don't make us take you in, too. That mare doesn't stand a chance without you."

Herb said, "Don't worry, Doc, it'll be fine. They just want to talk. I didn't do anything wrong."

Norwood placed a hand on Herb's shoulder and muttered some words, probably along the lines of *Don't talk. Lawyer up.* Except I'd say that, not the country boy veterinarian.

The horse trainer listened with his eyes, showing he was wising up by the second.

Then, Herb leaned away and said a little louder, "I'll be fine. I'm a citizen. I was born here." He nodded as if to reassure Norwood, even patted the veterinarian's shoulder, but the new tension around the horse trainer's eyes didn't match his words.

"Get back to work, Doc." The state police detective ordered, "Olmos. Today."

Herb stepped away from the veterinarian, opened the gate with its elaborate chain wrap clip, and joined the detectives whose chalky smiles didn't meet their eyes.

I needed to be inside the fencing perimeter. If I were busy, I could stay. The police could order farther away than beyond Hazel's window seat.

Time to double down with a bluff. "If that valuable show horse dies of colic and orphans that maybe-even-more-valuable foal because you guys didn't let a vet do his job would be lousy PR. Especially in Kentucky. Worse, if it gets out on the internet." I nodded toward Norwood. "He needs another pair of hands."

Marvin stood with his hands on his duty belt. He seemed to be considering my offer. "Nice try, but she hasn't been a show horse in years. She's a broodmare. Yet, you have a point. Deputy—" He'd pointed at the new deputy. "Get in there and help that vet."

After a visible gulp, he said, "Yes, sir." He fumbled with the gate latch. He hadn't paid attention to Herb's elaborate slide and wrap technique to chain the gate shut. The deputy's clumsiness with a detail of equestrian life, or any contact with livestock, pulsated.

Like Gordon, the new deputy was a basketball Kentuckian, not a horse Kentuckian.

I folded my arms and planted my heels. "If that mare doesn't survive, that'd be a shame, but a great story for Lexington news, what with all the big farms there, tourism, and the in-your-face horse culture. You're a horseman. Wouldn't you agree?"

I gave him a moment to ponder Lexington media poking around Blanchard County, especially TV news crews poking mics in people's faces.

Clanking from the gate rang out as the poor kid with a badge struggled with the latch.

I added, "Not just media pros like me, but social media. Citizen journalists. Do you want a bunch of rabid bloggers with their own agendas taking to social media about Blanchard County? Like they do with the walking horse crowd? Let alone racing?"

Marvin leaned in and said, "Do you really know much about horses to help? The truth. Now." He jerked his chin over toward the barn and pond. "We're following a tip on evidence here."

My mind snagged on his use of "evidence," but I bet he was luring me into another game of Cop Keep-Away. *What evidence? What tip?* Then, he'd say *it's an ongoing investigation*, all following the script.

The mare pawed the sand arena. Sweat frothed on her black coat. The sun was high and warm to the point of hot, but the temperature wasn't what caused her equine version of flop sweat.

Time to ditch the script.

I said, "He hasn't tubed her yet, right?"

He rocked back and studied me. "Then, you know what all could happen," he said, "This could get messy and ugly fast. She and that foal could freak, and it could get dangerous, too. You in for all that?"

Sick of talking sideways, I said, "I've seen people blown to bits."

He stood taller in a recoil. His gaze veered from my eyes to a far point on the hills past the pond beyond the ring. "Go in," he said. He cleared his throat. To the deputy, he called out, "She's cleared. Make sure she goes nowhere else but that turnout."

To the crestfallen deputy, I said in a soft voice, "Pardon me," so he'd stand aside. With an even more confidential tone, I told him, "Every gate and every latch is different. Varies from farm to farm. Gate to gate, even."

I opened the latch and dragged open the gate, which emitted a metallic squeal I hadn't heard when Herb had gone through the gate. I stepped inside the ring.

The ground under my boots changed from packed dirt to deep sand footing, enough that my boot heels sank and stretched the calves of my legs, just like a walk on the beach.

On my way across the ring, I strained to see what I could of the pond, what the divers were doing.

A cranky horse doctor waited for me. "You work for me now, not the paper," he said. "Understand?"

Hard to believe we'd had a moment a couple of days ago. "Point me where to help."

"We've got one horse in pain." Norwood's voice pulled me up like a riding horse. "The other, too young for manners. They both are armed with teeth and hooves. Do I have to watch out for you, or can I do my job?"

"I'm big on situational awareness." Which would be easier now without a big Nikon at my eye, as there'd been overseas. "Give me her lead rope."

He passed it to me, and said, "Stand on the same side of her as me. Hold her head steady and up. Don't let her drop it."

Until the little equine family was out of danger. Then the story was fair game.

He smeared lube on the end of clear vinyl tubing. He touched her nose, both stroking it and then softly plucking at both nostrils.

I broke my own interview rule and filled the silence. "Interesting timing. A horse is colicking—a mare with a nursing foal—while cops are also searching the property." I let the words trail off. "For a coincidence, it's big."

Norwood swiveled to shoot me a scowl. "We save her first." His voice was grim. "Afterward is when we wonder what happened."

He ignored me and stroked the mare's face. I couldn't help but think, what a slick play it would be, when framing a horseman for a crime, to make sure he's so distracted while cops were executing a search warrant on his property that the patsy wouldn't even think to call a lawyer.

But that would require the framer to know a warrant would be served.

I didn't have time to consider the depth of that particular rabbit hole, especially with my cover as an amateur vet tech.

Norwood's gaze never left the horse. He said in a soothing tone, "Let's lower the volume. Now." More for her benefit than mine.

He stroked her lowered brow around its faint white star. Her ears drooped and the skin around her eyes sagged. I scanned along the length of her topline to see flanks heaving with labored breathing and lathered sweat inside her hind legs.

Even to my unschooled eyes, she needed a miracle. If what Hazel had said earlier was true, all Herb could afford was a miracle. And soon.

Norwood said, “Try to hold her steady but let her flex her neck. Helps with the tubing.” He rested his forearm over her head between her ears and threaded the clear plastic tube into her opposite nostril with his other hand.

The mare worked her jaws and flung her head high and from side to side as he threaded the tubing down her nose. I had to shift my balance to keep her level. She fussed and then swallowed and chewed. The tubing glided deeper, sliding off from its coil around his neck.

He said, “Can you see the tube going down her esophagus?”

What? Was I supposed to be watching? He should tell me these things. “Can’t you tell?”

He gazed at the mare’s nose and smirked. “Thought you’d want to notice. It’s not something you see every day.”

He took the non-horse end of the tube from around his shoulders, stuck the free end of the tube in his mouth as if he were siphoning gas out of a car. His cheeks hollowed as he sucked on it, and then he blew into it.

Even though I knew that had been coming, I cringed. But I also had expected stomach contents to come out. Both mine and hers.

The noon siren screeched an extended wail, the noise piercing my body in a direct hit.

Twenty-Seven

White heat flashed. My heart flailed against my ribs to make a run for it out my throat. *Take cover. Take cover.*

Escape routes? Too exposed. Except for under the truck next to me.

I dropped face down and scooted under the white truck. Filling my mind, a voice from memory, Master Sergeant Stewart's clipped British accent chanting the procedure:

Lie on stomach.

Cross legs at ankles.

Hold mouth open.

Hands on back of your head. Fingers laced.

Ya geeks can get new hands.

Sand rasped my exposed skin and smeared grit on my lips.

The tang of fuel oil penetrated my nose and spiraled like a sidewinder missile hellbent on my guts.

I'd taken cover under a giant gas can.

I waited for the next mortar to hit and hoped it wouldn't slam into my cover.

Where was the shockwave from the first strike?

Are the bombers waiting for the first responders to detonate another device?

Solid hooves stomped near my ears. *Oh, God.* Not a cart horse. A crowded market.

Collateral damage. Civilians, children, livestock, and wildlife? Here in the busy market?

I had to shoot pictures from under the truck. My hands released my ears to pat the sand like a pinned alligator. My camera. *Where the hell was my camera?*

A male voice. The authority of a sergeant. "All clear." The words more intelligible. "It's over." Then, "Avery, you can come out now," in a kind tone.

My hearing. I still had my hearing. Still sharp. No muffling, nor fullness between my ears.

Tears spilled down my face and stuck grains of sand to my cheeks. All I could see were boots with white paper pants. A DoD forensics guy. Had to be.

Damn, how long had I been under that truck?

Shame slid over me. I'd never live this down. It'd spread through the journalist corps like mono.

Tears of shame stung my eyes. I couldn't look at the man. Couldn't. "Is my camera out there?"

"No. But it's okay." He emphasized that last phrase with a southern linger. "Come on out."

I skooshed out from under the truck, a low rider for a military vehicle. Ahead, a stretch of sand. Farther away, yellow flowers splotched a sea of lush green.

I opened my teary eyes.

No flames and black smoke. No destruction.

I rolled over to see an azure sky with cottony white clouds.

Blinking couldn't stop the flow of tears. Relief, release, grief, fear, shame. All of it rose from my heart and down my cheeks.

A puff of cooler but still warm air blew across my face, across the hot wet streaks. A soft chamois brushed along my cheek. A muzzle with billowing nostrils at the end of a long tan face leading to brown eyes ringed by black skin. Horse breath smells sweet. Darkness descended. My nose got lipped. Moisture remained.

"Hey. Cut it out." I pushed the small equine face away from mine. Next time, she'd try a taste, or a sharp nip. A foal exploring.

I elbowed my way to a half-sitting position. Dizzy. Depleted.

A man wearing a ball cap and coveralls stood next to a horse.

Recent memories emerged, re-shaped, and returned.

His face woozed into focus.

Norwood Ward. What was he doing over here?

"Better now?" His gaze skimmed over my hands and eyes in a swift assessment much like a visual triage. "I know a lot of guys who've been in the Sandbox and hate that siren, too. Even guys who'd been in Viet Nam."

He stole a worried glance toward a black horse, the one I'd heard stomping. Probably ran away from her cart. What about her driver?

A sheen of sweat covered her sagging body. Wait.

No protruding hip bones. No sagging back. A fully fleshed body with a smooth but sweaty coat. Not an Iraqi street vendor's cart horse.

Ahead, I spotted the fleet of parked police cruisers and evidence squad trucks. No visible cops, probably because they all worked down at the pond executing a search warrant.

I leaned against the truck in relief. Good. No one wearing a uniform had seen me duck under the truck.

Then, I spotted the young deputy. He stood in front of the wire fence with his feet planted farther than shoulder-width apart. His fingers gripped the wire that crosshatched the fencing. The morning sun cast a diagonal shadow off the top of his head, leaving enough of his face lit to show his mouth gaping open.

"Miss Sloane?" The young deputy called out through the fence links. "Do you need an EMT?"

I ached to slink under the truck again but waved him off with a shake of my head. "I'm good." The urge to beg him not to tell anyone swept through me. Especially at the sheriff's department.

The young deputy unpeeled his fingers from the fence and shifted toward the barn entrance.

A guy in a navy polo shirt hauled a handcart loaded with a plastic household storage container big enough to hold a winter's worth of sweaters. Inside the transparent container, sludgy pond water sloshed and concealed the evidence found. The diver in an orange dry suit emerged from the barn.

"The cops collected some evidence from the pond." My voice had come out raspy. "Look."

"Not our problem," Norwood said. "Have you returned to us now?"

"What if this whole sick horse thing was a diversionary tactic? Could she have been deliberately poisoned? To target Herb for the fall guy?"

Of course, he wouldn't take my observations seriously. No one would.

Twenty-Eight

After the danger and manure had passed in the practice ring, Missy and her foal dozed in a stall with fresh bedding. The mare stood with her head in the far corner. Her foal sprawled on the soft bedding. Both slept. Finally.

Norwood had taken off in the vet truck. Most of the cops left not long after I'd been released from veterinary service. The cops had run police line tape from the barn down to the pond. The remaining deputies ignored my questions about what had been found in the pond.

An informational lock down, but maybe not just a Team Cops vs Team News situation anymore, either.

My official sources had seen me flip out. I'd ducked and covered under a truck. In the Middle East, it'd make a funny story among a legion of funny stories about people whistling through close calls in a graveyard. Here? Where odd behavior set you apart from the herd of people going along "just fine"? Unprofessional to the point of unhinged behavior.

I felt more slithering shame about first thinking of myself, instead of Herb, who had yet to return.

Was he still with the cops? Had he been taken into custody?

That left me the babysitter of a sick horse until Hazel came down from the house, or for the farm hands to be released from the police, whichever came first.

At least I was away from questions, like, *what happened to you out there?*

An older sedan arrived. Out of it came a slender Latino woman in hospital scrubs with two boys and a sturdy older woman in capris and an oversized floral tee.

The older boy, probably in his early teens, had his father's square face. I'd seen him before, from a distance, working with his dad by the pond. The younger, with curls, about kindergarten age, had the delicate chin and thickly lashed eyes of their mom.

"Who are you?" she said with a challenging up-and-down look at me. "Where's Herb? Why are there police cars out here?"

Hadn't he called her? Then again, if he were smart, his call would have been to a lawyer. Who still might have called his wife instead. I introduced myself and mentioned where I work, to identify myself as a journalist. I added, "I also live in Hazel's trailer. You must be Herb's wife. Has he contacted you?"

She wasn't listening but checking her phone as it buzzed. She ignored the call. My colleagues and competitors, maybe, after her for a reaction quote.

"No. Should he? I'm his wife, Estrella. What are you doing here? Why are there police here?"

"Let's let the boys look in on the mare and foal while we talk over here." Her nose wrinkled. When I saw Wesley lift the little one by the waist to peer into the stall, I signaled her with sideways jerks of my head.

She sidled over with tight lips and a sharp stare.

"So," she spat out before I could start. "Doris Caldwell finally talked police into raiding show barns? She's been calling off the hook. That freakin' pest. Of course, they wouldn't start with the big money barns. Especially after—"

I raised my hand to dive into her rant. She talked even faster than I did, at such a brisk clip I would have sworn she was Yankee-born like me.

"I don't know what you think is going on, but this is what I know. I happened to be here when some of it went down. Remember." I held out the press pass so she could read it. Which I realized too late looked like I was badging her.

She folded her arms in a challenging huff.

I said, "I'd like to speak privately with you."

She twisted her mouth and bored holes into me with her gaze. "The boys. I can't leave the boys."

The boys busied themselves with the horses. I stepped closer to her and said, "I need to tell you something you may rather they not hear from me." I added, "Wesley seems to work here with his dad, so I'm guessing he can keep the little guy busy?"

She shot me a glare and then said to her son, "Wesley. Watch him, while I talk to this lady."

We stepped around the corner of the barn, outside. She folded her arms, tapped her right foot, and waited.

"The police were here to execute a search warrant," I said, glancing into the interior of the barn for deputies. "Cops from different jurisdictions. They apparently found something in the pond. Herb left with them. He's not back yet."

"Which horse did they take?"

Horse? Hazel had fretted about the horses. How many times, how many people, did I have to tell, it's not about the horses.

"No horses," I said, sounding sharper than I'd intended. "The police searched your barn and pond and found something they're interested in. If Doris is calling you, maybe it's for her day job as a lawyer. Maybe you should call her back."

The horse trainer's wife retreated a few feet away with her phone.

Hazel arrived with a bag of knitting and asked the boys at the stall about their day at school. Wesley, polite with Hazel, stole worried glances at his mother, who listened to her phone and covered her other ear with her free hand. Her shoulders trembled.

Wesley needed a distraction.

"Wesley?" He nodded but regarded me with more sidelong suspicion than the cops had earlier. "I'm Avery, another one of Haze—Mrs. Ward's—tenants." I had to add, "I work at the newspaper, too. You help your dad, right?"

Another nod.

"Take me through the barn and tell me if anything's missing."

With his back tall with pride in how he helps his dad and my heart feeling sad enough I made myself hide it, I remembered what Cathy Epperson, the coroner, had told me about the murder weapon and what Hazel had said about what was being searched for in the warrant. I said, "Where do you guys keep stuff like lawn tools?"

"This is a barn," he said with teenage disdain before adding, "ma'am," with the hastiness of someone who'd slipped on the manners front.

"I'm from the city. Humor me. Something like a pitchfork? A manure fork?"

Manure forks or rakes, designed to sift stall bedding and hold manure clumps, looked and worked like a cat litter scoop had a baby with a leaf rake. Too light to have killed a man the way Cathy the coroner had described.

I just couldn't bring myself to add or *a shovel*. Saying shovel would've felt like a leading question.

A tool found on property Herb manages would cement a frame job.

Wesley's sneakers scuffed on the change in the barn's flooring. Larger than Kinsale's posh stallion barn built to impress, let alone isolate stallions from mares, the Ward barn was more of a kluge as it had been added on over the years. We turned down another wing with a wall still holding an old-style wall phone complete with stretched out curly cord.

"I don't have to look," the boy said. "We didn't get our scoop back."

That might be a shovel, but I played up my city folk vibe to be sure. "What's a scoop?"

His big eyes blinked and told me he'd bought my ignorance. "A shovel. A big one with a flat head. This'uns old, too. Heavier than the new ones."

I held out my hands, like the fish that got away, to show the approximate size of the plastic box I'd seen the state police carry out to their evidence truck. A box with what looked like pond water but had some heft. "Something about that long?"

"Yeah. My dad's big on that 'always be prepared' stuff. He must be the only one because everybody at the show there is always forgetting stuff and borrowing ours. Then they don't bring it back. And it's always the ones who can afford the stuff." He scrunched his nose in distaste.

The scoop may have returned, but not in the way they'd expected it to be returned. Nor in the place where Herb kept it.

I kept my voice level and even, "Do you remember who borrowed it that night?"

He studied the grass around the soles of his sneakers.

After our tour, Estrella was still on the phone. Hazel sat in the plastic lawn chair and bounced the little one, who was really too big for that, while he giggled up and down on her knee.

Would the boys remember these last seconds of normalcy before their mother revealed their father was in big trouble?

Herb's wife put her phone away. Her eyes went hard in her ashy pale face and she trembled more with rage than fear. "My Herb needs a lawyer. My Herb who doesn't even fix his horses. Tells the truth and does his job. I keep telling him to go to a tech school. Go to cooking school to work with my father. Forget this ambling horse stuff. No matter what we do, we're all guilty—of everything. No matter what."

Hazel said, "I can watch the boys if you need to do some things," in a masterful sweep of understatement.

Estrella said to her oldest son, "I have to leave for a while. Your father needs you to keep an eye on the barn. Do your chores and mind Mrs. Ward."

Wesley dared to say a faint, "I don't need watching,"

Her cocked eyebrow scowl proclaimed, "no arguments." He nodded, but a frown of concern creased a face too young to be burdened with adult woes.

With Hazel minding the ranch, I was free to return to my day job. "I'm headed to the sheriff's department, too. Want a ride?"

"Do you think I'm stupid?"

"No. I could drive while you make phone calls. If they arrest him, yeah, it'll be in the paper. Because it's public record. But I'm hoping it doesn't come to that."

"Thanks, but no thanks." Her voice was clipped. Her eyes narrow. "You understand."

"I'll see you there."

Twenty-Nine

While driving past the older part of the humongous cemetery across the street from the farm, I checked in with Gordon. My editor, my sounding board, my supposed buffer between management and the public. By tradition and newsroom structure, he had a right to know updates.

He was also my friend, even if he couldn't afford anymore to be mine.

He answered the phone. "Where are you? What's happening?"

"The cops carried out a transparent plastic storage bin." Fatigue thrummed through me. I added, "I couldn't see what for all the murky pond water. No one's talking. Except maybe Herb, who the police took away."

I left out the shovel part, not to keep secrets, but to wait until I could confirm. An old voice inside my mind insisted I shouldn't care. Reporter-editor conversations used to be sacrosanct. Or I'd been naive. I wished I didn't have to be so careful around Gordon.

"Good Lord." His voice modulated in shock and awe. "They took him away right after you got there? You've been gone for hours. He hasn't been back?"

"No, and I don't think he's been home because I just met his wife and family." I added. "Doris has been blowing up his wife's phone. I don't know why they're keeping him for so long, unless he's in custody. Which would be nuts because I don't think he did it."

"Avery, they wouldn't keep him without evidence."

"Wouldn't they?" I lobbed a softball, "Maybe because he doesn't look like most of the residents of the county."

"C'mon. Herb grew up here. Everybody knows him. I'm sure he's just being interviewed."

My brain parsed his tone to determine if he believed what he said. I wasn't sure. No matter how long I'd known him. I paused, difficult, to let him say more.

Then, he added, "Find out if they got the murder weapon."

"That's the plan, but don't be surprised if they don't release info until they release the search warrant affidavit." The affidavit was the filed paperwork explaining the probable cause for the search and the parameters. I also wanted to keep my knowledge of Hazel's possession of a copy of the search warrant confidential.

I heard typing clacking in the background. "Until there's an arrest," he mused, "it won't be released." A quick conversational veer. "Now you can get to the Mount Carmel elementary school. They're having a wolf program. Can you imagine? Wolves. Here in Blanchard County. Much cooler than coyotes," which he pronounced in the cowboy way as *ki-yotes*. "Get some photos with your phone."

A splash of mental cold water. "*A school program?* I'm on my way to the sheriff's department to find out what's happening to Herb Olmos. If he's a suspect in a murder. Which, I repeat, is ridiculous. I saw him that night after the murder. Still in his show clothes. He's a one-man band doing all his groom work. He was rumpled. Sure. But spotless. Do you know how filthy you get when you bludgeon someone to death?" I cringed but added, "Big yuck."

"No," he said with a sad lilt. "And that I know you know, makes me sad." But his voice went firm. "The program starts soon. See ya afterward."

Before he could end the call, I said, "Hello? Search warrant, police divers, and evidence collection. Did you hear me tell you they took him with them? Don't you want me to get official confirmation about developments?" I thought about my stint as a temporary vet tech. "You don't want to know what I shoveled to get as deep on the inside of this story as I am."

"The police are slow when they're filing charges. Wolves? Now that's timely. School will be out in a couple of weeks. Between Memorial Day and the fair in the summer, you'll be praying for a school program. Our readers will love the wolves. You'll see."

I waited a moment so I could land my next question. "More than they loved the funeral coverage? Did your uncle really get complaints? Or was it just him marking territory?"

He said, "You covered world news for so long you don't grasp the concept of community news."

"Send Wilbur. Or Justin. Please. Sure, they shoot wide, but you'll spot something great somewhere in their images. Make them do the cropping."

Bossy enough, Avery? Dial it down. I added, "Just an idea."

The faint background noise of typing stopped. Then, my editor said, "If you can get there before the program ends. All I need is a photo with a caption, not a story."

He reminded me when the elementary school dismissed and added a little back timing. "That's the best I can do."

I noted the time. Good thing Estrella chose to go alone.

"You won't be sorry," I stated.

I didn't hear, but felt, my old friend's sigh of resignation. "Just go."

Click.

His wariness burrowed under my skin. Was Gordon less worried about what Kinsale could do to me than what our paper's owner-publisher could do to him?

Passing the tall sandstone columns of courthouse square made me think I needed to know more about the county, even the region, to learn more about who pulled the rope that pulled the strings.

I drove into the sheriff's department parking lot. Before going in, I checked my phone. Something Sylvana Dobbs had said at the Fairmont House, another time when I'd done a public duck-and-cover, floated into my memory.

Cy had judged the horse show and named Kinsale's former maid's horse the night's champion over Kinsale's prized stud horse.

Was Kinsale egotistical and petty enough to resent that tie? How far would he go for retribution? Was that what had nagged at Gordon?

I had to keep in mind, just because I didn't like Kinsale—yadda, yadda, yadda.

Estrella Olmos stepped through and out the sheriff's department's glass door. She clutched her phone.

The lobby of the sheriff's department wasn't the best place to hold a conversation you didn't want to have overheard.

She stared straight ahead but didn't show reaction to my approach. "You mind Senora Ward. Mami loves you."

I'd get one shot at this, so I inhaled and set off. "How's it going?"

She said, "Horses colic from all sorts of things. Tree huggers don't accept that."

Here we go again. *It's not about the horses.*

I ticked off various causes of colic. "It's spring. She's nursing and dehydrating. She hasn't been drinking because she hasn't felt thirsty. Something she ate. Something she ate too fast. Causes of colic make a long list."

I left out my suspicions about poisoning. The Olmoses could hear that from their veterinarian.

I tilted my head toward the sheriff's department glass doors and said, "Did anyone in there tell you they found something in the pond?"

She shot me a glare, and stayed silent, but I continued. "Whatever it is fits in one of those under-the-bed plastic storage bins, like you'd use to store sweaters." I decided to stick with what I'd seen, rather than what I knew. Or thought I knew.

She flipped her wrist at waist level with her body between me and the view from inside the sheriff's department to shoot me the bird.

I couldn't help but smirk. "No need to hide that from the cops. They'd be happy to join in."

A white luxury import sedan rolled into the sheriff's department driveway and eased toward the visitor's spaces. Soon, the driver would be out of the car and heading toward the door. Considering the model of car, I didn't think it belonged to a deputy.

In all seriousness, I said, "If what I think is going down is, then Lexington media will be out here any minute. They will be all over," I made air quotes with my fingers, " 'the police have a suspect' story line. They won't start with innocent-until-proven guilty, even though it's the law. I believe he's innocent."

Great move, Avery. Accuse the other paper of no objectivity and kick it to the curb yourself.

The vehicle shut off its engine. The driver would be at the entrance with us any moment. "I saw him at the fairgrounds after the murder. His show clothes were wrinkled, but not the mess I'd see if what they're liable to pin on him is true." I added, "This is way too big to be about the horses."

The white car opened and a woman with a tan leather briefcase emerged. Doris Caldwell had switched the casual hippie grandma jeans for a gray suit and pumps.

"Estrella," Doris called out as she approached across the parking lot. "Legal aid sent me to represent your husband." She swung her attention to me. "Hello, Avery. You'll pardon us while we take care of business."

Estrella held out both hands as if to ward off the lawyer. "No. Not you." She backed away from the woman and said in a hushed tone as if she were consigning a demon to hell, "You don't like horse show people."

The woman, the source, who'd flaked on me and left me with coffee and rubber eggs at the truck stop said, "That doesn't matter now. My job is to defend your husband aggressively. I do my job."

I wasn't buying her line, either, although I suspected there weren't a lot of local alternatives who weren't part of the good old boys' club. I made sure to cover my own tush, and said, "Off the record, are you really her only option?"

Doris cast me a dismissive sniff. "It's not your concern." She returned her attention to Herb's wife. "Senora. Olmos—Mrs. Olmos—Estrella. I need a word with you. Privately."

The trainer's wife folded her arms. "Not you for my Herb. I want another lawyer."

Doris shot me a glare. "I'd appreciate you respecting my client's spouse's off-the-cuff comments as off the record."

"This is a public area," I said. I couldn't blame Estrella, but a new lawyer might cost money the Olmos family didn't have. Better lawyers always did.

Doris held out her hand, palm down, as if to direct her client's wife to speak more softly. "We'll talk about that later." Her small eyes slid over toward me. "More privately."

Estrella's arms waved, her hands slashing the air like a saber. "You already think my husband is guilty of hurting his horses just because he's competitive. You were talking trash around town about how he won the stake class the other night. Why would you fight for his innocence here?"

And people thought I had an impulse control problem.

The journalist in me mused about an opinion piece about the impact of loyalties and feuding, but Gordon was already alluding to all the capital and goodwill I'd been burning.

Deputies gathered in the lobby. Any weakness in Herb's support team could be used against him.

Even though he'd lawyered up, I could imagine someone finding a way to say to him, *Dude, your defense lawyer is here but, heads up, it's Doris Caldwell. Yeah, the lady who hates your guts because of what you do for a living. I know, right? You'd be better off taking your chances with us. We can help.*

In the interest of closing a case, they'd help him right into a prison cell.

I said, not knowing who was or wasn't trustworthy, "Thank you, Counselor. I'll be calling you later for an update." To Estrella, I said, "It's her job to help. It's my job to tell her the *Tribune* is watching." Then, I shot a smile at Doris and headed for my car.

Considering how uninterested Kinsale was in the story, my promise felt empty.

Maybe the rest of the *Tribune* wouldn't be watching, but I would.

Thirty

Moments before the "Learn About Wolves!" program ended, I arrived at the Mount Carmel school. I grabbed photos of awed schoolkids and the regal but bored wolves. After getting caption info from their handler and making a few indirect inquiries to the grateful teachers, they told me neither Wilbur nor Justin had shown up.

I texted the photos to Gordon, as a preview of coming attractions.

I left messages with Doris and Marvin, but no response so far. I thought about doing an end run around Doris because I suspected Hazel had Estrella's number.

Driving past the old part of the cemetery and approaching the curve where the Ward's barn lay, a light beckoned from inside the open barn door.

No cars or trucks sat on the parking area out front. Nor was anyone taking saddled horses toward or away from the riding ring. Just an open door with an inviting light.

Barn time. Just what I needed to soothe my nerves, still jangling after the siren went off and my argument with Gordon.

I pulled in and parked my car. Maybe Hazel, who'd taken over to watch Missy and her foal after I left, had stayed.

Inside the door, the white noise of horses chewing and the rustle of them nosing through hay comforted my ears. I felt lighter, just at the sound.

Over a faint soundtrack of bluesy guitar, horses chewed and rustled through their bedding. My heart rate slowed and peace washed over me, like a welcome sip of brandy at the end of a long day.

I stepped inside the wide door, peering down into the shadowy gloom of the long and wide barn aisle. "Hazel? Are you still here?"

My eyes adjusted to the softer light inside. A truck sat down toward the end of the aisle.

"Mom's up at the house," said a male voice with a southern lilt.

My skin tingled and fired in a warm sequence I didn't need. Especially with a man I suspected was unavailable, let alone gay. In the Bible Belt. He fit in less than I did.

I tamed my wayward hormones and called out, "Norwood? Where are you?"

"Down here," he said. "With Missy. In the big foaling stall where she was."

I followed the trail of his voice and the music through the wings and corridors of the Ward barn.

I called out, "How is she?"

"Come see for yourself."

When I peered into the stall through the door opened far enough for a human to slip out, the foal stood on stilty legs and tottered toward me. I hung my arm and open palm down over the low wall to present the back of my hand to the foal for inspection.

"Hey, little girl." I pitched my voice low and soothing. "Crazy day, huh?"

Missy turned her head my way and flicked her ears to assess my threat level. She must've recognized me, as she heaved a deep breath and smacked her lips toward the foal. The mare cocked her far hind hoof to rest on its tip and then murmured to call her baby to her side.

Oh. Right. She remembered the noon siren and panic it caused. I settled my nerves, and I withdrew my hand.

Norwood lowered his hands from the mare and backed away, but never shifted his gaze from the pair. He seemed to pull his breathing and energy into a deep regular rhythm matching Missy's in a moment feeling like private silent communion.

I kept my voice low and said, "She looks no worse for all the wear."

Norwood arced one arm as a gentle brace under his patient's neck while the other traced circular patterns on the big muscle below her withers, like a human's shoulder. With each complete circuit, he shifted his hand nearby to draw more circles.

I recognized it as a massage technique I'd seen done at the lesson barn back in the day.

"Wow," I maintained the FM radio murmur. "Bodywork. Maybe a little energy work, too." Gay and into alternative medicine in the Bible Belt. How did he manage living here, let alone stay in business? "Do all your patients get the best from East and West?"

"The Olmoses are good people. And Missy used to be ours."

"She's stayed all in the family." Which explained the mare's comfort and safety with Norwood, even if he was her veterinarian.

He ran both hands down Missy's back, from the base of her ears down to the base of her tail, as if he were flicking off bad mojo. He stepped away, shot me a smile that sizzled straight through my core, and said, "Yeah."

I gulped too late to hide my shudder. My body was insisting I find a friend with benefits and soon, but it kept pointing me toward poor choices. I doubled down into reporter mode. "Any news yet from the tox screen?"

He slipped through the gap of a stall door, then closed it and latched it with an old hook latch too low for nimble equine lips. "Labs for people are slow. Labs for animals are slower. Plus, we'd have to run separate tests for each suspicious substance. The list of possibilities is just too long."

No surprise there. My pesky hormones noted he was within arm's reach and staying put. "What if you told them it might be pertinent to a murder investigation?"

"Uh, excuse me?" An eyebrow quirked below the bill of his cap.

"Did you save her food and water? For tox screens?"

He edged away and the longing returned. "Who's going to pay for that? And which toxin would we look for? I checked out her hay to make sure it was okay in case it was a bad batch."

My gut didn't have to tell me there was more to that story.

My gut managed to speak over my hormones. He's lying. The old thrill of the hunt distracted me from attraction.

I thought about the murder weapon in the pond. "Is this barn ever locked? You should harden this target."

He tilted his head and squinched his eyes as if I'd said something ludicrous. I added, "Anyone could walk onto this property, almost at any point."

"It's possible you watch way too many action movies," he said with raised eyebrows and an amused smile. "I'll look into your suggestions." The most polite brush-off ever.

I went straight to my point. "If I were to tell you I think Herb is innocent, what would you say?"

He nodded and his mouth tightened. "I'd agree."

I kept an eye on the mare in case she sensed any tension in him. Animals could read us. Prey animals, like horses, were like children in a dysfunctional household. They sensed oncoming danger.

Yet, I believed he was hiding something.

"The search warrant timing is suspicious. What are the odds of a colicky horse while a search warrant is being served?" I continued, showing the cards I held, and added, "And I believe there's a reason you don't want to talk about it."

Leaden fear sank through my stomach. Unless I misread Norwood, I might be in danger. The weapon had been found on his family's property. The police had taken his tenant. He'd know how to poison a horse. He was hiding something.

And he was white, part of a long-time, land-owning family. Herb could be a handy convenient brown guy to pin a murder on.

Was Norwood giving his patient a little extra TLC? Guilt would be a good reason.

But that would mean I was alone in a barn with a killer.

My heart rate picked up and not because my hormones were confused. This could be bad. Very bad. I'd let down my guard and was trapped.

So distracted, I'd even forgotten to note the nearest exit.

He put both hands on his belt. The magic smile had left. He narrowed his eyes. "Who's asking me all these questions? An interested neighbor? Or a reporter?"

I watched him, but widened my gaze to assess the area for self-defense weapons of opportunity. Even if I pivoted and ran for the door, he'd be on me in a flash.

I backed farther away, talking the whole time. "I have to check in. With my editor."

Shut up, Avery. Don't babble. He's already seen you melt down. Don't do it again.

He swung his gaze to meet mine and said, "I found him. There. At the fairgrounds. That night."

Longing reached between us, but the ring of truth shot through me like lightning.

My reporter conscience demanded I get confirmation. My hormones insisted I comfort him. But for the moment, I opted to let him talk.

His shoulders bobbed a clueless shrug. "I've seen plenty of death in my life, but that was the worst. It weighs on my mind. It's different when it's someone you know." He all but scraped the toe of his boot on the floor. "I figured you'd understand better. I know you've seen bad stuff, too."

Exhausted emotionally and physically, the words tumbled from my mouth. "My Iraqi fixer and his family died because they helped me and other American reporters. I was on an assignment with a unit of Marines checking what we thought was an IED strike." My voice tightened but I couldn't stop talking. "I didn't know where my fixer's family lived. They didn't have to be in the Sandbox. They'd moved from Detroit to be with the grandparents who wouldn't leave."

The tears gushed out. I sputtered, "Why wouldn't those old folks leave? Who the hell moves to a war zone to be with family?"

I hid my face with my hands to contain the tears and snot. My knees wouldn't keep me vertical. I slid against the wood of the stall and sagged.

Arms encircled me and tucked my head. Into his neck, I said, "All they did was take jobs with us Americans. Because of their jobs, they were targeted."

I sobbed into his shoulder and let the pain gush out. When I caught my breath, the old wood felt hard against my arm. The emotional pain ached and called me away, anywhere but here.

But Norwood's neck smelled of horses, leather, and salt. Maybe the latter came from my tears.

My arms wrapped around his shoulders.

He didn't flinch.

I found an alternative to the pain.

I said, trying to modulate my voice from tears to inviting, "Let's go where we won't spook the horses."

He whispered in my ear, "There'll be another time."

The horses rustled and whickered as if someone showed up who'd brought them food before. From the enthusiasm I heard in a couple kicking stall boards, someone who'd brought treats.

"Norwood?" his mother called out.

His eyes squeezed shut. His shoulders shook from suppressed laughter. "Down here, Mom. In the foaling stall." He stepped away from me.

She padded along in her sneakers and zigzagged across the barn aisle to peer into each stall. "I'm checking on the horses." When she zigged our way, she said, "Oh. Avery. I didn't expect to see you here." Then, "Are you alright?"

Norwood's gaze slid my way, then shifted as if he felt embarrassed. To his mother, he said, "You don't have to do these walk-throughs."

She peered into another stall. "What about Herb's new horse, the one he beat Kinsale's stud horse with. He couldn't have started clean. He'd need periodic tuning up."

Norwood's mouth compressed as if he held back words. "He's fine," he said in clipped tones. "Nobody does that anymore." He stepped closer to her, spoke in a lower voice, and said, "Herb doesn't use abusive training techniques. If he did, I wouldn't rent him stall space."

Hazel swung her attention to me. "How about you, Avery? Are you feeling better? This has been a rough day for everyone."

Great. She'd found me hitting on her son. Aside from the whole "consenting adults" thing, she'd probably seen my freak-out dive under the truck earlier, too. No telling what she'd hash out with her with good friend

Laverne. Then, Kinsale would hear about it. Maybe not the climbing over each other part, but definitely the ducking under the truck part.

"I'm fine, too."

Just peachy.

Thirty-One

I headed for my car to move it to my parking space on the other side of my trailer. In the shadows facing the street stood a blank manila envelope braced against my driver's side tire. I slowed my pace to allow my eyes to adjust to the dark.

No printing.

Had Hazel left it? She would've said something.

Norwood? Likewise.

My insides quivered then hardened with a plan.

Call EOD. Explosive Ordinance Disposal.

You can take the girl out of the war zone but not the war zone out of the girl. Except I wasn't in a hot zone.

I'd be calling local police, probably deputy sheriffs.

A shiver. I didn't trust the cops. They'd destroy it, per procedure. Or laugh. I'd never live it down.

Without touching the package, I squatted and squinted to examine it in the dark. Slim. Just papers. Not enough room for an explosive, not any that I knew of.

Documents from an anonymous source?

But if someone wanted to reach me, I could be baited with information.

Whoever left it wanted me to open it. If someone wanted to kill me, they could've just hidden the bomb in the underside of the car.

Whoever left it didn't want me to call the cops, either, or they would've left it at the office. Or put it in the mail. Then again, mail was subject to federal laws.

The barn fronted a busy two-lane state secondary road. Across the street lay the dark cemetery. On the side of my car where the package lay propped against the wheel, anyone could've left it.

But who? And when? While Norwood and I were half-flirting? Had Hazel seen it? Or even someone driving by?

Whatever was in the envelope was meant for me alone.

No other thing to do but to move my car to my parking space and take the package indoors.

Before opening the suspect package, I hit the lights in my gingham-world kitchen. If the worst happened and I survived, a fire might consume all the merrily spiteful daisies and gingham. Insurance money would fund Hazel's redecoration.

I held the package at arm's length as if that would really protect me. Hindsight pointed out I should've come inside first for gloves before picking up the envelope. Let alone kept it outside to open.

Enough foolishness. If the envelope deliverer wanted me dead, I'd be dead already.

With the sealed package upside down, I tapped the top flap end against the counter so the contents would shift in reverse. I used scissors to snip a thin slice across the bottom.

Nothing happened. The package lay open with a menacing slit, hinting that danger lurked inside.

I leaned over to peer into the gap.

The beam from the over-sink light fixture revealed papers and something slim and dark, like a flash drive, in the bottom.

Enough farting around.

I pulled out a short stack of papers.

One was a printout of an old news story from a Connecticut newspaper. The headline, page one, just below the masthead: "State's Attorney Dies in Fiery Crash."

My chest contracted. Dread sank from my clenched jaw into my stomach.

I snorted in bitter annoyance. Someone had done some homework. To what end, I had no idea.

I girded myself and slid my attention past the text I didn't need to read. Nor did I need to see the spot news photo of the charred mangled remains of his car.

The other "art" for the piece was my father's post-law school head shot, a grainy black and white photo. Short, dark all-business hair, rectangular wire-rimmed glasses, and a wide tie.

My mother had said once, other than their wedding pictures, his student portrait was her favorite photo of him. She'd tucked a tiny color print of the portrait into her wallet and kept it even after she'd remarried.

I only remembered him from photos.

I shook off the nostalgia. Time to forge ahead.

I flipped over that first page for the next.

A handbill for a fundraiser. This sheet featured a picture of me as a toddler in a frilly dress. Lots of dark curly hair. My eyes, said to be my father's eyes and similar to the ones I'd just seen peering through old wire rims in his photo, crinkled with joy and my mouth quirked in laughter. Whatever the photog had done to get me to smile had been hilarious.

Wait. That didn't happen.

The photog, an impatient older dude, couldn't make me laugh.

My father had stepped up. He'd danced. I remembered him pointing his finger in the air, in a pose I'd later seen Travolta do in photos for the old disco movie.

The all-too-familiar pang of memories out of reach. He'd died two years after that picture was taken. I think.

A revived memory that should've felt like a gift, but didn't.

The fundraiser handbill advertised a spaghetti supper at a church along with a street fair to raise money for my medical expenses.

That fancy baby dress and happy smile hid a congenital heart condition. If my knowledge of my life served me, that photo was taken before I was diagnosed.

I'd needed open heart surgery to repair a hole in my heart. Had I been born later, doctors would've let it heal on its own.

If not for the fading scar on my chest and my obsessive avoidance of junk food, I'd forgotten it all. Or kept myself too busy to think about it.

I clawed into the envelope for the hard plastic at the bottom. A thumb drive.

Basic computer security be damned.

I palmed the drive, jammed it into the side of my laptop, and booted up.

Two files, an MP4 and a PDF, which I opened first.

Only a few words of cut-out type, large font and bold faced:

"Back off the story or this video goes to the media."

You dumbass. I'm in the media. I clicked on the video file. Grainy, like old home video digitized. I clicked the audio on.

My knee jerk bravado drained.

The screen showed two cars, a long black sedan and a smaller white car like a two-door coupe. Engines idled. The shadowy profiles of men stepped in front of the headlights.

The stockier man with wide shoulders stood braced with his back to the big car. The headlight beams skimmed over slicked silver hair.

The younger, more slender man in front of the coupe, had long hair. Not the alpha in this situation, his shoulders hunched while his head stole furtive glances to each side. A glint from his face suggested wire-rimmed glasses. Under them, a dark splotch suggested a Tom Selleck mustache on a wiry body.

Considering I was watching them more than thirty years later on tech the likes they never could've imagined, the young man had a right to be afraid. He was being watched and filmed in secret.

Something familiar. I knew this man. Somehow.

My nose for news twitched, but rising stomach acid warned me I wouldn't like it.

Over the idling cars, the more moneyed man spoke. "Glad we could help you patch up your little girl. Family is all that matters."

The younger man lowered his head and shook it. "Screw you," he said, followed by a loud bleep to cover the form of address. He straight-armed out a briefcase by its handle.

"Whoa! Sloane! Nice talk for a family man. Thanks to us, you might see her walk down the aisle someday. Won't that be nice?"

Another man stepped from the shadows and made the exchange. The well-tailored man spoke with mock indignation.

The mustached man shoved his hands in his pockets and backed away toward his car. "Are we done?"

"For now." Arrogance wafted from his words like strong cologne.□

The younger man stepped forward and shook his index finger at the crew near the long car. "No," BLEEP, "Not for now. Just this once. That was the deal. I'm through."

The smaller man pivoted to return to his car. Its headlights illuminated his face behind the wire-rimmed glasses.

My chest shrank and hardened against my breath. My head spun in a vortex of present and past and new, inconceivable information.

He'd lost weight since law school. Grown his hair long. Swapped out the Mad Men tailoring for flared pants.

I sucked it up and played the video again. My heart told me who spoke the other words, but I didn't want to believe it.

So, I watched it again. The tall man was straight out of a casting call for a mobster, complete with a tailored suit, a black luxury car, and a glinting pinky ring. The angry scrappy dude mouthed off with his old beater car behind him.

When I got to the speaking part for the man with the mustache, I clicked "pause" in a string of freeze frames.

What did his office at court think of the hippie clothes? Then again, maybe they all dressed like that then. Or those were his after-hours clothes?

Even more inconceivable, what had Mom, who shopped at Talbots and Lilly Pulitzer, thought of those clothes?

Focusing on the clothes was easier.

It couldn't be him. But the car behind him was the same white Chevy he'd died inside.

I froze the screen on the clearest image of his face.

It was him. My father, the state's attorney, who by day was a crimefighter righting wrongs in a late-night meeting, let alone handing off something, to a mobster.

Thirty-Two

A new element entered my war zone nightmares, my father. Not the geeky wanna-be Kennedy pictured as a law school grad, but a rumpled, casual '70s dude with the mustache and longer hair, like an edgy hippie.

Another innocent—wait. Maybe he hadn't been so innocent as I wished. But he was still collateral damage to my life thanks to a decision he made to help me.

I tugged on leggings while wondering about the nature of innocence. True innocence. Unlike the many civilians I saw unlucky enough to find themselves in the line of fire, my father had been coerced into ignoring his conscience, made vulnerable by a stroke of bad luck.

My congenital health defect.

I'd struggled to compartmentalize. I laced my sneakers and thought of Sandy, my fixer, whose family had insisted on coming home to Baghdad to be with other family, because they couldn't afford to get them out. With the best of intentions, they decided misery needed company. Just in time for war.

Or maybe innocence laced with naivete?

Get moving, Avery. My sneakers padded along the carpeting through the gloom of my trailer. The overcast sky peeking through the backlit gingham curtains at my kitchen window mercifully spared me the mocking of cheery checkerboard pattern and embroidered daisies.

Through the door and onto the deck, moist morning air filled my chest. I eased some gentle upper body stretches while gazing at the horse pasture filling the horizon. Mist lingered over the hills and trees. My eyes made out dark cylinders on stilts, horses grazing in the fog.

Herb, I hoped, was back home with his family. Not yet arrested, but all signs pointed toward him as a classic fall guy.

Someone with juice was making that happen. Serious juice with connections to east coast crime. Out here, among the wide-open spaces and placidly grazing livestock in the Bible Belt.

Had to be Kinsale. Who was he in bed with?

I clambered down the short wooden steps—thump, thump, thump—before my shoes hit grass. Nice and easy, I trotted toward the state road, already busy with sedans and pickup trucks speeding a bit more than prudent for the curves. If you've been driving these roads all your life, like most of these locals, you can rely on muscle memory to zoom along in your sleep. I jogged in place while I assessed the traffic rhythm and spacing.

After a plumber's truck careened by around the bend, I made my move to run across the state road. With lungs burning, legs pumping, and scar tissue itching inside my leggings, I ran like hell across the road to the cemetery.

Running farther from the traffic noise, deeper into the empty cemetery, I mulled over how I'd determine the identity of the criminals in the video with my father. They still had something to lose or they wouldn't have edited their own identifiers out of the video. They'd been less generous about my father's identity. That had been all too clear. So was the implication that they killed him, which may explain why they were so modest.

A pre-emptive strike, releasing the video to my old colleagues at *News-World* would take the swag out of their case, but I couldn't do that to my mother. Or to my father's memory.

Let alone all the cases he'd prosecuted. All would be questioned in appeal. By dragging my feet or even complying with the threat, I was doing the Connecticut State Court of Appeals a favor.

Or was I? If he'd sent innocent men to jail as criminals? How long had it gone on?

I had to know who the criminals were. The luxury sedan purring in the background indicated they were successful. Still active enough to threaten while fear identification almost thirty years later.

Who was safe enough to ask? I could send Cori, the local librarian, into a search, except I couldn't be sure she could keep a secret, considering how gossip fueled the town.

If Kinsale were mobbed up and word got out that I was, more or less, calling their bluff? Besides, the Blanchard County Public Library couldn't have the resources.

But I knew who did. The riskiest of them all.

I'd have to think about it, whether or not to contact an old New York friend who followed the local gang scene like a soap opera.

After a mind-clearing run down the lanes winding through tombstones, I made another mad dash across the road and to home. Soon, some of my McNulty's stash brewed and diffused the aroma through my kitchen. While showering, I second- and triple-guessed what I'd decided to do.

I booted up the computer and snipped some frames from the video, especially frames that showed the most detail of the faces of the criminals in question.

While in the shower, I mentally ran through the wording of the email I'd send. Unless I caved and backed out. Then, I pulled on a black sleeveless tee and pants, practical mourning attire.

Recently, there'd been a lot to mourn.

Back at my laptop, I re-cropped the best stills I could grab from the video. For this copy, and purposes of clarity—so I thought—I edited my father out. The only subjects in the video who needed identifying were the thugs. I knew the identity of the civilian and it broke my heart.

I sent the photo to my phone. My primo coffee churned in my stomach. No need for more caffeine to infuse me awake. I dumped the rest of my mug into the sink and watched my precious elixir from New York pour down the drain.

Back at the computer, with the email still open, I bookended my request with the hashtag for "off the record." Then, I backspaced over the last bit and spelled it out. I needed to be clear.

I added two photos of the two goons. With my cursor over Send, I hesitated a moment.

There'd be no taking this back.

Had I said what I needed to?

I was essentially sending this to the media myself. To Sal Vecchio, my old boss at *News World*.

For a foreign desk editor, he was all about New York City, especially tri-state crime family history. When the Latin and Asian mobs hit the news more, his brain almost exploded and then he dove in, but his first love was the Italians, what amounted to his shadow folk who he insisted invented mob culture, although I'd told him culture was a flattering term for meathead criminals.

I'd only half been busting his chops.

So, with a few clicks, I made sure the goons didn't have full control over this story. They were counting on me letting them railroad Herb Olmos, thirty years and a thousand miles away. Ha. They didn't know who they were dealing with.

Then again, I didn't know, either.

The coffee in my stomach needed something to fight with. The Quik Stop would be open. I backed my car out onto the state road, busier now as the morning woke.

I yanked my car's gear shift from Reverse to Drive. Everyone, including the bastards who sent me this information, counted on me to be responsible with it. To be a good journalist.

Their definition of responsible may not have been the same as mine.

At the Quik Stop, I glanced through the front plate glass window to see Gordon sitting hunched on a stool at the counter.

An empty stool next to him beckoned. So did the memories of shared dilemmas over beers and pizza. How to handle demanding professors. What to do about sources. Alternatives to stories dead-ending.

But that was all over now. Regret squirmed through my stomach.

Not that long ago, before I'd gone rogue, we could've whistled through the graveyard of my childhood by joking about "threatening home videos from the mob." Except I'd have to explain why I received those threats.

Someday we'd talk about it. But not today.

I pulled open the glass door. Gordon remained hunched over his plate with his rounded back to me. He gripped his coffee mug in both hands under his chin.

Loss washed over me like high tide. With my arm holding the door open, I bobbled in hesitation. A week ago, Gordon would've been my go-to. Calling him hadn't even occurred to me. I'd gone to Sal, my old boss. A subject matter expert, but I'd already bypassed my old friend, who, when last we spoke, was pissed off at me.

Much slower than I'd approached the door, I stepped inside the greasy spoon and headed through the tables to the counter.

The cook and his line staff looked busy enough not to eavesdrop. I headed for the vacant stool and perched next to my boss. "Why are you here at the counter instead of at home?"

He stopped blowing on the coffee in his mug. He didn't look at me but gazed unfocused at the pass-through window where some cooks worked the line. "Shannon had to go help her aunt in Nashville. She's having cataract surgery."

I glanced at what was left of his plate. "But school's still in session. Teddi, too?"

He shook his head and gazed at what was left of one of the breakfast specials. Gordon had made a dent in the split biscuit swathed in creamy sausage gravy, probably off limits at home. A sunny side up egg and a slice of bacon remained. "School. Not much longer left in the year. Shannon's parents are keeping her once school lets out."

I eyed the lone slice of bacon. Forced myself to look away. "Right." I shifted conversational gears. "Too bad Shannon's aunt couldn't schedule her surgery for after school ended," I said with faux cheer. "You could've made it a family trip."

Without looking at me, he said, "I also have a reporter I have to stay and watch. She's more trouble than Teddi."

Ouch. His flat tone stung more than his words. I wanted to sting in return, but it was Gordon. "All the more reason to get away."

He propped an elbow on the counter and turned toward me. "You should take another run at that reservist home from Iraq. Jerry Johnson." He returned to his plate of congealing grease.

Leaden resentment hit my gut. "Terry Johnson," I said with no cheer in my voice. "His name is Terry."

What kind of editor jumbled names like that? Especially hometown names? A race thing? No. Not Gordon. His lapse could've been anything from a brain fart to a carb coma, or even a jab at me.

"So, what's the problem?" Gordon broke the yolk on the remaining egg and watched it seep across the plate. "His story's not big enough?"

My breath caught in my throat. I glanced around at the other stools for other customers busy talking to each other or poking on their phones. The counter staff was busy and so were the line cooks.

I leaned closer to Gordon and murmured so nosey ears wouldn't hear. "Herb Olmos's trouble is crap. I have info I can't talk about yet. Big stuff." Well aware of how dodgy that sounded, my voice faded and creaked. I cleared my throat. "And it rattled me."

Gordon's gaze never left his plate. "Cy, then Herb. Countless troops and civilians in Iraq before that."

Pain shot from my jaw to my head. My mouth flexed, as if words wanted out, but for once I changed my mind. Instead, I said, "I saw Herb working on his horses that night. He was spotless after he'd supposedly bashed in someone's brains. Unless he's got enough money to have a second riding suit he could change right into—and who'd do that; you'd change into jeans and a shirt—let alone enough time to wrinkle up the fresh one like that one is." I added, "I believe he's innocent."

His shoulders rose then lowered as if they'd released air. "I heard a lot of unlesses."

I winced and took a deep breath to suppress my urge to attack. "I'm gonna find out who's out to get him. But first, I'm going to talk to Terry." My voice punched the correct pronunciation of his name.

The server came by. I ordered two black coffees and an oatmeal without milk, but with nuts and strawberries to go.

Gordon concentrated on his biscuits and white gravy.

I filled in the silence. “Plausible deniability. Good move. Big Daddy can’t smack your knuckles.”

“Take your food and go.” Icicle tone.

I hopped off the stool with the cardboard tray with two cups placed diagonally across from the other. “When did you start fighting harder for comfort than the truth?”

Then, I realized I was doing exactly the same thing by sitting on the video. I believed I was determining what was the truth. That I was being responsible, not evasive. Or was it delaying the inevitable?

Gordon swigged some coffee and asked, “When are you going back to the war?”

Thirty-Three

Out in the Johnson family backyard, Terry and I sat across from each other at a warping wood picnic table. His daughter, Shanice, sat in the middle of a nearby sandbox equipped with plastic toys. She filled buckets and played with plastic horses with comb-able pink and yellow manes and tails. Terry's mother was away at work.

"My mom wants this interview. Thinks it'll help me out in the county. With jobs. And with people on those jobs. I don't know what got into her head."

Who was I to argue? Let alone screw this up, as self-interest chimed in. "Maybe it will. It couldn't hurt."

But odds were, everyone in the county knew who Terry Johnson was. Newcomers would see his photo in the story. I suspected, with our readership, his abundance of muscles and melanin would count more than his words.

"I'm no hero." He tapped his thumb on the handle of his ceramic coffee mug. "A hero wouldn't jump every time that damn noon siren goes off." He tightened his lips and lowered his head to shake it once or twice in each direction.

"I hate that horn, too. Why don't they decommission it or update the system?"

He scrunched his nose and shrugged his bulky shoulders. "That's just the way it is. Always has been."

"Right," I said with an eye roll of dismissal. "Tradition first, last, and always." We sat here in an awkward interview he didn't want in an attempt to make his life easier as the powers-that-be, who he hoped to impress, embraced a structure of what they called "traditions" which didn't include him in any way he'd want.

He shot me a slit-eyed stare. "Just cuz they're not your traditions don't make 'em wrong."

Crap. I'd misinterpreted. I'd soon be explaining a second failed-interview attempt to Gordon. That I still cared felt both pathetic and like I still had hope.

"Point taken." I raised my hands, palms out, in the jazz hands version of surrender. "Every place has traditions it's willing to fight to protect."

He settled his bulky frame into a more neutral position. "Damn straight."

I repressed my sag of relief. The interview was back in play.

I'd stowed my notebook and phone recorder away to let our conversation loosen up.

Soon, Terry's real story came out in vignettes and pieces, tracking along a storyline I'd heard time and again from other veterans. Jobs were scarce and spotty, so he'd enlisted in the Marines because not only did he want to serve his country, but, well—The U.S. Marines.

As he spoke, I remembered Gordon referring to Terry as a reservist.

Oops. Details, Gordo. Details.

Terry's story continued. The sharp excitement of deployment turned into stretches of boredom punctured by the horrors of war, spitting in the eye of his action-hero dreams. He signed on for another tour and served as an MP. As the calendar ran out, all he wanted to do was protect his buddies and, almost as an afterthought, make it out alive.

What he didn't say, but I suspected, as much as he'd missed home and his family, he'd return to the Sandbox in a heartbeat for another tour to help not only the buddies he'd left behind, but his fellow Marines.

Not what his mom, nor my big boss Kinsale wanted to read. Or Shanice, after she learned how to read.

Kinsale wouldn't want this account of the war in his paper, even if it explained why someone home with family would want to go right back into the suck.

Terry's real feelings ran counter to my mission's goal.

Later, Terry himself might not prefer to see what he'd told me, in print.

But I'm not supposed to care, just report.

"Thanks for talking to me as a person." I didn't add, as a buddy. Too weighted, too new. "We'll need to spend a little time talking about things you don't mind being in the paper." My sympathy for his position and my stern journalism ethics battled in a fierce tug-of-war. Then, I said, "I can talk you through it."

In my imagination, a gaggle of my journalism school professors waved their hands to stop me. Also, a memory of Gordon's voice, sounding tired, *We still have to live here.*

He said, "I'm no hero. My wife even ran off with a Jody."

He used the military slang for guys back home who were busy stealing girls from serving troops. The androgynous name also worked for female troops.

"You know that has more to do with them than you," I said as much to myself as him.

Maybe with repetition, I'd believe it.

His gaze reassessed me. "Hmm. Sounds like you know about that, too. You look more like a grunt by association by the minute."

Dread slithered in my chest, like a snake coiling and writhing, warming up its muscles for a fast escape.

I remembered the mantra I lived by halfway around the world under a harsh unforgiving sun: *I may be among them, but I'm not one of them.*

Taking photos is so much easier. You can hide behind the camera. Interviewing takes a chunk of your soul. Nobody tells you that, even though j-school professors lecture about detachment and objectivity. In the field, face-to-face, you have to give a bit of yourself to get.

These days, thanks to my recent decisions, my imaginary professors were swigging cheap gin.

I heaved a deep breath of determination and resignation. "I'm not sure how long it was going on. Some people blew off steam in the war with choices they wouldn't have made at home. The last dot fell into place when I was stuck in the hospital."

"After you got that body art," Terry added. He wagged his finger toward my legs.

Sharp and wary, I searched his eyes for the leer. The last time I'd seen Terry, I'd rolled up my pants leg and flashed him some skin, what was left of it. Other men might have wondered how far the scars traveled up my leg, but concern coming from his eyes told me otherwise.

I took a swig of coffee before saying, "Let's go back to the subject of my divorce." Somehow, the relationship seemed more important.

Terry said with a scowl. "So, he left you while you were laid up. For reals?"

"The vows say 'in sickness and health.' Nothing about collateral damage." I flashed a fake giddy smile. "Loophole."

His mouth tightened into a line as flat as a Ka-Bar combat knife. "That's cold. Didn't you want to kill him?"

An astonished snicker slipped out of me. "How?"

Uh, oh, Avery. Wrong answer. In this circumstance, replying "No" would be correct.

I decided to roll with it and continued, "You could say my schedule was too full. Surgeries, treatments, physical therapy, other tests. Plus, I spent a lot of time hooked up to tubes, bandages, and beeping monitors. Where was I gonna go? What was I gonna do?"

His nod to encourage me to continue included a grim mouth suggesting he was giving me silent "atta girls."

I said, "Why did you ask? Did it occur to you? To kill Jody. Or whatever his name is?" Or her? But my instinct told me not to inquire about gender choices where everyone embraced conservative values. "By the way, I'm asking you off the record. We are gonna have to get back to business soon. I'll have my notebook out and everything."

His hand swatted the air as if he were shooing away a fly. "Nobody I care about any more would miss him. But I'd watch him and wait, knowing I could kill him with just one blow at any time."

A chill shot through me like a jagged bolt of frozen lightning. A marine who was a little girl's daddy had just confessed to stalking The Other Man. Terry, as a trained U.S. Marine, was walking, live ordinance. One half of a perfect storm, a miserable Marine with a philandering wife.

For how long had he lurked in the dark and imagined killing that mook?

The flush creeping up his neck indicated it was still going on. Probably after Shanice went to bed, especially on nights his mother went out to meet friends or to a book club.

My newfound family drama issues, thanks to the blackmail material I'd just received, tugged on my mental sleeve and reminded me I'd shoved it aside.

Damn. I'd enjoyed about an hour of war stories and avoided dwelling over my own new domestic drama—the one I never knew I had. Until last night.

I controlled my breathing and words. "You know you can't be stalking this guy, right?" I said as if he'd confided a guilty desire, more of a venal sin than a capital crime. "Please leave that guy alone."

His nose wrinkled. He cast me a sideways "just teasing" glance that I didn't believe. "I won't do nuthin' to him. I just like having the power, holding that power over him, and him not even knowing it."

The thundering inside my head drowned out anything my ears could hear. "Still too risky. He's not worth it."

"He ruined my family. Dammit. I get she was stressed out and lonely. I can't blame her, but I can't forgive her."

Which doesn't mean you don't love her still.

Shanice gripped her toy horse by the barrel and rocked it over the sand like a stiff-legged Arabian horse bounding over the dunes.

"You are irreplaceable to your daughter. And to your mother."

He sagged, as if I'd snatched away a comfort. "I know. I'd lose my baby. She's the most important thing in my life now." He added, "I have to remember that."

The little girl rocked the model horse onto its squared hind legs as if it were rearing. Near the corner of a house, a yellow butterfly flitted around a spear of bleeding-heart blooms waving in the gentle breeze.

"I look around here and see a pretty sweet situation while you figure out what's next." I tap danced as fast as I could, and not just to save my interview. "You know I'm a voice of experience, and the way I see it, you've got two really great—wonderful, really—reasons to forget the stalking and focus on the next chapter of your life."

He tapped his mug once, like a judge's gavel, on the old wood. "We got a little time before that siren goes off. You might want to ask me those questions Mr. Kinsale wants me to answer."

I picked up my notebook and phone recorder. I knew I'd only get this one shot.

Thirty-Four

Back at the office, with a queasy stomach, I picked through a draft of my Terry Johnson interview. He'd agreed to a photo with Shanice in his lap. In the one I chose, she had asked him a question and they'd made eye contact for a laugh they shared.

We'd massage his wartime experiences, but not to play nice with Kinsale, who wanted a hero story, but to softball it so Terry wouldn't need to relive what amounted to be the darkest and, yet so far, most exciting period of Terry's life.

Complicating matters, Terry's lingering rage at his ex, the mother of his daughter, still tugged at my heart and subconscious mind.

At least I didn't have a child, nor other sustained ties with my ex, except for memory. Did I miss him, He Who Shall Not Be Named?

Back then, I'd had too many issues—doctors, physical therapy, the nightmares—to go all early Taylor Swift on steroids with weapons.

Nor did I fantasize about violence toward the woman who broke us up. Yeah, the betrayal burned and left short-term scars. Once the sour adrenalin ebbed, I realized she'd been part of his own pattern, like I'd been, only he'd kept me for longer.

At least I wasn't seeing The Other Woman everywhere, like Celia, the woman who'd accosted me on the steps of the funeral home at Cy's funeral mistaking me for the other woman.

A discomfort I couldn't place itched through me. I needed another perspective. I saved what text I'd written and shot a glance toward Laverne, who was taking a classified ad from a wrinkled man in overalls and a plaid work shirt. He could've placed it online or phoned it in. But if he owned a computer, forget a smartphone, I'd be surprised.

I pushed my chair from the desk. This was either a good idea or a good idea about a week too late, considering my boss was angry with me.

Gordon hung up his phone. In about six steps, I sat in front of his desk. I said in a low voice, "What would you do if Shannon left you for someone else?"

His eyes went wide enough to push the color from his face. "She left to go help her aunt." He blinked twice. "Where did that question come from?"

I didn't want to lie, and I couldn't betray Terry's confidence, what with him finally talking to me, marine to—well, Another Person Who'd Been There Too.

"Forget I asked." I braced both hands on the chair arms to stand. "Brain fart."

He rocked to lean in his swivel chair. "Lemme guess. Terry Johnson skunked you again?" A teasing grin creased my boss's face but didn't reach his eyes. "No. Wait," said the man who'd known me—and thought he'd known me—for a year and a half of school "This has to do with the McCoy story." He tilted his head to assess me from down his nose. "You can't leave it alone. I might as well accept it."

"This is a small town. How do you not know about Terry Johnson?" My turn to wag a finger. "Oh. Right. You don't run in the same circles." I used the euphemism. "Let alone live in the same neighborhood." I could dog whistle right back at them. I slathered my words with disdain. "Imagine that."

He flicked an "oh please" glance at me. "The last I heard, Terry Johnson had a little girl. Maybe before marriage, maybe not—"

I rushed to say, "Not that there's anything wrong with that."

Gordon raised both hands as if to surrender. "And then the mother up and left while he was overseas."

"Avery, honey." Laverne drawled at me with her left hand braced on her hip and her right holding a manila interoffice memo envelope. "It's about time we had a talk."

Gordon said with a little whine, "Don't spin her up."

I wasn't sure who he was talking to. Me or his office manager who I always kept forgetting was his aunt.

But I would be happy to spin up Laverne. "Silly me. I thought Gordon and I were having a private conversation."

She waved her hand with a scrunched face. "In here? An open office?"

To her, I said, "I'm listening."

"Let's go out back." To him, she said, "We'll only be a minute. Maybe two. Be a dear and watch the phone."

She flung the steel door open to the alley, which ran parallel to our street and behind the storefronts. A cat slunk away from the dumpster behind the Quik Stop four doors down at the corner. The reek of stale leftover cooking grease crowded my nose. I knew from being places where I'd smelled much worse, that if I hung tough, my nose would ignore the stench.

I said, "Go ahead. Spill."

"Not until I say my piece."

What? After dragging me outside? "What happened to *Trib* teamwork? I'll just throw a little extra in the cuss box. A charitable contribution, not an investment toward future swearing."

"You think you were a big deal because you covered war. Well, why didn't you tell the stories about the good our boys did over there? All we ever heard was the bad. Then Gordon somehow talks Clark into hiring you and, just our luck, somebody got killed in Blanchard County, so you're focusing on the bad here, too. There's plenty of good around here. Why can't you focus on that?"

Her gaze drilled down into my soul.

I said, "What about that story about Cy McCoy's life with horses? Or even the interview I did with him when he won Teacher of the Year? And right this moment, I have notes on that new Youth Arts Crew *and* a feature about a hometown hero from that very same war."

Except my mouth went sour on that sentence. Terry and I had massaged that story.

Laverne folded her arms, and then said, "Do you want the skinny about Herb or not? Tell me why you're all fired up about this."

I thirsted to shock her. "From the way Cy died, his killer would have been covered in tissue, shattered bone, cast-blood, even flying brain matter."

She paled a little. Inside my gut, satisfaction settled in with comfort, only to spark a pang of shame.

Come on, Conscience. She had it coming.

I continued, "When I saw Herb Saturday night, he was wearing a vest, shirtsleeves, and tie, all a little rumpled. I'm betting it's what he wore into the show ring."

Laverne waved off the theory with a flash of pink nail polish. "Riders take off their show coats and hang them up between classes so they don't get rumpled. They're expensive with long hems, almost like tunic tops, so if you sit in them, the cheaper ones get mussed, especially on young trainers who show a lot of horses, like Herb. But you don't know nothing about that cuz you're one of them snooty hunter-jumper people up north."

Her last sentence landed another punch. After my mother remarried, she made sure my stepsisters, not only got to take riding lessons, but got to ride in horse shows.

"We" could afford it then. An old sore point I preferred to repress and deny.

I had to maintain.

"Like I said, if you bash a man's brains in with a garden tool and then chop on him for a while, you're gonna get messy. In all sorts of places."

No flinch this time. She folded her arms and said, "Like I said," she echoed with emphasis, "they take off their jackets. Maybe he'd already taken his off when you saw him?"

"He had taken it off and he was working on his horse. His vest, shirt, and tie were clean. Maybe he'd pulled on a hazmat suit for a murder?"

"State police found the murder weapon in the pond where he rents stalls." She stepped closer, getting into my face. "Come to think of it, that's where you live, too."

I held my ground. "Are you suggesting I could've done it, too?" The police were looking hard at Herb. That wouldn't stop them from looking at someone else. Like me, who may have left a stray hair in Cy's car when he drove me to the dealership after lunch to pick up my car.

"We don't know you. Gordon and Shannon only knew you for—what? Maybe a year? A long time ago. For all we know, you could be capable of anything. And from the way you act, that wouldn't surprise me in the least."

"So, I may be capable of murder... and you brought me out to a lonely alley?"

"You'd do nothing of the sort after Gordon and them all witnessed us coming out together." She jerked her chin toward the office door. "You're too smart for that. Anyway, I hate to pee on your parade, but I know for a fact Herb could have killed that man."

The man who cooed over his horses and sent his family home from a horse show to keep them safe. "Hello? Have you met Herb?"

Then again, the kind Terry Johnson doted on his daughter and was a trained marine with kills he'd never mention. Killing in war was one thing. Killing as an act of rage? Only where strong emotion churned. Terry had admitted to stalking the man who'd stolen his wife.

Laverne continued, "Start with testosterone. Add ego. Then that whole Latin macho thing. Herb got into Cy's face at the last horse show last year."

Nice play, wrong target. If I called her out on her bigotry, she'd walk away and tune me out and feel superior. "Lots of people argue," I said. "Even white people. Just like us right now."

"Maybe where you're from. Definitely online, especially those tree huggers with crazy ideas about how we keep our horses. But if one told another, 'Stay away or I'll kill you,' and the one that got told died, then the speaker would be a suspect, right?"

More information was more information, even if it didn't support my theory. As a journalist, I should've expected that. As much as part of me thirsted to throw down more with Laverne, I had to gather myself together and stay on point. I said, "So, what were Herb and Cy McCoy arguing about?"

"I was just a passerby, a lookie loo on the way to get a Coke. I didn't hear it all. Herb's wife was yelling at him, too, to stay out of it. She could handle it."

"Still could be anything." But I doubted it. Those words and that kind of territorial energy suggested one thing. The same vibe had come off Celia at the funeral. And Terry.

Small town. Small circles.

No way could Cy have been Terry's "Jody."

I hadn't asked Terry what he'd been doing the night of the horse show, even though I'd asked almost everyone else except Laverne.

Going berserk on a guy with a shovel wasn't a marine's style. Bare hands and bare knuckles, even a knife. A lot of men in the area wore folded hunting knives on their belts. I doubted Terry had been at the horse show, but I knew someone else pulsing with betrayed rage.

"What do you know about Cy McCoy's ex, Celia?"

She waved her hand as if to dismiss me. "I don't know much about that bunch in Lexington. Mavis used to be Clark's housekeeper and Cy's momma, his cook. Both of them up and quit to move away to take other jobs. I can't imagine why. Clark and Polly treated them like members of the family."

"Family paid by the hour," I added.

Laverne ignored me and continued, "Then, Mavis hit the lottery big."

"So, Mavis set Celia up in business?"

Laverne flashed a nodding, knowing smile. "You do know more than I'd thought. A little beauty shop in Lexington." She heaved a resigned sigh, "I reckon I have to spell it out for you. The story is, Cy liked women a little too much for his own good. Married, single, white, black, brown—he didn't care. As long as they were beautiful. I figured he made a pass at you during that interview. Especially with you now on a tear to hunt for his killer, I figured y'all connected. Or hooked up." Disdain filled her voice. "Whatever the kids call it now."

Unease scratched around inside my throat. Why hadn't I noticed this? Years of working in a male-dominated field, in a war zone where testosterone not only romped unchecked but was rewarded, and this hadn't crossed my mind.

Unlike the man Laverne described, Cy had been calm and cool. We'd even talked about my ex.

I struggled to keep my mind on task. What else hadn't I noticed? If he'd been a womanizer, how had he remained a teacher, let alone an honored teacher? On a more personal note, had he been such a hound, why hadn't he hit on me after dinner?

I stilled the wilder questions flailing inside my mind. "We conducted the interview as fellow professionals." Even the business dinner we shared, which I opted not to mention.

Laverne's smile lit as if for an aha moment. "Oh. He *didn't* make a pass at you." She reached out and patted my forearm. "I'm sorry, child. I reckon you didn't suit his taste. I'm sure you've been told your beauty is of the quiet sort. And you're single." She wrinkled her nose and scrunched her shoulders in glee. "Too risky for him. You might've wanted more commitment, even if you are a New York liberal."

She had no idea who she was dealing with.

I wasn't about to tell her, no matter how much I relished having the last word.

With a mysterious smile, I kept my gaze on her and dug into my pants pocket for my phone as if it had vibrated. I slipped a glance at the screen and then quirked my smile into the creepy zone.

"Thanks for the chat," I said. "Gotta hit the street."

Despite whatever else had been on my calendar, I planned to go beyond "the street" onto the highway. First, I'd look for contact info for Mavis, even if I had to ask Hazel to consult her Christmas card list.

I needed to check out a hairdresser.

Thirty-Five

A quick web search on my phone showed me Celia's business wasn't simply "a beauty shop," as Laverne had said. Nor was Celia a hairdresser.

The Glow Salon and Fitness Center was a family-owned business with Mavis Clement as CEO, which gave me tips on how to contact the family's—maybe even community's—matriarch.

On the website, Louise, the former Kinsale cook, was listed as head dietitian. Celia was the aesthetician, and her brother was the personal trainer. In the photos of the hair stylist and massage therapists, I spotted family resemblances.

The website had said walk-ins were welcome. I planned to be one. But I also left a message with the desk to pass on information to Ms. Clement that I'd be in town that day, maybe even a client at the salon.

On the highway to Lexington, my phone rang. I glanced at the caller ID on the phone stuck to the dash to see "Salvatore Vecchio." I tapped my earpiece.

My former photo desk editor's voice sounded as New York as a tugboat horn. "You don't call. You don't write. Until you want something." He *tsked* with too much *brio* to not be busting my chops. "Worse than my kids."

I'd missed that give-and-take. "Your number hasn't showed up in my call log lately, either, pal."

"How did you get that picture?" Straight to the point with intensity setting off my internal alarms.

"Who are those guys?" I managed to squeak out. I hoped Sal mistook my shallow voice for a bad connection.

"Who are those guys?" His voice swerved into the shrill zone. "My God. How could you not know?"

Oh, crap.

"We don't share the same historical interests. Who are they?"

"Believe it or not, it took me a while. I almost didn't recognize him. This is an old, old picture. Believe it or not, the guy in the suit is old man Rikesi."

Shock snatched away my breath. Not just a criminal, but *the* criminal.

"*The* old man Rikesi?" *Please, Sal, mistake the rise in my voice as excitement, not dread.*

"Old Dom was a big dude before he got old. I mean, really old, like he is now," he said with inordinate cheer coming from a man who reread *The Godfather* like most other people reread *To Kill a Mockingbird* or *Gatsby*. "The last of the old school dons." Sal's voice went wistful on that last sentence.

My throat went dry and my palms slicked with sweat. I straightened my fingers on the leather-wrapped steering wheel and then wrapped them again.

"Yo, Avery? You still there?"

I ended the call.

A tidal wave of nerves swept over me. Too much. It was worse than I thought. My father. *The Rikesis.*

A car horn blasted me back to the present. A jolt shot up through my spine. Drivers here didn't honk their horns like northerners did.

Swerving around me on the right, a massive white Cadillac SUV sped by. Its elegant driver with her silver hair set off by her tan flicked a gaze down her nose at me and my tiny car. Stuck to the rear bumper was a pristine, not ratty with age, sticker for Reagan.

Maybe I'd better leave the fast lane and pull over to gather my wits.

I drove my car onto the highway shoulder and rolled to a stop. I put my car in Park, folded my arms across the steering wheel, and rested my forehead on the back of my hand.

The freaking Rikesis. Who'd run New York and New Jersey back in the day. One of those old crime families now deemed defunct. Even quaint by mob geeks like Sal.

What had my father done for the Rikesis to pay for my surgery?

I needed my mind clear. To stay present. To make a decision.

Alone. No calling anyone for advice. No *just asking for a friend.*

Traffic whizzed past me with bigger engines roaring. The wind they stirred up shook my car. A tractor trailer almost rocked my small car hard.

The police were focusing on Herb, but I didn't believe he'd killed Cy. I just couldn't prove it.

My obsession made about as much sense as home movies from the mob. Why had they kept the footage, guys whose fathers and grandparents refused to use a phone, like in *Goodfellas*?

Maybe the cops couldn't prove Herb did it, either, but not without leaving his character as collateral damage.

On the other hand, if I proceeded with my own investigation, I'd upend or destroy my family's and my father's reputations. I'd cast doubt on all my father's old, closed cases. Those doubts would trigger appeals and lawsuits.

I heaved a deep breath to still the shakes. I tugged a water bottle from the cupholder, grasping the bottle so hard the plastic crunched.

Had my father let someone guilty go free? Or an innocent to jail? What had he done for the money to pay for my surgery?

Then, something had gone wrong. He'd complied with them, but implication from the extortion package was he'd died at their hands and they'd gotten away with it. For years.

Weirder still, did the Rikesis realize their threat to me implicated one of them?

A deep drag from the water bottle refreshed my dry mouth. I let my gaze relax, to look around.

On my side of the highway, billboards announced the next exits' offerings. Chain hotels and chain fast-food joints, some national, some more regional. One promoted "old-timey country cooking." Its logo included a sketch of a plump woman in a homey dress and a full apron, her white hair tucked into a bun.

A nostalgic fantasy to women living in capri pants, sneakers, or cowboy boots with little time to cook.

Had my father felt he had a choice, what would he have done in my shoes. If he hadn't had a sick child to protect.

I like to think he would've done his job.

Part of mine, because the story fell in my lap, would be to check out his story. Some how, some way.

After this road trip.

Closer to Lexington, the farmland, promoted by the tourist bureau, yielded to car lots and national chain big box stores. The Mini Cooper dealership where I took my car was nearby, as was the bookstore where I'd run into Cy and the restaurant where we'd grabbed dinner. Increased traffic slowed my progress.

On the northeast side of town, older stores and buildings greeted me, including strip malls. I spotted the sign for the Glow Salon & Fitness Center about the time my nav system announced I had arrived at my destination.

The glass front revealed a reception area sectioned from the treatment rooms with tall shelving holding beauty products. Two slim young black people, a woman and man in their twenties, stood behind the desk. In front stood a woman client consulting her phone as if booking a new appointment. I pulled the glass door open and stepped inside.

Almost cooler than the air conditioning was the mellow instrumental jazz. The young woman with gleaming box braids and flawless skin the color of a dark brown imported English saddle glanced at me and smiled.

"Avery Sloane for Celia." I'd tried to make an appointment to see Mavis to no avail, so I scheduled a facial.

She checked the schedule on the desk computer. "Celia will be with you in a moment. Please relax while you wait."

No relaxation for me. Had to be on my game. "Thanks. Standing's good. Long drive."

I tucked myself into a corner where I could pop out the door. I scanned for a second exit which would've been through the salon fitness center. The gap past the partition led to the salon and, presumably, a delivery entrance.

The woman paying with a credit card said her smiling goodbyes and see-you-next-times and then spun on her sandals to give me an odd look.

"You?" I heard Celia before I saw her. "What are you doing here?"

She stood with lab coat open and the collar twisted as if she'd tugged it on in a hurry.

"This will be your easiest appointment ever." My voice sounded hoarse. "All I want to do is talk to you. I'll still pay for booked services." I offered a what-can-it-hurt shrug. "My plastic's still good."

"Don't you people have a rule about not paying for news? Or has that lame paper you work for gone full-on tabloid?"

"I'm not paying for news. I'm paying for a facial. But I'm willing to save your effort and products to talk."

"Are you sure you don't want a facial?" she said as if she'd like to have me at her mercy. "That sun damage could use some plumping up. We could start shrinking those pores, too."

Yay. Thank you for noticing. "Not today. Thanks. Today, I just want to talk. Just for a few minutes." Her lips compressed, her mouth tightened, so I added, "I'm missing something. Alright? Something I'm not seeing. I was hoping for your or Ms. Clement's perspective."

She heaved a sigh and then said, "Come on, then. Let's get to it." She gestured with a graceful arm and a hard glint to her gaze.

She opened the door that admitted me deeper into the business. The salon and fitness center may have looked like a cozy hole-in-the-wall place from the front, but it ran deep into what had once been a box store.

I followed her down a narrow corridor with the several closed doors suggesting treatment rooms. Not knowing if anyone would pop out of the doors sharpened my situational awareness.

The walls without doors displayed a gallery of high-resolution photographic portraiture of elegant African men and women wearing regal headwraps matching the fabric prints of their outfits. Intricate gold jewelry glinted on ears and fingers.

I could hear the bass of rap and the clink of weights a few steps down the hall. Celia opened a door with an "Authorized Personnel Only" sign before I got to see the fitness area. I half expected a supply or a break room. Instead, the room was an office with a sleek table and a closed laptop computer facing two straight-backed chairs. I spotted another door on the other side of the office by the desk.

Celia closed the door and gestured toward the sofa on the wall opposite the desk. Above the sofa hung another gallery, this time, an arrangement of family photos, some snapshots, some studio portraits, and some old celebrating milestones like graduations and weddings.

I squinted at the signature in the lower right corner. "I may not be a photographer, officially, anymore," I said, "but these portraits are breathtaking. Gorgeous work." I didn't recognize the name.

She crossed the room to one of the dining room chairs facing the desk and turned it to face me. She said, "The photographer is talented. A distant relative in Senegal."

I stopped admiring the photos. "I'll just dive in. The police are sniffing around Herb Olmos for Cyrus's"—I made sure to use the more formal first name—"murder." No softening that. I added, "Do you have thoughts on that? Off the record?"

She wrinkled her nose in distaste and even huffed. "I'm not into that horse stuff."

Interesting how she mentioned the "horse stuff" first, like most of the Blanchard Countians.

"But you know he had some role in the horse community, probably from Cyrus's role. That the person of interest is a brown dude sounds a bit too convenient. Don't you think?"

Her left brow arched. "I'm sorry you drove so far to see me," she said as if she wouldn't be sorry if I spontaneously combusted, "but I don't have anything to tell you. Let alone for a newspaper fishing for scandal. Especially not for some white savior wanna-be."

I didn't take the bait. I liked her attitude.

"You had plenty to say to me at the funeral. Enough to make me suspect Cy had a thing for other women. Maybe he chose the wrong woman? Or maybe you think he was killed for something at the horse show? Like a ribbon. Again, what you tell me is off the record."

I'd been willy-nilly generous with off-the-record lately. I'd have to correct that bad habit. On another story.

Time to go for a pressure point. "Did you kill your philandering ex?"

"Hell, no. Don't think I didn't want to kill him last year when we broke up. I sure as hell wouldn't have done it last week at one of those horse shows."

Through an assessing squint, for good or ill, I said, "I heard the show horse your aunt just bought caused an upset and a stir that night." I shut off and waved my hand as if to erase the air. By leaning into the horse angle, I was now as narrow focused as those horse-obsessed Blanchard Countians. "Who else would've had an argument bad enough to lose it and want him dead, do you think?"

She ticked off on her fingers as if she could count plenty of reasons. The one she mentioned was, "One of those crazies fighting over the kinds of shoes horses wear?"

"Someone would kill over that?" came out of the mouth of the former war photographer still carrying shrapnel coated in dirt halfway around the world from a millennia-old conflict.

What she said put my thoughts into words. "For some people, it doesn't take much."

Her gaze slid past my shoulders. She pressed her mouth shut. Her emotions welled behind the barrier of mascara and threatened to spill down her cheeks.

I broke my own rule about letting them fill the silence. I heaved in air and hoped I'd get through what I had to say.

"I got cheated on, too," I said. "We met in Baghdad and then ran off to Jordan to get married. I thought I'd changed him." I stood, and added, "But that doesn't matter. Here? Now? I still believe the cops have the wrong man."

I leaned forward. "I believe the cops have the wrong suspect. They say they're following the evidence, but I'm not so sure. I think there's a lot here I'm not seeing. I want to find out what really happened. It won't be easy."

My mind flashed on that grainy still image of my prosecutor father dealing with gangsters. I added, "And it'll cost me. Big."

Going against the wishes of my immediate superiors. Maybe prompting the release of the story that would recast my father as one of the bad guys.

She unfolded her arms to fan her eyes. "You think you know a person." With tight lips and a clenched jaw, she shook her head as if she were squeezing back tears. "Give me a minute."

Her eyes glistened behind her elaborate mascara and eyeliner, but she maintained. "I found out Cy preferred cheating with married women because they weren't interested in commitment. Called it his 'catch and release' program. Like we're catfish or bass."

"Catch and release" stuck. I'd heard it before and recently. Common, but not that common. I'd deal with that soon enough. I asked, "Why'd he get engaged then?"

"I have no freakin' idea. You want some herbal tea? Coffee?"

I waved a "no thanks" and lowered my voice into a sympathetic purr I didn't have to fake. "So, why did you zero in on me at the funeral?" I raised my left hand. "Like you said, no ring?"

There was no more white skin from the desert tan. Not even an indented ring mark. Like I'd never worn a ring, like the marriage had never even happened.

Celia pulled me out of my spiral of self-pity. "I'd heard about a brunette woman from the north. Not Ohio or Pennsylvania north. More like New York or New Jersey north. Big city. When I heard you talking on the steps of the funeral home, I was sure it was you."

Sylvana popped into my mind. Another brunette living in the area. Talking about good Italian food. Cavalier "catch and release."

Couldn't be.

I said, "Lexington's full of people from other places. The colleges. Horse racing—"

"Horses. Yeah. And kids. This one had kids. Lived in Blanchard County, too. Shoot! Cyrus and those damn ambling horses. He loved those horses and even that tired Old South scene. They still play Dixie at those horse shows. Can you believe that? Hangin' on to the past like the future'll drown 'em."

After I left the salon-gym, I sat in my car, pulled out my phone, and thought about what all I'd learned.

The mystery woman I'd been mistaken for was from New York or New Jersey. She had horses. Kids. And was about ten years older than me.

I didn't like where this was going. The web of connections taking shape, but there they were. At the truck stop, Sylvana had used the term "catch and release."

I rolled the dice when I circled toward Man O'War Boulevard.

I didn't have time to go in with intel. Calling anyone on the staff, like Wilbur, or especially Gordon, would get me scolded or ratted out to Kinsale. Besides, anyone at the *Trib* only had our own news story files and basic internet access, not Lexis-Nexus.

Not even the county library had access to the database I needed, but I was on leave from a place that did.

I called a contact at my old office, but not Sal's department. The clerk who answered had been my intern when I worked in the city for a few weeks.

I told her the same search parameters I'd told Sal and then a little extra. Sylvana's name, her current husband's name. Also told her Sylvana was an artist and her husband Joe or Joseph worked for the—I had to think of the mall anchor store—and threw that in.

Come to think of it, I wasn't far away from the mall.

Thirty-Six

After parking my car, I waited in the department store office while listening to elevator music and wondering how I'd introduce myself.

Hi. I'm Avery Sloane. I'm friends with your wife. Thought I'd stop in—

Maybe not that one. Dropping by a new friend's husband's office—a man I'd never met?

I should've texted Sylvana. A friend would do that, give her friend a heads-up. Or not even go. I'd have time to call her after I left. Maybe before he called home with a "Guess who I just met?"

Except he'd tell her it wasn't an accidental encounter.

So, Introductory Sentence. Take two.

Hi. I'm Avery Sloane. I'm with the Blanchard County Tribune, *and . . .*

And, what? What business could I be there for?

This may be Lexington, a big city by comparison to tiny Bowmansville, Blanchard County's county seat, but Dobbs may have picked up the small town propensity for blabbing. Like Harlan Davenport and Grace Johnson, he could call my office and rat me out to Gordon. Or, more likely, over drinks with Kinsale at the nineteenth hole after golf at the Fairmont House.

My skin crept with the "bad idea" warning. That night at the lake with the bruschetta, Sylvana had told me a bit about him. As the phrase "catch and release" had stuck in my mind, so did her phrase "sweet mope."

What damage could I do, playing a crazy hunch to satisfy my curiosity? I could see how it played out and then make a spin control plan.

I had to see for myself if I thought Joe Dobbs was capable of killing a man.

"Hello. I'm Joe Dobbs."

Sylvana Dobbs's husband was a pale balding Charlie Brown with glasses in an inky blue suit, a striped tie, and a starter paunch.

I stuck out my hand for a networking handshake. "Avery Sloane. I'm in town on business and thought I'd introduce myself. Sylvana has told me so much about you. You have a lovely home."

My voice felt off, thin and edgy. A deep breath firmed my handshake.

I'd told the truth. Or close to it. Stopping by was the neighborly thing to do. And I was depending on his own sense of southern business manners for him to not punt me.

"Yes. Of course." His eyes darted around as if he had a million places to be. And he probably did. "Please do come to my office for a moment."

Perfect. "I can only stay a moment." I wanted to see his office, what he'd display for business contacts. Family pictures or an ego wall? "I don't want to keep you from your duties." I didn't remember his home showing much about him. Maybe his workplace would show how he presented to other people.

I followed him past the counter checkpoint into the maze of offices. I tried to notice how his minions reacted as he walked past. Would they dive into busy work? Or shoot furtive glances our way? They kept busy at their stations.

While we walked, he commented on my lack of a southern accent as a lead-in to ask where I was from. I told him Connecticut and New York and omitted my detours into the Middle East. I told him I'd met Sylvana through her work with the Youth Arts Crew and remarked about her rapport with the kids.

That was my plan. To talk up Sylvana, so he didn't get the wrong idea that I might be flirting.

His office featured a coffee-bean-brown leather sofa with two armchairs upholstered to match.

"Please have a seat." He walked around his desk to his chair, the doing-business position. "I was about to have some coffee, Miss Sloane. Would you care for a cup?" He headed, or more like trundled, toward a single-cup coffee maker on the counter of a cabinet of dark wood.

His diction carried a trace of Massachusetts in his soft "r," but the way he accented certain syllables indicated his voice was absorbing southern cadences.

"Just a quick cup," I said, remembering my manners to accept what's offered. "That would be great. Thanks!"

While we chatted, I scoped out what décor hung on walls. Two large fine art photographs of iconic Kentucky scenes. One of mares and foals grazing on lush grass under blooming spring trees, another of an old barn surrounded by fields of wildflowers.

No trace of Sylvana's edgy art. Probably smart, considering the store's area and demographic of upscale conservatives.

I scanned for family stuff that managers set out so their staffers called on the carpet could see signs that, yes, they were relatable. Family folk. Just like them.

And sure enough, there it was. In a folding double picture frame standing open like a book on the windowsill behind his desk, images in full view of who sat in the dual chairs.

On one side was an elbows-up portrait of Rick holding a bat as if he were waiting for the pitch. But he looked grim and all-business as if he dared the pitcher to strike him out. An embroidered orange and black Blanchard County Demon cartoon menaced from his shoulder.

Next to the baseball shot was the picture I expected to see, in some form or another, a portrait of Lexi with a dark liver-chestnut horse with a half-moon shaped star. They stood cheek to cheek, nuzzled against the side of a gleaming show bridle topped with a cream-colored vinyl browband matching the cream-colored braided ribbons hanging from its forelock and down its mane. Like a good hunter rider, her hair was up and sleek, with tasteful makeup under a grey derby hat topping a grey suit with a cream tie and vest.

With Dobbs basically sitting next to the pictures, which child was his and which he'd gained by marriage, was obvious.

But Sylvana's photo wasn't next to him. There was no hint of her, except for that sly predatory glint in Rick's eyes near the bat.

I made the usual social noises about his nice-looking family. Yes, thank you, he was proud of them. My heart warmed and I couldn't suppress a smile because of the way his eyes sparkled when he talked about both of his children, the fair-haired horse princess and the dark-haired jock.

I had to pony up, too. A good interview is often an exchange.

No. No children of mine, except for nieces and nephews far away. I didn't add that they thought I was nuts because their parents and grandparents did.

That's when I spotted the photo standing in the corner by his desk.

There she was.

Sylvana with her tumbling curls and direct gaze in a moody headshot for an artist.

He, of course, said that he looked forward to my company at dinner when he was in town, but, of course, he was very busy and retail hours ran long. Hint, hint.

I may have been lying when I told him I looked forward to dinner. After this, dinner with the Dobbses might be swept off the table.

After a few polite sips of the coffee, I uttered the expected "thank you for your time" and "catch you laters."

Then, I rushed to my car where I could call Sylvana. I pulled out my phone. While I had been sipping black coffee and assessing Dobbs's photo collection, my former intern had left a voice mail message. She had results for me, but too much to leave in a voice mail.

While still in the parking lot, I called her back. Instead of my former intern's breathy voice, my old boss's voice boomed into the phone. "So," Sal said with a boom of a challenge in his voice. "What gives you the right to call my intern to do some research for you?"

Thirty-Seven

I gulped at hearing from my old boss under circumstances beyond my control.

"She used to be my intern," I said. I should've expected him to find out. *News World* was a lot like a small town.

"Why do you have her looking into the Rikesis?" He may have been busting my chops again. Or not.

That department store coffee rose in my throat. "The Rikesis? Whoa! Dude. I asked about some woman named Dobbs down here in Kentucky."

"The plot thickens." Triumph lilted his voice.

The coffee in my stomach burbled like a volcano's simmering caldera. "Hardly. I was asking about the wife of some businessman from the north. Gotta be a mistake."

"You're lying through your teeth. I know you hung up on me. How long have we known each other? You gotta spill." His voice modulated with mischief. "Spill to me."

"Are you gonna put her back on so she can tell me what she found?"

"I don't have to." He cleared his voice. "About your Sylvana Dobbs. First off, the easy stuff. She was married to one of the old man's crew. One of his last crews. An enforcer."

A truck zoomed past me. My little car rocked it its wake.

Sylvana the artist as a mob wife didn't make sense, but my guts twisted to suggest otherwise. "Can't be." I said with good cheer I didn't feel. "My

Sylvana Dobbs is an artist and stay-at-home mom married to a guy who runs a department store down here."

I stopped short of telling Sal I'd just met the store manager, her second husband.

"Lemme guess. A Wal-Mart or a Dollar General?" His voice sounded merry, in dishing-the-dirt mode.

Annoyance gave me an inner twist. Had I felt insulted on behalf of my new neighbors? Had I, in the old terminology, gone native?

I said, "This one's more like a Macy's."

"Well," Sal returned us to the subject at hand. "This Sylvana Rikesi-Pascatore had some shows in SoHo—"

Blood pumping to my brain put Sal's voice in the background of my mind. As if in the distance, I heard Sal going on about "shows in the Meatpacking District" and "back when more blood ran in the streets than expensive high heels." Then, "weird 'found artifacts' sculptures with water faucets and rebar."

He stopped talking. My turn to speak.

"So, she's a Rikesi." I let some air surround that statement. "Lots of upstanding people have the same last names as criminals."

"She's the old man's great-niece." A beat of silence. "Are you two friends?"

I ignored his last crack. The old classic mob guys wanted their wives and girl children to keep their hands clean. "What happened to her husband? Pascatore?"

"Died in prison. Shanked. The obit says he was survived by his wife Sylvana and their son Michael Richard."

Richard. As in Rick. I gripped the steering wheel as hard as my sweaty palms would allow.

Yet, here I was again, enabling Sal to wax poetic on his favorite subject. He was lapping it up, too. Too bad I wasn't ready to give up everything yet. Although if the story were true, the day was coming.

Back to dishing dirt about the mob with Sal. "So, assuming this Sylvana is your Sylvana, Husband Number One dies. She meets Husband Number Two, and they move away. Do you think she wanted to get away from her family? I mean, this is the kind of place where the marshals take people in witness protection."

"Good memory. Hey, WitSec sent Henry Hill—you know, Ray Liotta in 'Wiseguys,'—to rural Kentucky."

Before I could respond, Sal rumbled an evil laugh. "Can you imagine? Some poor schmuck rats out the Rikesis, so the marshals move him to Buttcrack, Kentucky, to keep him safe. And then he runs into one of the peripheral mob princesses. Would that be rich, or what?"

I thought about the first time I met Sylvana at the Fairmont House. A busboy had dropped a tub of dirty dishes, sending me under the table, before he took off running across the tennis courts.

Which of us had freaked out the most? Me, when I heard the dishes crash and had a flashback? Or him, upon seeing Sylvana? A former mob widow.

A rush of sympathy for Rick hit me. We had more in common than I'd imagined. Our fathers had been taken when we were young and his mother had remarried and improved their family situation, both financially and from a stability standpoint.

I said, "Got anything about the boy? I only know him as Rick. How old was he when his dad died?"

"Yeah. Hang on." I could imagine Sal hunched over at his desk and scrolling down info on his monitor. "He was a little guy. About one. Wait. Two. Dammit. Math in my head."

"Your phone has a calculator. So, her daughter by Husband Number Two is about fourteen. Do you have a picture of Husband Number One?"

A pause with background clicking. "A mug shot. Hang on . . . wow." He paused a moment and then posed a hypothetical, "Damn. Who looks good in a mugshot?"

The con's son Rick was building some junior smolder already in his teen years.

I said, "Email me what you've got. But to my personal email. Especially that picture of Husband Number One."

"Why can't I email this stuff to you at the Mayberry Messenger? Is that how you're exploring life options during your leave of absence? Running down wild leads?"

I smiled at the second snarky slight. I was becoming too attached to my current surroundings.

"More or less. This is a less-than-blessed enterprise project."

"Listen, kiddo, if you've really got some kind of Rikesi family connection there, you know we want in."

"Of course. You want a taste. Tell me again how we're different from them?"

"Very funny. What is this story anyway?"

Good question. A murder of a horse show judge or an honored teacher? A random killing in a parking lot with a bit of extra rage or a hate crime? A romance gone seriously wrong? Local yokels or some kind of long-distance mob vendetta?

So, I only said, "I wish I knew enough to distill it down to a slug." I could've mentioned the murder but, if I had, he would've expected an update yesterday. No reporting, even off-the-record, until I knew for sure.

"Fine. Keep me in suspense," he said with some resignation. "But be careful. It's all fun and games until someone ends up dead. Do you have any backup down there? Wait. You're in Podunk where that Gordon Hulett's from. His dinky paper. He's a big dude, sure, but he'll be no help. When push comes to shove, hicks stick together. Watch yourself."

And yet, without me telling him, Sal had summarized one of my situations. Gordon and Kinsale, my allies here, vs the Rikesis. Figuring out the connection was liable to get me killed.

Did I want the threat against me to include Gordon, Shannon, and Teddi? Kinsale with his money and station was probably untouchable. Little people like me and the Huletts were all too accessible.

After chiding Gordon for having lost his journalistic nerve, I was beginning to understand, as I was on my way down the slippery slope myself.

"I understand," I said. I slipped the car into gear. "I'm on my own."

The wheels of my car hummed on the asphalt. We could leave our pasts, maybe even try to tell them to "sit and stay," but the memories and problems shadowed us, ready to pop out and surprise us.

Back on the highway and headed home, my phone dinged. The photo from Sal had arrived. I pulled over onto the shoulder to check out Vincent Pascatore's mug shot.

His square chin and quirked full lips oozed Bad Boy heat. His black eyes lasered the darkness of an angry soul. I'd seen eyes like his in the Middle East. Cold. Shut down. Not the thousand-yard stare of someone who'd seen some shit, as the saying went. Something else. Deep, cold, and primal.

I'd seen it in guys who proclaimed they used violence for a greater purpose for a cause but considered war permission. Like Bond's "license to kill" but with too much enthusiasm.

I realized why I was so insistent on Herb Olmos's innocence. Not just his rumpled, but not bloody, horse show clothes he'd worn. Nor his "Howdy, neighbor," attitude.

Herb didn't have the killer instinct in him.

Vince Pascatore was a killer all right. Plus, an older, wirier version of his son Michael Richard, whom I knew as Rick, except his son's face held some innocence.

Sylvana wanted to leave criminal life far north of the Ohio River, but the shadows of city streets followed her south to the country.

Like how memories of conflict zones followed me home like hungry ghosts with late-night cravings.

After I turned off the exit, the state road took me past the usual chain restaurants and motels found at highway exits and into farmland cloaked under darkness.

I needed to decide soon how I would approach Sylvana. She would find out I'd spent my time in Lexington meeting her husband. That could be no big deal. Or seal my doom.

I remembered a photo hanging on Sylvana's fridge, a family portrait gathered around a horse looking over a black plank fence. Sylvana, all wild hair, muscled arms, and gleaming sculpted jewelry. Her sturdy, balding second husband smiled with an arm around their daughter who shared a mix of his features and Sylvana's and the broad shoulders of the teen with handsome Sicilian features.

Rick was Rick Dobbs. Not Rick Pascatore. Joe Dobbs had adopted him.

Husband Number One was a hot criminal. Husband Number Two was law-abiding and generous.

Would he be enough for the flashy, vivacious Sylvana?

I felt more than saw headlights filling my rearview mirror. High like those on a big pickup truck and closing in.

I checked the road for the solid line indicating a no-passing zone. No line at all. I eased over to let the truck pass. It lingered with its grill close to my rear bumper.

Ghostly fingers brushed my neck under my hair. Dread sank from my throat down into my stomach.

A driver minding his own business would've passed already.

I wrapped my fingers around the leather-wrapped wheel and used my fingertips to flick on my brights. I shoved my foot on the accelerator, stomping it.

The sporty compact engine growled in response. The blazing headlights in my mirror shrank. My own car's headlights showed pavement branching off, a turnoff I passed.

"Take it, you bastard," I muttered at the headlights growing in my rearview. "Turn off."

Except the headlights grew. The truck caught up and followed me.

I steered the car into the middle of the road. They'd have to veer out to the wrong side of the road, let alone go off the road, to drive on my left to run me off the road.

At the next wide spot, I'd swerve out to do a j-turn, double back their way, like the submariner's "crazy Ivan." I'd pass them, see them, maybe be lucky enough to glimpse a plate number.

A clunk from behind rocked my head to thump the headrest. I released my grip on the steering wheel with my left hand and swatted the mic to use the voice command, "Call sheriff's department."

Behind me, a big engine roared. Those morons. Those headlights. They had to see me tap my headset to activate. My hand jittered along the button.

Dialing.

One, two—come on. Dispatch, pick up.

"Sheriff's department. Fortner speaking."

A harder crash from behind. My head snapped forward, then back to whap the headrest. The car hopped. The wheels left the pavement. Headlights cut a sweep through the dark across asphalt, then grass, then down toward the flat stone wall. An old thick-trunked tree stood on my side of the fence.

The stones would splat me like a kid's juice box.

All that came out of my mouth was, "Fortner—"

Thirty-Eight

I came to with a headache throbbing to a musical beat.

Weird. I'd laid off that level of partying.

Sweat broke out on my skin, prickling with heat. I gulped stuffy heated air.

The urge, the need, to kick off blankets and peel off garments almost overwhelmed me. But I didn't know where I was. Or who I was with.

Stripping off to cool off could ruin my reputation and attract unwelcome physical contact. I'd spent too many nights on assignments where I'd been embedded in units with lonely horny guys trained to be predators, their only restraint being military discipline.

I opened my eyes to total darkness. Nervousness squiggled at the base of my throat.

My shoulders stretched and found aches. Narrow straps cut into my wrists. I flexed my feet, but they wouldn't move. Lashed together.

This wasn't a flashback. I was tied to a chair.

A hot spear of fear sizzled through me. I sucked in a sharp inhale. Fabric brushed my lips and skin. Rough, loose fabric around my head like a bag. Or a scarf.

A few musical notes wove past the pounding headache. Reedy notes and hollow drums, harsh and fast. Middle eastern beats. Men talking fast, too fast for me to understand.

What I'd always dreaded had happened.

They had me.

Every horror story from captured journalists, both what had been released to the public and private tearful venting spilled in a dark bar over vodka, flashed through my mind.

Ransom demands. Beatings. Forced and false confessions to spying or committing atrocities. The excited groping of the American whore. And then, why stop there? Once the thrill is gone, it'd all stop with beheading, live on the internet.

A couple of understandable words surfaced. Was that Pashto?

Hairs on the back of my neck made my scalp shiver. Tied to a chair was bad, but tied to a chair in Afghanistan near the Pakistan border?

I strained to hear Urdu, the official language of Pakistan. *Please let me hear Urdu. Please let it be Pakistan, not Afghanistan.* As if one were better than the other, really, for a kidnapped journo.

Whatever the case, the Taliban had me, and I was on the way to their turf in Pakistan.

If I could make them see me as a person, not an infidel or a hostage or a bargaining chip, I might get through this.

Then again, woman. Taken by the Taliban.

The Master Sergeant's voice pushed to chime in with a gem from my security training, but a thought pushed him aside.

I hadn't been gagged.

I stilled my trembling long enough to issue a greeting. "*Salaam aleikum, habibi.*" Peace be with you, my friend.

They ignored me.

Not unexpected. I was a woman. A Western woman.

I repeated my all-purpose greeting. Like "ciao" or "aloha," it worked as "hello" and "goodbye."

Weaving through the atmospheric din came the realization that Arab world men had been speaking around me. Or, rather, off to my right. And they had multiple accents.

I strained to sort out different words, any keys to their identity.

The name of an Egyptian pop star.

A guy speaking Turkish had embarked on a passionate yet defensive rant about how deeply he loved her.

My head quirked to the side, as if to help me figure it out. So, a holier-than-them-all Pashto-speaking Taliban was waxing poetic about an Egyptian pop singer famous for her sensual performances?

Yeah, I'd been out cold, either from a whack on the head or some kind of drug, but the conversation whirling around me made no sense. Next came two guys speaking Egyptian and haggling over a deal. Something about brass?

Funny. From my standpoint of frightened restraint, wasn't I the most valuable commodity present? Available for ransom from an American news organization.

The heated conversations switched again. Guys in classic Arabic. Then, back to Turkish. All Middle Eastern men speaking in accents from regions that didn't get along.

Yes, the enemy of my enemy is my friend, but these guys had held tribal grudges against each other for millennia. All in several different conversations. From sexy pop singers to haggling over brass trinkets.

My panic faded into weird confusion. I sniffed the air in case I was surrounded instead by secular thugs smoking something recreational, something taboo. All I picked up was my stale coffee breath.

Then, I recognized a rant I remembered from the news, a voice I recognized as a Palestinian politician.

Growing strength from solid certainty reeled back the fears fighting to fragment me. The soundtrack of my captivity was different speeches or conversations edited together. An audio clip reel from the Arab world.

Back to the pop singer's super fan.

Weird.

Whoosh. Another room, surrounded by journalists fresh from New York, Los Angeles, and London, all fired up to cover the world's biggest story and fronting casual slouches to hide our unease.

The Master Sergeant strutted the room with bombast and bristle. *Don't you gormless pencil pushers try to escape unless you know where you are and where you can run to.* He prowled the room hunting for nervous tells. *Be the trained observers you keep yammering you are.*

Another memory surfaced, of the huge pickup truck looming in my rearview mirror. My taillights gleaming off new chrome. Not an old beater.

I wasn't in Afghanistan or Pakistan.

I was in Kentucky. Maybe near Bowmansville, where I'd been living and working.

Not a war zone.

The pickup's lights had seared into my rearview mirror. I'd slammed into the low stone wall. An airbag exploded in my face.

Someone had run me off the road, kidnapped me, gone to a lot of trouble to gaslight me. Like that old movie in which the husband convinces his wife she's going mad.

Not only was I being gaslighted, but by someone who thought every speaker from the Arab world sounded alike.

I had to get the hell out of here.

Except for that audio looping, maybe I was alone. I wiggled to assess my injuries.

My shoulders strained from the zip ties clamped around my wrists behind my back. I wriggled numb fingers. Shifting vinyl chafed my skin. Salty sweat stung the wounds.

Man, it was hot. Whoever had me paid attention to detail, except for a lack of appropriate regional cooking smells. I was sweating all over and about to make my own body odor.

I'd have to cut the damned restraints. My fingers strained for a thin metal edge within reach. Nothing.

Seeing would make escape faster. Could I get this damn hood off my head without my hands?

I smacked my dry lips against the folds of fabric sticking to the perspiration on my face. My head throbbed with the twisting, turning, tilting back, and gumming at the fabric. I tasted salt from sweat, along with a bitterness and grit I'd rather not try to identify.

Hair clung to my lips. I hoped it was mine. I spat it out as best I could. Then, I nodded and rocked my head back and forth, like a headbanger chick, even tried to snake my head around in the bag.

My reward for my efforts? Failure, plus dizziness swirling my brains in the dark. My heart hammered so hard my pulse filled my ears.

My kidnapper would return soon. I was still exactly where they wanted me, except for one thing. I now knew I was on American soil.

A door hinge creaked. I stilled my breath to listen.

A latch clicked. Flooring creaked from heavy footsteps with the sound growing closer. Heavy plastic crinkled.

That creeped me out more than anything. A drop cloth under and near my chair?

The other person stood out of reach but nearby. As if waiting.

Would my original plan work now? Try to come off as a person, not a captive? Could I negotiate my way out?

I braced my voice with false confidence. "Just let me go," I said into the bag over my head. The words croaked and creaked.

I repeated them with more projection to get past the soundtrack and added, "and this never happened."

Silence.

I added, "Please," an even-toned 'please,' as if I were asking a waiter for the check.

No reply. No footsteps closer. Another squeak zinged down my nerves. This one was metal against metal and higher than the floor.

Items in a wooden box rattled, as if a hand rifled through a junk drawer. A male voice snapped an expletive. In English and with the force of a city street.

The drawer slammed shut hard. The contents rattled.

My captor was American. *Try again.*

"You win," I said. "Epic prank. You had me going. Untie me. We'll call it even."

A male musk, with a spicy top note, wafted my way. Like a body spray.

"Look." Deep breath, count to four. Exhale, then count to four. "If you can set me free and make sure I don't get hurt badly enough to need professional treatment, no cops ever need to know. I'll even tell them I fell asleep at the wheel and hit the stone fence."

Shut up, Avery. Stop adding stuff you can't deliver. Tied to a chair and blindfolded for no telling how long after a car wreck, I had no idea about the true extent of my injuries. Stupid, stupid.

I'd even given them the option to go ahead and kill me.

"You'd do that?" a familiar male voice said in the darkness in front of me. Amazement rose with a grace note of naivete. Definitely young. "You'd forget the cops?"

Thirty-Nine

Man, that voice was familiar. Teenage even.

The bag dragged over my head and hair. I took my first breath of fresh but humid air. A harsh single source of light beamed at the floor, burned my eyes, and squashed what glee I couldn't suppress.

A rectangular shape. A phone flashlight. A here-I-am beacon brighter than the Christmas star.

I blinked and squinted. "Thanks, but damn, that's bright." I had to keep him on my side. "Turn that light off. Might give us away." Someone else could come or even be well on their way.

"But I can't see where I'm walking." A hint of a young male whine?

Still couldn't figure out who he was, even though the voice sounded familiar.

"Turn off the flashlight," I said, abrupt. *Keep it soothing, Avery, he's a kid.* "Your eyes will adjust."

My eyes cooled and adjusted first. Who the hell was my rescuer? A dim red light illuminating his face like firelight.

"Rick?" I said over the still loud mixtape loop of Middle Eastern conversations. "What are you doing here? We gotta get out of here." We. We. From here on out, it'd always be "we." Somehow, I had to get him on my side.

He held my blindfold as if he'd unveiled a surprise. He said, "Holy crap. I gotta turn off that racket." He pivoted away, toward a waist-high but wide, dark silhouette. My eyes adjusted to note the sheen of an open laptop monitor on a kitchen counter.

"No!" I coughed from forcing my voice. "Leave it on. It's cover. Can you do something about these restraints?"

Shapes formed in the room. Old-style chrome kitchen table and chairs. Uneven plastic shimmered on the floor. Doors cracked open to what looked like bedrooms and a bathroom. Smallish windows letting in some moonlight.

"Okay," he said. "I can see now." He shoved what was in his right hand toward my face. The shadows of wire clippers nestled in his fingers. "Hold still and be quiet." He dropped to a crouch at my feet. He pawed around my ankles to find the zip tie.

I stayed quiet.

His voice came from behind me. "This is crazy. Geezus. The heat's cranked up in here. It's freakin' May. Who runs a heater in May?"

Below me a snap, loud enough to sound like the crack of a tree limb in the silence. My legs relaxed yet burned as circulation returned to them. My knees opened in relief. Cool air snaked inside my pant leg. In moments, I'd have to stand and move fast.

"Thanks." I flexed my ankles to speed the reawakening. My feet responded with pins and needles and fire.

"Shh. Geezus!" Impatience pitched his harsh whisper. "If they come back and catch us, we're both toast."

They? From the guy who'd just used a flashlight to sneak in? Even scarier, sending my breathing shallow, was, when would they return?

What to do next flashed through my mind. How had he known I was here? Was he one of my captors but with a conscience? Could I knock him out and run away on my own?

Another plasticky snap from behind me. My hands dropped away from each other.

My shoulders returned to a normal forward position. I creaked my arms to a normal position toward my front, only to feel the prickly warmth of sensation returning to my arms with a vengeance. I rubbed my wrists, slick with sweat stinging the abrasions I couldn't see.

I was free, but I had no idea what Rick's role was in this whole thing. Rescuer? If I had to fight him, could I? No weapons of opportunity revealed themselves to me in the dim cabin light. Even if I could sucker punch him and hit him hard enough to slow him down. "Gormless pencil pushers" like me weren't taught hand-to-hand combat techniques aside from don't get caught.

Time to see how this would play out. I said, "How do we get out of here?"

"Stay close. Don't knock anything over."

I let Rick blaze the trail through the cabin. No moonlight penetrated the darkness. That he knew his way around told me something I didn't want to accept. The knowledge tapped with impatience at my gut. I'd do something about it. Soon. If I blurted out my growing suspicions I had to ignore, I'd go nowhere fast. First, I had to get off the bounds of the property. Wherever I was.

We went out a rear door that opened to a small clearing that led to the woods. With the blaring computer audio fading behind us, the song of bullfrogs ponging got louder. I inhaled humid air carrying a rich peat that suggested more canoes and burgers, followed by the alarming flash of a memory of red wine and bruschetta.

The lake. A lake. Maybe Bowmansville Lake. Where the Dobbs family had a cottage.

"No matter what you step on, or in," he said in a whisper, "be quiet."

Snap under my feet. Had to be a branch.

I risked a glance toward the cabin. Maybe the chattering audio, now fading behind us into the woods, covered the racket of our escape.

We dodged trees and bushes reaching out for us and climbed a steep hill. Never before had I been so aware of the tactical advantages of stealth.

"Watch out," he said. "There's all sorts of squirrelly shit living out here."

The least of my worries, City Boy.

A clearing opened around a compact SUV with a gravel road leading from it.

He opened the door. "Let's go."

I hesitated. My skin prickled. What was his role in this? He knew that cabin all too well. Was I escaping one captor for another?

Rick's cooperation and my safety probably hinged on me pretending I was clueless about who'd kidnapped me. No questions. But no questions might look suspicious. I opted to ask about something expected.

"Where are we going?" I climbed into the SUV and eased the door shut behind me.

"I'll take you to the bus station in Lexington. I don't carry enough cash for a plane ticket," his words ran together at this point, "and I didn't think we had time to look around for your bag and your credit cards. Sorry."

Nor my phone.

He started the engine and was smart enough to ease the SUV out without hitting the lights.

Keep calm. Keep cool. *Breathe.* But with my gut cramping, belly breathing didn't work.

After a few yards and a turn, he switched on the headlights.

What could I say? How could I say it? Just to keep him talking. "So, bus stations and plane tickets. I'm guessing this wasn't a prank?"

The SUV rocked and dipped on the curvy narrow roads by the lake. Still in the lakeside subdivision, I glimpsed flashes of street names I'd remembered from staring at the county map hanging on the *Tribune's* office walls. I recognized "Cygnet Cove" and "Kildeer Run."

He switched gears. Then, he smacked the gear shift handle. I jumped.

He said, "What was she thinking? That you'd go bonkers just because they made you sweat and listen to Towel Head TV? Geezus!"

The subdued glow from the dashboard lights showed me his face. His eyes opened wide, maybe less to see the road than to face his worries.

Then, his voice veered tone as fast as his turns. "Did you mean what you said about the cops? As in, no cops?"

My mind assessed my situation with the clinical detachment of a battlefield computer. His mother, Sylvana, had kidnapped me or had me kidnapped. How far would she go? Especially with Rick talking about me lamming it out on the bus.

I couldn't keep that promise to keep the cops out of it. Not for long. Funny, the lies I'd told over the years to get at the truth.

Except this lie, that I'd be silent to the cops about him, might save my life.

Anyone else involved? The deal wouldn't apply. But would he go for that deal? To free him on the grounds I'd implicate someone else in his life.

We'd left the lake area and were headed along the road with the cemetery, my trailer, and, eventually, town.

He didn't press me for an answer, and I was glad. Because everything I knew implicated his mother.

Had she killed Cy McCoy? Wrestling scrap metal and welders gave a girl some mad upper body strength, maybe enough to bludgeon a man with a heavy shovel? All it'd take would be a first sucker punch. Yet . . .

Breaking me out of a captor's cell and driving a getaway car was a young male athlete with bulky shoulders and a thick neck. I'd seen a photo of him swinging a baseball bat. Was he on steroids? What if he took enough to have killed Cy in a fit of 'roid rage? Would I need to worry more about getting away from him?

And how far would he go to protect his family?

"Like I said. No cops." I'm not a fool. I chose to lie. "Just get me to Lexington." Closer than Louisville. Lexington had phones I could use to call the cops.

He and his sister would go into the custody of their dad, who surely wasn't part of this craziness. Or was he? I didn't have a stellar track record with my observations.

He slapped the steering wheel with a meaty hand. "Cuz I'm serious about no cops." The dash glowed enough to let me see veins standing out on his neck.

"No cops."

Instead, I checked the side mirror for lights and then swiveled at the waist to look behind us, which also allowed me to keep him in my line of sight. We'd left the secluded lakeside neighborhood and headed toward dark pastureland.

He'd been looking in the rearview. "Where are they? Why aren't they chasing us?"

Unless we were supposed to get away.

Yet, my breath caught as if the thought snatched it from mid-air. My stomach flipped and twisted like a plane landing at the Baghdad airport to dodge rocket propelled grenades.

What if they'd doctored the car? Would Sylvana do that? Who was the crazy one now?

From pretty bad to way worse.

In the Smart Girl's Guide to Avoid Serial Killers, "don't get in the car with a man" is rule number one.

I glanced at the roadside to figure out where I was.

Bad news and good news.

I recognized the voids left by the black plank fences bordering the Ward Farm.

I didn't have butterflies in my stomach as much as a swirling vortex. I had to escape my rescuer.

I rested my right hand near the door handle. Swung my gaze around to see into the night. Now or never. Alive or dead. I popped open the car door. Felt the damp night air blow past my face. I flung myself from the seat into the dark Kentucky night.

Forty

I tucked my head under both raised arms as I hurled out of the SUV into the darkness flanking the country road.

My pulse thudded in my ears. Seconds crept while I felt suspended in mid-air. I squinted one eye, my right eye—my camera viewfinder eye—for a peek.

A glimpse of asphalt, flanked by a pea gravel, then a slope into a ditch. My left shoulder hit the pea gravel, slamming air from my lungs.

I skidded on my side across the nubby gravel until the slope. I slid down the hill toward the shallow water filling the bottom of the ditch.

The gloopy mud I'd splatted into felt chilly and gross. I flipped over to my hands and knees to crawl farther away. Humid night air warmed my face.

Above me and to my right, tires squealed. Panic sat on my chest and squeezed my throat. The night sky spun around me. As long as I stared at the stars and didn't rise to peek over the edge, he couldn't see me.

A car door popped open, the keys-in-ignition bell dinging. Over the racket, Rick shouted. "Avery? Avery!"

He called out again, "Where are you? What the—? Don't be stupid."

So, he didn't quite know where I was? I froze, not wanting movement in the dark to betray my position.

Now what?

He ranted, peppered with obscenities, and then, “Are you crazy?” More swearing and a thump making me think he’d kicked the SUV’s tires.

We both knew then I’d break my promise and call the cops.

The closest phone was Rick’s, but no way. Where was I? I thought about the road away from the lake toward Bowmansville. Much of that property bordered the Ward Farm.

But I’d have to leave the ditch.

To leave the ditch, I had to tone down the reflection from my skin, runoff mud from a cow pasture or not.

I jammed my fingers into the gloopy mud and flipped my hand to smear mud all over my skin. I had to bring myself to smear it on my face, too. *Think of it as a facial that could save your life.* I held my breath and smeared the goop on my face.

My immune system inoculated for the bacteria thriving in a war zone had better be ready for stateside.

My sharp inhale revealed no stink. Just fresh, more or less, mud with some decaying vegetation. A cow pasture on the other side of the culvert probably drained into this ditch, too, providing a smellier variety of decayed vegetation.

No time to worry about bacteria on my face. I eased myself into a crouch and dared a glance toward him.

About twenty yards away, he stood outside the SUV and faced away from me. He pivoted and swiveled to scan the field ahead.

“Where the hell are you?” He sounded louder, angrier, closer. The keys-in-ignition bell dinged like saccharine klaxon. He swung his arm from the shoulder to slam the passenger side door shut. The key warning still clanged, connected to the open driver’s door. He swung a leg and kicked the right front tire again.

His tantrum provided cover. I had to move, somewhere, even if down the ditch toward the way we'd come. I shifted only to hear the mud suck against my skin. Good thing the car engine still ran. Rick might not be able to see me, but without the car noise, he might hear me.

He'd be searching the dark for me. I had to move, but to where? Not out into the field ahead. He'd think of that. Behind us, back where we came? Would've been nice to have a plan beyond just get away.

The word "gormless," popped into my head. Something about don't escape unless you know where you're going. Delivered in a sneering northern England accent.

I could claw my way out of the ditch behind Rick—because only a moron would run back in the direction from which we came, so it was an awesome move—sneak around behind him, steal the car, and drive to the cop shop.

If I were fast, if I didn't slip or make noise.

Way too many "ifs."

A dark pickup slammed on the breaks behind the SUV.

Now Rick had company.

Was it the black pickup that ran me off the road?

Did it matter?

I ducked into the culvert and crept through the bog toward a clump of trees by the fence line.

Above and away from me, a car door popped open. More dinging of a key warning alarm.

"What's wrong with you?" A sharp-voiced Sylvana, sounding more distant as I crept away along the culvert. "Thinking with the little head?" The smack of a hand slapping skin.

Then, louder, she said, "Avery! I know you can hear me."

With the sinking feeling of my escape plan falling apart, I listened from my hiding spot in the culvert behind mother and son, my kidnapper and her son, my rescuer whose motives were suspect.

Rick spoke in response to his mother's interpretation of his rescue or kidnapping of me, that he'd had other plans for me, rather than taking me to a bus station.

"Christ, Mom, I don't have to take it. Especially from an old lady like her? With some of the hot girls around here? *Mom*, I have standards."

As they argued, I reassessed my plan to jack Rick's car. They were too close.

I began creeping my way away from them.

"You ruined my plan. It was working, too." She continued her scolding.

Good. The more they focused on each other, the farther away I could get. I didn't dare stand up, in case I attracted attention.

"That was your awesome plan?" Rick's voice vibrated with self-righteous rage. "You told me you had a good plan."

"It worked. See? She went crazy. Who jumps out of a moving car?"

"She sounded okay when she was talking."

"Are you sure you weren't thinking with your—"

"Like you have a lot of room to talk."

I dragged myself away from eavesdropping and got a move on. The soggy ground squished with each step. My clothes wicked moisture from the boggy culvert.

Where was I in relation to any houses? I shuffled through my memory of the big map on the wall at the paper. The road to the lake ran along a property line of the Ward Farm.

Get to a house. Pound on the door. But the Dobbses, acting more and more like the legendary Rikesi crime family, wouldn't back off if I involved others. I'd put innocents in danger, too.

Sylvana and Rick would follow me or know the area well enough to predict where I'd run.

"Avery?" Sylvana's voice, modulating with phony friendliness. "I know you're out there." Impatience sharpened her voice, "Avery!"

They still couldn't see me. Not only was I glad I'd smeared myself like a commando and hadn't gone blonde, but I'd also continued the Manhattan custom of wearing all black. Which didn't matter as the mud I'd caked myself in itched as it chilled.

"This is crazy, ya know," she said, as if they were on a mad impromptu midnight taco run, "running out in the dark. With cow shit everywhere."

If I weren't careful, they'd smell me if I made it out of the cow pasture. Had to get some distance between us.

I crept down toward a clump of trees and bushes by the road. The wire fence twisted through the vegetation, making the obstacle shorter.

I clambered out of the culvert, crunched down the wire, and threw a leg over the fence into the pasture. The rough underside of the plank scuffed my cheek.

"Fine." Sylvana shouted, answering her own question. "Just walk away. Alright? We can all walk away. No harm. No foul. Just forget everything that happened tonight. The deal you offered Rick. It's back in play."

My deal had also been a lie.

We all had too much at stake to let bygones be bygones.

Let alone the poor sap the cops had been circling for murder. How had I gotten into this mess?

I rolled over and then doubled into a crouch, to keep my face turned away from their voices. My eyes adjusted to the dark. I had put more distance between us.

But not enough.

Sylvana called out into the darkness. "Every family has secrets, Avery. Dirty laundry. Some things are permanent stains. You know what I'm talking about."

Her words, laden with meaning, sent a chill across my skin, almost making the mud harden and crack.

Not only was she too close, if I could hear what she said, but I knew without a doubt Sylvana knew my new secret.

Her grandfather knew my father, paid him off for the surgery that saved my life. Payment for services rendered. No telling what. Yet, somehow he'd pissed them off enough to kill him.

Shame and frustration shivered with my fear. My prosecutor father not only knew gangsters but was beholden to them. All because of me, to pay for an operation to save my life.

Bottom line—he was dead because of me.

I was the only person who could stop them.

I had to get away from them and report.

I had run away to escape tedium and expectations at home to cover war. Funny how I hadn't run away from war but had been too damaged to stay. Then, I had run away from the noise of the city to a peaceful land with horses only to find, not only more conflict again, but peril. And it wasn't just me. With Herb standing accused and his family on the brink of ruin, I had to save them, too.

Like a mouse avoiding a vigilant cat, I crept along the shadowy tree line. My feet crunched on old leaves. Snapped dried twigs. I wheezed with nerves and stumbled in the dark.

Would Sylvana and Rick be determined enough to catch me by following me? Depending on their vanity to keep their shoes clean was a thin tactic. Mud was one thing. Cow manure?

I had stepped through worse for a day at work.

A little cow manure wouldn't keep them from protecting their futures.

Still, I could end my pain about my father, my nightmares, and return to them. I knew too much. Maybe they'd even do the Bond villain thing and tell me their entire plan as sort of a goodbye gift. Then, they'd kill me.

After Iraq, wasn't I living on borrowed time anyway? An IED hadn't taken me out. How many chances would I get?

Around me, the cicadas' singing and chittering ebbed and flowed. Cattle groaned and rumbled with the occasional distant moo. A bullfrog ponged out his song and reminded me to watch out for a body of water, like the pond where Herb had exercised the horse only a few days ago. Which meant I had to be close to the barn.

Ahead, the big Ward barn stood on a hill, silhouetted against the sky, against the clouds. Tucked in beyond the trees near the barn stood my trailer and Hazel's house.

I crept around the wide thick oak near the pond where I'd watched Herb work horses in the water.

With the tree between me and my pursuers, I leaned against the knobby bark, caught my breath, and assessed up my options.

Where to go? Home?

Now, I was totally without a phone because I didn't have a landline. I hadn't thought I needed one, because I had a cell, which was wherever Sylvana had stashed it.

Note to self. Always have a backup phone. A burner. A landline.

If I got out of this.

Plan B. Go home and get on the laptop to call the Blanchard County Sheriff's Department via voice over the internet.

Which would take a lot of time. My pursuers had cars and better knowledge of the area. They could drive instead of slog through a dark pasture. Then, they'd isolate me in my own home.

Unless Hazel heard something and got nosey. Then, they'd have her, too. A home invasion.

I'd lead Rick and Sylvana, willing to kidnap and maybe even murder me, to an innocent. Like my old fixer, Sandy, who'd been murdered because he'd helped me.

The barn. I'd seen a landline in the barn, an old wall phone with the spiral cord. Unlike Kinsale's barn, which was up to date with modern conveniences, the Ward barn had a do-more-with-less vibe. If any place had an operational landline, it would be that barn.

I made it into the rear door of the barn, left open so horses and cattle could come and go. I tucked my body along the inner frame to catch my breath.

My eyes adjusted to what light slipped through the windows. The hum of horses munching, shuffling through wood shavings, and snoring greeted me.

First one dark horse head popped over the stall's half door, then another. A series of silhouetted heads with perked ears and wide nostrils checked me out. What if they called out looking for food? My breath caught at the thought.

Good thing I'd never fed them or they'd be whickering and kicking at their stall doors or feed buckets. Also, I hadn't come through a door they expected people to enter.

The phone was around the corner from what I knew of as "the crosstie room." I patted the walls to help my eyes find the phone. My shaking fingers snatched it from the cradle, only to find no dial tone.

Clutching the useless hand set I leaned against the rough wood and slid down like undercooked spaghetti. My shoulder throbbed in protest. My legs crumpled under me. The mud on my skin dried and itched.

Now what? Dash past the riding ring, go around Hazel's house, break into my house to Skype the sheriff's department?

A familiar woman's voice, raspy with sleep and age, called out.

"Who's there? Mighty late if you have horses here." Her voice modulated with a veiled threat. "Sing out now."

Hazel? Oh, no. Not Hazel.

Forty-One

The horses recognized her, too. They nickered and rumbled with suppressed excitement. Finally, someone useful who knew the way to the feed room.

I called out, "Get out of here, Hazel. Call the cops."

I slipped into the tack room and tucked myself under the shelving holding the grooming potions.

"Avery?" Surprise lifted her voice into a shock.

Much louder, forcing my voice. "Go now. *Go.*"

I heard a smack, a squeak, and the soft thud of a something falling and landing.

"Didja hafta hit her, Mom?" Dismay throbbed through Rick's voice. "She didn't see us."

Sylvana called out, "We have your landlady."

My eyes and heart sank in dismay. Another innocent. Like Sandy and his family, in the wrong place at the wrong time because of me.

Rick's voice swooped in amazement. "What did she think she was gonna do with a shotgun?"

A shotgun? Why not just call the cops and watch from the safety behind her sheer curtains?

"How long have you lived here?" Sylvana harrumphed. "Kentuckians."

"Why'd ya have to hit her?" His voice veered into a whine. "She was one of my best customers. She gave me sweet tea and tips."

His mother ignored him by calling out, casually, as if she'd spotted me out in town. "Avery?"

"Mom, she's not even in here. Let's go before anybody else shows up."

"She's here." Sylvana sounded in charge. "Avery—" No more questioning tone, but more of an order. A click, then the ratchet of a shotgun racking.

My heart almost leapt to land in my throat and cut off my breath. Was Sylvana so hardcore she'd shoot Hazel? She'd left the Rikesis for what she must've assumed would be a safer life.

Plus, the sound of a shotgun blast in the middle of the night would carry. It'd be like calling 911. But then what if they hit something or someone?

The faces of all the young lives Sylvana's poor choices would damage flashed through my mind like a slide show. Rick's. Her daughter, Lexi's. And the kids of her precious Youth Arts Crew.

Sylvana's voice called out, "Come on out, Avery." Her voice carried through the dark barn. "Let's get out of here. Your landlady will come to thinking she slipped and fell."

Riiight. We'd all leave together, except for Hazel who'd be out cold on the barn floor and then wake up to wonder where her shotgun went. Sure.

What kind of damage could being knocked out do? Blunt force trauma wasn't so great for the young, either.

I had to decide what to do. So far, Hazel wasn't in additional danger, especially if she lay there and stayed quiet. If she'd been wise, she would've called the cops from the house. She'd suspected the intruder had been someone she knew, who'd answer when she'd called out.

Sylvana said, as if biting off each word and as if in hopes I couldn't hear, "Let me handle this."

Horses shuffled their bedding. Some munched hay and sloshed water. Another kicked the wood of the stall in a demand for food.

Sylvana spoke again, “I know you’re in here.” Her voice echoed the kicking horse’s impatience. “Somewhere.” She added, “This is between us. Let’s all get out of here and let the old lady wake up on her own.”

Rick again, “I’m just saying, not everyone I cut grass for is that nice. And nobody around here tips. Except her. Down here, it’s not like New York where people tip. Ya know?”

I appreciated his hindsight kindness toward Hazel, but what the hell was wrong with him?

“Shut up,” Sylvana, with her voice on the edge of losing it, said to her son. A moment of horses chewing, then she said in a lower voice, “I’ve got this. Keep an eye on her.” Then, louder, “She’s light. Rick can carry her. We may take her with us. Avery, I’m losing patience.”

I leaned against the wall and pulled the old journalist’s trick, let ’em keep on talking. I let Sylvana stew in the silence. If Hazel had done the smart thing first, the law would be on the way.

“But once the old lady wakes up,” she called out to me, “you’re both out of time.”

Forty-Two

Tucked in the shadows of the crosstie room, I listened, partly to maintain the silent treatment to avoid betraying my position, and to listen for any stirring from Hazel, knocked out somewhere in the barn.

Sylvana called out again. "Rick was taking you to a bus station, but I can do better. I can get you on a plane." She laughed shrill and hollow before saying, "Hell, I'd rather go with you, and not just to keep an eye on you. I could use a vacation." Her closing sentence had been loaded with fatigue. I'm sure she'd love to get away.

Right. We'd catch American to LaGuardia. Then, we'd go in together on buying the Brooklyn Bridge. Maybe the sellers would throw in a chunk of Williamsburg, too.

I strained to hear what was going on with Hazel.

Sylvana's voice swelled with exasperation. "This *place*. If I weren't married into this life?" The question hung in the air, like mine and Hazel's fates.

Then, her voice turned triumphant. "That's it. You're staying for *him*. That's why you keep this crappy job. For him."

What? Him? Him who? What the—

"He's not the type," scorn dripped from her voice, "to be happy with catch and release. Would you, who's covered the biggest news of our time, be happy spending the rest of your life keeping the books for a *veterinary practice*?"

What the—?

Oh. *Right.* That damn wine and bruschetta on her deck by the lake. Some sassy talk about how good and unrecognizable Norwood had looked at the funeral. When Sylvana and I were on the way to friendship.

She'd play any angle to get a rise out of me. For me to give away my position. Soon, she'd send Rick after me.

Let her. Why not kill time? If Hazel had had any sense, she called the police before heading to the barn with a shotgun. The longer I worked through that thought and Sylvana still chattered, the less likely the property owner had called the cops first.

"For chrissakes, Avery. What are these people around here to you but a punchline? This is your opportunity to get the hell out of here."

And let Herb take the fall? Not a chance.

But that was knee-jerk bravado. A twinge of guilt pierced me anyway. She had a point.

I'd often assumed the worst, that parochialism threw up impenetrable walls around my perception of narrow minds. Overseas, I was more generous with my benefit of the doubt. Back home? Not so much.

The cops weren't coming, I realized with a chill. I was on my own.

And Hazel was way too quiet. Had they hit her harder than they'd led me to believe?

I had to check on Hazel. To get her some aid.

My shoulder ached where I'd landed adjacent to the road. My skin itched where the mud dried. Considering I'd thrown myself out of a moving car, I was damn lucky or I had injuries adrenalin masked.

To think I could've been asleep enduring sweaty nightmares about war and collateral damage.

I couldn't have another innocent's death on my head. Maybe them killing me was my time? I'd cheated death so many times. Sometimes, living to tell the tale is a burden. Time to unload.

Time to trade myself for Hazel.

But it would cost them. I hadn't figured out how yet.

I called out, "Let her go."

"Then stop screwing around already and come on out," Sylvana said. "Come out and we won't hurt her."

I stepped out into the barn aisle. Sylvana held a pistol. Rick had the shotgun.

I said, with my hands at shoulder level and palms out. "Let me take a look at her. Reporters headed toward hot zones are trained in first aid."

"That's ridiculous," Sylvana said. "No way. Stay there and keep your hands up."

I stopped mid-step. "Oh, yes way. Before you head over to a conflict zone, you get training. The Brits started it, and now we have security companies training over here."

Sylvana didn't need to know I knew more about staunching blood loss from penetrative injuries like gunshot or shrapnel wounds than blunt force trauma.

She waved with the pistol in a lowered but ready position. "Let her sleep. She's better off."

"I agree to your proposal," I said, as if we were negotiating where to go for dinner. "Let's get out of here. She can wake up thinking she fell. No harm. No foul." I stepped forward. "This is between us."

Sylvana waved the pistol in a jerky gesture toward a powder blue robe in a heap by a stall. "Go ahead. Nice and slow."

Hazel lay on her side with her cheek on the barn floor. I crouched at her side and touched her neck to feel her pulse. Still kicking. Judging from the red spot on her cheekbone, she was going to have a shiner from conking onto the floor.

She opened the eye turned toward me, caught my gaze for the length of a heartbeat, and closed it again.

I creaked to a standing position and said, "Good news. She's still alive. Out cold. Let's get out of here before she wakes up."

Sylvana angled her head to Rick. "Find some leg wraps."

What? *Leg wraps?* We had to get out of there. Hazel could let the cops know what was happening.

Rick waved the shotgun like someone holding a hockey stick, not a firearm. "Polo wraps? Or vet wrap? Assuming I can guess where they keep that stuff here."

"It doesn't matter," Sylvana said through gritted teeth. "All these ambling horse barns are alike. Hell, they probably have a roll of plastic wrap somewhere. We need to tie Avery's hands."

I chimed in again. "No need to go to all that bother for me. I'm going willingly. Remember? And we were on our way out the door."

"Get enough leg wraps for gags," she said to Rick. "Find some nasty ones with liniment, or better yet, mustard oil. One of those noxious concoctions they use instead of training. Bound to be plenty of that stuff. Kerosene, too. We can leave these two here."

She was planning to burn down the barn.

Rick half whined, "I don't know where that stuff is in this barn. I mean, look at all the crap lining the shelves. I don't know half of what that is."

A strong voice startled all of us. "My boys don't fix their horses."

The air seemed to whoosh out of the room. Aw, hell. Hazel couldn't keep her mouth shut. What was it with these horse people? Like street kids, they had to defend their honor over their lives.

To my sinking dismay, my landlady sat up against the wall. "No way. These horses aren't just compliant. They're clean." A glint of righteous triumph lit her eyes.

Thanks to Hazel's itch to defend her boys, my plan of getting out of there and leaving her to call the cops fell through with a leaden thud.

"Welcome to the party, Hazel. I'm guessing we won't find diesel fuel in this crosstie room, either? Rick. What did I say? Get busy."

To my shock, the Hazel who'd successfully played unconscious flipped into conscious and spitting mad. "They're not just compliant. Herb's the cleanest trainer for miles," she said with the pride of someone who'd forgotten she was a captive.

Great. I couldn't help but shake my head.

Sylvana waved the pistol at us. "Then, you two are going into the crosstie room. Rick," she said a little louder, "after you get the leg wraps, go siphon gas out of lawn mower. If there's a gas can, get that, too. I know you know where that is."

A chill shot its way down my spine. My mind pulled at me. I dug my fingernails into my palm. Must stay present.

All this hunting and fetching would take time. And that time could be on our side. More time for Hazel and me to live. Provided someone came for the late-night check. Unless that was Hazel. Then, we're screwed.

"Mo—om?" Rick's question vibrated with suspicion. "What are we gonna do with the gas?" As if he were hoping she wouldn't say what he was afraid she'd say.

Sylvana stated, "Barn fires happen all the time."

Hazel gasped.

Rick said, "But what about the horses? And Mrs. Ward?"

I had a feeling who the weak link was. Could I get them to turn on each other? He had the shotgun. He also wasn't leaving to get the leg wraps or gasoline.

"Rick," I said, "what will Lexi say if a barn full of horses burns, and they all die? Especially horses she knows? Maybe even fed treats to? You know it'll break her heart."

He shifted in the shadows.

I kept talking. "Even if she never finds out you and her mother did it," I hit the next word hard, "you'll know who did. How will you face her?"

"I'm protecting her," he said. "She doesn't need to know." He pivoted to shoot a pointedly disgusted snort toward his mother. "About a lot of things."

"Shut the hell up," Sylvana said to me. To Rick, she said, "Someone needs a gag. Grab a handful of leg wraps."

I didn't have much time. I said, "All you wanna-be bad guys think torching is the answer for getting rid of a body, but you forget. Gasoline fires don't get hot enough to burn the big bones."

"She's right," Rick said, as if a light had switched on. "I saw it on TV."

"So what?" Sylvana, unimpressed, watched us. "No one's here that isn't expected to be here. Except maybe for her."

It was working. I didn't have much time. "Rick, if you make sure we live, I'll tell the police you helped us. You helped me already. That counts as points in your favor. She's going down for killing Cy McCoy. Don't let her take you with her."

His harsh laugh woke me like a slap. "You don't know shit."

I inhaled a gulp of air, along with hay dust and horse hair.

Sylvana may have kidnapped me, but when I'd been in the truck with my so-called rescuer, my lizard brain had warned me Rick was dangerous. Made me jump out of a moving truck.

What made a woman plant evidence? Kidnap people? Convince a nearly adult child to go along with a desperate foolhardy cover-up?

The realization sank down my spine, down to the primitive level. One of the most primitive relationships ever. Blood all right, but deeper than blood.

With my vision jittering in rhythm with my pulse, I shifted verbal tap-dancing gears. "We can still protect him. He's not yet eighteen. A good defense lawyer can leverage that." I stopped short of saying your family. "You have resources to help him."

Like corrupt judges. Family-funded Congressional seats. Even a young Connecticut state's attorney for a while about thirty years ago. But all that support was up north. Or was it?

"Shut up," Sylvana swung her pistol toward Hazel. "Rick, point the shotgun at Hazel."

"Mrs. Ward?" His voice quivered with horror. Rick planted his feet, kept the shotgun low, and said to his mother, "When did you get so bad you want me to do bad things?"

"I'm not making you do anything except have a hand now in cleaning up the mess you made." She swung her pistol to indicate Hazel. "I said, point the gun at her."

While she spoke, I crept forward, just a few inches. Then froze. Trying to control my breathing. Enough air not to pass out, but not a big enough breath to indicated I was up to something.

He raised the gun toward Hazel, kind of half-heartedly. "I'm sorry, Mrs. Ward. I never meant for you to get hurt."

Before Hazel could respond, Sylvana jumped in.

"None of this would've happened," Sylvana said with exhausted rage dragging on her voice, "had you not been so impulsive."

"Me?" he mocked.

I crept closer again. It was working. They were turning on each other. I just had to keep my mouth shut. I ached to ask for clarification, but survival came first. Truth later.

The shotgun Rick held, wavered. "I was protecting you. Us. Our family."

"Like hell you were."

"You weren't thinking, either. At least, not with the big head. After Dad has given us everything?" He was on a roll. "You know a local jury won't convict me for that. You know how they are down here."

Sylvana's laugh went fast and sharp. "Yeah. I do. You're an outsider from the north. No matter how much juice I can add."

His shotgun wavered away from Hazel, who I tried not to look at.

"But we're Rikesis." His voice dripped disgust, "You were banging a *mouli*."

Sylvana wasn't even looking at me. "We moved away from family so you wouldn't be drawn into the life. And now you think like a redneck boor."

Rick stood tall with his shoulders wide and the shotgun drooping. "I'm a Rikesi. So are you. Maybe you forgot. My real father was a Rikesi." He managed to stand taller.

"He was employed by the Rikesis." Sylvana's shoulders sagged. "I'm the Rikesi, and I wish to God I weren't."

I closed in. My hands were together, palms pressed together in a prayer position. Knowing if she shot me, I'd die for sure. And, so what? No more nightmares. Maybe the noise at this hour would draw neighbors or passers-by on the state road. Hazel would be saved.

Sylvana pivoted to me. "What are you doing? Praying for mercy?"

I powered my steepled hands between her arms and forced them apart. Sylvana dropped the gun.

It thudded on the rubber matted flooring. We dove for it, scrambling where horses pooped.

We both clutched the pistol in our hands when I heard the newest deputy shout, "Police! Put the gun down! Now!"

Forty-Three

Three F-16 Falcons, streaking high above my head, sliced the deep blue sky with fierce screams of fury and force. I braced for terrified shrieks, moans of pain, and wails of grief. I waited for rising columns of smoke and searing flames.

Instead, giddy applause and whoops of pride. Exuberant faces squinted at the sky. Fingers pointed to track the jet trail. Children waved small American flags on top of reedy sticks.

Pinpricks of sensation returned to my fingers, slippery with sweat yet still pinching my phone.

I shifted to grab a couple of flag-waving, happy crowd shots, but my finger stuttered on the shutter a moment too long and, worse, fired off a burst.

Good going, Avery. Your photos used to win awards.

Across the street, a little boy in shorts and a T-shirt, covered his ears and squeezed his eyes shut. That shot, I grabbed.

Yeah, kid, I know how you feel.

After the flyover, the Blanchard County Memorial Day parade continued marching past me at my spot east of Courthouse Square.

Ahead of me, floats built on the decks of flatbed trucks by merchants and community groups fluttered with tissue-paper decorations. Vintage convertibles glided past with county officials or a smiling girl wearing a dress with a beauty queen's sash, all of them perched atop the back seat and waving to the crowd.

I'd grab just a couple more photos, enough for the special parade coverage the *Tribune* had promoted.

Toward the end of the parade, before the fire trucks, the mounted unit from the Blanchard County Saddle Club, all decked out in Western wear, clopped by. I lifted my phone to my eye.

Josie Kinsale sparkled like a rodeo queen in a blue and white spangly outfit on a golden palomino in black Western tack studded with silver medallions. She waved and beamed the megawatt smile only rich peoples' dental care could provide.

Behind her, Herb Olmos and his Mini-Me, his oldest son, Wesley, looked like cowboys cleaned up for town in their matching straw cowboy hats, red plaid shirts, and jeans. The manes of their two chilled out been-there-seen-that black-and-white paint horses wore fully bloomed red peonies, fresh from a yard garden.

A spark of anticipatory excitement stirred in my chest. Would he be there?

I almost didn't recognize him.

Instead of his usual ball cap, Norwood wore a black cowboy hat, deep indigo jeans, and a dark denim western shirt. No shadow darkened his sharp chin. He'd deemed the occasion important enough to shave for. Or he'd actually had a moment in his busy veterinarian's schedule.

The warm melty ache in my chest suggested, *yeah, he wears Western well.*

Who are you staying here for?

Sylvana's voice as she'd goaded me to threaten me and Hazel. Funny how Sylvana had known more about me than I cared to admit.

Coming to horse country to fill in as Gordon's temp reporter had appealed to me, but I hadn't spent much time with horses, considering how I'd ostensibly moved there for them. I'd change that in the ensuing weeks.

Still, that unmistakable ping of attraction made me wonder. Had Sylvana suspected what I didn't want to admit? Was my subconscious mind pulling the strings to plan my life around a man? A man I didn't know well?

My silly anticipation shrank and faded when I realized he hadn't waved at me. Had I waved at him? No. I was taking photos. What a relief. At least, I wasn't that far gone.

Ahead, he not only waved, but removed his hat with the hand not holding the reins, held his hat over his heart, and then bowed his head toward the reviewing stand on the courthouse steps.

Most of the reviewing stand's occupants were women. The contingent of Gold Star Mothers. Women with white hair sat in the front row while some sat in wheelchairs flanking the others. Behind them on higher tiers sat more-youthful women. All wore strained smiles.

Every one of them would have forgone the "honor" of a Gold Star, signifying a child had died while serving the military.

That he'd honored them made me all the more interested in Norwood Ward.

Far enough behind the horses not to spook them, rumbled a small contingent of fire trucks and a squad car.

By the time the official vehicles appeared, the crowd already thinned out to disperse to parked cars, Memorial Day sales, and picnics.

Spectators and some marchers returning to join their families along the route, surrounded and jostled me.

My chest labored to gather air. I had to get out of there, go somewhere quiet. I slipped my phone into my hip pocket. A touch on my elbow almost sent me rocketing toward those flying jets.

"Avery," said Grace Johnson calling out to stop me. Behind her, Terry carried Shanice, straddling his hip. Clutched around her tiny hand were two reed-thin sticks. Off one fluttered an American flag. The other held aloft a pony balloon.

She said, "Your story was lovely. Both for what you said and what you didn't say."

I nodded and hoped I didn't look as queasy as I felt. I grinned a bit energetically at Shanice and then said with more zest than I felt, "Did you see the horses?"

With wide eyes she nodded, and then glanced up as if to confirm with her dad. Terry's mouth looked a little pale around the edges. A discomfort with crowds seemed to be common among those of us who'd spent time in the Sandbox. Worse for the military.

"Crowds. Ugh." My face squinched. "Right?"

He replied with a bob of his shoulders and a shy smile, as if he was keeping it together for his little girl, to share the experience of a small-town tradition with her.

I edged away. "Sorry. Gotta go. Working. Enjoy the day." I waved at the retreating Johnsons with Shanice turning to give me a little wave.

"Avery?" Hazel wrapped me in a hug in her thin arms. A puff of coconut fragrance wafted from her hair. "How are you? We never see you anymore."

When Hazel released me and held me at arm's length, I spotted the faded purple and yellow of the bruises under her makeup, not far from the lines on her face.

Tears shot to my eyes. I hugged her again so I could turn my face away from the damage I'd caused. Had I not been in her barn hiding from Rick and Sylvana, she wouldn't have been hurt. When I looked at her, all I could imagine was how close we'd all come to dying. My actions had put another innocent at risk. Again.

And who knew what else was brewing up north after I'd disregarded the Rikesi's threat to reveal my father's secret.

I squeezed off tears. "I've been busy," came out of my mouth.

Laverne shouldered her way next to Hazel. "You're looking a little pale, hon." Her kindness without her usual edge of judgey contempt almost made me want to shape the sign of the cross with my two index fingers, as if to ward off a vampire.

She took my hand in both of hers. She pressed a thin metal key into the sweaty skin of my palm.

"Go cool off in the office." She squinted as if she could assess and diagnose. "Just lock the doors after you leave."

Gratitude almost shoved my swelling tears over the edge. I whispered my thanks. Hazel's attention veered from me to someone who called out, "Hazel! I hear you fought off murderers!"

Behind me, the crowd murmured. I sensed people shifting and parting. A soft clip clop grew stronger, louder.

Of course, someone was riding a horse back through the crowd. Sylvana's dismissive harrumph, Kentuckians, echoed in my memory.

From behind me, my name called out, not yelled but projected. "Avery," Norwood said.

He shifted his wrist to neck-rein his black horse to step toward me. One of the horse's ears cocked back to him, the other swiveled to monitor the crowd. "Avery. Wait."

My breath thinned like I'd reverted to age fourteen. I'd plunged into a rogue murder investigation, but was nervous about talking to a man I liked?

I said, speaking first to control the conversation, "What are you doing? Riding that horse through a crowd." His horse with relaxed ears and kind eyes looked calmer than me.

With a smile that flashed down to my toes, Norwood said, "He was a police horse in Lexington. Retired."

Almost imperceptibly, his body relaxed. The horse stopped, lowered its head, and tracked, with interested eyes, a passing child with a cookie.

Close enough I could be heard above the rumble of the crowd leaving, I stepped to stand next to the horse's neck, closer to Norwood, but away from hooves in case the horse needed to stomp away a fly.

Norwood said, "You can pet him."

With the hand not gripping the key Laverne had given me, I traced my palm along the graceful satiny neck. Norwood hadn't been wrong about how I'd feel. More centered, grounded.

Norwood said, "Between your schedule and my schedule, maybe we can go out for supper some time." I must've looked as dumbstruck as I felt. He added, "I thought we had a moment at the funeral. Wasn't the time or place."

We each stood our ground as if we were holding our breath. A spark of hope stirred my hormones again, but my brain kept them on a short rein.

"But we've had this conversation."

"You didn't answer." Some senior ladies walked by and smiled at Norwood, who tipped his hat. "Unless your silence was the answer."

My skin tingled as I remembered crying and then hitting on him to distract myself. Then, my skin crept. Then, a lot of men would've said, *Let's go.*

"After our moment in the barn—" I waved my hand, but not too wide not to spook the horse. "You still have to ask?"

He shrugged and leaned over the saddle horn. "I'm a touch old-fashioned."

Almost as if a personal bubble shrank around me, I stared at the horse's ebony satin neck and said, "I put your mother and your barn at risk. I'm sorry." Tears erupted like spring plants, but I bit them back. "I didn't know where else to go."

Great. Crying in front of everyone downtown. Must. Resist.

He lengthened the reins, then in a whirl, he swung his right leg over the horse's saddle. He dismounted with the speed of a teenage gymnast to land light on his feet.

I backed off. Don't touch me. Not in the small-town goldfish bowl half a block from Main Street. I was already notorious enough, even inserted myself in the story I'd been covering, not a cardinal sin for a journalist but bad enough.

"Text me," I said, "and we'll sync what we can of our schedules." I opened my closed palm with the key stashed inside and jingled it between my fingers. "I need to get back to work."

We both went our separate ways. With the crowd thinning, he climbed aboard the horse, and they turned to ride through town.

I headed straight to the newsroom's glass doors. My shaking hand skittered around the opening of the lock. Laverne's kennel-club-branded key fob bobbed and clacked against the steel door frame. Finally, the tip of the key slid into the lock. I twisted the mechanism hard, then slipped inside the dark office. With still shaking hands, I locked the deadbolt behind me.

The empty desks stood in cool half-light. The closed glass door and office front window muffled the passing street noise. Yet the ringing in my ears engaged and buzzed to fill in the silence.

My desk looked inviting, but too public thanks to the storefront window. Movement in here could attract attention out there. Some moron might even remember to pay his bill.

I could hide unseen behind the cubicle partition wall and collapse in Gordon's swivel chair. I hurried deeper into the office.

"Hello, Avery." Gordon's chair was already occupied by my boss's boss Clark Kinsale.

Forty-Four

My stomach shrank in betrayal. Laverne had set me up with Kinsale. We were alone.

He didn't seem the type to do his own dirty work, but I turned so I could see both the entrance and the rear exit to the alley.

I spoke first. "Did you see your daughter ride by?"

"Yes. She and Generator's Spark of Gold. He's always a crowd pleaser." A sadness veiled his eyes for a moment, then his practiced mask of a smile returned. He tilted the chair, braced his elbows and steepled his fingers. "I need to speak with you privately."

"On a holiday you could be enjoying?"

This had to be bad. I braced myself against the flimsier-than-I'd-like cubicle divider. Was that how it would end? Even though I'd caught the infidel invaders from the north red-handed, he still needed to take out the rest of the Yankee trash?

If this was it, I'd at least get the truth first. "Would you have let Herb take the rap?"

"You simply hurried matters along to their inevitable conclusion."

"Innocent men go to jail all the time." The words almost didn't pass through my tight breath. The big question. "What's your connection to the Rikesi crime family?"

"None, or so I thought. Mrs. Dobbs had told me her maiden name over lunch as part of her credentials for running the group. She'd also mentioned how she worked hard to distance herself from her family." He bowed his head and said, as if to himself, "Such a tragedy when family has been the toxic influence."

I went on the offensive. More or less. "Your full-time employee Crystal was at the parade with her new baby. She'll come off maternity leave soon. I'll be out of your hair in no time."

"Talk around town is that she wants more time with her new precious baby." He cast me a sidelong glance with a lordly smile. "Can you blame her?"

His "precious" comment stung, even though my biological clock only went off for hunger, thirst, and lust. I thought of Sylvana's appetites and assumptions, especially about me, that I was staying for, of all people, Norwood.

I popped a casual shrug. "Good for her."

"After she comes back to work," he said, "I expect you'll be returning to your old haunts?"

New York with its shoulder-to-shoulder crowds and screaming sirens? Home to a family who wouldn't like what might come to pass, especially if the Rikesis made good on their threats, because I was obsessed with following my nose? Or off to Afghanistan or Darfur with a camera, a sat phone, and a protective vest?

"I've kept my options open," I said with maybe too much *brio*.

"I understand the children in the Youth Arts Crew still want to organize a luminaria memorial for Cyrus McCoy?"

The children. Some of them were almost old enough to enlist and be deployed. "They plan to include his students. Will that be a problem?"

He tilted his head and smiled, like I'd seen Ronald Reagan do in a video of his famous "there you go again" moment at one of the debates. "Josie wants to hold a fundraiser. I think my wife wants in, too. And once my wife steps in, well," he chuckled to himself, "it's out of our hands entirely."

"Maybe one of them would like to lead the Youth Arts Crew? I hear there's an opening."

He said, as if watching video of my thoughts playing out across my forehead. "Too bad you're leaving. I think you'd be a good leader for the Youth Arts Crew. I would be agreeable to that, and you staying at the *Tribune* when Crystal officially resigns, but on one condition."

Before I asked about his sole condition, I said, "Group leader? Why me? I'm not an artist. I was a photojournalist."

"Potato, potahto. Call yourself an interim advisor then. Your article about the group suggested you'd be a good candidate. But remember there's a condition."

Condition. *Catch.* "I'm listening."

He said, "Go into counseling."

"Here? This town has therapists?" I half expected him to send me to a church, to a minister, who knew more about Bible verses than cognitive behavioral therapy.

"Gordon will assign you to a story looking into mental health support available here. I don't think we've run that particular story for a while. The rest is up to you."

I clutched at an excuse, any excuse, not to use a local therapist. "Won't my covering the therapy scene here muddy the waters ethically if I'm really shopping for a therapist?"

"You cover public safety, but you also call the police when you need them."

Point to Kinsale. Even if she'd just been doing her job, I owed Deputy Georgia Fortner lunch. "So, the *Trib* will pay me mental health benefits?"

"You're still officially on leave from *News World*. They pay."

I rubbed my nose. If I went back to NY, I could have my pick of shrinks. Here? No telling. If I returned to New York, I'd enjoy museums, pho joints, and fashion but also crowds, noise, and the accusatory stares of my mother and sisters.

So far, the Rikesis hadn't made good on their threat but not much time had passed, either. Maybe through online sources I could stealthily figure out some of my father's connection with the Rikesis?

"I'm in," I said.

"Good. Horse country is a lovely place to heal. You can do good work here. Even shape young minds. On some level, that worries me, but I also have faith you'll rise to your better angels."

Here I could fulfill my longing to get more involved in the horse scene. Maybe substitute riding for running alone in the cemetery. And maybe Norwood Ward would be worth getting to know better.

A pinprick of warning shadowed my relief. "So," I said, "are we done here?"

Kinsale said, "No one at the Sheriff's Department will tell you this. I believe, after all you went through, you deserve to know what happened with that misguided young man."

Forty-Five

Was his offer for real? "How do you know?"

"I've known everyone involved, except for the Dobbs family, all their lives. I knew their grandparents. And I play golf with various officials."

I dropped my usual filter. "Who'd take a chance on souring the jury pool, even losing the case, just to dish dirt on the golf course with a newspaper owner-publisher?"

"I'm a businessman. A pillar of the community. A lifelong friend with generations of friendship and *bona fides. You're* the journalist." He gazed at me with impassive entitlement. "What's the term you use? Off the record?"

I should've been overjoyed. Instead, I wondered how many filters what he was about to tell me had been through. How had the information changed? And what did he have to gain in telling me all this?

"I understand. They put you in a lousy position. Misery loves company, so you want me to help you carry around the secret, too. Many hands carrying a heavy load doesn't work well with secrets. You do know that?"

It still didn't make any sense. The court would have to change trial venues. But wait—I realized why I was about to learn.

"There's not gonna be a trial," I said. "They're copping a plea. Do tell. I'm all ears."

"Everything I tell you about this case is off the record. Do you agree?"

Oh, geez. Live by the sword, die by the sword. Still, with the right questions to the right people handled with enough finesse, I could get confirmation later. “Stop stalling. Spill.”

“Earlier on the night of the murder, before the storm hit, young Rick was on his way to return a barn scoop he’d borrowed from Herb Olmos. The boy, who’s known to be athletic and charming but not quite right, passed by his mother’s RV, which she takes to every horse show. As the rain began, he spotted Mr. McCoy bidding Mrs. Dobbs,” Kinsale paused as if he sought a tasteful euphemism, “a rather intimate farewell.”

For a teacher, Cy had been reckless with his personal and professional life. All too human and susceptible. He’d broken Celia’s heart. Had he considered her a “catch and release?”

As for Sylvana? I’d hoped it had been more theoretical than practice, considering her ego and thirst for status, especially while living and trying to work in a Bible Belt fishbowl.

Kinsale stared at me with a quirky smile. What the hell kind of reaction had he been expecting? Grief? Jealousy?

Not sure I was buying into all the, lemme lay the truth on you vibe, I said, “In my time in the barn alone with the Dobbses, Rick used a racial epithet in Italian to reference McCoy. That sounds like a hate crime. With federal charges attached. Any word on that? How would they plead that down?”

“Perhaps only if premeditated,” he said, as if he were guessing. Then, he returned to his topic, “The boy said he,” the man added air quotes, “lost his, well, let’s just say manure. Through pouring rain, he followed Cyrus to his car, confronted him, lost control, and used the barn scoop as a weapon.”

My imagination went to that bloody place. I shook my head. Good thing I didn’t have a similar war memory.

As the sheriff’s golf buddy, Kinsale knew a lot of details.

I'd follow the trail to see where it led.

"Sounds like," I said, "he stalked Cy through the parking lot."

I must've been channeling my father, the prosecutor.

Update. The dirty prosecutor.

All I said to Kinsale was, "Rick followed him to the car. In the rain. He had time to reconsider. He meant to take action. Premeditated."

A crime of passion, yes, but sheer cold rage with strategizing. First-degree murder, yes, and maybe hate crime charges. State and then additional federal charges.

"So, Rick," my turn for air quotes, "came to, gathered his wits after his bout of blood lust." One hand waved in the air as if ticking off a list. "Saw the carnage, realized what he'd done, freaked out, and then ran through the storm to Mommy. How could he really run home to Mommy after seeing her cheating, or thinking he saw her cheating?"

A sudden craving hit to see the smug Kinsale uncomfortable. "And what did you mean by 'intimate farewell?' A passionate kiss? Wandering hands? What?"

Yes. Do tell. Lots got talked about in those eighteen holes of golf.

Lots of off-the-record stuff, probably floating around town as we spoke. Why did we even publish a newspaper?

Kinsale ignored my question, but continued, "She couldn't bring herself to call the police. Her affair—perhaps even, affairs—would be revealed."

"Affairs?" I sounded as skeptical as I felt.

But yet, it was possible the plural could apply to Sylvana. She'd been a very busy woman, being a mother, a wife, creating art, and running a youth art's group. She'd had to have been a skilled time manager.

"Yes. Plural. With an independent contractor who'd been doing some remodeling work at odd hours. A man from New York. Said to have worked at Aqueduct." Kinsale said with snobby disdain.

"Does he drive a black pickup truck?" I thought about the truck parked near her motor home. She'd recommended his contractor services. I hadn't considered him as one of her squeezes.

I gave Kinsale a bit of a break, in return for all the juicy details I'd record on my phone to confirm for later. I said, "So, she panicked, thinking she was protecting her marriage, her family, and her standing in the community. Why didn't she just send her son where we don't have jurisdiction?"

Kinsale shrugged and said, "The school year. Finances. Perhaps she didn't want to involve her extended family. As she'd told me, they were estranged."

I didn't add what she'd told me. That they'd been putting old-fashioned ideas in the impressionable boy's head. Turns out, she'd been right to be concerned, but had intervened too late.

I wouldn't dish. I wouldn't be like the locals.

Had she not kept her son in town and improvised on the fly while living her life as usual, she might have pulled it off.

But she'd also told someone among the Rikesis. Perhaps the family archivist.

No. The mob wouldn't keep home movies. According to Sal's knowledge from his mafia fandom, most of the old-school dons knew better than to use phones. Which didn't apply to film cameras.

"You should also know," he paused before saying, "she considered you a threat. She was most insistent on you covering the youth arts group. You, specifically. Was curious about why you're here and not returning to the city or covering national or foreign news."

My hand swashed through the air in a dismissive wave. "You can't tell me she didn't con you, too. I half expected you to be up to your Adam's apple in this." I folded my arms, tucked my fingers inside the fold, held my breath and waited for him to answer my veiled challenge.

He said, "She was a desperate woman. Tried all sorts of things to get you out of the picture. Pulled some strings back home to get you a job at a magazine? Even that poor misguided boy of hers thought she'd gone too far. He rescued you."

Geez, what hadn't they told Kinsale?

What I chose not to mention, Sylvana had to know blackmailing me over my father's association with her family pointed a finger right back at her, but I wasn't ready to test that story with Sal, let alone confide in Kinsale.

If the Rikesis made good on their threat, the video on my hard drive would prove them as conspirators to cover up a murder in, of all places, Kentucky.

That meant, even with the old man in prison, they were still active with feelers across the nation.

Maybe even in this room.

That was a dragon to confront another day. A battle above my pay grade to fight alone.

I finally said, "She was desperate enough to make bad moves. Kidnapping and was considering felony arson. Short of double homicide." Me and Hazel.

My own desperation had led me to rash behavior mixed with tactical cowardice disguised as prudence. Although I preferred thinking of my choices as strategic decisions.

Adding fear and strong emotion makes a decision tree slippery.

His eyebrows shot up. "They were going to burn down the barn? Full of horses?"

A memory flash of a Baghdad cart horse in the wrong place at the wrong time when an IED went off tried to hijack my side of the conversation.

I dug my fingernails into my palm, focused on that digging pain, and noted the murmur of the celebratory crowd passing outside the office window.

I made myself say, "You told me the cops would've caught them anyway. Per chance, did your golf buddy tell you what they had?"

"DNA."

Made sense in a TV school of criminalistics way. "This soon? And it lasted through that storm? All the evidence probably washed into a ditch down the street."

"Not everything." He nodded once in a note of finality, but he had to know that wouldn't stop me from prodding.

I said, "Where did they find it? On the shovel? No. It had been in the pond. Wait. Rick went into his mother's RV to confront her. Oh, that's why she was remodeling her RV."

Bloody foot and handprints. No telling what other trace evidence had seeped through carpets.

His mouth twisted in disgust. He picked lint from his slacks. He pinched his normally tight mouth as if to hold back the words, plus he flushed red.

I sensed blood in the water. "Oh. Let me guess. The DNA had been under Cy's clothing," I raised my eyebrows, "after whatever preceded an intimate farewell?"

He flushed. "Indeed. Shall we leave it at that?"

His discomfort tasted delicious.

I added, "You are aware that, even though I agreed to this off-the-record conversation, I'll look for independent corroboration of everything you just told me."

He drew up to his full height. "Why? There won't be a trial. Once the details have been agreed to, we'll report the charges to which they've pled guilty" He shot me a hard glare. "You can't report any of this. If you find corroborating stories, I won't print them."

I'm not sure which red flag waved the hardest. I won't print them. Or there won't be a trial.

At least, I knew where I stood. I also realized I'd made a good choice in not sharing my newfound family drama.

Only to myself would I admit he had a point. I already had a lot to do in my spare time. Going to therapy. Running the arts group. Shopping for a replacement car and returning the rental. Fitting in the mythical work-life balance.

Let alone conducting my own long-distance investigation into my father's old cases.

The very video the Rikesis tried to use against me totally implicated them as well. In blowing up my family's reputation, they'd blow up theirs. We'd all go down together in a blaze of bad multimedia press. Had any of them considered that particular end game?

So, I was betting I had a little time, especially with Sylvana and Rick haggling for lenience, to look into things myself.

I shot him a smile and made eye contact. "What else am I gonna do?" I made sure my voice sounded like I was lightly busting his chops. "The sidewalks in this town roll up at five o'clock." Punctuated with a cocky New York shrug.

Deep inside, past my bluff, I came up with my first step. To beef up my internet security. Then, set up online notifications searches on my father's name.

Then I'd find secure sites to store copies of the media used to blackmail me.

If you enjoyed reading *Fatal Image*, you can help other readers decide if this story is for them, too, by posting a review on your favorite review site. Your review can be as short, or as long, as you like.

Also, for more about me and what I'm up to, sign up for my newsletter at this page on my website rhondalane.com/newsletter.

Thank you for reading.

Acknowledgements

Many generous people helped me over the years it took me to write this book. Some prefer not to be named. Of those who'd appreciate being named, I know in my bones I'm liable to miss someone. I apologize if that circumstance applies to you.

This is where most authors thank their author groups, and that list is coming, but there's someone else who belongs in the top spot.

My husband Rod.

This book would not exist without Rod's support, encouragement, and faith in my unconventional choices. Let alone his interest in technology when most people considered electronic devices toys. Without his influence, I might have rejected tech.

Among all the ways he's helped, I'm also grateful for his willingness to hold down the fort while I gallivanted off to do research or train with other authors at a police academy or attend some writer's group meeting or workshop or conference.

Thank you, honey. Your love and support mean more to me than I can say.

I'm also grateful to Cori Arnold and Allison Keeton, my critique partners. They gave me a lot of supportive fun and let me know when a scene didn't stick the landing. The dearly departed Lily the Lab, our silent partner, snuggled up to our feet under Allison's table.

Megan Ryder helped me get my manuscript out of Scrivener to send it to the following full manuscript beta readers.

Book doctor Jill Fletcher helped me see my blind spots.

Riding instructor Christine Lentz caught some horse-related mistakes.

Target audience readers Marian Lanouette and Kay Kendall brought great insights.

Kathryn Orzech clued me in on some punctuation problems lurking within my pages before they went to my editors Lisa J Jackson and copy editor Nancy Breininger.

I'm grateful to the Better Faster Academy coaches who gave me good counsel: Becca Syme, Terry Schott, Susan Bischoff, Milana Jacks, Ellie Zafiris, and Krystal Shannon.

Many thanks to equestrian fiction author Natalie Keller Reinert for showing me by example how beautiful interior design adds to a book.

Sarra Cannon's course "Publish & Thrive" helped simplify the massive task of learning business and self-publishing.

I'm grateful to the Sisters in Crime New England, Connecticut, and Guppies chapters; Mystery Writers of America NY/CT chapter; Connecticut Romance Writers of America; Charter Oak Readers & Writers with its workshops with Mary Buckham; Connecticut Authors & Publisher's Association; American Horse Publications; The Salon with Dr. Lindsay Byron, better known as Lux ATL, and her assistant Desiree Nathanson; "Rocky's Vision Writing" group with the Juicy reVolution; and Alessandra Torre Inkers.

My deep gratitude goes to the my late friend and artist with-a-pedigree-book Arlene Gray.

A fervent "thank you" to you all, including those relieved I didn't print your name.

About the Author

Rhonda Lane has been a stringer news photographer, a reporter with a split beat covering "cops & courts" as well as feature stories, and a TV broadcast technician for live and recorded programming.

For twelve years, she ran the horses-in-culture blog known as *The Horsey Set Net*. She is the author of the short story "On Like Donkey Kong," which appeared in *Fish Out of Water: A Guppy Anthology* edited by Ramona DeFelice Long. Her poem "At the Rail" is in *Track Life: Images and Words* by Juliet Harrison. *Fatal Image* is her first novel.

Her varied work history gave her unexpected training for a writer, especially in an age when writing and publishing involves multimedia technology.

As for her equestrian credentials, she grew up in rural Kentucky, but family circumstances prevented her from being a lifelong horsewoman. After a health scare in midlife, she entered the equestrian world as soon as she could.

She lives with her husband and their cats among an oak grove in central Connecticut.

www.ingramcontent.com/pod-product-compliance
Lightning Source LLC
LaVergne TN
LVHW090553110826
845146LV00001B/110

* 9 7 9 8 9 8 6 9 3 7 5 0 2 *